FOUR DEAD QUEENS

FOUR
DEAD
QUEENS

Astrid Scholte

G. P. PUTNAM'S SONS

G. P. PUTNAM'S SONS

an imprint of Penguin Random House LLC, New York

Copyright © 2019 by Astrid Scholte.

Map copyright © 2019 by Virginia Allyn.

Penguin supports copyright. Copyright fuels creativity, encourages diverse voices, promotes free speech, and creates a vibrant culture. Thank you for buying an authorized edition of this book and for complying with copyright laws by not reproducing, scanning, or distributing any part of it in any form without permission. You are supporting writers and allowing Penguin to continue to publish books for every reader.

G. P. Putnam's Sons is a registered trademark of Penguin Random House LLC.

Library of Congress Cataloging-in-Publication Data
Names: Scholte, Astrid, author.
Title: Four dead queens / Astrid Scholte.
Description: New York, NY: G. P. Putnam's Sons, [2019]
Summary: Keralie is the best pickpocket in all of the kingdoms of Quadara, but when she steals a "comm disk" and realizes a royal murder plot is afoot, she must learn who to trust and fast.
Identifiers: LCCN 2018016446 | ISBN 9780525513926 (hardcover) |
ISBN 9780525513933 (ebook)
Subjects: | CYAC: Kings, queens, rulers, etc.—Fiction. | Criminals—Fiction. |
Assassins—Fiction. | Science fiction. | Fantasy.
Classification: LCC PZ7.1.S336533 Fo 2019 | DDC [Fic]—dc23
LC record available at https://lccn.loc.gov/2018016446

Printed in the United States of America.
ISBN 9780525513926
1 3 5 7 9 10 8 6 4 2

Design by Jaclyn Reyes.
Text set in Horley Old Style.

To the queen in all of us.
May she be brave, self-confident, opinionated, unapologetic,
and determined to achieve her dreams.

ARA

CORRA

QUEEN OF EONIA

EONIA

Commuter

Canals of Ludia

LUDIA

STESSA

QUEEN OF LUDIA

The Cliffs

THE QUADRANTS OF QUADARA

Archia

The agricultural isle that values simplicity, hard work and nature.
Proverb: Trust only in what can be wielded by hand and heart.
Queen: Iris

Eonia

The frozen quadrant that values technology, evolution and
a harmonious society.
Proverb: A turbulent mind produces turbulent times.
A peaceful mind heralds peace.
Queen: Corra

Toria

The coastal quadrant that values commerce, curiosity and exploration.
Proverb: Know everything, and you shall know all.
Queen: Marguerite

Ludia

The pleasure quadrant that values frivolity, music,
art and entertainment.
Proverb: Life is for the revelers with open eyes and open hearts.
Queen: Stessa

QUEENLY LAW

Rule one: To protect the fertile lands of Archia, the queen must uphold the society's humble but hardworking way of life.

Rule two: Emotions and relationships cloud judgment. Eonists must concentrate solely on technological advancements, medicine and the community as a whole.

Rule three: To allow for a thriving culture of art, literature and music, Ludia must not be weighed down by the humdrum concerns of everyday life.

Rule four: Curiosity and exploration are at the heart of every Torian. This should be encouraged to promote further growth of Toria's burgeoning society.

Rule five: A queen must be raised within her own quadrant to learn the ways of her people and not be influenced by the palace's politics.

Rule six: Once a queen enters the palace, she is never to visit her homeland again.

Rule seven: A queen must produce an heir before the age of forty-five, to ensure her royal lineage.

Rule eight: A queen cannot waste time or emotion on love. She is forbidden to marry, for it is a distraction from her duties.

Rule nine: Each queen will be appointed one advisor from her own quadrant. They will be her only counsel.

Rule ten: The advisor from each quadrant must be present in all meetings and involved in all decisions to ensure the queens remain impartial.

Rule eleven: The power of the queen can only be passed on to her daughter in the event of the queen's death or her abdication.

Rule twelve: As soon as a queen passes, her daughter, or the next closest female relative, must be brought to the palace immediately to ascend the throne.

Rule thirteen: Only a queen may sit upon the throne. When she takes the throne, she accepts the responsibility to rule the quadrant until her dying day.

FOUR DEAD QUEENS

PART ONE

CHAPTER ONE

Keralie

The morning sun caught the palace's golden dome, flooding the Concord with light. While everyone halted their business and glanced up—as though it were a sign from the four queens themselves—we perched overhead like sea vultures, ready to swoop in and pick them apart.

"Who shall we choose today?" Mackiel asked. He was leaning against a large screen atop a building that displayed the latest Queenly Reports. He looked like a charming, well-dressed young man from Toria. At least, that was what he *looked* like.

"Choices, choices," I said with a grin.

He moved to drape his arm heavily around my shoulder. "Who do you feel like being today? A sweet young girl? A damsel in distress? A reluctant seductress?" He puckered his lips at me.

I laughed and pushed him away. "I'll be whatever makes us the most money." I usually picked my targets, but Mackiel had been in a good mood this morning, and I didn't want to tip the boat. He submerged easily into darkness these days, and I'd have done anything to keep him in the light.

I shrugged. "You choose."

He raised his dark eyebrows before tilting his bowler hat to further survey the crowd. The line of kohl around his lids made his deep-set blue eyes stand out all the more. Nothing escaped his scrutiny. A familiar smirk played at his lips.

The crisp Concord air was clean, unlike the acrid tang of seaweed, fish and rotted wood that pervaded our home down on Toria's harbor. It was Quadara's capital and the most expensive city to live in, as it shared boundaries with Toria, Eonia and Ludia. Archia was the only region separated from the mainland.

The stores on the ground level sold a variety of approved goods, including Eonist medicines, the latest Ludist fashions and toys, and fresh Archian produce and cured meat—all collated and distributed by Torian traders. Squeals of children, the murmur of business and sighs of queenly gossip bounced between the glass storefronts.

Behind the buildings rose an opaque golden dome, encapsulating the palace and concealing the confidential dealings within. The palace entrance was an old stone building called the House of Concord.

As Mackiel searched for a target, he held his middle finger to his lips—an insult to the queens hiding inside their golden dome. When he caught my eye, he tapped his lip and grinned.

"Him," he said, his gaze landing on the back of a dark figure who descended the stairs from the House of Concord into the crowded main square. "Get me his comm case."

The target was clearly Eonist. While we Torians were bundled up in layers to ward off the biting chill, he wore a tight-fitting black dermasuit over his skin, an Eonist fabric made of millions of microorganisms that maintained body temperature with their secretions. Gross, but handy in the depths of winter.

"A messenger?" I flashed Mackiel a hard look. The delivery would be of high importance if the messenger was coming from the House of Concord, the only place where Torians, Eonists, Archians and Ludists conducted business together.

Mackiel scratched at his neck with ring-covered fingers, a nervous habit. "Not up for the challenge?"

I scoffed. "Of course I am." I was his best dipper, slipping in and out of pockets with a feather-light touch.

"And remember—"

"Get in quick. Get out quicker."

He grabbed my arm before I could slip off the roof. His eyes were serious; it had been months since he'd looked at me that way—as though he cared. I almost laughed, but it lodged somewhere between my chest and throat.

"Don't get caught," he said.

I grinned at his concern. "When have I ever?" I climbed down from the rooftop and into the crowd.

I hadn't gotten far when an old man stopped abruptly in front of me and raised his hand to press four fingers to his lips in respect for the queens—the *proper* greeting, as opposed to Mackiel's middle-fingered version. I dug in my heels. My spiked soles gripped the well-worn cobblestones. I halted in time, my cheek brushing the back of his shoulders.

Dammit! What was it about the palace that inspired such slack-jawed stupidity? It wasn't like you could see anything through the golden glass. And even if you could, so what? The queens didn't care about us. And certainly not someone like me.

I slapped the cane from the old man's hand. He stumbled to the side.

He turned, his face pinched in annoyance.

"Sorry!" I said. I fluttered my lashes at him from under my large-brimmed hat. "The crowd pushed in on me."

His expression softened. "No worries, my dear." He tipped his head. "Enjoy your day."

I gave him an innocent smile before slipping his silver pocket watch into a fold in my skirt. That would teach him.

I stood on my toes to find my target. *There.* He didn't look much older than me—eighteen, perhaps. His suit clung like a second skin—from his fingertips to his neck, covering his torso, legs and even his feet. While I wrestled with corsets and stiff skirts each and every day, I couldn't imagine his outfit would be any easier to dress in.

Still, I envied the material and the freedom of movement it allowed. Like him, my muscles were defined from constantly running, jumping and climbing. While it was not unusual for a Torian to be fit and trim, my muscles weren't from sailing back and forth to Archia, or from unloading heavy goods at the docks. I'd long been entangled within the darker side of Toria. Hidden beneath my modest layers and pinching corsets, no one knew of my wickedness. My work.

The messenger hesitated at the bottom of the House of Concord stairs, rearranging something in his bag. Now was my chance. That old man had given me inspiration.

I dashed toward the polished slate stairs, fixing my eyes on the palace with my best imitation of awe—or rather slack-jawed stupidity—on my face, my four fingers nearing my lips. Approaching the messenger, I snagged my toe in a gap between two tiles and pitched forward like a rag doll. Inelegant, but it would do the job. I'd learned the hard way that any pretense could easily be spotted. And I was nothing if not committed.

"Ah!" I cried as I crashed into the boy. The rotten part of me enjoyed the thwack as he hit the stones. I landed on top of him, my hands moving to his bag.

The messenger recovered quickly, pushing me away, his right hand tightly twisted around the bag. Perhaps this wasn't his first encounter with Mackiel's dippers. I stopped myself from shooting Mackiel a glare, knowing he'd be watching eagerly from the rooftop.

He was always watching.

Changing tactics, I rolled, purposely skinning my knee on the stone ground. I whimpered like the innocent Torian girl I pretended to be. I lifted my head to show my face from under my hat to take him in.

He had that Eonist look, evenly spaced eyes, full lips, high defined cheekbones and a proud jaw. The look they were engineered for. Curls of black hair framed his tan face. His skin was delicate, but hardy. Not at all like my pale creamy skin, which flaked and chapped in the winter wind and burned in the blistering summer sun. His eyes were on me. They were light, almost colorless, not the standard Eonist brown, which guarded against the sun's glare. Did it help him see in the dark?

"Are you all right?" he asked, his face giving nothing away.

Eonists' expressions were generally frozen, like the majority of their quadrant.

I nodded. "I'm so, so sorry."

"That's okay," he said, but his hand was still at his bag; I wasn't done with this charade just yet.

He glanced at my black boot, which had scuffed where my toe had caught between the stones, then to my knee cradled in my hands. "You're bleeding," he said in surprise. He did indeed think this was a ploy for his belongings.

I looked at my white skirt. A blotch of red had spread through my undergarments and was blooming across my knee.

"Oh my!" I swooned a little. I looked up into the bright sun until tears prickled behind my eyes, then turned back to him.

"Here." He grabbed a handkerchief from his bag and handed it to me.

I bit my lip to hide a grin. "I wasn't watching where I was going. I was distracted by the palace."

The messenger's strange pale eyes flicked to the golden dome behind us. His face betrayed no emotion. "It's beautiful," he said. "The way the sun illuminates the dome, it's as though it were alive."

I frowned. Eonists didn't appreciate beauty. It wasn't something they valued, which was ironic, considering how generically attractive they all were.

I bunched the hem of my skirt in my hands and began pulling it up over my knee.

"What are you doing?" he asked.

I swallowed down a laugh. "I was checking to see how bad it is." I pretended I only then remembered where he was from.

"Oh!" I rearranged my skirt to cover my legs. "How inappropriate of me." Intimacy was as foreign as emotions in Eonia.

"That's all right." But he turned his face away.

"Can you help me up?" I asked. "I think I've twisted my ankle."

He held out his hands awkwardly before deciding it was safer to grip my covered elbows. I leaned heavily against him, to ensure he didn't feel any shift in weight as I slipped a hand inside his bag. My fingers grasped something cool and smooth, about the size of my palm. The comm case. I slid it out and into a hidden pocket in my skirt. As soon as he had me on my feet, he released me as though he'd touched a month-old fish.

"Do you think you can walk?" he asked.

I nodded but swayed side to side. Novice dippers gave themselves away by dropping the act too soon after retrieving their prize. And my knee *did* hurt.

"I don't think so." My voice was light and breathy.

"Where can I take you?"

"Over there." I pointed to an empty chair and table in front of a café.

He held on to my elbow as he guided me over, using his broad shoulders to navigate the crowd. I fell into the chair and pressed the handkerchief to my knee. "Thank you." I tipped my head down, hoping he'd leave.

"Will you be okay?" he asked. "You're not alone, are you?"

I knew Mackiel would be watching from somewhere close by.

"No, I'm not alone." I put some indignation into my voice. "I'm with my father. He's doing business over there." I waved a hand vaguely at the surrounding shops.

The messenger crouched to look under the brim of my hat. I

flinched. There was something unsettling about his eyes up close. Almost like mirrors. Yet, under his gaze, I felt like the girl I was pretending to be. A girl who spent her day at the Concord with her family to enjoy the spoils of the other quadrants. A girl whose family was whole. A girl who hadn't shattered her happiness.

That moment passed.

Something flickered behind his expression. "Are you sure?" he asked. Was that real concern?

The cool of the metal case pressed against my leg, and Mackiel's hot gaze was on my back.

Get in quick. Get out quicker.

I had to disengage. "I need to rest for a bit. I'll be fine."

"Well, then," he said, glancing behind him to the House of Concord, his hand on his bag. As a messenger, his tardiness wouldn't be tolerated. "If you'll be all right . . ." He waited for me to refute him. I might have oversold my fragility.

"Yes. I'll be fine here. Promise."

He gave me a stiff Eonist nod, then said, "May the queens forever rule the day. Together, yet apart." The standard exchange of interquadrant goodwill. He turned to leave.

"Together, yet apart," I recited back to him. Before he had taken a step, I was up off the chair and among the crowd.

I clutched the comm case in my hand as I ran.

CHAPTER TWO

Iris
Queen of Archia

*Rule one: To protect the fertile lands of
Archia, the queen must uphold the society's
humble but hardworking way of life.*

I ris shifted uncomfortably on her throne, rearranging her stiff
skirts. The midday sun streamed down from the domed ceiling, hitting the elevated golden dial beneath it. The nation of
Quadara was engraved upon the face, with thick ridges representing the walls that divided the land. An amber globe sat in the
center of the dial and fractured the sunlight into rays, highlighting
hundreds of cursive words etched into the throne room's marble
walls. The words reminded each queen, and those who visited
court, of the approved transactions between quadrants and the
strict rules the queens must abide by. Queenly Law.

The four thrones, and their respective queens, sat in a circle
around the dial. While the quadrants remained divided, the queens
ruled from the same court.

Together, yet apart.

Each looked out upon her section of the circular room, a
painted crest to signify where her quadrant began.

Iris's next appointment stepped from around the partition

that separated court visitors from the queens. She glanced at one of her sister queens, Marguerite, sitting beside her. Marguerite raised an eyebrow in amusement as the man bowed, his nose grazing the polished marble at his feet. He stood upon the Archian crest: a rural island bordered by branches, leaves and flowers with a stag atop a mountain, depicted in bold golden swirls.

Now thirty years old, Iris had not seen her homeland of Archia for twelve years. But for as long as she lived, she would never forget the crisp air, the lush forests and rolling hills.

When the man straightened, he still wouldn't meet her eyes. A shame, for she had lovely eyes.

"My queen," the man's voice trembled.

Good. Iris cultivated fear. A time-consuming but worthwhile pursuit.

She knew Archia could easily be perceived as the least formidable of all the quadrants, as Archians mostly kept to themselves, rarely crossing the channel to the mainland due to their general distrust for machinery. They focused on physical work and living good, if somewhat modest, lives.

"Speak." Iris waved a hand at the man before her. "I don't have all day."

A trickle of sweat ran down the man's brow and onto the tip of his nose. He didn't wipe it away. Iris twitched her nose in sympathy—the only sympathy he'd get.

"I have come here to ask you for power," the man said. She scowled, and he quickly clarified, *"Electricity*—we need electricity."

Iris had to remind herself he was the Archian governor, although the title held little authority in her eyes. The queens were the power. No one else.

Power was a game, and over the years, Iris had perfected it.

"*Need* electricity?" Iris leaned forward. "No."

While the other quadrants had electricity, Archia continued to use only what could be *wielded by hand and heart*—a traditional Archian proverb.

Finally, the governor brought a shaking hand to wipe his brow.

"Electricity would allow for machines," the governor continued. "The workers are struggling to keep up with this year's delivery schedule set by Toria. Please consider, my queen."

She sat back and let out a breathy laugh. "You know better than to ask this of me." It was true that Quadara's population continued to grow, and no matter what they'd tried, all quadrants other than Archia remained barren.

Quadara's divided nation was an ecosystem, each quadrant playing its part. Archia provided crops and natural resources; Eonia developed medicine and technology; Ludia provided art, fashion and entertainment; and Toria arranged imports and exports between the quadrants. And Queenly Law upheld the system.

Archia was the nation's only hope. Which was why Iris needed to protect her homeland at all costs. She couldn't risk over-harvesting the land with the use of machines. If they destroyed Archia, Quadara would starve.

While some might still consider Archia primitive, it was not weak. Not while Iris ruled.

The governor's bottom lip jerked outward. "I know we are not meant to take technology from other quadrants, but—"

"Then you bore me with this conversation because . . . ?"

"Perhaps you should allow this?" Marguerite asked. At forty, she was the eldest and longest-reigning queen, and often the voice of reason. Even though her last appointment for the day had been canceled, she continued to watch court with interest. Like all Torians, her curiosity for other cultures could not be satiated.

An utter waste of Marguerite's time, Iris thought. She snapped her gaze to her sister queen. "This doesn't concern you, Marguerite." Her tone was forgiving, though; meddling was in the Torian queen's nature.

Marguerite tucked a graying curl of auburn hair behind her ear. "You'll remember I asked Corra to have her doctors develop an inoculation to prevent the blood plague from spreading further. Sometimes we must bend the rules, but not break them."

Iris tilted her head to see Corra's braided black hair, tied up in the common Eonist way, her gold crown gleaming against her dark brown skin. But the twenty-five-year-old queen of Eonia did not glance back at the mention of her scientists. Stessa, however, the queen of Ludia, looked over and grimaced, as though Iris was annoying her. She probably was, for everything Iris said or did seemed to annoy the sixteen-year-old queen.

"An entirely different situation," Iris said to Marguerite, ignoring Stessa's glare. "The plague threatened to wipe out your people. The inoculation was a one-off intervention; it did not significantly alter your quadrant. Even if I allowed machinery for a short amount of time, how would we return to our old ways? I can't risk it."

Marguerite gave her an understanding, but amused, smile, as though she thought Iris was being stubborn for the sake of being stubborn.

"No," Iris said, turning her attention back to the Archian governor. "Electricity is not from our quadrant; therefore, we shall never have it. We will not be aided by machines and their automatic witchery."

Iris had seen what technology had done to Eonia, and she would not have the same happen to her quadrant. With their mostly frozen and inhospitable land in the far north of the nation, Eonia had no option but to focus solely on technological advancements, and even genetic alteration, to survive. In turn, they had lost a part of their humanity. Or so Iris thought. She couldn't help but look at Corra once more.

Iris did not miss the governor's glance to the string of electrical chandeliers hanging in the four passages that led to the central throne room. Iris knew it appeared as though she enjoyed the pleasures of all the quadrants, but the governor didn't know that Iris still read by candlelight and bathed in the natural warm springs in her private garden rather than use the palace's heated water system. She wasn't about to discuss her hygiene regimen with him.

When he failed to respond, Iris raised a brow and asked, "Anything further?"

The governor shook his head.

"Good," she replied. "And if anyone wishes to quarrel with my decision, then they know where to find me. The palace is always open to my people."

With that, she stood and stepped down from the dais, leaving court to her sister queens.

———

IRIS DECIDED TO SPEND the remainder of the day in her cultivated palace garden. Growing up, she had enjoyed countless hours in the immaculate grounds that surrounded her childhood home. It was there where she had imagined her reign and how she would rule an entire quadrant. Iris had been a solitary child, and while she had thought she'd prepared herself to be queen, she had not expected anyone could be capable of influencing her reign.

Or her heart.

The garden was located in the Archian section of the palace, split in four as the nation itself. The garden sat outside the golden dome, perched on the cliff overlooking the channel toward the neighboring isle of Archia. Long ago, one of her ancestors had demanded access to nature—to life. Queenly Law decreed the queens were never to leave the palace—for their safety and to ensure they weren't moved by external influences.

Iris would never set foot in her quadrant again, never soak in the beauty of Archia or see the stags and deer roam the mountains.

She sat back in her wooden settee; it sank into the grass while her black skirt swallowed the frame. She removed her heavy crown and placed it on the table beside her. She tilted her head, enjoying the sunlight on her pale skin. The warm springs bubbled nearby, reminiscent of the gentle brook that trickled not far from her childhood home.

This would have to do.

Also dictated by Queenly Law, Iris had been raised by adoptive parents outside the palace in the region she would one day rule. But while she'd been raised in a humble stone cottage, she'd never wanted for anything. She didn't know *how* to want for things she'd never seen, never experienced. She learned all she could about her land, the animals and her people. And Quadara's dark past.

Archia had been an untouched refuge from the nation's

troubles for hundreds of years; in fact, it wasn't until Toria had built their boats and traveled to the west that the lush island was discovered. The rest of the nation had grown desperate, their natural resources nearly depleted. And there was Archia, ripe for the taking.

While the distinct regions had each developed strengths and resources, they shared the same weakness. Jealousy.

And so began the Quadrant Wars. They lasted nearly a decade, with thousands of lives lost. During this time, the other regions attempted to conquer Archia. But their plans were foolish. As rearing livestock was foreign to Eonists, Torians grew restless and wanted to discover new lands, and Ludists didn't want to dirty their elaborate outfits by tending to the crops.

Then the founding queens of Quadara built the walls to separate the regions, finally ending the Quadrant Wars. The walls provided space to breathe, allowing the quadrants to continue to evolve independently, and harmoniously.

Archia was once again safe.

Iris left her homeland for the first time on her eighteenth birthday, when she had been informed her mother had died. She sailed across the channel on a Torian vessel toward the palace. She took to her new world and throne without blinking, insisting she attend court minutes after her mother had been laid to rest beneath the palace. That evening she had stayed awake until the early morning, reading books on Archian history and diplomacy. Nothing could shake Iris. Not even the death of her mother.

Iris opened her green eyes to the vibrant blue sky—enjoying the break from the enduring golden palace. With the palace enclosed by a glass dome, every room, and everything within it, was cast in a golden hue. Even at night, the corridors blurred into a deep amber, as though darkness would not dare caress the queens with inky-black fingers.

When Iris looked to the clouds in the sky, she thought of her father. Not the father whose blood she shared—a man who'd never been identified by her mother—but the man who had raised her in Archia. When she was a child, he'd told her about the queens above, the deceased queens who lived in the quadrant without borders, watching the relatives they'd left behind. When she was alone, she would look to the clouds and share her gravest fears and most wondrous dreams, knowing her secrets were safe with them. Her most loyal confidants.

Then she came to the palace and met the queens. They spent every evening together—often staying up beyond a "respectable" hour to discuss their childhood, families and quadrants. Iris was no longer alone.

Still, she often looked to the sky, but now she spoke to her father, long dead.

"Father, I have not wavered," she said. "Queenly Law is, and will always be, paramount. However, there are certain rules that pertain to the queens, to *me*, that I have come to see as irrelevant over the years." Even speaking the words aloud felt wrong. Iris shook her head. She would need to be stronger, be a woman with an iron backbone. "We are the queens. We should be able to change the rules that do not affect the quadrants and the peace we uphold. We should have *some* control over our own lives." She shook her head. "I will continue to fight for Archia and protect all we have, but I want more." She shook her head again, thinking of the governor's request. "Not more for Archia, but for me." She hated how weak she sounded.

"I have a plan." She let out a weighted breath. "I've been too many years silent. But no longer. Tomorrow things will change. Queenly Law *will* change. Tomorrow I will—"

A bee pricked her throat. An intense bite, followed by a dull ache.

Bees, and all other bugs and insects, were supposed to have been eradicated from the garden by a spray. *Another wonderful Eonist creation,* Iris thought wryly. Iris didn't object to sharing her garden with the creatures that *should* come with it. But the advisors had insisted it was best, for Iris's safety.

A smile appeared on Iris's face; perhaps nature had conquered technology in the end, beating out the spray. She couldn't wait to gloat about her findings to Corra at tonight's evening meal.

The bee's sting grew more painful, to the point where Iris was unable to swallow. Saliva pooled in her throat. Was she allergic?

She brought a hand up to the bite and found a gaping ridge of skin. When she pulled her hand back, it was darkened with blood. A wail gurgled from her lips.

A figure loomed over her, teeth gleaming with menace and delight. A thin knife reflected a slice of sunlight, dripping red.

Fury flashed through her as hot blood spilled down her neck. Her arms flung backward, knocking her crown to the floor.

An outrage! I am the Archian queen!

How dare someone cut my thr—

CHAPTER THREE

Keralie

Mackiel Delore Jr. sat at his heavy oak desk and rotated the comm case in his hand, his rings sliding along the metal surface, his brows low. He'd been strangely quiet since I'd handed it over, and during the long, cold walk back from the Concord, through Central Toria and down to the auction house located on the half-rotted dock. He hadn't been this quiet since the day his parents died.

His pale skin and dark hair held the only resemblance to his father. Painfully narrow, he wore a waistcoat to help expand his width, and a bowler hat added to his meager height. Still, he was a fragment of his father, of who he wanted to be.

Mackiel Sr. had wanted a formidable protégé. Instead, he'd gotten a waif of a boy. He worried Mackiel's presence would not instill the same kind of fear and admiration in everyone who'd dealt with him and his business of Delore Imports and Exports.

He'd been wrong.

Mackiel looked upon the comm case as though he was equally delighted and troubled by what might be inside.

"Are you going to open it?" I asked him.

"And tarnish the goods?" He wagged a finger at me, his expression lifting. "You know better than that, darlin'."

I hissed as I took the seat opposite him.

"Hurt yourself, porcelain doll?" he asked with a grin. "You should be more careful with *your* goods."

I rolled my eyes and gently rubbed my bandaged knee under my faded black skirt. My con clothes were at the cleaners; hopefully they could beat the blood out. It was my mother's skirt. One of the few items I had of hers.

It had been six months since I'd seen my parents. Six months since my father's accident. Six months since I'd fled my home, unable to look my mother in the eye, and shut off that part of my heart, never to look back.

"It was worth it," I said. I'd do anything for Mackiel. While he was only two years older than me, he was both a friend and a mentor. And the only family I had left.

He jerked his chin. "With you, it always is."

I ignored him. Mackiel was always joking, but this time I didn't know if it was a jibe or whether he actually wanted more from me, from *us*. I wondered what he saw when he looked at me. Was it the put-together Torian girl I pretended to be? Or a broken girl, *his* porcelain doll; all that was needed was a crack to reveal the darkness growing within.

I didn't question what he would prefer.

Mackiel's office was located in the attic of the auction house, overlooking the Torian harbor. The moonlit sails of the boats glowed like ghosts on the dark water. I'd often wondered why he'd chosen this room overlooking the sea. Was it simply because it had been his father's? Or did he want to confront his phobia of the ocean each day, hoping the fear would one day subside?

Mackiel scratched his neck briefly to check he was not, nor was he about to be, submerged in water. He was stronger than he gave himself credit for. Unlike me. I couldn't face my ghosts. Any space smaller than my compact quarters behind the auction house stage sent me running from the room. Simply thinking about tight spaces made my chest constrict.

Small breath in, small breath out. There's a way in, and always a way out. The mantra helped still any anxiety curling in my belly, like an agitated eel.

"How much do you think it will go for?" I asked, distracting myself.

He placed the comm case on the table and stretched out his other hand. "This is for you."

In his palm was a silver locket in the shape of a gold quartier, the currency that united Quadara. I reached for the locket. He grabbed my fingers in his. *There*—the darkness that lately plagued his expression bubbled to the surface, and my friend was gone. "You took too long out there," he said.

I pulled away from him, the locket in my grasp, and leaned back in my chair. "Too long for what?" I countered. "Has anyone else stolen a comm case without being arrested by Quadarian authorities?"

"Touché," he said, tilting his chair back, mimicking me. The wooden frame dwarfed him. The room had been built and furnished for a larger man—Mackiel Delore Sr. And everything was exactly as he'd left it, before the blood plague.

The plague had started as a seasickness contracted on a return voyage from Archia and had spread swiftly once the boat had docked and the crew had returned to their homes in Toria. The disease had been merciless; mere hours after you'd been exposed, blood would seep from your eyes and ears, before hardening. Mackiel's mother had contracted it first, then his father.

Mackiel had rushed to the Eonist Medical Facility in hopes of gaining access to HIDRA. The Holistic Injury and Disease Repair Aid was an Eonist cure-all—Quadara's most prized creation. But only one "deserving" patient could be treated each year, due to dwindling supplies. The queens decided who that patient would be. A criminal and his wife were not high on their list.

Mackiel's parents were dead by the time he returned home.

The only change to Delore Imports and Exports in the three years since his father's death was the menacing gleam behind Mackiel's eyes and the growth in his security team. His henchmen were out tonight, doing his bidding. More monsters than men—I hoped they'd forget their way home.

"Thank you, Kera," Mackiel said suddenly.

I glanced up. "You're welcome?" It came out much more like a question than I'd meant it to, unsure how to take his shifting mood. We'd been friends for seven years. Our thieving had begun as a thrill to chase and a game to play, which also happened to fill our pockets with cash. He'd been a lively, charismatic boy of twelve, promising wealth, excitement and fantasy. A world far from the one I'd known.

While a young Mackiel had boasted about playing with the latest Eonist technologies and eating fluffy Ludist pastries, I'd shivered in my parents' narrow, dim cottage and eaten my mother's stew made from week-old fish scraps. My father had inherited his shipping business from his parents, but the boat had been leaky and could barely weather the storms between Archia and Toria. We'd lived week-to-week, my parents always hoping for a brighter horizon.

Mackiel's offer to join the dippers had been a ticket to a new life. I'd taken it without a second thought.

But over the past year, something increasingly tarnished Mackiel's thoughts like the sea air tarnished the dock. Where was the boy whose smile lit his face as easily as the sun lit the sky? Was it his parents' death that continued to haunt him, as my father's accident haunted me?

Six months ago, I'd moved into Mackiel's auction house—to my own room, of course. I thought moving in would've brought us closer, back to our childish years, when we did everything together. But he still disappeared for days, never telling me why.

"You did well," he said with a smile.

I rolled my new locket between my fingers before attaching it to my dipper bracelet. He'd started giving me lockets for increasingly dangerous thefts about a year ago. The coin hung among my other conquests. "Thanks for this," I said.

"I have something else for you." He held out an envelope. Fear racked my insides.

I tore the letter open without further preamble. My mother's latest letter was short, but struck me between the ribs like a blow.

Dear Keralie,

Please come to the Eonist Medical Facility at once. Your father is dying. The doctors believe he has weeks remaining, maybe less, if he isn't allowed access to HIDRA. Please come and say good-bye.

I love you, Keralie. We miss you. We need you.

Love,
Mom

I clutched the paper in my hands, my breath leaving in gasps.

Although it was six months ago, I could still hear my father screaming my name. It was the last word he uttered, almost like a curse, before he was thrown from his boat and hit his head on a nearby rock. I would never forget my mother's tearstained face as she sobbed over his unconscious body before he was carted away to receive medical attention.

My mother had stayed by his bedside for two weeks. By the time she returned home, I was gone. She sent numerous letters to the auction house begging me to join her at the hospital's accommodation, knowing exactly where I'd fled to.

But she was wrong. She didn't need me. My father was on the brink of the next world because of what I'd done. They were better off without me.

Meeting Mackiel had set me on a path for a different life, and my father's accident was the final act to sever me from my parents and their oppressive expectations. I couldn't return to them now. Much as I might want to.

"Everything all right?" Mackiel's voice was soft.

I shook my head. "My father's dying."

"No HIDRA?" he asked, expression darkening.

"Doesn't look like it." My father was one of thousands on the waiting list. For years, Eonist scientists had tried, but failed, to replicate the treatment. Whispers had begun to spread that there were no doses remaining.

"Curse those queens," Mackiel said, slamming his hand on the table. "I'm sorry, Kera."

I took a deep, steadying breath. I'd used up all the tears for my father in the days following the accident. He was gone to me the moment he was thrown from the boat.

A vibration rattled the building as the weight shifted on the floor beneath us. The audience had arrived.

"If you're not up for tonight," Mackiel said, "I'll understand."

"And miss out on seeing who buys my comm case?" I forced a smile. "I don't think so."

He gave me a sly grin, his somber mood disappearing. "Come, then. Let's not keep our audience waiting."

———

THE AUCTION HOUSE was located on the dock at the far, and seedier, end of the Torian harbor. As a child, the old trading hall had seemed like a majestic palace with its high-arched ceiling and wide columns. Now I saw the truth. The building should be condemned. The salty air had rotted the pylons, slanting the right side of the building toward the sea, and the decay of wood infected every room, including the drafty lodgings I rented behind the stage. I was sure the smell of decay followed me like a shadow. How fitting.

The audience shuffled in from the slightly more stable section of the dock, which housed other Torian attractions: the stuffy gambling houses, courtly pleasure palaces, and the dingy, damp pubs that rose in between like fungus in marshes, forming Toria's notorious Jetée district. Our neighbors' hands as dirty as our own.

The auction floor became increasingly crowded until there wasn't enough room to breathe without warming the back of someone's neck. If one more body crammed inside, we'd sink to the ocean floor beneath us. While there was no ignoring the cacophony bleeding out of the walls and onto the dock, Torian authorities left Mackiel to his sordid business.

The Torian queen had been intent on shutting the Jetée down for decades. She'd recently revealed her plans to demolish the dock for "safety reasons," but we knew the truth. She was desperate to erase the blight on "proper" Torian society. Could that be what tarnished Mackiel's thoughts?

Mackiel wasn't alone in his concern. During the day, when most of the Jetée establishments were shut and everyone *should* be home in their beds, loud voices could be heard from behind closed doors. Angry voices. Voices from the business owners, demanding to take vengeance on their meddling queen. They vowed to run *all* Torian businesses into the ground if she succeeded. Despite what the queen wanted to believe, the seedy underbelly was the heart of the quadrant. Cut that out, and Toria would perish.

I didn't involve myself in palace politics.

I watched from behind the stage curtain as the audience forgot their manners—or rather the manners they pretended to keep while in public as hardworking and enterprising explorers and traders. It wasn't long until the true, darker desires were

27

exposed. Wide skirts pushed in among one another, hands groped for exposed flesh, while children weaved in and out among legs like rats navigating the sewers, hoping to get a nibble of the action. A perfect training ground for new dippers—any kids who managed to steal from the audience without getting caught were worth recruiting.

It wasn't difficult to see why my parents had warned me to stay away from this place as a child. But with their cottage located near the harbor, the auction house had never been far from view.

Growing up by the sea, I loved to swim, but I had always hated sailing. Being short made it difficult to reach the mast and my small fingers were inept at tying knots. While my parents could walk the deck as though they were on dry land, I'd always been off balance. I couldn't understand why they loved the seafaring life: the early rises, the bitter cold, and the tiring, relentless work for little return.

After a voyage, my parents would huddle by a fire—on the days we could afford it—and reminisce about the journey, while I would pray to the queens above for a storm to strike down the boat moored in the harbor. As I got older, I'd beg them to travel without me and would throw a tantrum if they insisted I come along.

For years, I didn't know there was another way of life, a life I would enjoy, a life I'd thrive in. Then I met Mackiel.

I don't remember much of my first visit to the auction house except the feeling. A tangible thrill ignited my body and senses. I didn't steal anything, merely swept my hands across ladies' bags and dipped into men's pockets. But I could have taken something, and that was illuminating.

Mackiel found me later that night, sitting on the dock with my legs dangling below, my cheeks flushed with excitement despite the cold night. He introduced himself, offering his hand and a job.

I pushed back thoughts of my parents, my mother's letter and the aching absence they'd left in my life. An absence I'd created the day I decided to follow Mackiel down a darker road. There was no turning back now.

Searching the auction house crowd, I wondered who would be the owner of my comm case and the chips inside, and what my cut would be. I imagined the flurry of bids it would ignite from those desperate for a glimpse into Eonist life and their technology. Like the other quadrants, Torians weren't allowed to use most technologies from Eonia, for fear that it would alter our society. But that didn't stop us from wanting a taste.

And that was exactly what the chips would allow. All you had to do was place the comm chip on your tongue and your senses would be transported to another time and place. A memory, which would feel like your own. A message from another life.

Mackiel was standing in the stalls crudely erected into one side of the building. Since his father's death, Mackiel had added a heavy red curtain to conceal the wares from the crowd, the auction house now looking more like a Ludist theater than a warehouse. Just the way Mackiel liked it, preferring the spectacle of life.

Mackiel saved the seats in the stalls for "valued patrons," those too proper to sully their clothing by mingling down with the commoners. He ushered a girl with a large royal blue bonnet to her seat, one hand on her velvet-clad arm, the other to tilt his hat toward her. She looked up at him. Even from here, I could see her sickening, adoring expression. I looked away as Mackiel glanced in my direction, not wanting him to see the jealousy heat my face.

"Move," Kyrin said, elbowing me. "My wares are up first."

I happily stepped aside; his breath preceded him by at least ten feet. His sandy blond hair was stuck up in odd directions, as though he'd been trying to imitate the current trend in Ludia. It looked ridiculous on him. We dippers traditionally wore conservative clothes and attire, allowing us to blend into our surroundings.

"Still stealing watches?" I asked. Unfortunately for Kyrin, his tall stature made him stand out, no matter what he tried. Although, I hated to admit, his deft long fingers could unclasp watch fasteners in seconds, the owner none the wiser. "How long does that make it now? Five years?"

"Shut it, Keralie," he bit back.

I shrugged, tucking a stray lock behind my ear. "It's all right. Give it a few more years, and you'll get there. You see this?" I held out my wrist and jingled my new locket at him, a sign of moving up the ranks in Mackiel's crew. "Want a closer look? It might give you some inspiration." Kyrin's leather cuff had only two charms to keep each other company, while I had struggled to find room for my latest success. My parents used to argue that sailing was in my blood, but they'd never seen how I could take a woman's bag from her shoulder or the glasses right off a man's nose. *Thieving* was in my blood.

"I don't need *your* kind of inspiration." Kyrin pushed my arm out of the way. "Not all of us are willing to wet Mackiel's whistle as you do."

"I do nothing but my job!" I'd raised my clenched fist before I'd thought about my next move.

Kyrin didn't flinch. "Right. You think we're blind?" He gestured to the dippers watching with interest behind him. "You get all the best jobs."

"*Because* I am the best."

"The best at sucking his—"

I lurched forward, my fist about to slam into his face, but I was jerked back at the last second by a hand covered in rings from nail to knuckle.

"What's going on here?" Mackiel asked, his eyes flashing between us, his full mouth pulled up at one side.

"Nothing," I replied, swallowing down my anger. I didn't want to discuss the rumors spreading about Mackiel and me until I knew where we stood. "I was just hearing about the gorgeous Ludist watch Kyrin acquired today." I gave Kyrin a sweet smile.

Mackiel grinned at me. "Is that so?" He tapped my dimpled cheek. "Sweet." Tap. "Little." Tap. "Kera." Tap.

I pulled my wrist out of Mackiel's grasp and stepped away, hating the way Kyrin's eyes lingered on the contact. Sure, there were the late nights in Mackiel's rooms, discussing the future of the auction house. But nothing had happened, although I felt us teetering on the precipice of more. Or at least, *I* was teetering. In the last year, he didn't seem to care as much about me anymore.

"What is it that I always tell you?" Mackiel's voice was melodic, but still authoritative. His deep-set eyes flicked among us all.

"Never detract from the wares," we replied in unison.

I kicked Kyrin's shin for good measure. He grunted in reply and took a step away.

"Very good," Mackiel said, fiddling with his bowler hat. "And we have a generous collection tonight. Let's stay on track, shall we?"

Generous? I caught Mackiel's eye. He hadn't answered my question about the comm case's worth and the chips inside. He avoided my probing gaze and scratched briefly at his neck, his eyes landing on me, then darting away again. Mackiel was never nervous, not when it came to an auction. This was what he lived for now that his father was gone.

"Places, dippers," he said. "Let's begin!" He swept onto the stage, his long coat flapping behind him.

"Mackiel seems distracted." Kyrin's breath wafted over me as he whispered in my ear. "Didn't put out last night?"

This time I went for Kyrin's toes with the spiked heels of my boots. I reveled in the *squelch* as the spikes pierced through the leather and into his skin.

"You bitch!" he yelped, hopping up and down on one foot. "One day you're going to get yours!"

I shoved past him and the rest of the gawking dippers.

"Maybe," I called back over my shoulder, "but you won't be the one to deliver." Not while Mackiel had my back.

I pushed my way to the entrance of the auction house to watch the proceedings from behind the crowd. Perspiration dotted my brow from the crammed bodies heating the cavernous room; the only relief was the salty breeze, wafting in through cracks in the timber floor.

A groan shuddered the building. The bidders quickly shuffled a little more to the left to balance out the weight.

"Welcome to my house!" Mackiel boomed, his voice filling the theater. "For tonight, you and I are family. And my family deserves the best!" It was his father's line, but the crowd still lapped it up as if hearing it for the first time.

His father had built this black market business from nothing. As a young man, not much older than Mackiel was now, he saw the opportunity to capitalize on the curious nature of his fellow Torians who couldn't afford to own a boat or purchase interquadrant approved goods. Instead, he provided the goods at a much lower price.

"You're in luck tonight," Mackiel continued, "for we have our best selection." He said this each and every night, but tonight it was true. Second only to the thrill of acquiring the wares was the clamor during an auction. I grinned in anticipation. The perfect distraction from my mother's letter.

"Before we begin, we must cover the auction guidelines." The crowd spread a groan like fleas on a stray dog. "Now, now," Mackiel tsked. "First business, then pleasure. That's what I always say." He grinned, and the crowd was back in the palm of his hand. Mackiel's proclivity for spectacle had increased the bidders by dozens, ensuring they didn't stray to his competitors after his father's death. In fact, some of his competitors were here for the show, keeping their quartiers warm in their pockets.

"Right then, as you know, we don't trade in full payments here; it's too tempting for those with sticky fingers." Laughter circulated through the crowd, the audience knowing full well how Mackiel "procured" the auction items, and the hypocrisy of it all. "That said, a ten percent down payment will be required to secure the bid. At the end of the auction, my darling dippers will follow the highest bidder home to collect the remaining quartiers. If you can't find the funds, the dipper will return with the wares, and the rest of you will have the chance to bid for it tomorrow night. But I don't give second chances to those who play games."

What Mackiel withheld from the audience was that his

dippers had one hour to return with the payment and then we were given a five percent cut for our troubles. New dippers often tried to pocket more than their cut or keep the stolen valuables for themselves. Mackiel used to banish any disloyal dippers, leaving no quartiers to their name, but now he used his henchmen to enforce his law.

A shiver ran down my back at the thought of their skin on mine, or worse, their whiteless black eyes upon my face. It had been two years since Mackiel had hired them and I was still not used to their presence. And I couldn't deny the impact they'd had on Mackiel. As a boy, he used to rescue rats from the Jetée sewers; now that was where he dumped the bodies of those who betrayed him.

"The henchmen got a little carried away," he'd say. But the darkness behind his eyes made me question who had in fact done the deed. I wasn't sure I wanted to know the truth.

Mackiel continued with the rules. "There will be no further negotiations after the auction is complete. If I see the ware appear at another house, well, let's say you'll never set foot in here again." He smiled widely, though the message was clear: the day you cheated him would be your last.

"Finally, my business and my service"—he grinned at the audience, his eyes glimmering—"and my presence are a luxury only Torians can enjoy, and should not be taken for granted. Remember, my name and my dippers' names are never to be spoken outside of my house. This is of the utmost importance."

The bidders grew restless as his speech wore on. They'd heard it before. They wanted to see what was up for auction. What relic or prize from other quadrants could they get their grubby hands on? Something to improve their life? Medicine, perhaps?

Something trivial to sit upon their mantelpiece, which they could brag about to friends?

Or comm chips—allowing them a glimpse into life in another quadrant—the perfect prize for any Torian.

My undergarments clung to my sticky skin. *Come on, Mackiel. Get on with it.*

"All right, then," he said, finally. "Enough business. On with the show!"

The crowd burst into applause as Mackiel yanked back the curtain to reveal the first item for auction. The early wares moved slowly: woven Archian blankets, handkerchiefs and scarves, and Ludist paintings, jewelry and hair tints. Hands rose in reluctance. No one wanted to spend their money too early. There weren't many bids for Kyrin's watch—the most common of pickpocket items. I chuckled under my breath. Kyrin wouldn't earn much tonight.

Frustration darkened Mackiel's expression, his brow low over his eyes. He wanted the best. But that was why he had me.

The bidders grew restless. They wanted more. Something they'd never seen before. Something from Eonia, the most different of all the quadrants. I shuffled my feet side to side to see between hats. I had no doubt Mackiel would leave my comm case—his top prize—till last.

The audience shifted like a disturbed sea as Mackiel unveiled the next item. A torn sleeve of a dermasuit. Not very useful, but at least more interesting than a watch. The crowd leaned forward for a better look, before raising their hands in earnest. I ducked to the side as the man beside me lifted his dank armpit in my face.

That was when I saw him.

He stood still in the middle of the crowd as everyone moved

around him. A scuffed top hat was pulled low over his black hair, and he wore a blue vest over a crumpled white shirt. But I knew who he was—his dermasuit was peeking beneath his collar.

The messenger.

He was here for the comm chips.

CHAPTER FOUR

Corra
Queen of Eonia

*Rule two: Emotions and relationships cloud
judgment. Eonists must concentrate solely
on technological advancements, medicine
and the community as a whole.*

The news of Iris's death was whispered in Corra's ear the moment she twisted in her bed, her eyes flicking open. She sat up in shock, her dreams fading into the dark bedroom. She'd retired to her room for an afternoon nap once court had concluded; the pretenses often exhausted her.

"What?" she asked, facing her fleshy advisor. He loomed over her, his hands stiff by his sides. "What did you say, Ketor?"

"Queen Iris is dead, my queen," he repeated, his eyes darting away from her bare brown shoulder. Sleep was the one time Eonists didn't wear their dermasuits, and it was a freedom Corra enjoyed, if not reveled in. She knew it wasn't very Eonist of her—she should be coy and conservative—but she didn't care. Especially not now.

"No," she said. "That's not possible."

"I'm afraid it's true, my queen. She was found in her garden a few hours ago."

"The doctors couldn't save her?" Corra's voice trembled.

"They were too late," he said, eyes downcast. "She was already dead." Even Eonist doctors could not resolve the finality of death, although they had tried. Once.

Corra drew herself from her four-poster bed, not caring her naked body was on display as she reached for her gold dermasuit, which lay across her dressing chair. It wasn't like the suit covered much more. She pushed her arms and legs through the tight-fitting material, the suit fluttering against her skin as it adjusted to her curves. She realized her handmaiden was also present, a young Archian woman with red blotches on her cheeks and glassy eyes, no doubt from crying over the news of Iris's death. Most of the palace staff were Archian, for they were no-nonsense, hardworking people.

Corra picked up her small gold watch—a coronation gift—from her bedside table, slipped the chain over her head and tucked it under the material. She turned to allow her handmaiden to knot her thick black hair into a bun and secure her heavy crown with pins. While her face was hidden, she squeezed her eyes shut, willing her emotions away.

"How did it happen?" Corra asked, turning around when she was composed.

Iris was still a young woman and her health was as strong as her resolve. Corra had never seen Iris sick, even with her Archian upbringing, which had sheltered her from all mainland viruses.

Surely this is a nightmare. Simply a vivid dream, she thought.

She wanted to climb back into her bed. Iris could not be dead. She was as permanent as the gilded walls surrounding her—protecting her—or she should've been.

Ketor was silent for a moment, drawing her eyes to his.

His ruddy cheeks were absent of tears. "She was murdered, my queen," he said.

"Murdered?" Corra's hand flew to her mouth. No queen had ever been murdered within the palace. Attempts had been made hundreds of years ago, when the Quadarian monarchs were free to roam their quadrants and the Quadrant Wars savaged society, but that was before Queenly Law had been established. Now to leave the palace was to forfeit the throne—ensuring the queens followed this crucial law. It was not only for their safety but to guarantee they were not influenced by the voices of the people. For the unhappy always spoke the loudest.

"I'm sorry to say it's true," Ketor continued. He remained distant, seemingly uncaring. Like Corra, he was Eonist. Queenly Law dictated a queen's advisor share her quadrant of origin, protecting the quadrant's integrity.

"Queens above," Corra said, leaning slightly against a bedpost to stay upright. Surely shock was allowed? "How did this happen?"

He cleared the discomfort from his throat. "It's grisly, my queen."

When he didn't elaborate, she said, "Tell me." This was Iris. She had to know.

"Her throat was cut, my queen."

A gasp ripped through Corra's body before she could stop it. She shut her eyes briefly once more to center herself and stabilize her emotions. Her chest felt unusually tight.

"Don't be vulgar, Ketor!" Corra's handmaiden admonished.

Corra shook her head, knowing her advisor was simply being honest. Eonist. "That's all right. I wanted to know. What's the protocol?" She needed to play along until her advisor left her side. Then her real emotions could show.

Grief. She'd never felt the weight of it before. It was rare for someone to pass unexpectedly in Eonia. Due to Eonist advancements, their lives were long, not cut short by illness or old age. Some had shorter lifespans due to genetic abnormalities, but their deaths were still not unexpected. Little was unexpected in Eonia. Corra would rule till her death date in her ninetieth year, although she was allowed to abdicate, if she so desired.

"The queens have been called to court before the nightly meal to discuss who will inherit the Archian throne," Ketor said.

Corra wouldn't have time to grieve.

"She has no direct heir," Corra said. Iris had claimed she couldn't find an appropriate suitor, no matter how many men had been paraded in front of her.

Ketor nodded.

"What will happen in the absence of an heir?" she asked.

"I don't know, my queen." His expression was frustratingly calm. "We must attend court at once."

While Corra's heart was splintered by the news of Iris's murder, she would not allow her stoic mask to crumble. To grieve was not Eonist. It implied feelings beyond general associations. Eonists were a unified people, but distant. It provided an environment where logic and knowledge reigned.

"Lead the way," she said.

———

MARGUERITE WAS ALREADY upon her throne when Corra entered court. She wore a traditional black Torian dress for mourning with a veil attached to her crown that covered most of her face. Corra wanted to run to the eldest queen, but she forced her footsteps to steady. Stessa had yet to arrive, no doubt ensuring her death mask was painted on in perfect detail, the Ludist custom of showing respect for those who had passed. The girl was always late to meetings, but for once, it didn't aggravate Corra. Sixteen was far too young to deal with such monstrosities.

When Corra neared the dais, Marguerite lifted her veil. Corra startled. The Torian queen's usually clear alabaster skin was blotchy, and her sharp features were softened from puffiness. She looked older than her forty years.

Marguerite stood and embraced her. Corra didn't register the contact until she was surrounded by her floral perfume.

"Are you all right?" Marguerite asked. "Have you eaten? You look unsteady on your feet." She pulled back, searching Corra's face. Corra willed herself to be calm, then nodded. The tightness around her chest had moved to her throat. Marguerite gave her arms a squeeze. Corra wished she could feel the warmth of the older woman's hands through her dermasuit.

"We must take care of ourselves, and each other, now more than ever," Marguerite said. "We are all we have." Sadness pulled at her brow and mouth.

"Yes," Corra replied, her gaze steadying on Marguerite's as she ignored the swirl of sorrow inside her.

The advisors had arranged three thrones close together on the dais to face one direction—Iris's quadrant. Corra had only seen the thrones encircling the Quadarian dial. She hesitated, unsure which throne to take. They all looked the same, and yet foreign, in that moment.

"Next to me, dear," Marguerite said, nodding beside her. Corra stared blankly. Iris should have been between them.

Marguerite took hold of Corra's gloved hand and gave it an encouraging squeeze. Corra pressed her lips together—not quite a smile, not a frown. She could sense Marguerite's disappointment; she wanted someone to grieve with.

She wouldn't get that from an Eonist. Emotion clouded thoughts, muddying logic and intellect, and that got in the way of progress.

Corra took a deep breath and sat down. Immediately, she was affronted by the view. Every day, Corra sat facing north and the beginning of her quadrant. Although there were no walls inside the throne room to segregate what was and wasn't Eonist, she believed she could sense where her quadrant began and ended. She loved Eonia, and it didn't feel right facing toward the west of the room—toward Archia and neighboring Toria. She could see the Torian crest painted on the floor, depicting a boat crossing an ocean. Framing the boat was one large fishhook, and on the other side, a spyglass—symbolizing the quadrant's focus on trade and exploration. Next was the Ludist section of court, denoted by a painted crest of ribbons, garlands and gems encircling the sun and moon—the picture of frivolity.

Corra pressed her fingers to the crest stitched on the shoulder of her suit: a strand of DNA twisting together to form a loop—symbolizing community—and willed stillness to settle upon her skin.

Beyond the painted crests stood the advisors. They were all talking at once, their faces drawn in concern. There had always been an heir to inherit the throne before the passing of a queen—part of Queenly Law. A queen must give birth to a girl before she turned forty-five. Even Corra's future daughter would be required to have her own baby girl before this milestone, ensuring the royal line.

Without a queen per quadrant, the borders that had safeguarded Quadara for decades would fracture and blur. No one wished to see the nation return to its combative past, and it was believed the quadrants, and their respective queens, maintained the peace. If Quadara weakened, they risked other nations turning their attention to the wealthiest continent. The palace, and the governing advisors, could not risk Quadara's future.

The advisors hushed as Queen Stessa made her entrance. Her short black hair was twisted and curled around her gem-laden crown, reminding Corra of a bird's nest. Dark red lines were painted in intricate patterns across her copper skin, leading down to her neck, where a ribbon was tied to symbolize the injury that had taken Iris's life. The rest of her outfit was subdued—for a Ludist—a simple brown dress to represent the earth to which Iris would be returned, although metaphorically in this instance. The queens were laid to rest within the Queenly Tombs, hidden in the labyrinthine tunnels beneath the palace.

Stessa bowed to her sister queens, shutting her brown eyes briefly to reveal red-stained lids. The death mask complete. A shudder ran down Corra's spine. She was glad Eonists didn't have such strange and opulent customs. To draw attention to yourself was disrespectful; you should be staying quiet and contemplative when faced with loss.

"Apologies for my tardiness," Stessa said, taking her throne. And though her face was an image of grief, Corra could see no lines pulling down the corners of her lips. The youngest queen appeared to be the least affected of them all. Perhaps it was because Stessa had known Iris for only a year? Or perhaps it was because Ludists took pleasure in the strangest of things. Everything a game, a reason to celebrate, flaunt an elaborate outfit and eat a wasteful amount of food.

Would Stessa fear her own death? Or would that be considered part of the game of life? Corra wondered. As an Eonist, Corra shouldn't believe in the queens above or life after death, and yet she did, hoping she would one day be reunited with her mother. And now Iris.

"Let's begin," Marguerite said in her commanding voice. It felt wrong to begin without Iris, as though they were sullying her memory. The advisors took their seats. While Marguerite's presence was reassuring, it was clear no one knew what to do or say.

"Well?" Stessa asked after a moment of silence. "What do we do now?"

Iris's advisor, a tall and stern-looking woman with a wisp of white hair, stepped forward. "I will speak for my queen and for Archia."

The sister queens glanced at one another before nodding.

"Go ahead, Alissa," Marguerite said, her shrewd eyes prepared to analyze.

"Thank you, Queen Marguerite," she said. "As you all know, Queen Iris did not have a female heir. She was trying for children, but she had yet to have a fruitful match."

A lie. The truth was that Iris never even tried to find a match.

Corra glanced at Marguerite. Marguerite also hadn't

produced an heir after years of trying. She'd been unable to carry to full term—even with the assistance of Eonist medicines. Whispers had spread through the palace that she never would.

There hadn't been fewer than four queens for over four hundred years—not since the tenth king of Quadara had taken a wife from each region of his nation. *To taste all that Quadara has to offer,* he'd famously said. When he had died unexpectedly and his four young wives had yet to produce any heirs, the queens decided they would rule in his place—one for each land of their origin. It had been the simplest solution.

Marguerite spoke, her shoulders inclined toward the advisors in front of her, her probing expression unchanged. "Surely we have prepared for such an event?" She glanced to her advisor, a tall man with a round and pleasant face named Jenri.

Jenri nodded. "Yes, that's correct, my queen. Queenly Law states that a female relative is allowed to take the throne in the absence of a female offspring."

Corra knew in these circumstances it wouldn't matter who this woman was, as long as they continued what the king's four wives—the original queens of Quadara—had started.

She could feel the tension; the palace needed an Archian heir, before the Quadarian people learned of Iris's passing. Only queens could uphold Queenly Law; without the laws, the nation would fall to disarray and give voice to those who questioned the relevance of the four queens and the walls in today's peaceful age. And it would further fuel the uprising stirring down on the Jetée in Toria; they wanted increased access to Ludia and Eonia, unhappy with their place in the nation's hierarchy.

Marguerite tried to keep her people appeased, allowing them to continue to run all trade for Quadara, but she knew they wanted more.

Alissa nodded to Jenri. "We will begin our search to replace the departed queen at once."

"Departed?" Stessa snorted. "Iris was murdered! Her throat cut! You speak as if she chose to leave us."

"I apologize for my wording," Alissa replied, lowering her eyes.

Marguerite turned to the young queen. "Stessa, this is a tough time for us all. Do not take it out on the advisors. They grieve as we do."

Stessa huffed. "Just because you're the oldest doesn't mean you can speak down to me. You don't rule me, or Ludia."

Marguerite held her hand out across Corra's lap to reach for Stessa. "That was not my intention," she said.

Stessa merely stared at Marguerite's fingers. "Well, try harder, then." Marguerite retracted her hand as though she'd been stung. "With one queen gone, you're already taking the opportunity to steer this toward your interests."

"My interests?" Marguerite sat back in her throne in irritation. "My interests are my quadrant, my sister queens and Quadara. That is all."

"Unlikely!" Stessa replied. "You see this as an opportunity to have more of a voice in court! You're Torian—of course you want to stick your nose into everyone's business. Why can't you leave us be?"

"Stop." Corra rose from her throne. "We can't turn on one another." Iris was the strongest of them all; without her, they were already falling apart. "Why has no one spoken of what happened to her?"

Marguerite turned from Stessa with a small shake of her head. The two had been close when Stessa had first entered the palace, needing a motherly figure, but now the youngest queen seemed to take offense whenever Marguerite spoke.

"I'm sorry, Queen Corra," Alissa began. "I didn't know you hadn't heard. It's terrible, but her throat was—"

Corra stopped her with a wave of her hand. "No. No one has said *who* did it. Why are we bickering like children when there was a murderer in the palace? Who *still* might be in the palace?" Was she the only one focused on the actual issue?

Stessa sank farther into her chair, curling into herself like a wounded animal. "A murderer?"

"One does not get murdered without a murderer," Corra said bluntly. "Don't be foolish." She had wanted to say *childish*, but that was an easy shot. And Corra was not hot-blooded. She was calm. Still.

Steady hand. Steady heart, Corra reminded herself of her mother's famous words.

"Of course we must find an heir for Archia," Corra said to the advisors, her hand on a small lump where her watch was concealed beneath her dermasuit, "but we can't forget what brought us here. We have to uncover who killed Iris and why."

"She wasn't very kind," Stessa replied quietly, studying her black-painted nails.

Perhaps she wasn't to Stessa, Corra thought. Iris had issues with the Ludist queen and her wavering temperament. She'd often said that Stessa was too young to take her position seriously.

"And she wanted too much from this." Stessa glanced to the words engraved on the walls surrounding them. "More than what's allowed."

Corra snapped her attention to the Ludist queen. "What are you talking about?"

Stessa glanced away. "You know how she was." But she left something unsaid, her black brows knitting together, her death mask cracking.

No one spoke in Iris's defense. Something inside Corra's stomach twisted and burned.

"Queen Iris was a good queen," Marguerite said finally, her voice steady as though she dared anyone argue with her. She addressed Alissa. "And Queen Corra is correct. We need to uncover how someone made it into the palace undetected and killed Queen Iris. How was this person not spotted? And how were they allowed to carry out such a ghastly act unnoticed?"

"I will investigate, Queen Marguerite," Alissa replied.

"No," Corra said. All eyes were on her. She lowered her hand from her chest. "We need someone from outside the palace, outside of Queen Iris's staff. Someone on the outside of influence." And suspicion.

The sister queens nodded.

"I will call an inspector immediately," Corra said. "We will uncover the truth."

CHAPTER FIVE

Keralie

I stared at the back of the messenger's worn top hat. What was his plan? Ask Mackiel for the comm case? Steal it back?

Unless he won the comm case in the auction . . .

There was no way he'd be able to afford it. The comm case was sure to ignite a bidding frenzy. People would fight for the chance to use unique technology from Eonia and *witness* the quadrant for themselves. While I'd never had the pleasure of the experience myself, I knew comm chips allowed Eonists to share memories as if they were your own.

The messenger was a fool to come here. Mackiel's henchmen wouldn't be far—the mere sight of them was sure to send the boy running back to his perfect, polished quadrant before they even laid a hand on him.

No one appeared to notice the messenger wasn't one of their own. But even if I hadn't seen the black dermasuit tucked beneath his collar, his movements gave him away. Calm and controlled. Not fidgety like Torians. We didn't have time to be still. We didn't have the luxury. And he was too clean cut. His sharp cheekbones, defined jaw and perfect skin stood out among the grimy faces in the crowd; the seafarers who hadn't had time to bathe before the auction began, bringing their sea-tarnished quartiers and the stink of fish along with them.

I waited for the messenger to reveal his plan, while he waited for his comm case to be unveiled.

Mackiel's musical voice filled the room. "And that, my fair Torians, is the last item up for auction this evening." Everyone groaned in response. He fluttered his hands at them. "Don't fret! Don't fret! For my dippers will have a mountain of goods from all the quadrants for tomorrow night." He tilted his bowler hat, his lips pursed. "No one misses out here!"

What? I tore my eyes from the messenger to glare at Mackiel. Where was my comm case? Mackiel never held on to a ware for another night, always sold it as soon as he claimed it, ensuring the owner didn't come to collect.

Like the messenger.

The audience began shuffling out the front door and back to their lives. The fleeting moment when they'd glimpsed another quadrant gone. I stepped to the side to let them pass. When I looked back to the messenger, he'd disappeared.

What was Mackiel thinking? Had he received an early offer? High-profile clients, those who claimed to be above all that the Jetée had to offer, were allowed to bid early so as not to be spotted in the crowd. Someone like Governor Tyne.

"You," a voice said from behind me. A breath tickled my neck. I spun.

It was the messenger. His dark curls were tucked under his hat, his moon-like eyes gleaming like a cat's in the dark.

Before I could reply, he pulled me into a side corridor by my sleeve and pressed the edge of a long cylinder to the base of my neck. And although such a device had never been against my skin, I knew the shape. An Eonist destabilizer. "Where is my comm case?" he asked.

I stood still, not wanting the current to spark my skin and travel to my brain, rendering me unconscious, or worse. Destabilizers were used by wall guards when someone tried to illegally enter another quadrant. On the lowest setting, it resulted in you losing consciousness, and the contents of your bowels. At the highest setting, it liquefied your brain and interior organs.

"I don't have it." I barely moved my lips, let alone anything else. I wanted to keep my insides where they belonged.

Where were Mackiel's henchmen when I needed them?

The messenger kept the destabilizer against my neck. "You played me. You stole from me. Tell me where the comm case is, and I won't be forced to press this button."

"Press the button, and you're shit out of luck." He flinched at my curse. Cursing wasn't allowed in Eonia; it betrayed emotion. But it would be the least of his worries when Mackiel's henchmen arrived. "You'll never find out where the comm case is."

He pressed the destabilizer harder into my neck. The current tingled my exposed skin.

"I need that comm case and the chips inside," he said.

"I'm telling you the truth."

"You have ten seconds."

"I told you, I don't have it."

He spun me around to face him. "Where is it, then? Why wasn't it up for auction?"

"Drop the destabilizer, and I'll find out."

He studied my face for a moment before loosening his grip. "Okay, agreed." He jerked his chin backstage. "Take me to it."

"Stay here, and I'll find out when it's going to be sold."

"No. That wasn't our agreement."

Ha, of course! Eonist morality meant their words were like a blood promise—a binding agreement. I could use this to my advantage.

I tucked a curl behind my ear. "You don't want to meet Mackiel, trust me. He'll gut you for coming here. I'll find out when the comm case is up for auction, and you can return to bid for it then."

He stared at me, his Eonist face still. "You want me to bid for an item you stole?"

I shrugged. "That's how it works."

"That's not how it works in Eonia."

I batted my eyes at him. "You're not in Eonia."

"That comm case and the chips inside belong to me. To my employer." He fiddled with a small device hooked around his ear, a comm line, allowing him to communicate with someone long distance—an Eonist technology.

"Now they belong to mine." I smiled sweetly.

"You don't seem to be understanding me."

No. This messenger didn't get it. Mackiel didn't take well to betrayal. I'd seen dippers kicked out on their ass for a lot less. I wouldn't—*couldn't*—go home. I'd take my chances with this messenger boy. And yet behind his calm Eonist appearance was a hint of desperation.

"I'm sorry," I said, though I wasn't. Not really. "You were my target, and the comm case is Mackiel's now. The only way to get it back is to win it at auction."

He must have realized I wasn't lying, as he released me.

"If I don't deliver that comm case," he said quietly, studying the moldy floorboards, "my job will be forfeited." He raised his eyes, rimmed with black lashes; a shiver ran along my back from the intensity of his expression. "Without work, they'll move up my death date."

Death date?

He noticed my confusion and clarified. "I'm as good as dead. Please, I'll give you anything you want in return."

I glanced around the auction house; the floor was a mess of food wrappers and globs of tobacco spittle. Stray dogs were sniffing out anything edible and pissing and shitting wherever they pleased. Without any wares on display and Mackiel's smoke and mirrors, the auction house's true form was exposed. And though it stank of unwashed bodies, dog shit and rot, it was home.

"I'm sorry." I meant it this time. "What's on the comm chips?" Coming from the House of Concord, the one place where Eonists, Torians, Ludists and Archians did business together, the memory had to be of high importance. Perhaps it had come from the palace itself?

"It's not my job to know, and it doesn't matter," he said. "I just need them back."

"Okay." I looked around for the other dippers, but they'd all left to follow the auction winners back to their homes for the payment exchange. I was the only one left behind. "Okay," I repeated. "Wait here and I'll go get it for you."

"No, I'll come with you." He pressed a button on the side of his comm line. "I'll have it soon," he said to the person on the other end. While Eonists don't get angry, the receiver's muffled voice sounded pretty irate. The messenger's eyes flashed to mine. "Yes, I'll deliver it tomorrow, first thing." The messenger pressed the button again, and the other voice went quiet.

That wasn't going to work. I wasn't *really* going to steal it back for him; I needed to get away and find Mackiel. He'd know what to do. "I told you, that's not a good idea. You stay here, and I'll get your comm case back." I gave him my sweetest Torian smile. "Promise."

"I don't believe you," he said.

I didn't blame him. "If Mackiel sees you with me, he'll know what's going on." I gestured to his clothing. "You may have the crowd fooled, but you won't fool him."

He stared at me for a moment before saying, "Be quick."

I was getting tired of people telling me that.

———

MACKIEL'S OFFICE WAS empty, but I knew he wouldn't be far.

Stolen wares were locked in a vault hidden behind a Ludist landscape—a maze of canals and bridges—a painting his father had stolen back when he was a fledgling dipper. We all knew what lay behind it, although we would never have dared open it.

I sat down in Mackiel's chair to await his return. The harbor looked different from here. Beautiful, even. If you ignored the smell, you could imagine overlooking a vast constellation, the boats' lanterns on the black sea like stars in the night sky. And Mackiel was king of this nocturnal kingdom. Until the Torian queen tore this place down.

"What are you doing?" a voice asked from behind me. I spun in the chair, a hand to my chest.

The messenger stood in the doorway.

"I told you to stay put!" I gasped for air. I wasn't used to being snuck up on.

"Did you get the comm case?"

"I got tired. Needed to rest first." I placed my feet up on the desk.

He stepped toward me, the destabilizer raised. "Stop wasting my time."

That was exactly what I was going to do until Mackiel and his henchmen returned. Instead, I accidentally glanced at the painting.

He noticed my mistake and approached the wall. He ran his fingers along the brushstrokes before removing the landscape.

"Oh, well," I said, looking at the bare brick wall behind the artwork. "I guess I *really* don't know where it is." I tried not to sound too smug.

"It's an Eonist safe," he said. He pressed his hand to the wall. For a moment, the bricks shimmered, as if something reflective lay behind them.

When had Mackiel upgraded to an Eonist safe? And why? It had to have something to do with the comm case and the chips inside. What memory did they hold that required this kind of security?

"Open it," the messenger said with a jerk of his head.

I pressed my hand to the wall and it shimmered again. "Does this look like something I can open?"

He let out an exasperated breath. "Open the vault, and I won't hurt you."

I held up my hands. "I'm not lying to you. I can't open this."

"You're a thief," he said, disgust dripping from his words.

"The best," I added with a grin.

"Then open it." He moved forward, the destabilizer pointed toward my head.

I took a step back. "Let's not be too hasty here. This is Eonist tech." I'd heard about Jetée businesses acquiring Eonist security to ward off other Torians. "I don't even know how it works."

"The vault is keyed to the thoughts of its owner. It opens only when the owner wants it to be opened," he explained.

"Mackiel will never open it for you." Where *was* Mackiel?

He continued, ignoring me. "The vault is built from micro-organisms, like the technology embedded into the material of our dermasuits. At the core, they're sentient."

"This is all very interesting"—I waved my hand at the wall—"but none of this is going to help. I'm a thief, as you said, not a therapist. I can't help unscramble, or scramble, a mind—whatever the case may be."

Hang on. I blinked. I couldn't scramble a mind, but I knew what could. "Give me your destabilizer."

The messenger looked at me as though I were mad. "No."

I placed my hands on my hips. "I can unlock the vault." Although I wasn't planning on it. Once I had the destabilizer, I could use it on the messenger.

He looked between the wall and his weapon, then aahed in understanding. Too bad he wasn't as dumb as his stony expression suggested. He removed his hat and ran a hand through his black curls. "Please move aside."

"Only because you asked nicely."

He held the destabilizer to the wall and pressed the small button at the base. A bright blue streak flashed before the bricks disappeared altogether, the microorganisms now unconscious.

And although I should've been concerned about Mackiel finding us breaking into his vault, I couldn't help but enjoy the buzz. I forgot where I was, caught up in the game.

The vault yawned back into the darkness. I squinted. It hadn't been this large the last time I'd been in here. Mackiel must have extended into the room next door—his quarters. Why hadn't he told me? And what else was he hiding?

The messenger flipped a switch on his destabilizer, and light bled out in a circle, illuminating the alcove in an instant. The closest shelves were mostly empty, making the silver comm case easy to locate.

I darted forward and slid the comm case into my palm before the messenger could reach for it.

"What are you doing?" he asked.

"Ensuring my safety." I stepped back out of the vault, my eyes fixed on the destabilizer. "We'll do a swap. You give me your destabilizer, and I'll give you the comm case." *Come on, come on.*

The messenger stepped forward but then stopped, his gaze trained on the office doorway. I turned reluctantly.

"Hello, darlin'." Mackiel was blocking the exit, a pistol in his hand.

The messenger held the destabilizer up, but it was useless against Mackiel at a distance. I'd seen more powerful versions that shot darts of voltage, but it was clear this smaller one was meant for hand-to-hand combat.

"Mackiel!" I said in relief. "Thank the queens above you're here. This messenger said he'd destabilize me if I didn't return his comm case."

Mackiel moved to stand behind his desk, his pistol unwavering. "Is that so?"

I frowned at him, confused by his cold reaction. I knew how it looked, but I would never betray Mackiel.

"Yes." Now was not the time to be playing games.

The messenger shot me an angry look, an expression I wouldn't have believed he was capable of making.

"Kera, darlin'," Mackiel mused. "My most daring, my most talented . . . my *best* dipper." He didn't say *friend*. I stayed quiet, unsure where he was going with this and scared by the deadly look in his eye. "*And* my best liar." He smirked. "I've trained you well."

Only then did I realize the pistol was aimed at me.

"What are you talking about?" I asked. "You know me. I would never—"

"Oh, be quiet!" he snapped. "I know exactly what you would and wouldn't do. Hand over the comm case. Now."

"What's wrong with you?" I asked. "You know I wouldn't betray you."

"Really?" He raised an eyebrow. "You're saying you'd never leave me for dead?" He scratched at his neck.

"That was years ago! You know that was an accident!" And what did that have to do with the comm case? What was so important about the memories the chips held?

"An accident?" He pursed his lips. "Like your father's? Many people seem to have *accidents* around you."

I flinched as though I'd been slapped. He'd never spoken to me that way. He'd grown cold, yes, but never cruel. This wasn't my friend. The boy I knew would *never* have thrown that in my face. He had comforted me after my father had been gravely injured. He'd given me a place to live when I couldn't face my mother. Why was he turning on me now?

"Give me the comm case before my finger slips," Mackiel said with a sly grin, "*accidentally.*"

Was I about to become another body to dump in the sewer? Was it really the henchmen or Mackiel who'd been getting "carried away"?

"Please, Mackiel." I held my hands out, my dipper bracelet dangling from my wrist. "Don't do this!"

He pointed the pistol at the messenger. "Move." He gestured to me with the barrel. "Stand beside her."

He always wanted to prove he was tougher than he looked. Would he kill me to do it?

"Quickly!" he said.

Mackiel had selected the messenger to steal from; somehow he'd known what was on the chips and how vital they were. Vital to the survival of the auction house, which was all he had left of his father. Was it a memory *from* his father? Surely not. But he obviously cared more about this comm case than our friendship. I would have to use that against him.

I shoved the window behind me open. "Come any closer, and I'll throw the comm case into the sea." I placed my hand out in the frigid air. "Then you'll have to take a swim to the bottom of the ocean to retrieve it." Both of us could use *that* day. The day he almost drowned.

"You wouldn't." Mackiel stopped dead, the pistol drooping a little in his hand.

"I thought you knew what I would and wouldn't do?" I glanced to the messenger. His face showed a flicker of fear. I was going to have to be brave for the both of us.

"Now, now," Mackiel said. Was that sweat beading across his forehead? "Don't do anything foolish." The sea would erode the chips; he wouldn't allow me to send these memories and his father's business to the ocean floor.

"Let us go," I said, "and we'll give you the comm case, and the destabilizer as a bonus, because we're such good friends." I showed my teeth, not quite a smile. "It will sell well tomorrow night. It will make your patrons happy. No one else has to know what happened here." That was why he wanted to get rid of us, right? His reputation. He would have his comm case back and whatever memories were on the chips.

Mackiel gave me a wolfish grin. "Give me the comm case, and I won't send two bullets to make a home in your belly."

He wouldn't.

Or rather, the old Mackiel wouldn't. He'd spent too many years pretending to be ruthless, too many years trying to impress his father with darker and darker deeds, desperate to earn his attention, his love. And since hiring the henchmen, he'd crossed a line that couldn't be uncrossed.

The metal case was cool in my palm, soothing. All I had now was the comm case and the chips within it. I needed Mackiel to care about me as much as he seemed to care about these chips. Only one option remained.

My eyes flashed to the messenger before I pressed the button on the top of the comm case. A hiss echoed as the lid lifted. Both Mackiel and the messenger froze.

"Careful, darlin'," Mackiel said, his voice low, his gaze darting to the open window and the water below. "Let's step away from the window . . ."

Before he could lunge for me, I picked up the four round translucent chips from inside the case and shoved them in my mouth. As the chips dissolved on my tongue, the embedded video links traveled to my brain, tapping into my synapses and taking hold of my senses. They transported me to another time and place. I was no longer in Mackiel's office.

I was in the palace.

And I was covered in blood.

PART TWO

CHAPTER SIX

Keralie

Images flickered through my mind like the Queenly Reports screened at the Concord. Only they were transmitted in red.

No. That wasn't right. The pictures were in color, but they were slick with blood. It was as though a red veil had been lowered over my eyes.

The flickering slowed. Scenes lingered. Images came into focus.

A column of pale unblemished skin. A slender silver knife. One quick slice. A mouth opens to form a scream. Blood rushing from a deep groove. A chasm of red.

Then.

Liquid gold turning red. First stagnant, then moving. Splashing, swirling, splattering over tiles, as though the liquid is alive. A head of dark hair submerges. A golden crown sinks to the floor. One last breath. A body turns limp, rising to the surface.

Next.

A flicker. Light. Heat. Bubbling and blistering skin. A hand presses to glass. A mouth opens. Begs. Brown skin is covered in ash, like dirt covering a grave.

And finally.

A body contorts. Shudders. Sweats. Limp dark hair is splayed against a pillow. Bile is expelled. Over and over. Skin turns yellow. White lips open. A final scream.

I wanted to turn away, but couldn't. They were there. Everywhere—the images. The crowns. Faces. Faces I knew all too well. Faces I'd seen many times on the Queenly Reports. They were there. All of them. All four queens—dead. Behind my lids. Inside my head.

How do you hide from your own mind?

Get out, get out, get out!

"WHAT HAVE YOU done?" a voice asked.

My father's agonized face flittered behind my eyelids, joining the queens.

Too much agony. Too much blood. *Not again. Not again.*

I wiped my hands on my dress, trying to get the blood off. But it wouldn't budge.

"Keralie!"

I gasped, pulling free from the darkness and decay. Mackiel's office came into view. I turned to the voice, rolling my head from side to side to disturb the images, like extracting myself from a bog. Now that the chips had fully dissolved and washed away with saliva, my senses returned. But not everything would fade.

"Kera." Mackiel stepped toward me, the pistol limp in his hand, his eyes eager. "What did you see?"

I'd forgotten he was there. I'd forgotten everything. Everything aside from the images. Those faces marked with death. What *was* that?

I looked at the messenger. His eyes were wide. Comm chips were perfect for one-off communication that left no trace. Perfect for recording the act of murder and mutilation.

"Kill me," I said to Mackiel, still blinking back to reality, "and you'll never find out."

Clearly, he wasn't planning to sell the comm case and these chips to the highest bidder.

What had he gotten himself into? His father never got involved in palace business. Ruling the Jetée was all he'd cared about.

I wished I'd taken one chip at a time, like you were supposed to—then I could've understood the memories better—but a part of me didn't want to know more. Too much blood. Too much death.

"Let's not do anything rash," Mackiel said.

"Rash?" I barked out a laugh. "You're the one holding the pistol."

"Point taken, darlin'." He placed the weapon on his desk, splaying his ringed fingers wide in surrender. "Better?"

I shook my head. "You let us go." I gestured to the messenger. "You let us live. And I'll consider telling you what I saw on those chips."

Mackiel's kohl-lined eyes studied the messenger. "I'll let *him* go. You"—his gaze flashed back to mine—"stay here."

But I didn't want to be in the same quadrant, let alone the same room, as him. There was something sinister about his expression—something greedy and hungry that made my skin crawl. This was not the boy who had cried for weeks after burying his father or cared for me after I nearly lost mine. But I couldn't let him see how much this hurt. Mackiel took your weaknesses and twisted them for his gain.

"No deal," I said.

"Now, now, darlin'." His words sounded melodic and soothing, but something desperate scratched at the surface. "You know I would never really hurt you. *Promise.*" But that was *my* word. A word I'd always used, but never really meant. "You know you can't go home." He wasn't referring to my lodgings downstairs.

I wanted to throw my hands over my ears; I wanted to scream at Mackiel for using my family against me. Instead I said to the messenger, "Come here."

The messenger hesitated, glancing between Mackiel and me. I shot him an annoyed look. Finally, he shuffled over.

"Kera." Mackiel's voice was lined with steel. "Let's sit down and talk about this for a moment." He removed his bowler hat and set it on his desk. Sweat glistened on his brow. I was making him nervous. *Good.*

"We've talked enough. You'll let us go, and you won't follow. Neither will your henchmen."

Mackiel shrugged his shoulders, two sharp points visible under his large coat. "I can't control their every movement. They're still free men, after all."

Free? *Hardly.* I ground my teeth. "Yes, you can. And you do. Don't play me, Mackiel."

"Me?" He pointed to himself and widened his eyes. "Never. Why don't we have a chat," he said, nodding to his desk chair. "Let's slow things down a little, make things more civilized." He grinned widely. "Dinner?"

The darkness that had been bubbling beneath Mackiel's surface for months was now revealed. His eyes narrowed. Movements frenetic. He watched me with the same intensity that he studied his targets. Calculated. *Yes.* That was it. But now I was the prey.

I had to go someplace where there was no chance he would follow.

"Sure," I replied. "But first"—I threw the now-empty comm case at his head—"duck!"

As he ducked, I pushed the messenger out the open window and into the black waters waiting below.

THE WATER WAS as freezing as I'd imagined.

Of course, I hadn't thought this plan through, and in the moments before I hit the ink-dark water, I questioned my decision. It was winter. It was nighttime. The water would be bitterly cold.

For the first time tonight, I wasn't disappointed.

The water punched my lungs. The waves were needles relentlessly stabbing my face, neck and bare arms. Salt burned my nostrils and stung my eyes. I wasn't sure if I was up or down in this weightless watery grave.

And while I should've struggled for the surface, I thought of Mackiel and that day seven years ago.

We'd only known each other for a few months when I'd suggested we jump off the Jetée. It was a simmering summer's day, and the water was the same crystal blue as the sky above. Mackiel had been hesitant. He was even narrower then, a thin reed of a boy. But I'd promised to look after him, boasting about being a strong swimmer. I'd spent every summer swimming off my parents' boat, and I could hold my breath for long amounts of time.

"I'll look after you," I'd said. "Promise."

And so we jumped.

When Mackiel had struggled and dipped beneath the surface, I thought he was playing. Mackiel was always playing. His face contorted, air bubbles sparkling up around me as he gulped like a fish. I giggled at his antics.

I realized my mistake when his face turned red, then blue.

I dove beneath and managed to pull him to the surface, tucked his limp body under my arm—he'd fit easily back then—and dragged him to shore.

He immediately spluttered the water from his lungs, but it wasn't until he smiled that I relaxed. He never believed in my promises again, as if I'd meant to hurt him.

A current tugged at my clothes, dragging me back to the present. There I was, surrounded by darkness. I kicked and kicked until my head pierced the surface. My gasp was a breath of fog upon the water. I looked around, searching for the gas lamps on the dock.

As I treaded water, I expected to become accustomed to the frigid pain. I didn't. And my skirts were intent on dragging me to the bottom of the sea to join the others who'd tried to deceive Mackiel. I imagined pale arms reaching up from the sea floor, ready to snag my boots.

A wave barreled into my back like a runaway horse, pitching me toward the dock.

No. It wasn't a wave. It was an arm, encircling me, weighing me down. Black hair bobbed above the water, pale eyes reflecting in the starlight.

The messenger.

Why was he trying to drown me? A body thrashing in red-and-gold liquid resurfaced in my mind. I wouldn't be taken down as easily.

I kicked, connecting with his stomach.

"Stop!" he sputtered. "I'm trying to help you!"

I gagged, my mouth full of salty sea. It shredded my throat on the way out.

"Your dress is weighing you down."

"Oblough." *Obviously*, I tried to say.

"We need"—he panted as he treaded water—"to take it off."

I nodded and reached around to the ties behind my back. Without the use of my arms to stay afloat, my head dipped below the water.

Two strong hands lifted me back up. "Stop!" he said. "I'll do it."

I tried to comment about him wanting to undress me ever since we met, but my mouth filled with more salty water.

He turned me in his arms, and I did my best to stay above the surface as he tugged at my corset. His valiant attempt to keep me from greeting the ocean floor with a sandy, salty kiss was taking its toll. We were sinking.

"Why is this so complicated?" he gasped. I thought of his dermasuit and the easy magnetic clips.

"Here," I managed to say. I pulled my sharp lock pick from where it clipped into my dipper bracelet. "Cut it off with this."

He wasted no time slicing through the corset. My outer layers floated away, and I kicked free. The relief was immediate.

Without the weight of my dress, I was able to swim easily. The messenger wasn't far behind. We swam toward the dock.

71

I was halfway up the dock's ladder when a voice sounded in the dark like a foghorn.

"Find them!" Mackiel ordered. "We can't let Keralie out of our sight!"

I shivered. He saved that tone of voice for certain people. Only two people, in fact.

His henchmen.

Slipping back into the water, I held a finger to my lips so the messenger would stay silent.

"I don't see them," came a low voice, the sound of footsteps on ice.

We were in deep shit now.

"What is it?" the messenger whispered.

I clamped a hand over his mouth, but it was too late.

"I hear them," the voice said. "They're in the water below us."

"I don't care about him," Mackiel said. "Get her. *Now!*"

A dark figure spiraled into the water, while heavy boots clomped overhead on the dock.

"Move!" I pushed the messenger away from the dock toward the shore. "*Move!*"

I swam as fast as I could, hoping the messenger would follow suit.

I made the mistake of glancing back. The messenger was behind me, as was one of Mackiel's henchmen. He was bald with two black eyes, all pupil, increasing his vision beyond the normal limits. His skin was yellowed and scaly and smelled worse than a half-rotted fish. He moved toward us like a ghostly sea creature.

"Swim faster," I shouted back to the messenger.

Mackiel laughed from somewhere above us. He wouldn't dare come close to the dock's edge and had sent in his henchmen to do the dirty work, as usual.

Something grabbed at my ankle. I shrieked.

"Don't know why you're always so jumpy around the henchmen," Mackiel said. "They're such charming fellows. Wouldn't hurt a fly." He laughed again.

If only that were true. They might've been nice men once, but under Mackiel's supervision, they'd morphed into something truly ugly. Or was it the other way around, and Mackiel was the true ghoul?

One of the henchmen pinned my legs together and pushed me into the side of a dock post. His black eyes reflected my terrified expression.

"Let go!" I cried.

"Give her 'ere," said a gruff voice.

I screamed as the first henchman pushed me upward.

"Don' worry, Kewawee," the second henchman slurred; the right side of his face had been eaten away. "We won' hurt you." He leaned over, revealing yellowed bone where half the muscle and skin had fallen from his left arm.

Before his bony fingers could clasp onto my shoulder, something leapt out of the water and smacked him aside.

The messenger!

He shoved the destabilizer against the henchman. There was a loud *zap*, and the remaining veins in the henchman's arm sparked blue, then black. The henchman's eyes rolled, and he tilted backward onto the Jetée, his body stiff as the corpse he smelled like. The messenger disappeared beneath the ocean's surface.

I'd thought the henchman was dead, until I heard him groan. The spineless Eonist should've used the destabilizer's highest setting.

"What's happening?" Mackiel asked. His voice sounded far away. He wouldn't risk seeing for himself.

The other henchman narrowed his black eyes at the water, attempting to see into the dark depths. I'd never seen the henchmen fear anything, or anyone. I squirmed in his arms, but he still wouldn't release me.

"Tell me!" Mackiel roared.

I bit down on the henchman's yellow hand. He let out howl like wounded animal.

Another *zap.*

The henchman jerked in the water, and my skin tingled from the close contact. His arms stiffened by his sides, releasing me.

"Come on," the messenger said, appearing beside me, the destabilizer in his hand.

He didn't need to tell me twice.

When we reached the shore, I pulled myself onto the sand and coughed up water. Rolling onto my back, I stared up at the stars winking down at me as if tonight were some kind of joke. I hoped it amused the dead queens watching from above.

The messenger loomed over me, blocking the stars. Water glistened on his defined cheeks and full lips, his black hair twisted like seaweed around his face. His eyes were milky pearls in the low light. While I felt like a half-drowned sewer rat, he looked like what Torian seafarers called a *lure*, a mythical creature who seduced men and women from their boats and into the waves, never to be seen again. My father used to call my mother and me *earthly lures*, persuading him to live a life on land. I wished we had succeeded.

"Are you all right?" the messenger asked.

I rolled onto my side, then tentatively stood. "I think so." I patted myself down. "Yep, all here."

"What in the queens' names *were* those things?" he asked.

"Mackiel's henchmen." I shuddered. "They're from *your* quadrant. That's the ugly side of trying to create a perfect world."

He grunted. "Eonia is hardly a perfect world."

Coming from his perfectly shaped lips, I found that hard to swallow.

"Eonist scientists were trying to create a replacement for HIDRA," I said. "They thought if they could cure death, then it wouldn't matter when all doses of HIDRA ran out. To test their serum, they destroyed certain parts of the henchmen, hoping they could revive the cells." I shuddered thinking of their ruined bodies. "It didn't work."

His eyes brightened. "You know about HIDRA?"

"Of course I do. Everyone does." That wasn't true. I knew about HIDRA because of Mackiel and my father, but I wasn't willing to talk about that.

"But what are the henchmen doing here?" he asked. "In Toria?"

"Mackiel knows the wall guards between Eonia and Toria, or rather, he knows all the guards' secrets and blackmails them into providing information about Eonist technologies that might be worth stealing." *Extortion is another form of trade,* he liked to say. "He forces the guards to let desperate Eonists cross illegally into Toria to become part of his employ. And there was no one more desperate than the henchmen."

Unfortunately, the henchmen hadn't realized that in deserting Eonia, they had merely stepped from one nightmare into another. Mackiel now controlled their every move. And while he provided lodgings, the henchmen weren't paid for their "protective services." Being alive in Toria, or mostly alive, was the only payment they'd get. The alternative was death.

"They do his dirty work and frighten the pants off of anyone who has the unfortunate pleasure of meeting them," I said.

"That's really sad."

I huffed a laugh. "Sad? Did you not see them? They're disgusting!"

"Yes, I saw them." A shadow cast over his face. "But surely they were men once."

"Yes, but not anymore." They'd wanted to improve their standing in Eonist society by volunteering for genetic testing; now they weren't even allowed out of the auction house in the daytime, in case they were seen by Torian authorities. Before the henchmen had fled Eonia, the scientists had planned to exterminate their failed experiments. If Mackiel was found harboring Eonist fugitives, it would be the end of his business. He had power in Toria, but not that much.

The messenger nodded. "I assume you want this back," he said after a moment. He handed me my lock pick.

"Thanks." I reattached it to my dipper bracelet, although a part of me wanted to throw it into the sea. I'd known something was increasingly off with Mackiel, but I'd never thought he'd turn on me.

I shoved my icy hands into my pockets. It was a little warmer, though still soggy in there. "And thanks for helping me."

"I wasn't about to let you drown." The way he said it was as though he wished he could have. He was still angry with me.

He began peeling off his Torian clothes to reveal his dermasuit.

And while I shivered in my wet undergarments, the snug material of his suit already looked dry.

"I'm sorry," I said, wringing water from my hair. "Mackiel told me to steal from you." I shrugged. "So I did. It's nothing personal."

"Nothing personal?" he muttered. "Because of you, and *Mackiel*"—his voice hardened on the name—"I've lost my commission and—" His hand stilled near his ear. "No," he whispered.

"What is it?" I glanced behind me, expecting to see the henchmen approaching from the water like half-drowned ghouls.

"My comm line." He ran his finger around his ear. "I must have lost it in the water."

"Shame."

"You don't understand." He looked at the sea as though he'd find it floating out there. "I need to check in with my boss. I need to tell him I failed."

I held up a finger. "From my experience, bosses don't deal well with failure. He's better off not knowing."

"I need to tell him something or I'll lose my job."

"I think that ship has sailed."

His nose twitched. "This isn't a joke. This is my life. What are we going to do?"

"*We?*" I stomped my feet; water seeped from my boots. "*We* do nothing."

"But you ingested the chips," he said. "And saw the memories."

The less I thought about the chips and those images, the better. I didn't have time to dwell on what I'd seen. I began walking up the shore to the nearest road; I had to keep moving or I'd freeze to death.

The messenger caught up to me with a few quick strides. "You ingested the chips to ensure your boss wouldn't kill you."

"Or you," I reminded him. "Now we're even. I saved you and then you saved me. A fair trade, I'd say. I assumed you'd prefer to be alive tomorrow than dead today." I scrubbed my hands over my eyes; salt scratched at my skin. I still couldn't quite believe Mackiel planned to kill me. I'd always known he was dangerous, but I thought our friendship protected me from the increasing darkness within him. After I'd ingested the chips, there was nothing playful in the way he looked at me. His ravenous expression would haunt me for days. "Mackiel would never make a deal that doesn't result in a win for him. I had no choice but to ingest them."

"Where are you going?" the messenger asked.

"Away from here." Although I wasn't sure where yet. "Away from Mackiel."

"You can't leave me."

I smirked. "If I had a quartier for every time a boy said that to me—"

He grabbed my arm, then quickly dropped it, realizing he was touching my undergarments. "I *need* those chips. It's the only way to save my job."

"And I need a warm bath and some Ludist candy," I said, and kept walking.

His brows furrowed slightly. "Don't you care about anything?"

That was funny, coming from an Eonist. "Yes, I care about staying alive."

"What memories did the chips contain? What did you see?" He looked at me as though he wanted to pull the thoughts from my mind.

"You don't want to know." I really didn't want to talk about it. Ingesting the chips all at once had muddled the story, but I'd seen enough to know I didn't want to meet the intended recipient. There'd been enough horror for tonight.

"But Mackiel was your friend." The messenger hovered beside me, like flies on a warm carcass. "Wasn't he?"

"Friends? Enemies?" I shrugged. "Who can tell the difference?" Apparently not me.

"What did he mean when he said you can't go home?"

I stumbled in the sand. The messenger caught my elbow.

"Nothing." I righted myself and shrugged him off. "I rented one of Mackiel's lodgings, that's all."

"Where will you go now?"

I threw my hands up. "Enough with the questions!"

The messenger stayed quiet for a moment before saying, "Torians trade in deals, correct? Your entire economy is based off what you can get in return."

That wasn't exactly how I'd have described Toria. It sounded cynical and selfish. "Why?"

"I want to propose something—"

"You can propose to me all you like. I'll never say yes." I flashed him a grin.

"I'm serious." And he did appear serious, his strong jaw more set than before.

I jerked my chin at him. "Go on. Propose away."

"You need a place to hide from Mackiel. And I need those memories."

I groaned. "I told you, they're gone now. Do try to catch up."

"I know that," he said quickly. "But they're not gone completely."

I slowed, turning to him. "What do you mean?"

He tapped his temple. "They're in there, in your mind." Wasn't that the unfortunate truth. "Which means if you were to relive them, I could rerecord them onto new chips. I could try to deliver them, again. I could save my job."

"Relive them?" I didn't want to do that.

"You close your eyes, think of the time and place of a particular memory and a recorder pulls the images from your mind. It's how we record memories onto chips in the first place."

"Will it make me forget what I saw?"

"No." He sounded sad, as though there was something he wished to forget.

"I don't want you messing around up here." I gestured to my head. "It's my second-best asset, if you know what I mean." I winked at him.

He ignored me, or perhaps he thought I had a facial twitch. "What choice do you have?" He nodded to my sodden undergarments. "You need clothes and a warm place to stay. I have both."

I looked him up and down. "I doubt we're the same size."

He didn't laugh. "Do you want to freeze out here and wait for Mackiel to find you, or do you want to stay alive?"

"I can survive on my own." Although I wasn't sure that was true. I'd always had Mackiel to lean on. And, before that, my parents.

"But do you want to?" he asked. His face was pensive, his thick brows low over his eyes. Of course an Eonist would offer assistance; unity and civility was their quadrant's focus. Still, the idea of a warm place to stay while I considered my next move wasn't such a terrible idea.

"Fine. I'll relive the memories."

But he sensed my reluctance and asked, "They're that bad?"

In that moment, I envied him not knowing what I'd seen. While the Torian queen had hung a heavy cloud over the future of the Jetée—and thus my livelihood—it didn't mean I wanted her dead. Even though I'd seen the memory of the four queens being killed—from the killer's perspective, no less—I still couldn't accept the truth. All of Quadara's queens had been murdered.

"Worse," I said. "They're deadly."

CHAPTER SEVEN

Stessa
Queen of Ludia

Rule three: To allow for a thriving culture of
art, literature and music, Ludia must not be
weighed down by the humdrum concerns of
everyday life.

Late in the evening of Iris's murder, the advisors chose one of the sparser meeting rooms for the Eonist inspector to conduct his enquiries. Now was not the time to convene in a room dripping with golden chandeliers, be encircled by gilded portraits of smiling queens or sit beneath a canopy of murals depicting the varied Quadarian landscape. Murder was a serious business, therefore sixteen-year-old Stessa had worn her most serious outfit—a fitted white silk pantsuit and a simple beaded necklace that wove into her hair and crown—*simple* for a Ludist. Still, the room was bathed in a warm glow, the glass ceiling allowing a view to the dome above.

Inspector Garvin sat on one side of a large polished wooden table while the sister queens sat opposite, their advisors in the wings. Stessa was unsure if anyone had ever chosen to use this small and boring room before.

She fiddled with her necklace, earning a look from Corra beside her. She knew what Corra thought, what *all* Eonists thought of her quadrant. Ludists were naïve, frivolous and shallow. But they didn't understand. Ludists knew the world was often cruel, that sadness often outweighed happiness and darkness could be a mere step away. But instead of wallowing in this knowledge, Ludists embraced all that was beautiful, light and pleasurable in the world.

And Corra hadn't seen how Stessa's hands shook as she dressed for the meeting. She hadn't seen how the news of Iris's murder had shattered Stessa's rosy view of the world. Stessa had never known real hardship and darkness. She lived in a world of laughter and light and she would hold tight to her traditions to get through this trying time.

The inspector placed a clip around his ear and positioned a translucent disc toward his mouth. "I've examined the body of Queen Iris," he said into the recording device. But Stessa didn't want to hear about how Iris had died, how her killer had sliced her throat so she'd bled out almost instantly. Instead, she studied the inspector.

He appeared middle aged, which surprised her. Corra had said he was widely renowned, solving all of his one thousand cases to date, and so Stessa had imagined an old man. Two deep furrows hung over his piercing black eyes, eyes Stessa was sure would miss nothing, *had* missed nothing throughout his career. His black hair had a peppering of gray at his temples, making him appear more authoritative. And intimidating.

Stessa's fingers itched for her black eyeliner. Something so unsightly could be easily fixed with a little dye. Although, she supposed, it did match nicely with his gray dermasuit.

While Stessa couldn't deny the inspector was attractive—in

that older man way—there was something off about his features the longer she looked at him. His ears were a tad too large, his nose a little too prominent—due to genetic *tweaking*, no doubt.

Worst of all, and the reason Stessa refused to shake the man's hand when introduced, was the extra bone in each finger. His hands were spiderlike, the additional length tapering off to a point, no fingernails in sight.

Eonists were obsessed with perfecting humanity through genetic mutations. Most genetic tweaking happened in the womb for specific vocations, as per the inspector.

With the majority of Eonia covered in snow and ice, Eonists had to find a way to survive their harsh environment. Over the years, technological evolution had turned toward exploring human evolution, which had led to genetic tweaking. Initially, it had only been to rid humanity of illness and disease, resulting in such treatments as HIDRA, but Eonist geneticists had pushed further, wanting to explore the limits of the human body.

Stessa had heard of geneticists tweaking their patients—or experiments—too far, and even pushing the boundaries of life and death while searching for immortality. Rumors had spread to the palace about some ghastly experiments, but the geneticists had been quick to destroy any evidence of such abominations before the palace could investigate.

Since then, Queen Corra had put stricter rules in place, ensuring the geneticists didn't push too far.

The inspector's hands reminded Stessa of a particular story called the "Tweaked Man," whispered in the Ludist schoolyards to frighten young children: a shell of a man who stole into children's rooms at night to seize their souls by caressing their temples with long fingers, searching for a suitable soul to satisfy his hollow body.

The echo of the story made the hairs stand on the back of Stessa's neck. She decided to focus on his better features, like his shapely bow mouth. She wondered if the lines around his mouth were smile lines, and if they were due to a particular person in his life. She doubted it. Eonists were assigned mates for effective breeding—not love.

Stessa's chest constricted at the thought of a life without love. She couldn't imagine it, although she'd often worried it would be her fate as a queen.

Stessa had grown up in a house warmed by love and affection, as present as the sun, the moon and the quadrant walls. Her parents had loved one another deeply and had instilled the importance of this emotion within their adopted daughter. *The* most important emotion, they'd often said.

Let love guide your heart, and everything else will fall into place.

It had been a year since Stessa's birth mother had passed away and she'd been forced to leave her family, and her life, behind. Still, not a day went by that she didn't think of her family back in Ludia.

In the first few weeks, Stessa had considered breaking out of the palace to be with her family. Her *real* family, not the cold, still woman she'd visited in the Queenly Tombs in the cavernous underbelly of the palace. She didn't even look like her mother. Stessa's dark eyes, copper skin and black hair contrasted against the pale blond woman. Their only shared feature was their petite stature.

She must've gotten her looks from her father, Stessa had realized, selected from a number of suitors during one of the annual matching balls. To be matched with a Quadarian queen meant a wealth of riches, with one condition—he could never lay claim to the Quadarian throne or his offspring.

Stessa knew her father had come from across the seas, from a nation united as one land. A nation of one ruler. A king. She couldn't imagine such a place. The quadrant walls maintained peace on the expansive continent. Without the walls, Quadara would fall to ruin, as it had in the years when the last Quadarian king ruled, and battles and uprisings were as frequent as lightning across a stormy sky. With Quadara's fragility laid bare, the neighboring nations had turned their eyes across the sea to the largest land. Something had to be done.

Then the Quadarian king died, and everything had changed.

Even though living under the reign of a king was inconceivable, Stessa had considered traveling to Toria to secure transport across the sea. She could live with her biological father. Anywhere but the palace.

But in her fifth week on the Ludist throne, Stessa saw an opportunity. An opportunity she couldn't let slip by. She could reclaim a piece of Ludia for herself.

She missed the labyrinthine streets and winding canals. She missed the sweet smell of perfume and pastries that constantly hung in the air. And she missed her friends and the nightlong parties they attended. Ludia was a metropolis region that never slept. Stessa was still not used to the quiet palace after midnight.

After reciting his findings into his recording device, the inspector leaned forward. "What concerns me is the efficiency of the murder." He cleared his throat. "I have no doubt this was premeditated." A shiver ran down Stessa's spine.

She glanced at one of the advisors—Lyker, her

advisor-in-training—a tall and striking boy with a square jaw, colorful tattoos climbing up his neck to his chin and a flame of red hair perfectly coiffed upon his head. A coif she'd ruined countless times by running her fingers through it as they lay in bed together. He briefly stuck his tongue out at her, before returning to his stoic expression. Stessa hid a grin.

Ludists loved meeting new people, especially other Ludists. Well, that was what Stessa had claimed when Lyker first entered the palace, her arms flying around his middle before she could stop herself. If she'd been smarter, she would've kept her distance. But she was her parents' child. Her heart ruled her emotions, and actions. He'd smelled of home—her mother's cream-filled pastries and the peppermint oil Ludists used to stain their lips. But his warning hiss came in time, as she'd been about to reach up and taste him.

She'd explained to her sister queens that she'd been overcome by the connection to home. They'd believed her, knowing Ludists were passionate and warm, and not knowing Stessa's ears pinked when she lied.

Corra raised her hand. *A stupid Eonist habit,* Stessa thought. She was a queen; she needn't ask permission for anything, especially now.

The inspector turned to his queen. *He would've been quite handsome when he was younger,* Stessa thought. Her gaze flashed to Lyker's, worried he could read the appreciation in her eyes, as he often did. She was devoted to Lyker, but that didn't mean she didn't like to look at other men. She was Ludist, and they all appreciated beauty. Lyker was no different.

But he was more sensitive than she was, and she often found

herself watching for his reaction. He used to be a street artist, painting poetry onto the sides of Ludist buildings. Each flick and loop of a letter constructed a city of thought and feeling. Without access to his art, he had no outlet. A wounded animal, ready to lash out at any moment. His temper burning as brightly as his hair.

Like her, he was too open to the world and consequently felt too much. Stessa hated to think what would happen when she turned eighteen and was forced to attend her first matching ball. She avoided the topic whenever he brought it up, but she couldn't avoid it forever.

"Yes, Queen Corra?" the inspector asked. Stessa made an effort to maintain her attention on her sister queen, rather than Lyker and the strange man opposite her.

"How do you know it was premeditated?" Corra asked.

"What else could it be?" Stessa found herself saying, without meaning to. She'd planned to stay quiet throughout the meeting, not wanting to draw attention to herself. Even though the inspector was here for Iris's murder, she didn't want his eyes to linger on hers. She wanted to retire to her rooms and wait for Lyker to join her, to still her shaking hands and tell silly jokes, to help her forget this horrid day.

"Why do you say that, Queen Stessa?" The inspector's eyes found hers. It was the first time he'd really looked at her, and his eyes were so black you couldn't distinguish the pupil from the iris. It reminded her of the blackest night, no stars to be seen. What gruesome acts had those eyes witnessed?

"Queen Stessa?" he prompted when she failed to reply.

She knew what he was thinking. What she'd previously said about Iris was blunt and callous.

Suspicious.

But he was wrong. She was simply being truthful. Iris would've appreciated that.

Stessa tilted her chin upward. She might not be *his* queen, but she was still *a* queen and deserved his respect. Respect was something Iris had mastered as easily as breathing. Stessa was young; it wouldn't be as easy for her to garner the same kind of respect, but she would try.

"Well, it's not like Iris slit her own throat," Stessa began. "And she couldn't go a day without causing an argument or raising her voice." She shrugged, jingling the bejeweled necklace, which sat around her shoulders. "That's all." She hoped to shift the focus from her.

"No one would kill Iris for being argumentative." Corra paused for a moment, then said, "Would they?" As if she couldn't imagine a crime driven by emotion.

Corra was blind to Iris's faults, seeing only the best in her sister queen, but she must've realized that Iris was disliked by many. Especially the staff who were not Archian. She had not been an easy queen to serve. Even though she lived in the palace, with all Quadara had to offer, Iris insisted everything be made by hand, to continue her Archian way of life. Her food, her clothing, even the utensils she ate with. She was stubborn and unyielding.

"You said it was premeditated, Inspector?" Marguerite asked, bringing the queens back on track. "How do you know that?" It was clear in Marguerite's eyes that she didn't want to shy away from any details, but it was not her job to solve this crime.

The inspector twisted his mouth before replying. "The wound," he began, "to her throat was precise, as I said earlier. Crimes of passion are not neat. There was only one cut, quick, clean, and true. This was planned. The killer wanted a quick death, most likely to ensure they weren't caught in the act."

Neat—*what a strange word to describe someone's throat being slashed,* Stessa thought with a shiver. And she knew the murder hadn't been as tidy as the inspector claimed, for she'd overheard the staff talking in the corridors about the discovery of the body. A handmaiden had found Iris in a pool of her own blood.

"What does this mean?" Marguerite probed. Corra's face was blank, as usual.

"It's likely we're looking for a trained killer, or someone who has killed before," the inspector said carefully, his eyes darting between each queen. He scratched at his chin with those awful long fingers. "An assassin."

Marguerite shifted uncomfortably. "Perhaps the killer was hired by a neighboring nation?"

He nodded. "It's possible. It's unlikely you have someone on your staff who knows how to kill that ruthlessly, that precisely." He glanced at the advisors behind him before leaning across the table to the queens.

They followed suit, leaning forward.

He lowered his voice, preventing the audience behind him from overhearing. "Have there been any recent additions to the staff? Anyone new to the palace?"

Marguerite shook her head. "Not for a while. Not for over a year or so."

His question began to burn within Stessa's chest. The inspector asked, "But there was an addition before that?"

Marguerite's eyes found Stessa's, then flashed to someone behind the inspector.

Lyker.

"Yes," Marguerite replied. "There were two additions to the palace over a year ago."

The burn in Stessa's chest flickered into fire. "What are you trying to say?" She jumped up, sending her chair into the wall behind her. The necklace's beads jingled around her face nosily. "That *I* killed Iris?" A bubble of laughter burst forth. "While I can't claim to have *liked* her, I wouldn't have killed her. I'm no assassin." She splayed her hands on either side of her as if her appearance were proof enough.

The inspector focused his gaze on her again, his lips pressed together. "We must examine every possibility," he said. "I'm sure you want to find the killer, Queen Stessa?"

Stessa pulled her chair back to the table and sat down, swallowing her anger and fear. "I do."

His long fingers created a steeple. "Good."

Stessa held back a shudder.

The inspector glanced at Marguerite and Corra. "In fact, I will need to speak with all of you. Everyone in the palace will be spoken to."

Everyone. Stessa forced herself not to find Lyker's gaze, which she knew would be focused on her. She bounced in her seat in agitation.

"We understand," Marguerite replied, her hand gently squeezing Stessa's shoulder to calm her. "We will do anything to ensure the assassin is found, for Queen Iris and Archia, before we notify the public of her death."

Stessa noticed Corra refused to look up from her lap, her hand in the middle of her chest, as though something were lodged there.

"Good," the inspector repeated with a nod. "Then I will begin my interviews with Queen Stessa."

Stessa squared her shoulders and leveled her eyes on his. "Go ahead, for I have nothing to hide."

If only that were true.

CHAPTER EIGHT

Keralie

When we reached a cobblestone road, I glanced around in the dim. Few gas lamps lit this part of the harbor. The road through the suburbs to Central Toria—which the Jetée workers called the Skim, as those who lived there only skimmed across the surface of life—was increasingly brighter. A literal light at the end of the tunnel.

The quickest way to Eonia was through Central Toria and the Concord, where the quadrants met.

"It will take hours to walk to the Concord," I said to the messenger. Staying in Toria gave Mackiel the opportunity to find me. I didn't trust him, not anymore. I'd never trust him again.

"Then we'll need transport," he said.

"A carriage," I replied.

"Yes, but where will we find—" he began.

"*There!* A carriage!" I'd never been so happy to hear the sound of hooves against stones.

The messenger squinted in the dark. "Where? I don't see—"

"There!"

Two white horses were visible in the night, pulling a small carriage. The driver blended into the darkness, as though the carriage were driven by a specter.

Better this ghoul than the ones behind us.

The messenger gestured to my undergarments and sopping hair. "Will they let you travel like that?"

"You have money on you?" I asked, and he nodded. "Then we're good."

The messenger pulled out a few quartiers; I was surprised to see the circular impression on the coins glimmer gold. Perhaps he did have the means to bid for the comm case, if Mackiel had ever planned to part with it.

As the carriage neared, I skittered onto the road and under the beam of the nearest gas lamp. I threw my hands up at the driver. "Stop!"

The driver pulled on the reins, and the horses jerked to a halt with a whinny. "Are you mad, girl?" he asked, taking in my appearance.

"Let us in," I said, clambering for the side of the carriage. I ignored the tumble of my belly at the sight of the small internal cabin.

"You'll wet me seats." The driver showed a few spoiled teeth.

"See this?" I grabbed the messenger's hand, the coins still visible in his fist. The messenger flinched at my contact. "They're gold quartiers. You can take them all."

"But I—" the messenger began.

I shot him a look.

"Please," I said to the driver, wishing I didn't look like a drowned sewer rat. I wasn't working with my best.

The driver glanced back over his shoulder before jerking his chin. "All right. Get on in, then."

"We need to get to the Concord." I scrambled into the cabin before he could reconsider. "And be quick about it."

The messenger slid in beside me. "That's everything I have," he said.

"You want to get away from Mackiel and his henchmen?" He nodded. "Then you pay." I rested my hand on the door handle and took a few steadying breaths. We were safe.

The carriage lurched forward, and the messenger placed his hands to the side of the cabin.

"First time in a carriage?" I asked. He pressed his lips into a thin line and nodded again as we jolted along the cobblestones. While Toria was more advanced than Archia, there were a few technologies we still couldn't afford. Like fast, smooth electric transportation. But Queen Marguerite talked of advancements. One such proposal was to demolish the Jetée to build a larger harbor for transnational trades.

I wondered if the news of her death had spread to the Jetée owners and if they were partying in the streets, or if the news had reached my mother at the Eonist Medical Facility. She always spoke so highly of Queen Marguerite and her plans to rid Toria of its seedy underbelly.

The sudden and overwhelming urge to be enveloped by her arms stole the breath from my lungs.

"We should be safe in Eonia," I said, wrapping my arms

around myself. "Mackiel won't venture outside his domain, and the henchmen won't risk returning there." I couldn't believe how the one person I'd relied on for years had suddenly become my biggest enemy.

I took another steadying breath as the sides of the carriage appeared to close in on me. *Small breath in, small breath out,* I reminded myself. *There's a way in, and always a way out.* I was not being punished. I was not trapped. My senses were not smothered by the stink of seaweed, blood and fish. *Not today. Not today.* There was plenty of room in this cabin.

But the deaths of the queens had resurfaced thoughts and images I could no longer suppress.

It was six months ago. My father was once again attempting to teach me the ways of Torian seafarers, hoping to lure me from Mackiel and his business. While I'd never explained my role as a dipper, my father had a fair idea of what I got up to. I tried arguing that the money I earned could be used for a better life, a bigger house, even a better boat. But my father wouldn't take a single bronze quartier.

"Hard work runs in our family, Kera," he said. "What you're doing is cheating, and what's worse is that you're cheating your-self. You could be so much more."

He didn't understand. I was exactly who I wanted to be and had everything I'd ever desired. Everything they could never have afforded. I wanted to share that with them.

It would've been a normal afternoon, the two of us bickering until nightfall. But then the boat came too close to the shore, strik-ing a nearby cliff. I had tried to hold on to the mast, but the colli-sion ruptured the boat, flinging us both from the deck. I landed on my father, incurring no injuries. He landed at the base of the cliff.

I'd thought we were okay, safe from the boat's destruction. But my father wouldn't open his eyes. Then I saw the blood, seeping from a deep gash at the back of his head.

I managed to pull my father's limp body into the protection of a nearby cave. I shivered in the oppressively small space, the dampness never allowing my clothes to dry, my shuddering breaths echoing in the chamber, only the sound to keep me company.

On the second day, I started hallucinating from dehydration. The rock walls would judder, as if they were about to collapse in on me. On the third day, I hoped they would.

When the coastguards found us a day later, they'd thought we were dead; we were both unconscious and covered in blood. It wasn't until they cleaned me up that they discovered the blood was all my father's. I'd never forget my mother's tearstained face when she saw us, the first of many tears she would cry over my father.

And now he was dying.

I wished I could take that day, and many others, back. I wished I'd never taken Mackiel's hand when he offered it all those years ago outside the auction house. But I couldn't blame him for what I'd done to my father. I'd always wanted more than my parents could offer. I'd wanted a different life. I had to live with the consequences.

"Hey," the messenger said, noticing my shaking. "Are you all right?"

I nodded, pretending to shift a hair back from my forehead while I wiped the sweat beading across my brow. My damp dress was becoming an icy coffin. I focused on not gasping for large terrified breaths.

Small breath in. Small breath out.

The cabin wasn't getting smaller. I would not be trapped here forever. I wouldn't be forgotten. I would not—

"Are you going to tell me now what you saw on the chips?" the messenger asked.

I tried to focus on the boy in front of me. "You won't believe me." But that wasn't true. I didn't want to tell him in case he left me behind. I didn't know if he was telling the truth about being able to rerecord the comm chips. He could be bluffing, making me spill before our deal was done.

"Why wouldn't I?" he asked, a tilt to his brow.

Never give up your leverage until you have the wares safe in your hands, Mackiel would tell us dippers. *A promise of a deal is not a deal done.*

I needed to get as far away from Mackiel and his henchmen as possible. And this messenger was my ticket out of here.

"I'll tell you when we're at your place," I said, ignoring the darkness creeping in at my periphery, desperate to take hold. *There's a way in, and always a way out.* I gripped the door handle harder.

"We'll be at the Concord soon," he said. "The quadrant authorities will let you through to Eonia, as I'm permitted to do interquadrant business; however"—he looked back at me—"while your quadrant may not care about what you wear, you won't be allowed onto an Eonist commuter train dressed like that."

He was right. I'd be detained before we got close to his lodgings, being such an unsightly scandal.

The darkness in my periphery reduced as a new target formed in my mind. My hand loosened on the door. "I'll have to acquire a new outfit, then," I said with a grin.

"Acquire?" He groaned. "I'm beginning to realize that look on your face means nothing good will follow."

I patted his shoulder. "You're a quick learner."

"If I was quicker, I would've avoided this mess by leaving you on your rear this morning." There was a small raise to the corner of his mouth. He was making a joke. Oh, bless. "But spare me the details," he added.

I nudged him good-naturedly with my elbow. "What's your name, messenger boy?"

He hesitated before replying, "Varin Bollt."

"Keralie Corrington." I held out my hand for him to shake. "A pleasure."

He didn't take my hand. I let it fall into my lap. I'd forgotten Eonists don't touch each other.

"What is that disgusting smell?" he asked suddenly.

I took a good long whiff, then immediately regretted it. "That's horse shit."

"I've never seen a horse before." Like a child, he peered out the window to try and glimpse the horse up front. Most of Eonia was far too cold for any animals to survive, and the rest was dense cityscape, or so I'd heard, having never visited the quadrant myself. "They're beautiful," he said. *Beautiful.* There was that word again. Before I could question him about it, he added, "But they smell foul."

I laughed. "They're animals, not machines. You can't control everything they do and when they do it."

Varin raised his eyebrows slightly before turning to look out the window. I couldn't tell if he was insulted by my Eonist jibe or whether he was being aloof. I'd never spent much time around those from the advanced quadrant. They mostly kept to themselves. And it was common knowledge that they considered Torians to be meddlesome, selfish and arrogant.

Varin brought a hand to his brow and began rubbing the bridge of his nose. Though I looked more ragged, it was clear the night had taken its toll on him too.

"I'm sorry," I said quietly, part of me hoping he wouldn't hear, but to alleviate myself of some guilt for what I'd done to him. But this was Mackiel's fault, not mine. He'd chosen Varin and his comm case. Even now that I understood the importance of the chips, I still didn't understand Mackiel's involvement.

"What are you sorry for?" Varin asked.

I chewed on the inside of my mouth. What was it I was sorry for again? "Um. Everything?"

He sighed. "Don't they teach you how to apologize in school?"

"Teach me to apologize?" I snorted.

"I thought all Torians go to school?"

"Of course we do." And I was sure my Torian education was much more expansive than one in Eonia. We didn't shy away from other cultures. "But we don't learn to apologize. We don't have the pleasure of being told how to behave and what to say. We have more important things to worry about, like learning to master the ropes on a boat and learn the call of the tides."

"*Pleasure?*" He scoffed. "Tell me how pleasurable it is to be locked in a small dark room anytime you show emotion."

I shuddered at the image of being locked in the dark. Perhaps there was one thing I had in common with this unfeeling robot.

"I—" But not knowing what to say, I snapped my jaw shut.

"We're brought up to feel as little as possible," he said, the passing gas lamps reflecting in his pale eyes. He squeezed them shut for a moment before letting loose a sigh. "It's seen as a form of evolved thinking. It allows us to focus on society as a whole, technologies and further advancements."

"So you *do* feel?"

"The longer you go without feeling, the less you feel."

When I raised my eyebrows, he continued quickly, "There's no crime in Eonia, no uprisings, no hate. Everyone has their role in society, and we're paid well enough. Eonia has eradicated envy, jealousy, violence, cruelty."

"Not all emotions are negative," I countered. "And you require emotion to appreciate beauty." I waited, testing him, but his expression didn't shift.

"You can't let in the good without the bad," he eventually said.

Would life be better if I shut off my emotions? Would it be easier? I couldn't imagine my life without feeling—the good *and* the bad. Would I have worked for Mackiel for all these years if I hadn't felt a buzz when thieving? Would I have tried harder to appease my parents and learned how to sail? Or would it have been easier not to care about my family at all? I wouldn't have minded giving up the ache in my heart whenever I thought about my parents, for one good night's sleep.

"Perhaps we shouldn't judge one another," he said after a while. "I'll help you, and in return, you'll help me. Why don't we agree that neither of us knows what it's like to live in the other's quadrant?"

I could agree to that.

While Varin might appear an unfeeling nitwit, there was something behind his expression and comments on beauty that made me question his claim of an emotionless life.

"RIGHTIO," THE DRIVER said, thumping on the top of the carriage. "We're here. Pay up."

Varin flinched at the driver's bluntness but leaned forward to part with his quartiers.

I slipped out my side of the cabin. The tightness around my chest unraveled, like a corset cut loose. I tilted my head back and took in a deep breath. I'd done it! I'd survived! A part of me wished Mackiel had been there to see me face my fear of enclosed spaces.

A very small part.

I glanced up, expecting to see ALL QUEENS MURDERED splashed across the screens that surrounded the Concord. But the Queenly Reports only displayed the previous announcements: *Latest Archian produce shipment delayed due to a shipping accident outside the Torian harbor. The five thousandth name has been added to the list for HIDRA, yet the queens confirm they will not be increasing the doses beyond one per year. Ludists set to cross quadrants with a new traveling show, as approved by the queens.*

The palace must be keeping the murders quiet, for fear of causing chaos.

"What are you looking at?" Varin asked.

"Nothing." I stepped away from him and the carriage. "I'll meet you at the stairs to the House of Concord."

"Where are you going?"

I gestured to my clingy undergarments. "To get clothes."

He looked around at the darkened storefronts. Closing time had come and gone. The House of Concord clock tower showed it was nearly midnight. "From where?"

"You don't want to know, remember?" I said, grinning.

He rubbed the bridge of his nose. "Don't take too long."

I curtsied, then darted off.

Breaking into a store was easier than stealing from a person. With people, you had to observe. Observe the way they walked: Did they cling to their belongings like a child to their mother? Did they swing their arms wide, allowing a hand to sneak in underneath? Did their eyes dart about, searching shadows? Were they easily distracted, the golden palace stealing away their attention?

Stores didn't have thoughts and feelings, backgrounds and motives. Stores only had locks. And locks were easy to pick.

I unclicked the lock pick from my bracelet. The weight of it in my hand released the last of the tension from between my shoulders. For the first time since the auction, I was in control. This was something I could do, something that wouldn't go awry.

I couldn't speak for what else was to come.

———————

VARIN FROWNED AS I skipped toward him, still high from my break-in.

"What are you wearing?" It was more an accusation than a question.

I spun, the short layered skirt flaring out, spirals illuminating on the material as I twirled.

"I thought it might be useful," I said. "If we find ourselves in dark places."

"That's Ludist clothing."

I pushed his arm as I passed. "Oh, don't be so Eonist. There's nothing wrong with a little bit of color and flare."

"Not if you're on the run."

I shrugged. "No one said I couldn't look good while doing it."

He looked me over. "No one said *that* looked good."

I couldn't help but laugh.

We walked up the House of Concord stairs, the palace dome glowing behind it like a giant gas lamp. I ducked my head, not wanting to be reminded of what I'd seen on those chips. It wasn't like I could go to the palace guards and tell them about the memories I'd ingested. I was a thief. I couldn't risk it.

"Ludists are a frivolous people," Varin said, "caring only for what they own, how they look and their next fix of entertainment."

I couldn't argue against that. Ludia was like Toria on Quadrant Day—but in a constant state of celebration. Ludists didn't know the drawbacks of returning to reality.

"Not everyone is blessed with superior genes." I wrapped a hand around his arm. "Some of us have to work at looking good."

His face colored in the dark.

"At least it's less distracting than what you were wearing before," he said finally.

"Less distracting, eh?" I pressed up against him to see his face darken further.

"Can you focus, please?"

"Sure." I winked at him. "I'm focusing on you right now."

He yanked his arm free.

"Oh, come on!" I said. "Lighten up, or are you not allowed a sense of humor either?"

He leveled his eyes on me. "Only if something is funny."

I clutched my chest. "You wound me."

He ignored my response. "Once we're at my apartment, you'll tell me everything you know."

"I haven't forgotten our deal."

"Good," he replied.

What would I do then? Once I told Varin what he needed to hear, he could kick me out of his place and onto the streets. But I didn't know the streets of Eonia.

I thought of all the times my parents had begged me to stay clear of the auction house and Mackiel, asking, *What do you want to do with your life, Keralie? Who you do you want to be?*

Without Mackiel, and my role as his main dipper, who was I?

CHAPTER NINE

Marguerite
Queen of Toria

*Rule four: Curiosity and exploration are
at the heart of every Torian. This should be
encouraged to promote further growth of
Toria's burgeoning society.*

Marguerite retired to her chambers after the inspector's initial inquiries. Normally, the queens would meet for dinner, but Lali had left a meal upon her large wooden desk. Lali had been Marguerite's handmaiden since she entered the palace, and the older woman always seemed to know what she desired. Marguerite needed the reprieve, returning to the one part of the palace that had always brought comfort.

Every wall in Marguerite's chamber was covered in maps, maps of each quadrant, the palace itself and even the nations beyond Quadara. Her parents had been cartographers, and Marguerite had loved maps since she was a small child, tracing her father's creations with her chubby fingers. Her parents had told her it was pertinent to extend her gaze beyond Quadara and understand the other nations to help inform the ruling of Toria.

Marguerite removed her veil and crown, letting her auburn

hair tumble free. While she ate the meal at her desk, the maps beckoned like windows into other worlds. She didn't feel enclosed by the palace's dome. She didn't feel alone. She remembered that Toria was out there; her people a part of her, who relied on her. She would make it through this tough time; she had to.

Know everything, and you shall know all was a favorite Torian saying of her father's. And although she had not wanted to know everything about Iris's death, she had stayed back to pepper the inspector with questions. She tried to forget this was her friend, and think of it merely as an interesting case. She willed her curious Torian nature to take over and force the sadness from her mind, but she struggled.

Marguerite and Iris were the closest in age and had spent the last twelve years ruling together. Marguerite did not know how to accept her friend's death. Iris had been a flame, strong and bright, and now, snuffed out.

Marguerite wished she could be more involved in the investigation, but the inspector wouldn't allow it. When she had offered to work by his side, he said it was better not to be tainted by her bias. Marguerite had scoffed at that. She'd spent the last twenty years in the palace. No one knew the place better than she.

"Which is the problem," the inspector had said. "I need to remain impartial if I'm to uncover the culprit."

The inspector's presence had the palace in a spin. Perhaps it was his long fingers, or the way his eyes seemed to pierce through you, and to the truth. But his presence did not disturb Marguerite. There was something fascinating about him and the way he moved through the golden corridors with almost a mechanical determination. She'd sent her staff to tend to him overnight, ensuring he ate and drank, though she doubted he would rest. Perhaps he didn't need to.

After her meal, Marguerite ran her hand along one of her favorite maps. It was an outline of Toria, depicting Central Toria, or the Skim—as some Torians called it—all the way down to the docks. Her fingertips lingered. She took a deep breath and closed her eyes. She imagined the smell of the sea, the squish of granules of sand beneath her feet and a sticky ice cream dripping in her hand. The dock hadn't always been tarnished by the Jetée. When she was a child, it had been a getaway from the hubbub of crowded Central Toria, a weekend escape. But the darkness and squalor were spreading. Marguerite had to put a stop to that, or her home might be destroyed by a few criminals, deviants, and frauds. Torians were better than that.

A flap of Iris's pale skin, leaking blood, flashed behind her lids.

Marguerite opened her eyes and sighed. Even the maps wouldn't calm her mind tonight. She removed her mourning clothes hastily and climbed into bed. Though the sheets were crisp and cool, Marguerite flamed hot. The image of Iris's cold, lifeless body once again floated behind her eyelids.

Marguerite had been the unfortunate person to identify her. She could not bear to think of Stessa witnessing something that horrid, and Corra had disappeared to her rooms shortly after the first meeting with the inspector.

A sheet had been pulled up to Iris's chin to conceal the wound, her purple lids covering her vivid green eyes. Marguerite had imagined she was merely sleeping and at any moment she would wake and demand to know why she was in the infirmary, covered only by a sheet.

Fatigue now tugged at Marguerite's body and mind. And

although she did not wish to admit it, she felt old—much older than her years.

She could not fathom why anyone would kill Iris. Yes, the woman was stern, but she was a true and loyal friend. Marguerite had always found her presence reassuring. Her strength tangible. Inspiring. Iris had been there for Marguerite in the hardest of times. She had a determination and a passion for life that Marguerite had never seen in anyone else.

Many of Marguerite's favorite memories within the palace were with Iris. They shared afternoon teas in Marguerite's chambers. Even with Iris's Archian distrust for machinery and travel, she loved to hear about how teenage Marguerite had joined her parents to tour the coast of Quadara to draw new maps. In turn, Iris would tell Marguerite about life in Archia and what it was like to breathe unpolluted air, wake to birds chirping and ride horses along undulating landscapes. Marguerite drank in Iris's words, always asking for more stories, more details.

Over the last few years, their relationship had begun to weaken. It wasn't noticeable at first, but Iris began missing more and more of Marguerite's afternoon teas. Iris was still as lively and present as ever, but there was a distance between the two women, one that Marguerite couldn't close.

She had wanted to ask what was wrong and why they'd drifted apart, but Iris wasn't known for opening up, and Marguerite worried she'd push her friend further away.

Had the Archian queen been hiding something from her? Something that led to her death? And if Marguerite had asked what it was, would Iris still be alive?

For the first time in her life, Marguerite found herself thinking vile, furious thoughts. Thoughts that were not logical and sound of mind.

She wanted the assassin hanged. She wanted to watch the life drain from his body until he was merely a shell, as Iris was now. Fury was a peculiar and overwhelming feeling, but something to focus on. Something other than the hideousness of Iris's death.

EARLY THE NEXT morning, Marguerite spread her hands on the table opposite the inspector. "Despite what you may have heard from Queen Stessa," she said, "Queen Iris had no more adversaries than the rest of us. I've made a list." She pulled a journal out from her dress pocket. "They're mostly people who have quarreled with Iris's decisions, but there is no one, I believe, who matches your description of a trained assassin. Archia is a peaceful quadrant."

"May I see it?" the inspector asked.

Marguerite nodded, sliding the book across the table. The inspector flipped through the numerous pages of names she had collated overnight. No matter how hard she willed it, she could not maintain the deep unconsciousness that she desired fiercely—a break from the sorrow. Her mind wouldn't stop running through Iris's murder over and over.

"Thank you," he said. "I will compare these notes to the testimonies I have recorded thus far." He tapped the silver comm case clipped into his dermasuit at the waist. Marguerite knew Queen Corra recorded her memories of court onto comm chips, in case she needed to refer to them at a later date. She wondered what it would be like to have such easy access to your memories and whether you could get lost in the past.

She mentally shook herself. Now was not the time for such thoughts.

"While it is true Queen Iris was blunt and often harsh," Marguerite said, "she was a good queen to her people. No"—she shook her head—"a great queen. Perhaps the best of us."

He tilted his head to the side. "How so?"

Marguerite wondered if he was appalled she had not named Queen Corra—*his* queen—as the best. She doubted it; being appalled would require emotion.

"Her focus was on maintaining Archia's culture," Marguerite replied. "It's tempting to want to share more across the quadrants, to help each other. And sometimes we do . . ." She lifted a shoulder in a half shrug. "But Archia's culture and history was Iris's primary focus, ensuring her people continued to work without the aid of technology, to protect the fruitful land. She did not always make the easiest decisions, but she made the right ones for her quadrant."

"And yet she wished to change Queenly Law," he said, his mouth close to the recording device.

"I'm sorry?" Marguerite startled. "What do you mean?"

The inspector pressed his lips together, as though he didn't care to share more information.

Marguerite pulled her black veil back to reveal her resolute expression. "We need to work together, Inspector." She leaned forward, her hands encroaching his space on the table. He probably thought she was simply being a nosy Torian, but this was Iris. *Her* friend. Marguerite would have done anything to learn the truth and have her sister queen avenged. "Let us help one another. We have the same goal."

The inspector leaned back but nodded. She let out a sigh of disappointment, wanting more of a reaction from him. Just like Corra, always maintaining a distance. "I spoke with the Archian advisor late last night. Queen Iris had scheduled a meeting in court to discuss Queenly Law. That meeting would've been held today. All queens were to be in attendance," he said.

Marguerite shook her head. "There must be some mistake. There was no queen more steadfast in Queenly Law than Iris." In fact, Marguerite had often argued with the Archian queen, suggesting their two quadrants have a more symbiotic relationship. Iris had firmly rejected Marguerite's suggestions.

"I believe my sources speak the truth," the inspector said. "Do you not know your agenda for court in advance?"

"No." Jenri hadn't mentioned anything this morning; the advisors' minds were still locked on the sudden, and shocking, death of Iris. "It changes often. We're usually informed of our schedule by our advisor on the morning of the meeting when we wake and are preparing for the day." Marguerite thought back to Iris's increasing aloofness. "I can't believe she didn't discuss her plans with me."

"You were close to her," the inspector remarked, holding the recording device nearer to his mouth. "You were friends."

She laughed. "You sound surprised, Inspector."

"Comparing the narrow-mindedness of Archians to Torians' desire to conquer all, then yes, I am surprised."

"Archians are not narrow-minded." She didn't bother trying to correct him about Toria. There was no love lost between Eonists and Torians ever since the Quadrant Wars, when Toria refused to offer Eonia access to their land and forced them to be landlocked onto a region surrounded by snow and ice. "And Iris was misunderstood." Marguerite chuckled at the thought of Iris hearing herself being called that. She would have threatened violence at such insolence. "Or maybe not, but I always appreciate her honesty and integrity." *Appreciated,* she corrected. That was going to take some getting used to. Iris was so present, so active, so alive—to think of her as anything else tilted Marguerite's world askew.

She clasped her hands together. "Integrity is a rare quality in this world, Inspector."

He studied her for a moment with his black eyes. A small shudder ran down her spine. Perhaps he affected her more than she realized.

"Even in Toria?" he asked.

She knew he was referring to the Jetée and how it polluted the otherwise virtuous quadrant. She was tempted to tell him of her plans to tear the place down, to prove her quadrant wasn't spoiled by a few rotten fish in a barrel. Instead, she merely raised an eyebrow. Iris had often remarked on Marguerite's ability to say more without using words.

"Do you think her honesty is what got her killed?" he asked after she didn't reply.

Marguerite thought of the way Iris had spoken to the Archian governor on the day she'd died, but he would not have killed her for it. No, it was something else.

"I don't think so," Marguerite responded. "She was as good at keeping secrets as the rest of us. As I said, she was a great queen. No one was more earnest in her position. Being queen was her sole purpose in life."

Marguerite often tried to imagine what that would be

like—the throne her only concern. While Marguerite's queenly duties were her top priority, her mind often flittered. Beyond the throne. Beyond the palace. And to her past.

Iris had known Marguerite's secrets and told her it was natural to think of her past—the what-ifs—but they were not worth dwelling upon. Iris was good at that. She placed her concerns in a box and shut the lid.

But what if her past had returned and demanded to be addressed? Was that what this meeting was supposed to be about? Change Queenly Law to allow Iris to return to Archia and reconnect with her past? Her family?

The inspector stilled, the recorder hovering in front of his lips. "Queen Marguerite," he prompted. "You mentioned secrets. What kind of secrets?"

Had she? It must've slipped out without her meaning it to. Marguerite didn't elaborate.

"You must tell me, Queen Marguerite," he said, his eyes narrowing. "You said we were to help one another."

"They are the palace's secrets, not yours." *And some are not mine.* She shook her head, her auburn curls sweeping across her cheek. "I cannot tell you any more than I could tell my subjects."

"Then we may never uncover Queen Iris's assassin." His tone was annoyingly complacent. Anger boiled through Marguerite's blood.

"You will," she commanded. When the inspector did not reply, she pointed at him. "It's your job. Can you imagine the chaos if the Archians hear of the passing of their dear queen and the person responsible is still roaming the streets, a free man?"

Fury burned across her cheeks and bubbled on her lips as she spoke more quickly. "Iris had no children. Not yet. Her advisor is searching for any female blood relatives to inherit the throne. But if Alissa cannot . . ." A breath shuddered through her. "If she cannot locate a female relative . . ."

Marguerite leaned back into her chair, not knowing how to finish that sentence. There had always been a descendant for each throne. It was Queenly Law. But Iris was stubborn. She had refused to have a child with any of the suitors presented to her across the years.

"Iris claimed to have a niece," the inspector said. Marguerite had yet to find her voice. She nodded in reply. "So far the advisors have yet to find any evidence of said niece."

"We should display a message on the Queenly Reports, asking for anyone with information to come forward. Information on the assassin or about Queen Iris's relatives. We need all the help we can get."

"No," the inspector said calmly. "No one outside the palace must know of Queen Iris's death. We cannot afford the risk of mass panic."

"We cannot afford *not* to!" Marguerite waved her hands wildly as she spoke. "Iris is dead! A queen, murdered. We must find the culprit, whatever the cost!" The inspector's stillness only seemed to anger her more.

"I'm sorry for your loss, Queen Marguerite." And though he evidently detected *her* emotion, his tone and expression remained Eonist, detached. "This must be difficult for you. Not only do you have to come to terms with Queen Iris's death, but that she was murdered and the assassin is still within these walls."

Marguerite's hands dropped to the table with a thwack. "What?"

The inspector's expression remained unchanged.

She gulped at the air, the room suddenly stifling. Her corset was too tight, the layers of her dress weighing heavily upon her, her crown heavy on her head. She wished to tear off the veil and throw it across the room.

"The assassin?" she managed to get out. "You believe they are still in the palace?"

"Yes," the inspector said. "The palace was closed as soon as the body—" He cleared his throat. "That is, as soon as Queen Iris was found, the guards closed the entrance, and everyone has been detained in the processing room. And she was found not long after her death."

Her blood still warm. Marguerite remembered the inspector passing on this gory detail in yesterday's meeting. "Then you know who it is," Marguerite said. "You've captured the killer?"

Please let this be over.

"We hope so. Everyone who was visiting the palace at the time of the murder has been apprehended until I can determine their innocence." He paused, and Marguerite felt that strange unfamiliar flare of anger heat her chest once more.

Why was he drawing this out? An Eonist should not be this cruel. Or perhaps he was that unfeeling; he did not realize the pain she was in and how every silence caused further ache to her heart.

"No one has left the palace," he said, finally. "I will find the perpetrator. They will not escape."

It was as though she had swallowed glass. The pressure in her chest moved, pricking the back of her throat.

"We should gather the queens." She rose from her chair. "We

need to stay together. I must protect them." With the assassin sharing the same walls, the same air . . . they could be in danger.

"No, Queen Marguerite." The inspector shook his head once. Sharply. "That is not a good idea."

"*No?*" If Iris had been here, she would have had a fit. No one told her no. Especially not a man.

"I'm afraid not." An expression crossed his face that looked almost like discomfort.

The anger was like acid burning holes inside her chest. "And why not?" she demanded.

"As you said, we must protect the queens. I can't allow you all to be in the same room until I determine none of you are responsible for Queen Iris's death and a danger to the others."

She gripped the table before her. "That's not possible. All three of us were in court when Iris was killed."

The inspector nodded. "While a queen may not have held the dagger, it is possible she arranged the assassination. Until I can determine your innocence, the queens are my top suspects."

Marguerite was not a fainting woman, but right then, she swayed a little.

CHAPTER TEN

Keralie

The House of Concord stole the air from my lungs. I'd never seen this much gold; my fingers itched to savor everything. And break off a bit for later. Within the House of Concord, you could see the start of the palace's golden dome and the dark structure behind the amber glass. I knew what lay inside: a palace awash in gold and death.

"Come on," Varin said, pulling my attention away. "We don't have time for this."

I shook my head, dislodging the bloody images from my mind.

With the Concord stores now shut, most people had already headed home to their quadrant. The gateway to Eonia was a sleek commuter platform leading toward a tunnel. I'd never crossed quadrants, and the thought filled me with excitement.

An Eonist guard stood at the entrance to the platform, destabilizer hanging from his belt.

"Permit?" he asked as Varin and I approached. I shrunk back

behind Varin's broad frame, hoping to disappear into the background. Perhaps Varin had been right about my outfit.

"I'm recording a message for my employer from Ludia." He nodded to me, then handed over a translucent square the size of a playing card. As the guard scanned it, the square turned solid, displaying Varin's picture and his job title below it.

The guard handed it back, and Varin's picture faded from view. "Go on," he said, inclining his head as an electronic whine echoed down the tunnel.

That was easier than I thought. He didn't even question Varin.

"Stand close and step in time with me," Varin said as we neared the commuter track.

"Step in time?" I looked around. The few travelers at this late hour stood stationary like part of the building. They stared straight ahead, while I watched the commuter appear from the darkness.

As soon as the doors opened, everyone stepped forward. At the exact same time.

I grabbed onto Varin's arm to ensure I wasn't left behind. He didn't shrug me off.

ALL EONIST EYES WERE ON ME. Or rather, my outfit. They thought I was Ludist, and the mere sight of me outraged them. I flashed a wide smile. Let them think I was Ludist. It was safer that way. Mackiel had no connections with Ludia. Hopefully I'd be lost to him.

The commuter picked up speed in the tunnel. Somewhere above us, my father lay unconscious within the Eonist Medical Facility, my mother hovering over his still form, hoping he'd wake.

The expansive building connected out from the palace and spread for miles before reaching the research precinct.

When the commuter exited the tunnel, I saw the beginnings of the great sprawling capital of Eonia, extending as far as the eye could see. The illuminated silver buildings blurred past the window, as though I was swimming through a silvery lake. I knew I looked like a slack-jawed gawker, unable to tear my eyes, or hands, from the glass, but I'd never seen buildings as high, or as thin. The structures in the distance looked like needles, poised to blow over in the wind. I wanted to ask Varin how they managed to stay upright at such a height, but his face was turned away as he stared out the other window. I thought he was warming up to me, but perhaps warmth was not an Eonist concept. I'd yet to see any flicker behind his eyes.

While the Eonists didn't appreciate my presence, no one dared to approach me. Nor did they speak to those around them. It was as though they were traveling alone, completely disconnected from each other. They stared straight ahead, while a few spoke softly into their comm lines.

Was this what Varin's normal life was like? Did he catch the commuter into the Concord every day, engaging with no one aside from his boss via a comm line? Sure, the Jetée was dirty and smelly, and everyone there had questionable morals, but we acknowledged each other when walking down the street. I knew most people by name, if not by reputation.

"Good evening," a smooth voice said. I startled as a woman in an off-white dermasuit blinked into being in the middle of the carriage. "Whether you are returning home or visiting from another quadrant," she said with a robotic, disjointed smile, "we welcome you."

"Welcome? Yeah, right. And please leave as quickly as you arrived." I snickered to myself. Eonia was known to conduct what they called "head counts," searching houses to ensure no one had snuck into their perfect quadrant, intent on making it their new home.

The man sitting beside me glanced at me in disapproval. I smiled serenely.

"Eonia is a harmonious community of wondrous accomplishment and outstanding technological development," the woman continued. "We do hope you enjoy your stay." For a quadrant claiming to focus on harmonious community, I'd seen little accord here.

"What is this?" I asked Varin. The woman continued looking ahead, a distant expression on her face.

"A hologram," he replied. "All commuter carriages have them. They're for general announcements." Hmm, still no announcements about the queens.

I put my hand through the woman's mouth and wiggled my fingers out the other side.

"Stop that," Varin hissed at me.

I studied her bland, perfect features. "Seems like a waste of technology to me."

Varin turned away as though I'd embarrassed him. Did Eonists feel embarrassment?

"You are now arriving in Eonia's first precinct," the holographic woman announced.

Varin stood. "This is our stop."

I hesitated before stepping through the holographic woman. Her face distorted as my body passed through.

"Weird," I muttered.

We exited the commuter. And though no snow fell from the sky, Eonia was easily twenty degrees colder than Toria. While I couldn't see where the city ended, I knew if we continued on the commuter to the end of the line, we'd reach nothing but white. Snow and ice.

I shivered, cursing my decision to steal the Ludist dress, and tucked my hands under my arms. I cast a sideways glance at Varin, wishing I had a dermasuit, but he was focused straight ahead, his arms and legs moving uniformly, almost robotically.

Few people remained on the streets at this time of night. Everyone on the right side of the street walked in one direction, while everyone on the left walked the other. The pavement was clean. Polished. Organized. A man dropped a Ludist pastry, which must've been purchased at the Concord, but before he could reach for it, a woman dressed in a white dermasuit swept it into a dustbin.

"Everyone has their place here," Varin said under his breath as I watched the woman scurry away to her next cleaning emergency. "Everyone plays their part."

"And if they don't?"

He glanced away. "Come on, we're almost there."

But I knew the answer. Mackiel's henchmen were a perfect example of not fitting in. They were dead to Eonia. Or at least, Eonia had *wanted* them to be.

Varin's apartment was on the twenty-eighth floor in one of the needle-thin skyscrapers. Inside, it was small, but not oppressive.

I'd thought Varin would sleep inside an icebox, or a coffin, but was surprised to see a narrow white bed pushed into an alcove in the far corner.

I ran my hand over a sleek metal kitchen bench. It set off some sensors: a trash can appeared below, a sink rose from the middle, and a drawer opened at the end of the bench, revealing stacks of Eonist food bars and sachets of vitamin replacements.

Varin sighed, then swiped his hand back over the bench to return everything to its place. I moved toward a collection of paintings along the left wall that stood out in the otherwise featureless white room. One painting depicted a section of the colorful Ludist canals, another, the Torian harbor at night, and there was also a wide vista of the Archian mountains. All the other paintings were of the palace's dome. I was drawn to the middle frame, illustrating a gray day, the muted palace dome glistening with rain. I ran my fingers over the golden brushstrokes, marveling at the texture.

"Pretty," I murmured.

"Stop touching things," Varin said. He pressed another button, and the paintings slid behind a cabinet.

"It's my job to touch things." I gave him a smirk, which he thoroughly ignored.

Aside from the paintings, there was a white couch placed against one wall and a small white table with one chair arranged in the middle of the room. With the paintings now hidden, the most striking thing about the apartment was the floor-to-ceiling window stretching across the far wall. The skyscrapers were alive with lights, appearing like a vertical gray sky. There was no such view in Toria; the streets were too narrow, the buildings too short.

"We should get started," Varin said from behind me.

I hadn't realized I'd migrated to the window, my hands pressed to the glass.

"It's so beautiful," I said without turning.

"It is, but it's not why we're here."

I glanced at him, wondering if he could really see the beauty in it, but he'd turned away.

Even with such a prominent view and solar heating to ward off the winter winds, I'd rather have been back in my parents' narrow cottage. I even missed my mother's fish stew brewing on the stove, sending wafts of tomato and spices throughout the house. And while I hated sailing, I loved the briny smell that came with it. Whenever the salty scent would flood in from the front door, I'd know my father was back, ready to spin tales of seafaring and turning tides with such skill it sounded like song.

I'd have given anything to hear his voice again. Now I never would.

"Ah," Varin said, drawing me from my memories. His face distorted in discomfort, his shoulders shifting a little. "I have to change before we can begin."

"Thanks for letting me know," I replied facetiously.

A slight crease formed on his forehead. "I don't have another room."

"Where's the bathroom, then?"

"Keralie." He said my name as though it were a sigh. "I need you to turn back around."

"Why?"

"Because it's rude to watch me change."

I laughed. "I meant, why do you need to change? I thought

your wonder-suit did everything for you . . ." I scrunched my nose. "Eww. Is that why there's no bathroom? It *does* do everything for you."

He held up his hand to cut me off. "No. There's a compartment over there." He pointed to a section of his wall. It probably popped out like parts of the kitchen. "But there's not enough room to change, and this suit needs a break from being worn." He pressed a panel by the side of his bed, and a rack of two identical dermasuits sprung out. "The organisms need time to rest." The muscles in his shoulders shifted beneath the black suit. "I can feel their exhaustion."

"That is disgusting."

"Can you *please* turn around?"

"Fine," I huffed.

He should've known better. As soon as the suit's clips clicked apart, I peeked.

His back was to me. *Good.* He'd learned I couldn't be trusted. Then he began pulling his suit down, revealing perfect, unblemished tan shoulders. I sucked in a breath as he pushed the material toward his hips.

Turn back around, Keralie. Turn around. Do the right thing. For once.

But I'd had a hard day, to say the least. I ignored that little voice and what was left of good Keralie.

His shoulders were muscular, defined, and the opposite of Mackiel's scarecrow frame. But Varin's shoulders weren't as square as Mackiel's; they were less assured, as though his job, life or *something* had beaten him down. I shook that thought away. Eonists didn't question their standing in life. Varin had made that clear.

I still couldn't tear my eyes from his body. He was beautiful—
no one would deny that—but a shell of a person. His eyes lacked
fire, and that was something Mackiel had in spades. Perhaps too
much.

Why couldn't I stop comparing Varin to Mackiel? Even
though I was free of Mackiel—for now at least—my thoughts
remained tangled in him.

"I can feel you watching me," Varin said, stilling his movements.

"What? No—I—" I stuttered, quickly turning to face the
glass wall.

I thought he let out a soft laugh but couldn't be certain.
I stayed where I was; the reflection in the glass provided a good
enough view.

"Okay," he said. "I'm done."

I bit my lip to hide my grin. "What now?"

My warm pinked cheeks probably gave me away, but he didn't
seem to care. He held out a small contraption. "It's a recorder," he
explained at my blank look.

"Okay. Let's get this over with." Although I didn't want to
leave this striking, but cold, place. Not yet. But no Eonist would
hire me; I wasn't engineered for anything. Perhaps Ludia would
take me in? While I didn't know of anyone who'd relocated to
another quadrant, it was possible. A few were permitted each year
through a lottery system. But to enter the lottery, you had to meet
the criteria of the quadrant you wished to relocate to. Eonia's was
pages and pages long, making it almost impossible to meet. The
way they intended it.

"Where do you want me?" I asked.

He pointed to the one chair in the room.

"What if you have company?" I took the seat.

He fiddled with the machine, his tall frame towering over me. "I don't." The machine made a few beeps, then a soft whirring sound.

"No friends?"

"No."

"Family?"

He pressed a few more buttons before replying, "No."

"Everyone has a family. You didn't spring from the ground like a mushroom." I cocked my head. "Did you?"

"I'm just like you," he replied, missing my joke entirely. "As hard as I might find that to believe."

I ignored his jab. "So, your family . . . ?" I prompted. Talking about family was dangerous. He could easily turn the question back on me.

"Men and women are assigned multiple birthing partners throughout their lifetimes, matched for genetic excellence," he said, gazing out the window. "Once the mother gives birth, the child is handed over to the schools to raise."

I couldn't reply. That was too cruel. How could the Eonist queen allow babies to be taken from their parents? What could they possibly gain from that?

He glanced back to me. "I suppose the children I grew up with are closest to a family."

I let loose a breath. There was hope for him after all. "How often do you see them?"

"I haven't seen them since I graduated school a year ago."

Okay, maybe not.

"And your mother and father?" I almost choked on the words.

He shrugged. "I don't know who they are. It doesn't really matter anyway. They were genetic donors, nothing more."

"That's terrible."

Something flickered behind his eyes—was it doubt? "If you have no personal connections, there is no reason for jealousy. We have no crime, no hatred, no sickness." He sounded like the holographic lady on the commuter.

"No family, no friends, no love," I said.

"Do you have all these things?"

"I have my memories. I had a happy childhood." I swallowed roughly. "I had a family that cared for and protected me." I'd thought I had Mackiel. Someone I loved. I guessed he was a fleeting part of my life, like my parents had been.

He blinked. "*Had?*"

I couldn't talk to him about my past. How could he understand my pain when he felt nothing? "Having something, even if in the past, is better than nothing at all."

"And you believe memories are enough to sustain us?" he asked. "Through the darkness?"

I'd known dark times; often *I'd* created them. Were happy memories enough, if you were never to experience it again? I hoped so.

When I didn't reply, he pulled out a black container and lifted the lid. Inside lay hundreds of clear chips divided into two sides. I picked one up.

"Is this what we record on?" I twirled the chip in my fingers. There was a cloudy dot in the middle.

"Not that one." He grabbed the chip from my hand and

placed it back into the right side of the container.

"Why not?"

He removed a chip from the left side and clicked it into the recorder. "That's not blank."

"What's on it? A memory to deliver?"

"No." He studied his recorder, avoiding my eyes. Hmm. He was hiding something. While Eonists didn't lie, they *could* conceal information. I grabbed for another chip, checking for the cloudy dot.

"So if I was to put this on my tongue . . ." I stuck my tongue out at him.

He reached out and touched my hand, pleadingly. "Please don't."

I held the chip above my lips. "Why not? What's on them?"

He shook his head slowly and let out a breath, as though he was tired or, rather, tired of me. "They're snippets of memories."

"Your memories?" Now *this* was interesting. What in Varin's life had he recorded, if his childhood was unremarkable?

His lips pressed into a thin line. "No. Often we make duplicates at work, in case there's a problem with the delivery." Before I could ask, he said, "We didn't make a copy of the ones you ingested. We were instructed not to."

That didn't surprise me, knowing what was on the chips. "Then you stole these? You stole other people's memories?" I wasn't sure whether to be disgusted or impressed.

His back went rigid at the accusation. "I didn't steal them. They were going to be destroyed. And there's nothing confidential on them." But there was no way of proving that; once he'd ingested the chips, the evidence was gone.

"Why keep them?" I asked. If they weren't confidential, then they were hardly valuable.

He hesitated for a moment. "We only have a short time to experience the world, and there's so much out there to see." He closed his eyes. "I'll never get to see it all."

This boy was sitting in this stark room, watching other people's memories to get a taste of a life he'd never live. It was pathetic, but also incredibly sad.

"When we're done," I said, "I'll record a memory for you to watch."

His eyes flicked open. "Really?"

"Sure." I had plenty of happy childhood memories to share. Someone should get a little enjoyment out of them.

"Thank you." He looked at me as though I was offering him gold quartiers.

"Okay, let's do this before I change my mind." All this talk about memories was reminding me of the blood-soaked images I'd been trying to suppress all evening.

Varin pulled out two sets of round pads, placing one set in front of me and keeping the other. The Torian part of me was intrigued as the machine hummed to life, wanting to know how it worked. And of course, wondering what it would fetch at auction. Varin pushed the hair back from his forehead and placed a pad against each temple.

"What are you doing?" I asked.

"I'm going to watch the recording," he explained. "To make sure you're giving me what I need." He was going to regret that decision.

He crouched beside me and placed the pads on either side of my head, biting his lip in concentration. Electricity, which I wasn't sure was from the recorder, sparked through my veins. His eyes found mine, and I sucked in a breath. Those strange, but beautiful, pale eyes. My gaze wandered to his lips. When I looked back up, I found he was watching my mouth. Something lingered behind his usual stoic expression. Something like desire.

His eyes snapped to mine, and he pushed away from me, the moment gone.

He cleared his throat. "I'm going to start the recording now."

"Good, that's what I'm waiting for." I stumbled over my words, my cheeks warming.

He nodded, short and sharp. "Start with the first thing you remember from when you ingested the chips, and the recorder will guide you to recall the rest."

I didn't want to remember. It was brutal. Bloody. Unbelievable.

"Ready?" he asked.

No. But I had no choice. Even though Varin appeared to be living a heartless life, I wasn't willing to take it from him. He needed this information. And I needed to stay far away from Mackiel.

"Yes."

I closed my eyes and remembered.

CHAPTER ELEVEN

Corra
Queen of Eonia

*Rule five: A queen must be raised within her
own quadrant to learn the ways of her people
and not be influenced by the palace's politics.*

A storm raged inside Corra, as though half her body was
on fire, the other half as cold as ice. And everything hurt.
Her head. Her chest. Her heart.

Her heart . . .

She couldn't dwell on it. Couldn't feel it. *Shouldn't.* And yet
she did. She felt everything with such a precise clarity, her head
pounded as though it might split in two to allow the pressure
to escape. *I am Eonist,* she reminded herself. *Detached, logical,
composed.* But with the inspector interrogating everyone inside the
palace, she knew her secret was bound to be uncovered.

Corra was Eonist, but only by blood.

Unlike her sister queens, Corra hadn't been raised in the
quadrant she would one day rule. Instead, she'd been raised in the
palace—her mother had been unwilling to part with her on her
birth date.

Eonists were not as unfeeling as the other quadrants believed.
Yes, they learned to control their emotions and suppress their

desires from an early age, but they were not immune to emotion, and certainly not to the strongest emotion of all. Love.

Corra had been told by her mother that she was a perfect newborn: silky dark skin, a smattering of soft black hair upon her head and the warmest large brown eyes anyone had ever seen. To see Corra was to love Corra.

And so her mother had decided to give Corra to her wet nurse, who had recently suffered a stillbirth. The nurse would raise Corra as her own, hiding her from the rest of the palace to ensure, when it was Corra's time to take the throne, that no one would recognize her. Everyone else would assume baby Corra had been sent to live with relatives as required by Queenly Law.

Corra's mother wanted to have an influence on her life, let her daughter see how she ruled Eonia, hoping that Corra could one day follow in her footsteps.

At an early age, Corra was told that her birth mother was the Eonist queen. The queen visited Corra only a few times a year, ensuring her presence within the palace remained a secret. But she never missed Corra's birthday. She would explain that while ruling your emotions was fundamental to Eonia's peace, it was also important to open your eyes to the other quadrants' ways of life. And that not everything stemming from the heart instead of the head was wrong.

Her mother would end each visit with the same words.

Be patient, child. Be calm. Be selfless. Wait for the right moment. Wait for your time. Rule with a steady hand. A steady heart.

It became a mantra over the years, informing how Corra should and shouldn't behave. When a young Corra desired the world outside the palace, outside the rooms she shared with the woman who'd raised her, she would hear her mother's voice.

Corra remained in those two rooms for her entire childhood. She played with the toys that wouldn't be missed, she read the digi-scrolls that had already been read. She devoured all she could about her quadrant through comm chips. The memories captured Eonia with such vivid detail she could smell the crisp air, see the sleek silver skylines and taste the unpolluted rain as it fell from the sky.

Her mother's voice had once again echoed in her head after the inspector's initial questioning.

Be patient, child. Be calm. Be selfless. This is your moment. This is your time. Have a steady hand. A steady heart.

But Corra couldn't shake the visions of Iris's lifeless body and her blood splattered against the flowers she loved so much, her crown discarded as though it were nothing. While she hadn't seen it with her own eyes, she'd heard it described so many times, she couldn't rid herself of the image.

Once in her rooms, Corra ordered her advisor to take leave. She needed time, space. Time to grieve. But Corra wasn't sure there would ever be enough time to accept a world in which Iris was no longer.

Be calm, child. Steady.

But she couldn't. Not this time.

There was no one here to see her break or judge her behavior as un-Eonist. Connected, emotional, passionate.

Passion . . .

Corra shook. She would never again feel Iris's soft skin against hers. Her pale cheek next to her brown skin. She would never again press her mouth to hers, Iris's pink lips on her curved mouth. They would never again share a breath as if they were one. She would never again see the way Iris's cold exterior dissolved at the mere sight of Corra. And all those cherished smiles for her. Only for her.

Now it was all gone. *She* was gone. And there was no getting her back.

Corra flung herself onto her bed, pressing her face into her pillow so even she couldn't feel her tears as they fell. Tears that shouldn't fall for another. And certainly not for an Archian.

She let out a moan, grief clawing her throat.

Like all queens, they weren't allowed love; it was seen as merely a distraction. For if a queen was to love another, she might place the love for this person above her quadrant. But for the years Corra and Iris had secretly been together, they'd built a fortress, not only making them stronger, but their quadrants too. Corra didn't believe Iris completed her, for Corra was complete, always had been—her mother had seen to that. But Iris was vital to Corra, allowing her to rule with a sense of ease. A sense of peace. Corra felt as though she was honoring her mother's wishes. Ruling with a steady heart.

Iris was the first queen Corra had met after her coronation, even though Corra had heard of Iris, or rather, had *heard* Iris's booming voice through the palace passageways across the years. Corra had never known anyone so completely ruled by their emotions. Iris hated easily, threw fits when she didn't get what she wanted, roared at anyone who dared look at her the wrong way or for too long. When they finally met, Corra had been shocked to see such a voice belonged to a woman so slight.

Iris had studied Corra before offering her a small pale hand to shake. In her other hand, she held out a gold watch. "For you," she'd said.

Corra took the handcrafted Archian watch, confused by the hour and minute hand displaying 12:30 with the second hand stuck horizontal—fracturing the face in four.

"It's broken," she'd said, her voice quiet, unsure of what to make of this fiery waif of a woman.

Iris's green eyes lit up. "It's to remember the time before this"—Iris waved a hand around her—"before your coronation. For that's what will make you a great queen."

Iris was no doubt referring to the years Corra was supposed to have spent growing up in her own quadrant. But instead Corra thought of her mother, to whom she'd said her final good-bye mere hours earlier.

Corra should've taken the extra time to compose herself. She hadn't been ready to speak about her mother, her past. Iris didn't know that Corra had known her mother her whole life and that she hadn't gone to school to control her emotions. All Corra had was what her mother had told her.

To prevent tears from falling, she found herself whispering her mother's words. "Be calm, child. Have a steady hand—"

"A steady heart," Iris had finished, her green eyes widening. "You knew your mother?"

Corra had shaken her head. But it was too late. Iris had seen past the mask Corra had perfected throughout her childhood and into adulthood.

Iris had squeezed Corra's arm. "Your mother was a great queen, and a fine friend."

It was too much. Tears fell from Corra's eyes before she could sweep them away.

She'd been terrified, but rather than turning her in, Iris vowed to keep her secret. "For we all have them," she'd said.

Their first meeting had shaken Corra. She knew she'd made a friend within the palace, something she'd dreamed of since she was a child.

Iris had been the only person, aside from her adoptive mother, to know Corra's secret. She began letting her guard down, allowing her emotions to show. Allowing herself to be *someone*—not only the controlled queen she was born to be. She laughed with Iris. She dreamed of nations beyond Quadara. She dreamed of love.

Corra's mother would never have denied her that, for it was love that drove her to protect her baby and have her raised inside the palace. Not every Queenly Law was correct. They had been established by four queens, angry with their dead husband, who had allowed Quadara to almost fall to ruin. They had outlawed love from their lives and made the quadrants their only priority, but Corra could not do the same.

And although her emotions had not been stamped out by Eonist schooling, there was no queen who knew more about the palace, Eonia and the other quadrants. Her adoptive mother wasn't Eonist. Like most of the staff, she'd been Archian, and she shared any and all information she acquired from other members of staff. Corra had also witnessed the shift of power six times. She'd heard about advisors trying to assert their agendas—if their queens weren't mindful.

The palace had been, and always would be, a part of Corra. As would Iris.

A steady hand. A steady heart.

But only Iris calmed her heart.

THE MORNING AFTER Iris's death, Corra's advisor informed her that the inspector wished to speak with her. Corra managed to pull herself from her bed, donned her gold dermasuit and crown and pulled her braided hair atop her head.

On the way to the inspector, she saw her handmaiden and Alissa in the corridor. Her handmaiden cradled Alissa's tear-stained face in her hands, her lips by her ear. They both paused when Corra passed by, bowing low in respect, but kept their hands tangled together—no reason to hide their relationship.

A tremor ripped through Corra, knowing she would never hold Iris again. And to hold her in such a public place had always been a dream of theirs. To be like any other couple in Quadara.

Corra was so distracted by her thoughts, she almost bumped into Marguerite as she made to enter the inspector's designated room.

"Apologies, Marguerite," Corra said, her voice raw from crying all night.

Marguerite was looking through her, a bewildered expression on her face. Her eyes slowly focused on her. "Corra," she said, as though she was only now realizing the Eonist queen stood in front of her.

Corra had never seen Marguerite this shaken. Like Iris, she was a strong queen. Corra wanted to ask if she was all right, but the question was absurd. Of course she wasn't.

"I'm sorry I didn't make it to dinner last night," Corra said. "I was exhausted." Exhaustion was allowed; grief wasn't, Corra reminded herself.

Marguerite looked at her for a long moment. Corra wondered

if her emotions were showing. After a while, the eldest queen smiled sadly. "I didn't either." She squeezed Corra's arm. "Tonight?"

While it would be draining to keep up the charade, Corra had woken with an intense desire not to be alone. "Yes," she said.

"Be careful in there." Marguerite nodded to the room behind her.

Before Corra could ask why, the Torian queen gave her arm one last squeeze, then retreated down the corridor, her long black skirt flowing behind her.

Iris and Marguerite had been close. Did she know Corra's secret? Was that why she was warning her about the inspector?

The inspector had his recorder looped around his ear when she entered the room. He stood and bowed deeply. Something flickered across his face whenever he looked at her—an echo of emotion, compared to when he addressed the other queens. *Respect,* she realized. As an Eonist, she was the only queen who had an impact on his quadrant and life.

"My queen," he said, bowing again as Corra took a seat opposite him.

"Inspector." She inclined her chin. "How is the investigation progressing? Any news?"

She wanted the killer found as quickly as possible, not only as justice for Iris but to be rid of the inspector and his probing inquiries. While no one inside the palace knew her secret, it wouldn't take much digging into her past to discover that her relatives living outside the palace had never met her. And Corra knew an Eonist inspector would explore all avenues of treason, from both inside and outside the palace dome. If anyone discovered where she'd grown up, she would lose her throne in an instant.

For the first time, Corra was happy the woman who'd raised her, as well as her birth mother, was long dead.

"I'm afraid I can't speak of my findings, my queen," he said. "Not while the case is still open."

And while we're all suspects, she thought. Being a queen wouldn't change that. After all, who had more access to the queens than their sisters?

She nodded. "How can I assist you?"

"You can tell me all you know about Queen Iris."

"I'm not sure I have anything else to add. Surely you have spoken to the other queens and advisors?" Corra forced herself not to bring a hand to her watch, for fear he might ask her what she was hiding beneath her dermasuit. His eyes would miss nothing.

"I have, my queen. But I wish to hear from you also." She wasn't sure whether it was because he trusted her opinion more, or whether he wanted to compare notes with the other queens. Likely both.

Corra told him what she knew about Iris. How she had come to the palace years before her. *A lie.* How she was closest to Marguerite. *Another lie.* And how Corra knew little more about her private life than what had been displayed. *The biggest lie of all.*

"Queens don't have private lives," Corra finished.

"Thank you, my queen." He seemed appeased. He would never expect an Eonist to lie, and certainly not the Eonist queen. "And do you have any theories on who might have wanted her dead?"

Corra swallowed. "I really don't know." She rubbed two fingers across her temples. "There have been threats to the palace and the queens in the past, but nothing recent."

"Is there anything else you think I should know?"

Corra paused, holding back the stories and lies, and actually considered his question—some truth to allow him to find the bastard who had slain her love. While she didn't want the inspector's attention on her, there was a reason she had asked for Inspector Garvin to take this case. He was the quickest and the best. Iris deserved retribution.

"In the last few days," Corra began, "before Queen Iris's death . . ." She paused again, watching as the inspector pressed something on the recorder around his ear. A flag, she realized. But flagging what? "She was short with everyone—shorter than normal. And she missed a few nightly dinners. We didn't see her unless she was in court."

"I've heard similar reports from the other queens," the inspector said. "Queen Iris wanted to change Queenly Law. She was to discuss it with you the day after she was killed."

"Change Queenly Law?" Corra repeated.

He leaned forward, eyes piercing. "Did you know anything about that?"

Corra said, "No, nothing." But that was another lie. She knew exactly why Iris wanted to change Queenly Law. *Rule eight.* She wanted to be allowed to roam the palace's corridors hand in hand with Corra. She wanted to spend her nights with her love freely, without sneaking in and out. Perhaps she even wanted to marry Corra. Now she'd never know.

Iris had often talked about changing this aspect of Queenly Law, but Corra had argued that it would reveal Corra's more devastating secret, that she had not been raised in Eonia. Iris had agreed to let it go. Or so Corra had thought.

The night before Iris's death, there had been a noticeable

difference in her mood. Even when they were alone, Iris's frostiness did not completely dissipate. Corra had asked what was bothering her, and Iris commented on how the throne diverted love—not that it made it more difficult, but it actually put a divider between two people. Initially, Corra had thought she was talking about their relationship, and she'd put her arm around Iris's narrow waist and told her that their thrones had brought them together.

But Iris had shaken her head. "It's not just us," she'd said. "All queens are denied love."

Corra had been confused. She didn't know that this rule was an issue with any of the other queens. Iris was not close to Stessa, the age gap and differing cultures too much to bridge, which left only the eldest queen. "Marguerite?" Corra asked.

Iris had only sighed and changed the topic. Yet there was something in her eyes that had told Corra she'd guessed wrong.

What had Iris known about the youngest queen?

"Anything else important?" the inspector pressed, bringing her attention back to him.

Before she could stop it, there was a prickling at the back of her eyes at the thought of that last night together. The last night they would ever have. Their last touch.

She needed to get out of this room. Before she broke apart and her secret was laid bare. She touched the face of the watch beneath her suit.

Of Eonist blood, but not of Eonist heart. That was what Iris used to say, late in the evenings, their arms and legs intertwined.

Her guise was slipping. She was not emotionless. She was not Eonist.

"No. I don't know anything else that could help you." Corra stood abruptly. "I must attend to my queenly duties."

The first tear fell as she closed the door behind her. She wiped it away with the back of her hand. She needed to talk to Stessa and find out what Iris had discovered about her.

And whether it was worth killing for.

CHAPTER TWELVE

Keralie

The first thing I remembered was the knife.

The hilt was small, easily concealed in a pocket or belt, but the blade itself was long and thin, like a needle. It glinted in the sun like a slit of light from a cracked door—so narrow it almost wasn't there.

The assassin held the weapon behind their back and approached a figure lounging on a wooden settee, the sunlight hitting sharp cheekbones. Skin so pale it was nearly translucent.

Her lids were closed as she tilted her face to the sun, completely unaware of the person closing the distance between them. The garden smelled sweet and earthy; various flowers emitted a fragrance that contrasted with the sterile palace hallways. The sound of the ocean crashing against the cliffs below had drowned out the intruder's entrance.

The assassin moved lightly, on the balls of their feet. It wasn't until they dragged the blade across the woman's milky white skin that she realized she had company.

Her eyes flew open: vivid green, matching her surroundings. *Queen Iris.* She didn't appear frightened, merely annoyed.

She wiped a hand across her neck. Only when she saw blood staining her fingers did her expression shift. She spun to the assassin. Rage lit her features, flushing her cheeks nearly as red as the blood cascading down her slashed throat.

Her mouth opened, but her eyes rolled back into her head. Her arms flung wide, knocking her crown from a table beside her, as she sagged to the floor. The assassin wiped the blade clean on a nearby leaf.

Someone gasped. It was not Queen Iris or the assassin. The noise came from nowhere and everywhere at once, disconnected from the ghastly scene.

All the blood brought another memory to mind, as though it were happening today and not six months ago. My father was lying on the rocks, his head lolled back, eyes closed. Blood was everywhere. On my dress. On my hands.

"Focus," I heard a voice say. *Varin,* I thought hazily. "Focus on Queen Iris."

The image of her split neck flooded back into view. The recorder pulled the next murder from my mind.

The assassin entered a golden room; the smell of flowers tainted the air. A girl sat at the edge of a pool, the water tinted gold from the surrounding tiles. The girl dangled her legs into the water, her black hair twisted into complicated patterns, her ornate red dress billowing around her. *Queen Stessa.*

The assassin approached; this time their hands were empty.

All it took was a shove.

The water shifted as Queen Stessa's body hit the surface. The assassin followed her in.

Hands pushed arms, legs kicked her body downward. The assassin climbed onto her back, sinking her to the bottom, heels hitting tiles. Dark hair swirled like water down a drain.

A perfect pink mouth opened wide, sending bubbles to the surface. The assassin watched as the queen's eyes glazed over. Her last breath shuddered from her chest.

Then it was done. A simpler kill. Cleaner than before, but harder. Physical, and more intimate—two bodies intertwined as they dipped below the surface. Only one to reemerge.

While the assassin watched Queen Stessa sink to the bottom of the pool, another disembodied sound echoed through the cavernous room. Ragged gasps grew louder and louder. Pain—*my* pain. *My* gasps.

"It's all right," Varin said. "You're fine." *Fine?* How was any of this fine? "Don't fight the recorder." I thought I could feel the ghost of his hand on mine, but I must've been imagining it.

The images moved faster now, the recorder coercing them from my mind.

Good. Take them. Take them all.

The assassin was in a darkened room. A figure slept fitfully in a bed, their hand clutching something at their chest, under their golden dermasuit.

Queen Corra.

Now in a different room, the assassin flipped open a lighter. Life and light bloomed into the night. With one small flick, the little flame soared across the room, finding a home in a bunch of acrid-smelling rags. Alcohol.

Seconds later, the room was aflame.

Smoke followed, infusing the room with gray. A voice cried for help amid uncontrollable coughing.

Another voice gasped.

Varin. I wanted to follow him, pull myself out of this nightmare and into the light, but his voice was a thread I couldn't hold on to.

Queen Corra banged her hands against a window, desperate to be free. The assassin watched from the other side of the glass, waiting for the life to drain away from her body.

Yes, the easiest kill. No blood, no fight. Only death.

The assassin walked away as the palace guards broke the glass, seconds too late.

Only one queen remained. Queen Marguerite.

In a small indistinguishable room, the assassin shook powder from a small silver vial. This would be the easiest kill yet, completely removed from the action.

But the assassin needed to watch. Make sure the poison did its work.

No—enough. I didn't want to relive any more. But the recorder wouldn't let my mind go. I remembered it all, and all over again. Quicker and quicker. More and more details each time, unable to detach myself from the despair.

I screamed.

The images swam together. Blood. Water. Fire. Darkness. Death. Arms. Legs. Neck. Abdomen. Knife. Hands. Fire. Poison. Merging together into a tapestry of death.

Then, nothing.

CHAPTER THIRTEEN

Stessa
Queen of Ludia

*Rule six: Once a queen enters the palace, she
is never to visit her homeland again.*

Lyker was waiting in Stessa's rooms when she returned from her interrogation with the inspector. Stessa wasn't stupid. She knew that was what it was. All the queens were being interrogated, under the guise of "gathering information."

"What are you doing in here?" she asked, quickly shutting the door behind her. "The inspector could've been with me! You can't be here."

He frowned but stepped toward her. "I was worried about you. Where have you been? Are you all right?" He'd pushed his shirtsleeves up to his elbows to reveal the colorful lines tattooed on his fingers up toward his heart. She knew he hated wearing the long sleeves of the advisor uniform.

"It's too dangerous with the inspector sniffing around." But her body automatically moved toward his. She forced herself not to trace the lines up his arms as she normally would.

He curled a short black lock of hair behind her ear and grinned. "I'll take my chances."

"We have to be careful, now more than ever. They're watching us. *He's* watching us." That man with his disgusting fingers. She couldn't believe she'd briefly thought him handsome. She shivered at the idea of his dark eyes, or anything else, upon her.

Lyker took her hands in his. "Don't stress, Stess." He grinned at his rhyming words. "If we act weird, they'll know we did something wrong."

"The inspector already thinks I killed her."

"How do you know?"

"I'm the newest queen. And you"—she pointed at his chest—"are the newest advisor. We're easy targets. Don't you feel them watching us?"

"You're being paranoid."

"I'm not. We have to stay away from each other. Just in case."

"Seriously?" he asked. "What's the point, then? After everything we've done to be together? After everything we've given up?"

Stessa hated that she'd pulled him from the world he loved so fiercely. A quadrant of art and color and music. But they'd agreed they would be enough for each other.

"That's just it, Lyker. If they find out about what we've done, what *I've* done, I'll lose my throne. Worse, I'll be locked up."

His hands were clenched at his sides, his temper rising. "But—"

"Please," she said, running her fingertips along his arms to soothe him. "For the length of the investigation."

"I'm worried about you. The other advisors believe Iris's murder was an inside job. I want to stay with you until this is over."

"You can't. And I'm a queen, remember? I don't need you hovering over me like I'm about to shatter. There are guards roaming the halls. I'll be fine." He had to realize that protecting their secret was paramount. They would be together in time. A few days would be forgotten in their lifetime together.

"This isn't getting any easier." He ran his hand through his coiffed hair.

"What are you talking about?"

"Us."

She grunted. "I never said this would be easy."

"I know, but it's nearly been a year. I'm not sure how much longer I can pretend to care."

Her heart stuttered, and tears swam in front of her eyes. "You don't care about me anymore?"

He swept her hands into his. "Stess, don't be absurd. I was talking about my position. Look at me"—he gestured to his colorful arms—"I'm not built for court, palaces and politics. I feel like I'm losing myself." His voice softened. "I can't lose you too."

"You're not going to." She wished she could offer Lyker a different future. She wanted to make him a priority, as he had done for her, but what choice did they have? She had no female heirs; she couldn't renounce the throne and leave Ludia without a ruler.

Stessa had heard from her mother that if you loved someone, you should let them go, but she couldn't face a future without Lyker.

"Be patient, please," she said. "We'll find a way to make this work."

He nodded but didn't look convinced.

She pressed her cheek against his chest, wrapped her arms around him and started humming their favorite song. The beads in her hair and around her neck tinkled as they swayed.

"As long as we're together," she said, "I'll make sure you don't forget who you are."

"And you? Do you feel like the same girl as before?"

Stessa liked being queen; she liked ensuring the other quadrants didn't ruin what she considered the perfect community. She liked being taken seriously. And, she had to admit, she liked the attention.

Was she the same girl she'd been in Ludia? *No.*

"Does it matter?" She stopped swaying and tilted her head back to see his expression.

"Not if you're happy."

Her mother had always told her that if she held love in her heart, everything else would fall into place. But Stessa's love for Lyker had driven her to commit sinister deeds, things her mother would never support. Ludists weren't supposed to be dark and devious. They were light, playful, carefree. And Lyker was the epitome of sunshine and warmth. But every day, she saw his light dim and darken, and every day another weight pressed on her shoulders.

"I'm happy when I'm with you," she said eventually.

"What if we leave the palace before the inspector finds out about us?" His voice was hopeful. He'd never wanted her to accept the Ludist throne in the first place, suggesting they run away. It might've been easier. He still suggested running once a week, but this was the first time she actually considered it. It had taken a few months, but Stessa had embraced her role as queen, especially when she had Lyker by her side. She wanted to be as respected as Iris, as knowledgeable as Marguerite and as composed as Corra. With Iris's murder, and the inspector's unnerving presence, Stessa questioned whether this was the life she really wanted after all.

"Where would we go?" she asked. "Everyone knows my name. And my face."

"You're the master of disguise." He grinned and tapped her nose, referring to the parties they had attended together dressed in elaborate clothing and makeup to fool their friends, only revealing themselves at the end of the night. "But we'd have to leave Quadara."

Stessa knew that would hurt Lyker. He missed his family, friends and the freedom to create art wherever he went. He'd given up everything to be with her. They used to laugh and smile every hour of every day. Now all they did was lie, scheme and worry.

He watched her, waiting for a response.

She let a breath slowly escape through her teeth. "We can't, even if we wanted to. They've closed the palace. No one in, no one out. Not until they find Iris's assassin."

"But you're considering it?"

Stessa didn't want to give up her throne, the power or the responsibility. But she couldn't give up Lyker. If the inspector found out the truth, she'd be separated from him forever. She bit her lip, unsure what to do.

"I want to be happy," he continued. "With you. We would be happier outside of the palace, I'm sure of it."

Stessa could imagine a simpler life with Lyker. A life where he could paint words of love on the walls of their house to the tune of Stessa's songs. She would miss the palace, but not as much as she missed her home back in Ludia. And Lyker was disappearing in front of her eyes. She had to make the choice. Her love for Lyker, or her position on the throne.

There was no choice. It was Lyker, always and forever.

"I think you're right," she said. "But we have to wait until they open the palace doors."

"Then we run?" His beautiful face was lit with hope. It was all he'd ever wanted, the two of them together, no one to force them to part. No more stolen kisses and midnight rendezvous. Time would be theirs. They could start a new life.

No secrets, no laws, no murders.

"Yes." She grinned up at him.

CHAPTER FOURTEEN

Keralie

*K*eralie.

Darkness was kind. Still. Free from pain. Free from all that blood.

Keralie.

I once knew a girl called Keralie. But I was no longer that girl.

Keralie.

Her life was kind. Full of love. Full of happiness and laughter. Then she shattered it. And there was no getting it back.

"Keralie!"

My eyes flew open. Varin's concerned face filled my vision. I was lying on a bed. Varin's bed. His eyes were wide, his face flushed, and his hair stuck in odd directions as though he'd been pulling at it. But his hands were now on mine. He quickly retracted them when he saw I was awake.

"What happened?" I asked, my voice raw, my whole body shaking.

"You were screaming and then you passed out." He pulled the pads from my temples. "How do you feel?"

I tentatively moved to a sitting position. "Like I murdered Quadara's queens."

"That's not funny." He frowned. "Here." He offered me a glass of water and a food bar. His hands were shaking, and he was breathing heavily. He was in shock. I knew how it felt.

My stomach was too agitated for food, but I gladly accepted the glass.

"Why didn't you tell me what was on the chips?" he asked while I drank. "Why didn't you warn me?"

"I did warn you." I placed the empty glass on the floor and rubbed my forehead. I wanted to crawl back into the darkness. It was too bright here. "And if I'd told you, you wouldn't have believed me."

Now that the memories had been untangled, they were impossible to ignore. Each and every queen, dead.

He flew off the bed and began pacing the room. "You knew this all night, and yet you said nothing. They're our queens!" He ran a hand through his already tussled hair. "The very foundation of Quadara is at risk."

"I needed to make sure you upheld your end of the agreement. I relive the memories, and you help me hide from Mackiel. I was keeping my end of the deal."

He let out a racked breath. "I don't want to deliver these chips."

"Who are you supposed to deliver them to?"

"I don't know. I only know I was supposed to deliver the

chips yesterday morning at the border to Ludia. But before I got there, I found my bag empty."

I gave him a sheepish grin. "Do you usually know the contents of the comm chips?" I thought back to his memory collection.

His eyes locked on mine. "No, I don't."

"Then why did you watch the rerecording this time?"

"When you first ingested the chips, there was this expression on your face . . ." He let out another breath. "I had to know what you'd seen." Curiosity. Well, that was something I could relate to.

I bit the inside of my cheek. "Now what? You *need* to deliver them, right?"

He nodded slowly, but there was uncertainty in his movements.

"You want to do something about it, don't you?" I said with a groan. "You want to take the new comm chips to the palace authorities."

"Don't you?" Something flickered behind his eyes, something that seemed like drive. Passion. Emotion. Very un-Eonist.

"What can I do? These memories must be to confirm the assassin has completed the job. The queens are dead."

"We could still help!" He gestured at the new chips. "This is evidence!"

"We only know how the queens died, not who did it."

"We know someone was meant to receive these chips and be notified of their deaths. That's one person involved we know about."

"Two," I reminded him. "Mackiel. He wanted me to steal the comm case from you and then refused to sell it. He *has* to be involved."

"Yes."

I shook my head. "That's not enough."

"Why haven't we heard anything?" Varin asked. "Why hasn't the palace sent out a warning?"

"Perhaps they're worried about the panic the news would cause? We'll probably only hear once the new queens are upon their thrones. They might not even tell us the previous ones were murdered. They'll probably say it was some kind of accident." I leaned back into his bed; it was surprisingly comfortable. Fatigue weighed down my eyelids. A few hours' rest. That was all I needed.

"We should go to the palace," he said. Of course, he decided to be chatty now.

When I didn't reply, he continued, "Information like this, *powerful* information, which could be used to bring this murderer to justice, will be valuable to the palace."

I sat back up. Now he was speaking my language. "How valuable?"

"Enough to ensure you never have to work with someone like Mackiel again."

Working for Mackiel hadn't been just about the money, but Varin wouldn't—couldn't—understand that. He accepted his position in the world, while I had rebelled against mine.

"I'm a criminal," I said with a shrug. "The palace isn't going to give me anything, even if I do help them find the murderer."

"Keralie." The low intensity of his voice sent a shiver down my spine. "Do you want to be a criminal?"

Why did everyone assume I wasn't exactly who I wanted to be?

"Keralie," he said again when I didn't reply. This time his voice was soft.

"What?" I snapped.

"Fine. You don't have to come with me."

I didn't want to go anywhere. I wanted to stay here, on this comfy bed, far from Mackiel. But I also wanted to know how this ended up. I wasn't sure if it was merely curiosity or my long-delayed conscience emerging. Perhaps both.

But what if the palace *did* reward me? While I didn't really need the money, there was something I desperately wanted. Needed. My family.

If the doctors were correct, then my father had weeks to live. I didn't know much about the palace, only that they continued to deny access to HIDRA, despite my mother's best efforts. Perhaps I could change that? I could barter the information on the assassin for a dose of HIDRA. If my father was revived, I might be able to forgive myself.

"For argument's sake," I said, twisting a lock of hair around my fingers, "if you were to go to the palace with the comm chips, what would you say?"

I thought I saw a hint of a smile, but then it was gone. "That I have evidence on who the murderer is," he said.

"Really? I've seen the memories twice now, and I still have no idea."

"What are you suggesting, then?"

I put a hand to my chest. "I don't believe I was suggesting anything. I was merely inquiring about your plan."

"All right, theoretically, then, what would *you* do if you were to go to the palace with this?" He held up a silver comm case.

"I wouldn't." I put my hand up as he opened his mouth to interrupt. "I'd gather more information first." I smirked. "If I wanted a reward."

"Okay." He stepped toward me. "And how would you go about that?"

"You never steal from someone without knowing more about the situation and person—by watching them." An early lesson from Mackiel.

"We're not stealing from anyone."

I waved a hand. "Same difference. As you said, we know one person who is involved—the person who was meant to receive the comm chips." He nodded, encouraging me to continue. "If I were to do this, *theoretically*, then I would arrange to redeliver the comm chips in order to meet them. That way, I'd know who was pulling the strings. *That* would be valuable information to the palace." Hopefully valuable enough to access HIDRA.

Varin nodded as if he was considering my plan, but the light behind his eyes told me he was impressed.

Not that I was trying to impress him.

"Okay," he said. "I find out more information about the intended recipient of the comm chips and then take that information to the palace."

"You need to make the delivery spot somewhere more public this time," I said. "Safer." Somewhere Mackiel wouldn't be.

"Okay," he said again, putting the new comm case with the chips into his messenger bag. "Thanks for your help." He headed for the door.

"Wait!" I cried, jumping from the bed.

He stopped but didn't turn around. "What is it?"

I'd hoped to be free of these memories once they were out of my head. I'd hoped I could forget what I'd seen. But I couldn't. I wasn't free. I was tied to these four dead queens, whether I liked it or not.

But now I had a plan. Not only a plan to help the palace, but to help my father and restore my family. I squeezed my eyes shut, imaging my mother's arms around me, welcoming me home.

My heart fluttered inside my chest when I replied, "I'm coming with you."

CHAPTER FIFTEEN

Marguerite
Queen of Toria

Rule seven: A queen must produce an heir
before the age of forty-five, to ensure
her royal lineage.

Marguerite took a deep breath, waiting for the moment Iris would pass by.

Her body.

Her friend was gone.

Iris's death procession would be the fourth Marguerite had attended since entering the palace. Usually, they would wait for the new queen to be in place upon her throne, but with the inspector's plan to pull Iris apart for clues, they had moved ahead and set the ceremony for only twenty-four hours since she had been found dead.

Iris should've been then laid to rest within the palace tombs. Instead she would return to the inspector, and he'd poke and prod her with his implements in that cold and sterile infirmary of his. "She cannot rest," he had said. "*We* cannot rest. Not until the assassin is found."

And while Marguerite understood the need to find answers, she wished it did not cost Iris her final dignity.

The death procession was not complex. The body of the

queen was to be placed in a glass coffin, adorned with what she loved, and then carried through the palace by her advisor, hand-maidens and close staff. First, she would be moved through the Archian corridors, then the Torian corridors, and so forth through the different parts of the palace. She would then be returned to the infirmary, as promised to the inspector.

Marguerite shook, her fists clenched by her sides.

The palace was in chaos. Every conversation carried Iris's name, every whisper spoke of her death. And there was the inspector, seemingly everywhere at once. Always with his questions, and yet no answers to Marguerite's.

Marguerite had spent the morning reliving everything she could remember over the last few weeks for the inspector to record onto comm chips for later ingestion. Marguerite shivered at the thought of him watching her memories through her eyes. But she would do what she must to ensure the culprit was found.

Regardless that the queens had told the same story—they had last seen Iris in court that day, after she had declined the Archian governor's request for electricity—the inspector continued to focus on the monarchs. His black eyes narrowed when they entered a room, his lengthy fingers twitching at his recorder whenever they spoke. Yet Marguerite knew they were without guilt. She could not imagine a queen carrying out such a monstrous act upon her own sister.

The swish of footsteps on the marble floor brought Marguerite's attention back to the procession. The Archian advisor appeared first. Behind followed two of Iris's handmaidens. They wore matching black dresses, skirts long to the floor, leaving a dark interweaving trail of material behind them. They carried the coffin as if it weighed nothing, and yet their faces were drawn in such grief,

Marguerite worried they would collapse. When they neared, their eyes found the Torian queen and they tilted their heads in respect.

As in the infirmary, Iris appeared as though she were merely sleeping. She wore a white lace dress, hands placed on her stomach, cheeks dusted with pink. Her fair hair had been braided into a long plait and placed across her neck to hide the garish wound.

Iris would have hated her advisor deciding what she would wear and how she would look. *Completely undignified,* she would have said. *I am queen. I decide what I wear and where I go!*

Marguerite dabbed a handkerchief under her eye. She would miss the whirlwind force that was her friend.

Flowers and vines surrounded Iris's body, her beloved garden to be part of her final resting place. On top of the glass were hundreds of burning candles; the dripping wax would seal the lid shut, although the inspector would reopen it shortly.

As Iris's body passed, her voice sounded in Marguerite's head. The last words she had spoken to her. "I'm tired of court," she'd said. Her bright green eyes had flashed.

"You are always tired of court," Marguerite had replied with a smile. "And yet you still bear it."

"A foolish waste of our time." Her fury didn't flinch at Marguerite's comment. "I have much more important things to do."

"Such as?" Marguerite had been intrigued. As far as she was aware, there had been no major conflicts within Archia.

Iris had shaken her head. "You wouldn't understand."

Marguerite knew she did not mean to be cruel. Clearly, something had weighed heavily on Iris's mind in her last hours, although it would not have been the Archian governor who aggravated her so. It had to be something to do with her desire to change

Queenly Law. Something that resonated more deeply. Personal.

And yet Queenly Law dictated the queens were not permitted a personal life, for fear it would detract from the duties to their quadrant. The original four queens of Quadara had thought their king's attention was too divided. Not only across the quadrants but among the wives themselves. And the queens' dissatisfaction with their husband affected their thoughts, diverting them from their duties. Preventing future queens from having such distractions was key to upholding peace in Quadara.

Years ago, Marguerite had thought a personal life was possible within the palace. During one of the matching balls, she'd met a suitor and fallen quickly for the man with fair curly hair and kind blue eyes. He was the first—and only—man to ever show her affection. And it had been intoxicating.

When Marguerite was a young girl, she was taller than she should've been, and all her features were hard angles. *Scarecrow,* the kids called her. *Clothes hanger.*

When she was brought to the palace as a young woman, everything shifted. The staff spoke of nothing but her stunning beauty. Her long legs, small but elongated frame, sharp cheekbones and prominent profile. What a beautiful queen she would be. Yet the years of being torn down and made to feel smaller than the rats that haunted the Jetée could not be undone. Marguerite's past had made her who she was. When the staff called her striking, she heard *severe,* knowing her features were hard and sharp and not the typical Torian beauty.

So when Elias, son of a wealthy Torian banker, had attended the matching ball, she had no hope of rebuffing his affections. He was sweet and considerate and spoke of nothing but her beauty.

For once she believed the words, for no man had ever uttered such compliments.

But marriage was forbidden by Queenly Law.

Marguerite had tried to reason with her advisor. She had wanted more with Elias than a matching to produce offspring. She wanted to share a life with him. She wanted to wake to his handsome face and fall asleep to the sound of his breathing. She wanted to see him hold their child and help raise her together.

But her advisor would not yield. "If we cave on one rule," Jenri had said to her, "then all others could be called under question. If we shatter Queenly Law, we could shatter Quadara's stability."

Marguerite had been heartbroken. Until she missed her monthly period. And the next. And the next. She was pregnant. And nothing would stand between her new, growing family. She would find a way to keep Elias within the palace, even if she could not call him husband.

Elias had been given a room until the child was born. A male offspring would be raised by relatives outside the palace or by the son's father, with no claim to the throne. But the palace doctor had informed Marguerite that she was carrying a girl.

The day she ran to Elias's rooms to tell him the news of her pregnancy, she could've been floating—her smile so wide it was painful. But she had never really known pain, not living in the wealthy part of Toria with her adoptive parents.

Until that day.

When she reached Elias's bedroom, she opened the door without knocking, unable to contain her excitement. And there he was, his golden chest bare, his dark lashes resting against his prominent cheeks. Marguerite's heart swelled, until she saw the naked girl beside him. She didn't recognize her—her face was pressed into his side. It didn't matter. Their entwined bodies told her everything she needed to know.

He had never loved her. He had come to the palace for the status, and for the payment of being matched with a queen.

She would not let him see her tears, and left before he realized she was even there. It did not matter anymore. His part in the matching process was complete.

From that day, Marguerite vowed to keep her baby from this treacherous place, ensuring she would never be seduced by the palace and the lure of the throne. Everyone's motives became muddled when you were queen. Her daughter would be raised without any knowledge of her heritage, allowing for a simpler and, hopefully, happier life.

She told the palace doctor she'd lost the baby, and she hid the truth from her sister queens behind large billowing skirts. While Iris had not been in the palace when Marguerite had given birth to her daughter, as the two queens grew close over the years, Marguerite had told her the truth.

Marguerite had thought her stern sister queen would reprimand her for breaking such a vital law, but Iris had said, "You followed your heart, like we Archians do. You did what you thought was best for your daughter."

"What about what's best for my quadrant?" Marguerite had asked.

Iris had placed her pale hand on Marguerite's. "You will make it up to them."

And Marguerite had. Every day since, she devoted herself to her quadrant. Not only to Toria, but the nation as a whole. She learned everything she could, absorbed as much information as possible. Most nights she spent studying not only Quadara's history, but the world's.

Seeing Iris's lifeless body pass, Marguerite was happy her daughter would never feel the pain of losing a sister queen.

The day after Marguerite's daughter was born, she was smuggled out of the palace with the help of her loyal handmaiden, Lali. Upon Queen Marguerite's instructions, her daughter had been given to a childhood friend in Toria—someone who had been kind when other children had called her names. Her friend had vowed to find a family unconnected to Marguerite, who would never speak of her true parentage.

The palace would be lost to her. And she would be free.

Marguerite spent most of her days trying not to think about her child. She would be seventeen this year. *Seventeen*—nearly the same age as Stessa. She could not help but compare her daughter to the young queen and wonder what she was like and where she was now. And Iris was no longer here to tell her the past was not worth dwelling upon.

Marguerite gave her lost friend one last long look, hoping she was happy in the next life. And knowing that, one day, they would meet again.

This thought had prevented Marguerite from reaching out to her daughter across the years. In the next life, they would meet, and Marguerite would explain why she had hidden her from the palace and the throne. She had done it out of love. And love was a powerful thing.

But as Marguerite knew, it could also be terribly painful.

CHAPTER SIXTEEN

Keralie

We left Varin's apartment under a curtain of darkness. I wished we could've slept, but it was nearing morning and Varin's new delivery time. As the sun rose behind the silver buildings, the light fractured into streams. I wondered if I'd ever see this stunning city again.

Once we'd taken our seats on the commuter, Varin used his backup comm line from his apartment to communicate with his boss. While Varin's expression remained clear, he blinked rapidly.

"What did he say?" I asked once he ended the call.

"Our buyer will be there." He averted his gaze and watched the buildings fly by.

"Is that all?"

"He's already deducted yesterday's cut from my wage and is considering letting me go."

"Maybe it would help to speak face-to-face once this is all over? Explain what happened. You can even blame me." I nudged him good-naturedly.

"That wouldn't help"—he glanced over—"as I've never met him."

"Huh?" How could you work for someone you've never met?

"We're assigned our jobs once we graduate from school." His broad shoulders slumped as though the reminder of his past weighed him down. "I was assigned work as a messenger. I check in with my boss each morning." He tapped his ear. "And he informs me where to collect the comm case and where to deliver it. After a successful delivery, the payment is transferred into my account."

"No co-workers, then?" I could do without working with dippers like Kyrin.

"I work alone."

But it wasn't only that. Varin did everything alone. For a quadrant so focused on community, I would've thought they'd encourage relationships.

"Did you ever want to do something else?" I asked. "Other than being a messenger?"

"When I was younger . . ." He ran a hand through his hair. "It doesn't matter. We're assigned our jobs based on our genetic makeup. I was always going to be a messenger."

"But when you were younger?" I prompted. Surely he was allowed to dream of more?

There was a ghost of a smile on his face. "I wanted to be an artist."

I'd never heard of any Eonist working on anything remotely creative. "What kind of art?"

"Landscapes, portraits, still lifes." He shrugged slightly. "Anything, really. I want to capture everything while I can."

"The paintings in your apartment," I suddenly realized. "*You* painted them." He nodded. I'd assumed he'd bought them from a Ludist artist. "They're incredible, Varin. Really."

"Thank you," he said, short and sharp. But I could tell he wanted to say more, so for once, I remained quiet. "I like how art captures not only the exterior, but also the feeling and mood of the artist. Like a memory." The smile on his lips was more obvious now.

"You paint what you see on those stolen chips," I said.

"Yes." His cheeks colored. "So no one will forget them."

"And yet you paint the palace more than anything else." I remembered the detailed brushstrokes and care he'd given the subject.

His pearlescent eyes locked on mine. "It's the most beautiful thing I've ever seen. I don't want to forget it."

I laughed. "You see it every day as a messenger when working in the Concord."

"There's a difference between being somewhere and *really* seeing it. My art helps me see behind the surface of things."

Paintings were all about the surface, and yet, I understood what he meant. His artwork appeared to be much more than something to decorate the walls. They were a part of him, laid bare on the canvas. Now I wished I could go back and study them again to understand him more.

"But none of that matters," he said, his handsome face clouding.

"It doesn't matter that you're talented?"

"Eonia doesn't value art." He studied his hands. "I am, and only will ever be, a messenger."

I didn't know what to say. He seemed defeated. Then I

remembered his hidden compartment. Was he ashamed of what he'd created? Or was he concerned about being found out as different from other Eonists? Eonia didn't like different.

"What did you want to be when you were younger?" he asked, looking at his hands.

"A thief."

He let out a breath through his teeth. "Why do you always lie?"

"I'm not lying." And I wasn't. "I've tried to be other things. I failed." Spectacularly.

My parents had never understood why I hated sailing so much. And I had never understood why they loved it. Their shipping business caused much grief and cost so much time and money, but they wouldn't let it go, even as it was dragging them under. Even when I would return home with a handful of quartiers from a night at the auction house. It was like the boat was a part of my grandfather, which my father refused to let go, as long as it existed.

"Would you try again?" Varin asked, pulling me from my thoughts.

"No." And I'd had enough of this conversation. "Sometimes we fail because we're not meant to succeed."

"Sometimes failure is the beginning of success."

"Where did you hear that?"

"Queen Corra, during one of her broadcasted speeches."

I swallowed, unable to stop Corra's screaming, blistering face from appearing in my mind. "She was a good queen." I didn't pay attention to Quadarian politics, but she seemed to be generally liked by her people. At least, they weren't rebelling against her. Unlike Queen Marguerite. The workers of the Jetée were sick of her meddling, of her trying to erase their existence. Could they have been involved in her death?

"I can't believe she's dead," Varin said. "I can't believe they're all dead." Did the images haunt him as they haunted me? When would they begin to fade?

I shook my head. Neither of us had time to allow the reality to sink in. I hadn't even considered how this would affect Quadara.

"We won't fail, Varin. We'll find out who did this."

We got off the commuter at the Eonist gateway. At this early hour of the morning, the House of Concord was silent and still. Only a few Quadarian guards stood by, ready to check permits at the quadrant gates.

Soon the House of Concord would fill with people. Would they sense something sizeable had shifted within Quadara?

In the low light, the palace dome appeared to glow like a muted gas lamp. It was the illuminated heart of Quadara; extinguish it, and the entire nation would fade.

"We're running late," Varin said with a pointed look at my elaborate Ludist shoes as though they were the reason.

I slipped them off my feet to keep up with him. "Will your boss really kill you for failing to deliver the comm case?"

He focused straight ahead, his strides purposeful. "He won't kill me, but he'll fire me, and if I don't have a job, my death date will be reset."

"Death date?" He'd mentioned something about that back at the auction house. "What is that exactly?"

"Every Eonist has one. It's set at your birth date."

"When you're born?"

He stopped, and I jolted to a halt beside him. "Eonia is concerned about overpopulation. More than anything else. Over sickness. Over progress."

"What does that have to do with death?"

He ran a hand through his hair, pushing back a dark lock from his face. "As soon as we're born, Eonist geneticists run tests to see how healthy we are, determining our susceptibility to certain diseases and conditions. Our results are compared to the children born in the same generation. And from that, our death date is determined."

"Right," I said, though I didn't quite understand how that related to his job.

Talking about his death date had changed his expression— almost as if he felt something. But he started moving again before I could pinpoint what.

"I don't get it." I wished he'd slow down. "How exactly can they determine what you'll die of and when?"

This time when he stopped, I nearly flew into him. His hand settled on my elbow to prevent me from tripping. "No." His lip curled slightly. "They don't determine when we'll die. We're *told* when we'll die. It's not a predicted fortune, it's an order. The test determines how long we'll remain healthy for, and from that, they set our expiry date."

A gasp lodged in my chest. "They kill you?"

He nodded once, short and sharp, then continued moving again as if we'd never spoken.

I scrambled on the polished marble floor, grasping on to the truth. "They kill you when they think it's the right time?" My breath came out in bursts, not from exhaustion and lack of sleep but from shock. "How can they do that? How can they determine when it's the right time? When is it ever the right time?"

"I told you. It's the way our population is kept under control, to ensure our quadrant's future. It's how we flourish."

I snorted. There was nothing *flourishing* about the Eonists. Controlled. Perfect, maybe. But suppressed. Smothered. No wonder Varin watched glimpses of another life and painted what he would never see.

I hadn't witnessed any joy in Eonia during my short overnight stay. Their quadrant was undeniably stunning, and yet they were skimming over the surface of life, never really connecting to their environment, and certainly not to each other.

What was the point of it all? Where was the thrill of anticipation I experienced every evening at Mackiel's auction house? Where was the drive and desire to know how everything worked and what it was worth? Sure, the Jetée was dark and dirty, but we all felt something. We cared. We *lived*.

"I thought you agreed not to judge," he replied.

"When's your death date?" I asked, unable to help myself.

"I'll live until I'm thirty."

I stumbled. "Thirty?"

"It's shorter than most Eonist lifespans, yes."

I grabbed his arm and twisted him to see his face, but it was blank, his eyes not meeting mine. He couldn't speak callously of his own death. No one could.

"No, Varin." I shook my head. "No. That's shorter than my quadrant's average lifespan. That's shorter than all the quadrants'."

He rubbed the bridge of his nose. "I have a condition. It's not terminal, but it's a tax on society. So—"

"They'll kill you for being a burden?" I spat the words at him. What was wrong with me? I should have been nicer to someone who'd told me he had little over a decade to live. But I was enraged, and his lack of emotion enraged me further. "That's ridiculous!" I wanted to shake him to make him see the truth. Not what he'd been brainwashed into believing.

"We don't have time to discuss my death date."

I laughed cruelly. "Yeah, you do. You have about twelve years. Why not talk about it now?"

"You don't understand."

"No, I really don't. This isn't normal, Varin." And his reaction was even less so. "Why don't you run? Escape Eonia?" He had access to the other quadrants as a messenger—he didn't have to take his chances with the wall guards.

"Where would I go? What would I do?" Something behind his question made me believe he'd at least thought about it. "Eonia is everything I am and everything I will be." But he wanted more; his collection of comm chips and paintings proved that.

"Until they kill you."

"Come on." He touched his messenger bag. "I need to find out who's behind this."

"The queens are already gone," I said. "We can't save them."

"I know."

"But you want to help the palace find the assassin. For what purpose? Justice? Revenge?" I spread my hands wide. "Why do you care so much for your queen?"

"Why do you care so little for yours?"

It wasn't that I hated Queen Marguerite, but she was trying to destroy the Jetée, my home—my *old* home. "You seem to care more about Queen Corra's death than you do your own death date. They're already dead; *you* are not."

Varin studied the floor.

"Varin. Varin, look at me."

He hesitated but eventually lifted his head. I wanted to reach out and touch him, but didn't. His brow was low, his full lips turned downward. Even his moon-like eyes seemed dimmer.

"Why?" I asked.

"Why what?" His voice was full of exhaustion. Despite his tall frame, he looked insignificant. Sure, we hadn't slept all night, but there was something else there—years of fatigue. When he spoke about his art, I'd seen glimpses of a boy who wanted more than this life. But without hope, he'd been worn down, any fight left in him eradicated. Taught not to care, taught not to want. While I knew the feeling of being exhausted and infuriated by the hand you'd been dealt, I'd let it fuel me, while Varin had let it burn him down to nothing. But he had dreamed once; he'd had hope once—that had to be inside him. Somewhere.

"Why don't you care about your own life?" I asked. "Why don't you fight for yourself?"

"I do." But there was little fire behind his words.

I shoved him in the chest. "Then prove it!"

"Why?" He turned the word back on me. "Why do you care?"

Good question. "Torians are curious creatures. *Why* is our favorite word." But I knew that wasn't the real reason. I wanted

Varin to break free of the cage he'd put himself in, because I couldn't break free of mine.

"I want to help the palace find the killer, as it's the right thing to do," he said finally.

"Right thing to do," I muttered under my breath. How disappointing . . .

"And," he said, his expression resolute, "if I help the palace, they might help me."

"What?" Did he say he wanted to do something for himself? I rubbed inside my ear. "Can you repeat that? I've suddenly gone hard of hearing."

A smile played at his lips. "The palace might help me with my"—he swallowed—"health issues. If we help the palace find the assassin, they might change my standing on the list."

My chest tightened. "The list?"

"For HIDRA. I've never even been high up enough to be assessed."

I merely nodded, my head feeling disconnected to my body. "Right," I said numbly. "HIDRA."

I wanted to ask more about the list and how to advance it, but I couldn't let him know I was also after HIDRA. For it was the one reward we couldn't share.

———

"YOU CAN'T COME in," Varin said when we reached one of the meeting rooms inside the House of Concord. He pressed his palm against a panel, which pinged and displayed his name, occupation and quadrant on a screen above the door.

"Try to stop me." I shoved by him before he could block the entrance with his frame.

"For the queens' sake, Keralie, I mean it. They'll be expecting me to deliver the comm case alone. They'll suspect something is wrong."

I shook my head. "I'm not leaving. You're already a day late; they know something went awry. And you need my eyes."

Varin startled. "What?"

"It's my job to analyze people and understand their weaknesses."

He shook his head, placing his messenger bag on the long metal table in the middle of the room. "My boss told the buyer there was a mix-up that caused the wrong chips to almost be delivered. I don't need you here." Well, that hurt.

"Fine. I won't interfere, but I'm not leaving either."

"What are you suggesting?"

"You're not the resourceful type, are you?" I didn't wait for his reply. I looked around the room for somewhere to hide.

Aside from the large table and surrounding chairs, the room was rather empty. Shelves lined one wall, stacked with books about interquadrant negotiations and law. Beside the shelves were metal drawers, lining the middle of the wall.

I slid the latch to the side and pushed one drawer up to look inside. A tightness clamped across my chest and throat at the sight of the confined space. My breaths started coming in gasps. I closed my eyes, wishing there was another way. Either I'd get in or I'd leave Varin alone with the mastermind behind the queens' murders.

I placed one leg inside. I wasn't going to leave him alone in this—as he was alone in everything else in his life. We were in this together now.

"That's an incinerator." The shock was evident in Varin's voice. "Have you lost your mind?"

"It's been suggested once or twice." I squeezed the rest of my body into the tight space. Ash tickled my nose. My chest and stomach constricted; my cheeks flashed hot. I pressed my hands to either side of the incinerator to prove to myself there was plenty of room. Any movement in my periphery was my imagination.

Small breath in.

"It's used to destroy confidential materials directly after a meeting," he said, his voice pitching higher.

Small breath out.

When I didn't reply, he added, "It gets up to more than a thousand degrees in there."

There's a way in . . .

"I'll be fine," I said, sliding the drawer down—and with it, my way out. "Just don't turn it on."

CHAPTER SEVENTEEN

Corra
Queen of Eonia

Rule eight: A queen cannot waste time or
emotion on love. She is forbidden to marry,
for it is a distraction from her duties.

C orra knew her mask was slipping. It wouldn't take much
more than a passing glance to realize she was running on
raw emotion—emotion that should have been extinguished
through years of schooling. She was tired, a bone-deep tired, and pain
and anger were the only things fueling her body into action.

But she didn't take the time to hide it. She had to find out
what happened to Iris. And Stessa was the only lead. Iris had
known something about the sixteen-year-old queen. Had Stessa
silenced her?

Corra barely registered that there were no guards posted at
Stessa's door, nor her advisor. She didn't bother knocking, instead
flung it open with such force it almost rebounded back toward her.

Stessa let out an ear-piercing shriek. For a moment, this distracted Corra from the fact that Stessa was in the arms of a man.
Lyker—her Ludist advisor-in-training. His shirt was off, revealing a complicated pattern inked onto his skin.

"I was—I . . ." Corra couldn't think what to say. All the words spinning through her mind as she walked the hallways to Stessa's rooms had vanished. Corra blinked, unable to comprehend the scene in front of her. She knew Ludists were impulsive and passionate, but she'd never considered *this*.

"The throne diverts love," Iris had said on her final night. This had to be the secret Iris had uncovered about Stessa. A secret worth killing for.

Stessa pushed Lyker away with such a ferocity that he stumbled. "This isn't what you think!" she cried to the Eonist queen.

Corra shook her head in disbelief. "Do tell me, then," she said, finding her words, "what your *advisor* is doing in your bedroom, without a shirt and with his *tongue* shoved down your throat."

Before she replied, Stessa made the mistake of looking at Lyker.

"Stessa," Corra said. "How could you? You know Queenly Law."

Stessa let out a resigned breath. "Lyker was my boyfriend from home."

Corra took a step back, remembering the day Lyker had arrived in the palace, and Stessa's warm embrace, claiming that was how Ludists greeted each other. "You lied to us?"

Lyker quickly buttoned up his shirt. "I'm sorry, Queen Corra. We tried to stay away from each other, but we couldn't. Young love and all that," he said with a grin, aiming to lighten the mood.

"Don't." Corra held up a hand before addressing Stessa. "You know it's illegal to be in a relationship, let alone with your advisor. You spend too much time together, time that should be spent focusing on your quadrant, not on *this*—" She gestured between them. She was angry. And it felt good, the weight of her grief shifting into something purposeful. But still, she had to be careful, and not let the anger show.

"Please, Corra," Stessa said, her bottom lip quivering. "Please try to understand. Love is powerful. It's not easy to shut it out once you've let it in."

"How did this happen?" Corra asked. "How did *he* get here?" The less she looked at Lyker, the better. What was the girl queen planning?

Stessa's eyes wouldn't focus on Corra when she replied, "There was an opening for a Ludist advisor. Lyker applied. That's all." But the way she'd said it—*that's all*—it was as though she was trying to cover up something.

"Demitrus . . . He fell ill, out of the blue," Corra said, speaking of the previous Ludist advisor. The one Lyker had replaced soon after Stessa had entered the palace. "Queens above! Tell me you weren't involved!"

"I wasn't! I mean, I never meant to hurt him," Stessa replied, pulling at one of the beads entwined in her short hair.

Corra wasn't sure if she was more shocked by her admission or the fact that she wasn't trying to hide her wrongdoings. "You poisoned him."

Stessa nodded, although it hadn't been a question. "I didn't know how badly he'd be hurt. I wanted him to fall ill and leave. That's all."

That's all.

"He never recovered," Corra said with a heavy sigh. "He is still unable to leave his bed." The old advisor had been a kindly man, a Ludist who'd tired of the partying scene and his quadrant's focus on appearance. He wanted to give more to his nation. And Stessa had gotten rid of him. "How could you?"

Before Stessa could reply, Corra blurted out, "Did you kill

Iris?" Seeing Stessa in the arms of Lyker and hearing the truth about Demitrus, she was certain she'd uncovered the truth. "You wanted her gone. You can't deny it."

"Don't be ridiculous," Lyker said.

Corra's eyes flashed to him. She'd almost forgotten he was there, but Stessa spoke up. "Don't speak to Queen Corra like that."

A small part of Corra softened at Stessa's defense. But that was all it was. Defense.

Did Iris also know about Demitrus? Had Stessa killed her to defend this secret?

"I did not kill Iris." Stessa's expression shifted. "And I didn't mean to make Demitrus that unwell."

"You hated Iris," Corra said. "And she knew your secret, didn't she?"

Stessa had always made it clear she wasn't a fan of Iris's. *It doesn't make her guilty, though,* Corra thought. And she had no evidence. Even though there was motive, it didn't mean she had anything to present to the inspector. After all, he'd said a trained hand had sliced Iris's throat. Poisoning Demitrus was careless; *an act of passion,* the inspector would deem it. Stessa was no trained assassin, nor was Lyker. Unless they had managed to fool everyone about that too.

It was possible, she supposed.

Stessa squared her shoulders, Lyker standing strong behind her. "I know *your* secret. Would you kill me for it?"

Corra's breath stuttered. But which secret? Her hand fell from the watch around her neck.

A wicked smile played at Stessa's lips. "Tell anyone about me and Lyker, and I'll be forced to spill your secrets too."

"This isn't a game!" Corra said. Everything was pliable to the Ludists; of course a Ludist would not abide by the law, even Queenly Law. Stessa was too young to put her frivolous background behind her and value the throne as required.

"No, it's not." Stessa's eyes watched her coolly. "But you broke Queenly Law first."

A shudder took hold of Corra's body. *No.* Stessa couldn't know. Couldn't know Corra had grown up inside the palace. That she felt and grieved. She'd be ruined. Deposed. And worse, her mother's legacy would be tainted.

"You loved Iris," Stessa said, eyebrow raised.

Corra struggled not to let her relief show. It was better she knew that secret than the other, more devastating one.

"In your way," Stessa continued, "as much as any Eonist can really love anyone." She looked back to Lyker. A meaningful exchange passed between them while they entwined their fingers together.

Corra bit the inside of her mouth. *Fine.* Let her think that. *Not of Eonist heart.*

"What proof do you have?" Corra asked. "It's my word against yours."

"We don't need proof," she said. "*You* are all the proof we need."

"What are you talking about?"

"You record your memories onto chips each evening, do you not?" Stessa tilted her head. "I'd wager Iris appears in many of these recordings." She grinned, knowing she had Corra trapped.

Even with Iris dead, the revelation of their relationship would still spell the end of Corra's reign. Aside from romantic relationships being forbidden, having close ties to another quadrant was unforgivable. Even though her relationship with Iris had always been separate from their thrones. Who would believe that now that Iris wasn't here to support her claims?

She was alone in this.

"What do you want?" Corra hated how defeated she sounded. She'd come here to uncover Iris's killer, but now she was at the mercy of this girl queen and her boy advisor. The girl who'd almost taken Demitrus's life to have her boyfriend by her side. Such recklessness.

Stessa looked to Lyker once more, and though she was furious, Corra felt a twinge deep inside, knowing she would never again exchange such a look with another person. They loved each other; it was clear in their every movement.

"Don't tell our secret," Lyker said for Stessa, a smirk upon his lips. "And we won't tell yours." Anger burned within Corra. How dare Stessa let Lyker speak for her!

Who was really in control of Ludia?

But she couldn't risk her throne to out the girl and her advisor. She had to protect her mother's legacy.

Corra shuddered, hating herself for what she was about to do. She glanced at the golden dome above, hoping Iris wasn't looking down upon her at this very moment. She'd failed her, time and time again.

"Fine," Corra said. "I won't say a word to the inspector, or anyone, about you and Lyker and what you've done. But this must end, understand? Lyker must step down from his position and return to Ludia."

Lyker shook his head. "No."

This time, Stessa didn't reprimand his tone. "Never," she

agreed. She wrapped her free arm around Lyker. "Nothing can tear us apart."

"It's forbidden." Corra managed to keep her voice even.

"At least we're from the same quadrant," Stessa said. "We have the same goals. Unlike you and Iris."

Corra wasn't really from anywhere. The palace was an in-between place, and without Iris, no one understood her. Sometimes Corra wondered if she even knew herself. All she knew was that when she was with Iris, she was happy. And it was not an emotion she wanted to quash.

It hurt to look at Stessa and Lyker. She couldn't be in a room with them any longer.

Before Corra left, she said, "Continue this relationship, and someone else will find out. First Iris—"

"Now *you.*" There was a sinister gleam in Stessa's eye. "Don't forget what happens to those who uncover the truth."

Corra slammed the door behind her, her body shaking. Stessa and Lyker might not be Iris's killers, but they were just as dangerous.

CHAPTER EIGHTEEN

Keralie

The insides of the incinerator pulsed in my periphery, as though it were alive. I couldn't . . . I couldn't think of anything but the walls pressing in, my lungs responding in kind. Fear skittered across my skin; a cold sweat trembled my shoulders. Soon my whole dress was damp and clingy.

No way out. No way out.

And Varin wouldn't stop pacing the room, his footsteps tapping in time with my increasing heartbeat. I peered through a small vent in the door, but I couldn't make out more than a dark smudge.

"Quit it," I whispered through the vent. "I can feel your nerves from in here. You need to act normal."

"Normal?" he whispered back. "We're about to meet with the person who may have orchestrated the assassination of the queens, and I may have the only evidence to convict them. And you're in an incinerator. How can I act normal?"

The feeling of being trapped felt too familiar. The size, the darkness . . . it haunted my dreams. Bile rose in the back of my throat as memories of the cave rolled over me. The smell of salty blood and sea spray. The clammy air, my lungs dragging as I wept. My father helpless in my arms.

My hands began to tremble, rumbling the metal door.

"Keralie?" he asked. "Are you all right in there?"

"That almost sounded like concern," I replied, my breaths coming in short gasps. I pressed my fingers into the vent to feel the air and remind myself of the world outside. A world I would soon return to. "Just focus on your inner Eonist, and you'll turn back into a robot."

I wished I could turn off my emotions. My memories.

The sound of the door opening silenced Varin's reply.

"Good morning," Varin said to whoever entered.

I bit my lip, listening for anything that could help us. Anything else we could take to the palace.

Focus, Keralie. Focus. Don't think about the silver coffin you've climbed into.

"Take a seat, messenger," said a voice. Female. Clearly angry. Definitely not Eonist.

"Yes, ma'am," Varin replied.

Two chairs scraped against the tiled floor as they took their seats.

Only one woman? Surprising. I'd expected a whole enclave to be guarding the comm case and the secrets it held. Although . . . Two against one . . . I preferred those odds.

"Apologies for the delay. There was a mix-up with the delivery." Somehow he managed to keep his voice steady.

"You have my comm case?"

"Of course. Here." I heard the comm case slide along the metal table. I wished I could see what was happening.

The case clicked open, and I held my breath. This could all be over quickly. And I had no doubt this woman would be armed. This was a secret worth killing for. Hot fingers plucked at my chest like a Ludist musician on guitar strings. Perhaps this plan was madness, after all.

"Four chips," the woman commented. *One for each queen.* "How interesting . . ."

Silence. *Come on, Varin. Do something! Be brave. Be* something*!* Varin couldn't let this moment slip by, could he? This was *his* plan, after all.

"Is everything all right?" Varin asked, finally. *You can do it. Be brave.* "If you tell me more about your source, I'll check with my employer. But everything should be correct."

"More about my source?" the woman repeated.

"Yes. The person who sent you this message. If it's not what you were expecting?"

"It is," the woman said. "But you are not."

"I'm sorry?"

"Why are you asking questions about my chips?" the woman asked. "You're not paid to think. You're paid to deliver. Why do you care what's on them?"

Shit.

The room was hushed, as if submerged in water. It was far too hot in the incinerator. Sweat pooled between my hunched shoulders. Had the woman turned the incinerator on?

"I don't," Varin said, but nerves were playing games with his voice.

"Eonists don't lie," the woman said, her voice turning steely. "And yet you're clearly lying to me now."

"No." Varin sounded too defensive. "I mean, I'm a little curious, but—"

She laughed. *"Curious?"* The way she said the word, I knew she was all too familiar with the concept. Which meant she was Torian. I hoped for all our sakes that she didn't know Mackiel.

The door opened, and I let out a breath, thinking the woman had left. Although we hadn't learned much, at least Varin had a good look at her. Hopefully that would be enough to go to the palace authorities with. I made to open the incinerator when another voice interrupted. A melodic voice. One I knew all too well.

"Need some help in here?" the voice asked.

Shit. Mountains of horse shit.

"Mackiel." The woman sounded surprised to see him. "I told you I would handle this." Mackiel was high on the Torian queen's wanted list. It was dangerous for him to be this close to the palace.

"But I didn't want to miss out on all the fun," he said. He sounded calm, in control, like he always did.

What could he possibly have to do with the assassination of the queens? Had he been the one to organize the assassination? Then why had he asked me to steal Varin's comm case in the first place? I knew he hated Queen Marguerite for what she was planning to do to the Jetée, but why kill the other queens? Was it because they'd denied him access to HIDRA to save his parents?

"Hello, messenger," he said. "It's such a pleasure to see you again." He didn't sound surprised to find Varin.

I shuddered inside the incinerator. I had to stay quiet. Absolutely silent. I couldn't save Varin, but I could still save myself.

"Hello, Mackiel," Varin said softly. I wondered what flittered through his mind. Did he fear for his life? Or was fear an emotion also stamped out? How could his voice remain impassive?

"Where's Keralie?" Mackiel asked.

"Who is—" Varin began.

"Don't play dumb," Mackiel replied. "You're cute enough for it, but you're an Eonist, and Eonists are not dumb."

"I don't know who you're talking about," Varin replied. It sounded believable to me, but Mackiel was not easily fooled.

"She's not here," the woman said. "But the boy knows something."

"Keralie told you what she saw?" Mackiel asked. He sounded unconvinced.

"No, she wouldn't tell me," Varin replied.

"Ah!" Mackiel said. "Now, that reeks of my sweet Kera."

"But he was asking about the chips," the woman said, sounding confused. "He *knows*."

"Yes," Mackiel agreed. "He must have rerecorded them from Keralie's memory, didn't you?" I knew the expression he'd have—the expression I saw every day, pulling the truth from those who didn't want to give it. And there'd be that smile, that charming smile, which assured you everything would be okay if you followed him. Told him the truth. Trusted him.

Don't tell him, Varin, I begged. Nothing good came from telling Mackiel the truth. *He'll use it against you.*

"Yes," Varin said. A part of my chest collapsed. Why couldn't he be stronger? "I rerecorded them from her memory. Therefore, the chips are as they once were. The transaction is now complete."

"Hmm," Mackiel said. I could hear his rings clack together as he entwined his fingers. "Silly pretty Eonist. You think if you're polite and helpful that all will be forgiven. That's how your world works, isn't it?" I could imagine Mackiel's grin widening with each word. He'd be enjoying this. Twisting the truth was his favorite game. "But you're not dealing with Eonists. You're dealing with a Torian. You're dealing with me."

"I don't understand," Varin said.

"You've set me behind schedule," Mackiel replied. "And I don't like to be kept waiting."

Varin's voice wavered when he said, "I don't have anything else to give you."

"Are you sure about that?"

"I—I . . ." Varin stuttered.

"How about we make a new deal," Mackiel said. "Tell me where Keralie is, and I won't kill you."

I held a trembling hand over my mouth to slow my panicked breathing. Darkness crept in from the sides, threatening to swamp my sight.

I hoped Varin remembered what I'd said about Mackiel. He couldn't best him. Varin was dead, whether he gave away my location or not.

"I told you I don't like to be kept waiting," he said, his fingers tapping on the table. "So, before I lose my temper, which is never pretty, tell me where Keralie is."

"I don't know," Varin said. "I recorded the memories, and she took off. She didn't want anything more to do with me. Or you." It sounded like something I would do.

But Mackiel knew me too well. "What did you give her in return?" he asked.

Damn it. Damn him! He'd created me and knew exactly how to destroy me. *Stupid, stupid.* Mackiel was a child of greed and deception; how could I expect loyalty from someone bred from such darkness?

Varin's voice broke when he replied, "What do you mean?"

Mackiel laughed and I could picture him putting his hands behind his head and his feet on the chair next to him. The image of control.

"What. Did. You. Give. Her. In. Return," he replied, drawing each word out. "Keralie does nothing without gain. She's always been that way, ever since I met her. So what was it?"

Varin didn't reply.

Mackiel took a deep breath. "I know more about my dippers than they know about themselves. And I know more about Keralie than any of the others. When I met Keralie, she was a scraggly girl of only ten. You wouldn't have looked at her twice. But now? She's a shining star. The moon on a clear night. The sun on a summer's day. You can't not look at her. And even an Eonist has to see that. Aside from her face, her beauty, there's one thing that makes the girl who she is. It's her family." He laughed. "Oh, I'd like to take credit for it all, but there's no denying we're all a product of our upbringing. No one more than Keralie. Perhaps you wouldn't defend her if you knew the truth?"

I wanted Varin to tell him to shut up, but he said nothing. *Coward.*

"Keralie is the spitting image of her father," Mackiel

continued. "Of course she doesn't see that, but everyone else does—or did. They're both incredibly stubborn." His voice hardened. "Did she tell you what happened to him?"

No. I bit the inside of my lip. *Don't tell him. Stop!*

The walls of the incinerator shimmered. My head grew feverishly hot. Black spots filled my vision. I was moments from passing out.

"No," Varin said. "She said she had a happy childhood."

"*Had?*" Mackiel asked. "Yes. Until she ruined everything." He paused for dramatic effect. *Bastard.* He was enjoying this performance. "Keralie is like her father: intelligent, determined, ambitious. But she never wanted to follow in the family business. While the sea called to her father, the Jetée calls to Keralie." I could hear the grin lining his voice. "But her father refused to give up, making her join him on his journeys to Archia, hoping she would warm to the ways of the ocean. One afternoon, while upon the water, Keralie decided to force her father to give up on her and allow her to be who she wanted to be."

What do you want to do, Keralie? Who you do you want to be?

I pressed my hands against my ears. I didn't want to hear it. I didn't want to remember. But I couldn't block out Mackiel's words, or the memories of my father's terrified face, the blood and the fear.

"But how do you force your parents, the people who have loved you, raised you and sheltered you your entire life, to give up on you?" Mackiel asked.

Varin didn't offer an answer.

"You turn into the darkness," Mackiel said. "You show them you are beyond their reach. Beyond saving."

No. I couldn't breathe, nothing but dust and rubble in my lungs.

"Keralie was steering her parents' boat," Mackiel continued.

When would he stop? "Her father no doubt thought he'd already turned her face toward clearer skies. Then he realized they were sailing too close to the cliffs."

I squeezed my eyes tight, but it made it worse, bringing the images to life as Mackiel revealed my secret.

My father grabbing for the wheel, me pushing him away and jerking the boat closer to the cliff. The sea pummeling the rocks, spraying our faces with salt. Determination thrumming through my veins, propelling me into action. My teeth sinking into my bottom lip. Thinking, I'll destroy this boat. *This stupid thing that my parents care about so much, which costs so much time and money while we still struggle year by year. They will never let it go. They will never see the truth. But I'll show them. There are easier ways to attain wealth. I'll destroy this boat, then we'll all be free.*

I'd only meant to clip the cliff, damaging the boat so it couldn't be repaired. But I didn't know the power of the water; how could I? I'd spent all my time blocking out the lessons of the ocean my parents had tried to teach me.

When we hit the cliff, it sounded like an explosion.

I'd never forget my father's expression as we were thrown from the rupturing boat. He was terrified. Of me.

Mackiel finished recounting the story. "She wanted her parents to see she would do anything to destroy the future they saw for her—a future she desperately didn't want. And her father was in the way of that."

He made it sound like I'd wanted to hurt him. But I hadn't. I'd wanted to remove the one thing in their lives that caused uncertainty. Without it, they would see that I could help them, provide for a better life. If they would only let me.

Instead, I'd caused more pain and heartache than I ever could've imagined.

"What happened to her father?" Varin asked.

"He's in a coma and has weeks to live. Only HIDRA can save him now, but the palace won't help the father of a criminal." His voice turned icy.

I desperately wished to see Varin's expression. Had the story changed his opinion of me? Would he now give up my location, knowing I had purposely destroyed my family's business and critically injured my father? Would he now abandon me and go to the palace for HIDRA alone?

"Why are you telling me all this?" Varin's voice sounded strained.

"An Eonist has no business with a girl such as her." Mackiel almost sounded soothing, understanding.

"Tell us where she is," the woman said, "and we'll forget all about you."

I held my breath, waiting for Varin to reveal me. I wouldn't have blamed him.

"I told you," Varin ground out. "She left after I recorded the chips."

I didn't dare let out a breath of relief. Not yet.

"Mackiel?" The woman sighed in frustration. "We're wasting our time."

But Mackiel said, "We don't need him to tell us where she is."

"We don't?" she asked, clearly confused.

He laughed. "As I said, I know Keralie's moves because I taught them to her. I made her. My porcelain doll."

A lump lodged itself in my throat. Ash clung to my lashes,

nose and mouth. I swallowed down the desperate urge to cough and sneeze.

The woman asked, "Where is she, then?"

Someone began moving around the room.

"Keralie knows better than to leave her target unsupervised," Mackiel said, his voice back to full melody. He was toying with me.

My sweat turned icy in the small space.

"Enough games," the woman snapped. "Where is she, Mackiel?"

"Before I say, I want to ensure there's no evidence of our meeting. Messenger"—I could hear the grin in his voice—"place the empty comm case in the incinerator and turn it on."

My throat began to burn.

"Messenger?" Mackiel repeated. "Did you not hear what I said?"

Varin had two options: Reveal my hiding place or keep to his story and let me burn. A part of me wondered if he'd be happy to be rid of me, now knowing I deserved it. The other part knew that being an Eonist meant he could never injure or kill another human being.

I slid the drawer open.

"Hello, Mackiel," I said. "Did you miss me?"

CHAPTER NINETEEN

Stessa
Queen of Ludia

Rule nine: Each queen will be appointed
one advisor from her own quadrant.
They will be her only counsel.

*C*ome to the baths.

A thrill ran through Stessa as she read the words on the scrap of paper, which had been left beneath her pillow, the cursive clearly Lyker's. It had been weeks since he had left her a secret message.

Passing notes had begun as a game at school. The rules were never leave the message in the same spot, and never allow anyone else to find it. Sometimes they failed and the notes were discovered, but they never included names, to ensure they couldn't be incriminated. Back then, the messages had been a lifeline for Stessa. Her secret within a secret life.

Stessa had told Lyker of her royal lineage the day she learned she would have to leave home to claim the Ludist throne. She was nine, and the thought of leaving her family had sent a flow of hot tears down her cheeks, tears that refused to stop, even when she'd sat in her seat at school. Her neighboring classmate was Lyker.

When she loosened her plaits after school that day, a sliver of paper fell loose.

Why are you sad? the curling script had asked.

The next day, Lyker had found a scrunched-up piece of paper in his left shoe. How she'd managed to put it there, he never found out. But he would never forget her words.

I'm the next Ludist queen.

He had sought her out at school, wiping her weeping eyes with his sleeve. "Cheer up, Stess," he'd said. "You're still you. You're still my best friend." She'd cried harder then, wrapping her arms around his lanky frame.

She told him about Queenly Law and how she would be required to leave her old life behind and never look back.

He'd squeezed her tighter then. "I'll come with you," he'd said, not understanding how difficult that would be. "You can never get rid of me."

She had smiled, flashing the gap between her teeth.

And in the years when their friendship had turned into love, their messages were essential.

Stessa's parents had warned against forming close ties, as it would only make it harder to leave. But they didn't understand; anytime she thought of leaving her home, her friends, her family, she would break. And only Lyker knew how to put her back together with his smiles and silly jokes.

Everyone treated her like the future queen she would one day be, but Lyker always treated her like the girl she'd always been. The girl who wanted to sit by the canals and write music. The girl who wanted to attend all the parties, her makeup perfectly applied, dressed in the fanciest of dresses. The girl who wanted to enjoy everything her quadrant had to offer. A life of color, laughter and love.

And she wanted to share that life with Lyker. A boy who saw the world as she did: something to revel in. He was the center of any party, the teller of tales and the heart of every warm touch. His artwork decorated many Ludist streets; even when Stessa walked alone, she was surrounded by his presence.

When Stessa's birth mother, the queen of Ludia, had died, fifteen-year-old Stessa had reluctantly traveled to the palace, leaving a brokenhearted Lyker behind. She swore their separation would be temporary. She would find a way to bring him to the palace.

In the five weeks they were parted, Stessa wrote herself letters, hiding them around the palace, pretending they were from her lost love. They made her happy, until she realized she might never see Lyker's fluid writing again, never hear his low laugh or feel his hand in hers.

Stessa was not a violent person. Nor was she ruthless. But she had to be ruthless, one time, if she wanted to be reunited with her love.

She had quickly surmised it was the advisors who had the most contact with the queens, who were almost always by their sides. Her advisor, Demitrus, was an old man in his seventies and, in Stessa's eyes, ready to retire. At his age, to fall ill would not be suspicious. She checked all the Ludist perfumes and products she'd been allowed to bring into the palace. Most were safe, simply root dyes and natural minerals. But there was one that warned against ingestion: Stessa's hair dye. She didn't know how much to put in his drink. To be safe, she emptied half the bottle.

She had wanted only to make him ill; she never expected there to be piqberry in the dye, which was commonly used in acidic cleaners.

Demitrus was sent to the Eonist Medical Facility to be monitored. Doctors thought he would pass away, and perhaps that would've been kinder. Instead, he spent his days coughing up blood, while his family argued their case for him to be bumped up on the waiting list for HIDRA. But there were more dire cases than his, and so they waited for next year's dose or perhaps the year after.

Stessa had been tormented by her guilt, unwilling to venture out of her room for days. Everyone thought she merely wept for the man who had been kind to her during her first few weeks in the palace. When the queens told her the time had come to choose a new advisor, Stessa had asked for someone closer to her age to ensure the situation with Demitrus could not be repeated. The queens had been sympathetic, especially Queen Marguerite, who had immediately taken a shine to the young queen.

Stessa had recorded a message to be displayed on the Queenly Reports, asking for any Ludists with political aspirations to come to the palace. She knew Lyker would be watching for any sign from her. Within days, the applicants arrived for further assessment. Lyker was the first to step forward. She'd been shocked, and hadn't recognized him at first with his signature tattoos covered by long black sleeves. He looked a shadow of himself, all color stripped away. Still, he was there. And when his gaze caught hers, his smile was blinding.

After a week of pretending to assess the other hopefuls, Stessa declared Lyker to be the next Ludist advisor-in-training. Once he'd moved into the palace, he made up for lost time; his first letter slipped into her throne between the padded armrest and wooden frame.

And although they spent nearly every waking moment together as advisor and queen, Lyker continued to hide messages for her, to remind her that he would always be by her side. And to remind her she was still Stessa. The girl he loved.

After a few months, the letters had stopped, and Stessa worried Lyker was no longer interested in her, perhaps too distracted by the power of his position as advisor-in-training. When she'd asked why, the reason had been simple. He'd discovered that the palace guards checked the trash. At night, Lyker drew his words of love onto Stessa's skin with his fingers so no one would ever find them.

Stessa wondered why Lyker had requested her presence now. She hadn't heard any news about the assassin; it was too soon for the palace to have been reopened.

The baths were located on the far side of the palace, and the farthest from her rooms. It was a perfect place to meet. No one would think to look for her there, for neither Stessa nor Lyker knew how to swim in deep water. No Ludist did. Shallow canals wound through Ludia, allowing them to cool off in the mid-summer heat without being fully submerged. Water was an enemy; it flattened hair, ruined makeup, made you remove clothing and jewelry. It made you plain. And that was not the Ludist way.

The baths were located in a cavernous room with a golden mosaic-tiled ceiling. A few small baths encircled one large pool in the middle. Each bath was lined with gilded tiles, shading the water gold. The center of the deepest pool darkened to a rich amber.

Pretty, Stessa thought. The mosaic tiles reflecting in the water reminded Stessa of the canals and how they reflected the colorful buildings along the bank. She could see why Lyker wanted to meet here.

The only other time Stessa had visited the baths was during her first day inside the palace. Demitrus had shown her all of the royal facilities, trying to warm her to the golden cage she would now call home. She'd barely glanced at the room back then, not caring how wonderful they claimed the palace to be. She missed her parents. She missed Lyker. She wasn't sure she wanted to be in a world without them.

Now Stessa studied the various glimmering pools, wondering if the other queens frequented this place. The room was warm, as though Stessa were swaddled in a thick blanket. Heat radiated up from the tiles, drawing her to the main pool's edge. Sweat trickled between her shoulder blades underneath her ruby-red dress.

She removed her shoes and stockings and sat upon the pool's ledge, slowly lowering her feet into the cool water. She let out a contented sigh. Once her feet were submerged, she wanted more water to wash over her. Her perspiration made her skin feel sticky and her dress tight. The outer layers of her makeup began sliding off her face like shedding skin.

Where is he? she thought. It was unlike Lyker to be late.

It had been difficult to sneak away with the increased security, but Stessa was used to running about the palace with the queens none the wiser. Except for Iris—she'd known her secret. And she'd kept it until her dying breath.

One evening, Iris had grabbed a bread roll from Stessa's plate, her appetite much larger than her petite frame. When she bit into the fluffy white bread, she was surprised to find a scrunched-up piece of paper. The instructions had told her to meet in the royal ballroom at the stroke of midnight.

Iris had ventured to the ballroom, unsure who she'd find. When Lyker had turned at her entrance, Stessa's name on his lips, their secret was out.

Initially Iris had been furious with her much younger sister queen. She yelled and swore and scowled. Stessa had tried to reason with her, tell her she'd known Lyker before entering the palace and it was not merely a fling with the new advisor.

"It is against Queenly Law," Iris had said. "You are young; you don't yet understand its importance. You can't break a law whenever you like."

Stessa had wanted to tell Iris she wasn't so young that she didn't know her own heart. But she stayed quiet. Iris already thought she was impulsive and reckless. She had to prove her love for Lyker was more than a fleeting fantasy.

"Come with me, Iris," Stessa had said. Lyker had followed behind, remaining silent.

Once in her rooms, Stessa had gone to her crowded dressing table.

"Now is not the time to play with your makeup," Iris had remarked.

Stessa had ignored her, opening one of her makeup tins. Inside were thousands of pieces of paper. "Here," she'd said, shaking the paper onto the floor like confetti.

"You kept them all?" Lyker had asked. It had been dangerous bringing the letters to the palace, but Stessa had needed a piece of Lyker with her; it had made her feel less alone. And his handwriting was beautiful, poetic, like the poetry he wasn't allowed to squander his time with inside the palace.

Iris bent down to pick up one of the pieces. "What are they?"

"Letters." Stessa smiled down upon the scraps of paper, a fragmented love poem. "From Lyker. It began when we were children."

Iris didn't reply, her fingertips flitting over the paper as she read. Some were private moments, but Iris needed to know the truth.

After a while, Iris had sat back on her heels. "I'm sorry, Stessa."

Stessa's heart had dropped. It hadn't worked. Iris didn't care about her relationship with Lyker. She would turn her in to the authorities, and Lyker was sure to be banished from the palace.

"I'm sorry this has been hard on you." Something had burned beneath Iris's petite features. "It's trying to be separated from the ones we love. But why should we be kept apart? We are queens, after all." She had taken Stessa's hand then. "I promise not to speak of your secret."

Stessa had thought Iris meant her family as "the people she loved," but at the next nightly dinner, she had watched Iris interact with Corra. While it was almost imperceptible, there had been a difference, a lightness that had colored Iris's features and brightened her green eyes. When Iris had turned to speak with her advisor, the light had dimmed. It could've been mistaken for merely affection for her sister queen, but Stessa had suspected something else. For it was a look she had often seen in Lyker's eyes. A look of love and desire.

That night, Stessa had followed Iris back to her rooms. She needed to know. She'd wanted to believe that Iris wouldn't tell anyone about Lyker, but out of all the queens, she'd seemed most married to Queenly Law. She didn't have to wait long. Corra arrived around half an hour later. Stessa had been initially shocked they'd both broken Queenly Law, but this worked in her favor. She'd confronted Iris the next morning.

Two weeks later, Iris had been murdered.

Stessa ran a hand across her perspiring brow and scowled at the white cream coating her palm. She would have to reapply her makeup when she returned to her rooms. She swirled the water around with her fingertips and watched the cream dissolve.

The door to the baths opened. Stessa sat upright, but didn't turn around. Not yet.

"You're late," she said. "You know I don't like to be kept waiting." But her voice was light. Playful.

She turned after a silent moment, annoyed he hadn't spoken.

"Oh!" she cried when she saw it wasn't Lyker. "I thought you were someone else." She scrambled to her bare feet. "What are you doing in here? And—" Before she could ask anything further, she was pushed in the middle of her chest. She soared backward and hit the water with a painful *whack*.

Stessa's indignation at being pushed into water while fully clothed was soon overcome with dread. She'd fallen into the deep middle of the pool. She reached for the edge, her arms and legs thrashing.

"Help!" she cried. She tried to stay afloat. "I can't swim!"

A moment later, she was joined in the water. Stessa held out her arm to be brought to safety, but instead of being pulled to the pool's ledge, the arm encircled her waist and pulled down.

Stessa let out a cry, but her scream was washed away with bathwater. It tasted like chemicals. She thought of poor Demitrus and tried to spit the water out, but there was only more to meet her open mouth. Her thrashing arms and legs collided with her attacker as she tried to right herself. The attacker's arms loosened. Momentarily free, she scrambled for the edge. Her black fingernails gripped the golden tiles.

Stessa opened her mouth to scream for any nearby guards, but a hand clamped down from behind. Another arm pulled her backward. The arms were solid, muscled. Stessa was no match.

She thrashed, but with the attacker clinging to her back and her wet, heavy dress, she began to tire. Her head dipped beneath the water, dislodging her crown. She reached down as the crown sank to the bottom of the pool. When she glanced back, she couldn't distinguish which way was the surface. All she saw was gold. And two eyes watching from above, expression blank.

A lick of flame built within her chest, throat and nose, her arms and legs leaden.

No! No! This can't be happening. She was too young. Too beautiful. Too loved. With a full life to live. Why would someone do this to her?

As Stessa's heels hit the tiles at the bottom of the pool, she looked up to the water's surface and reached out with one hand. The assassin stood on her shoulders, pinning her down. She bucked, trying again to dislodge the weight. But she was weak, her legs collapsing beneath her.

Her last breath burned its way out of her lungs, sending bubbles to the surface. The assassin finally released her, but it was too late.

She wished she could leave Lyker one last message.

CHAPTER TWENTY

Keralie

Mackiel tipped his bowler hat as I climbed out of the incinerator. "Hello, darlin' Kera. It's wonderful you could join us."

I recognized the woman next to him as the informant who worked on the wall to Toria. What was she doing here?

"You knew I was in there the entire time," I said to Mackiel, keeping the table safely between us.

The woman asked, "Is that true?"

"It's what I would've done." Mackiel shrugged. "And I thought it would be more fun to smoke her out. It *was* more fun, wasn't it?" He grinned.

Talking about my accident had never been about getting Varin to betray me. Mackiel wanted to remind me about my father. He wanted to remind me how I'd hurt the people I loved the most. But why? If he was planning to kill us both, why waste his time?

"What now, Mackiel?" I spread my hands wide. "Shoot

us, then shove us into the incinerator to ensure no one finds our bodies?"

Mackiel tapped his lip. "Thank you for the suggestion, but I'm not planning to be rid of you." *Yet,* his words promised.

"This isn't our normal business, Mackiel," I said.

He brushed invisible lint off his black coat, which I'd stolen for him over a year ago. Was anything actually his? I looked down at my gaudy Ludist outfit. Was anything mine?

"*My* business," he said, "is anything and *everything* lucrative. You know our world, darlin'. You know only the most cunning survive. And in these times, we have to be more ruthless than ever."

He was right. We had to be ruthless to survive. *I* had to be ruthless.

"We don't involve ourselves with quadrant politics and palace laws," I said, stalling.

"The queens got involved with us first," he replied. Then this was about the Jetée? I still couldn't imagine Mackiel, the young boy I'd grown up with, to be the mastermind behind the murders of all four queens.

"Why did you make me steal the comm chips in the first place?" I asked. "If they were always intended for you?"

The woman beside Mackiel stiffened. He replied, "Who said the messages were intended for me?"

"If they weren't, then who were they meant for?"

"I would hate to speak on someone else's behalf, but I'm afraid the intended recipient can no longer speak for himself," he replied. The woman beside him grinned manically.

"You killed him," Varin said.

"I did nothing of the sort," Mackiel replied. "But the henchmen might've got a little carried away. You know what they're like." Again, he blamed the henchmen. Did he even realize the darkness he'd invited into his life? While his father had been treacherous, devising a plan to murder the queens was a step too far. Something he could not come back from.

"Why are you doing this?" We'd come here to find out more about who was pulling the strings, but now I wanted to know why Mackiel was involved and why he'd dragged me into it. "What have you been promised for the comm chips?"

"What it's always about." He rubbed his fingers together. "And I've evolved beyond petty stealing." *Beyond his father's work*—he didn't have to say it. "Don't be cross you haven't caught up"—the right side of his mouth twisted upward—"yet."

"You're still trying to best your father," I thought out loud, ignoring his last jibe. "Still trying to do something he wasn't powerful enough to do."

Mackiel's kohl-lined eyes narrowed. "*Don't* speak of my father."

"One of your little rules," I said in a singsong voice. "I'm not playing your games anymore. I don't have to abide by your rules." I paused, then whispered, "You can't make your father love you, Mackiel. He's dead."

Mackiel lunged for me across the table. The woman pulled him back by his arm. "Enough," she said. Her hand hovered near a pocket inside her jacket. "We need to leave, Mackiel. We've been here too long." She glanced at me.

His serious mood faded and he nodded. "All right, then." He gestured toward the door. "Time to see your favorite henchmen."

He wasn't planning to kill us here, or perhaps he couldn't

face killing his closest friend, after all. But I couldn't trust him, not again. But what defense did we have? We'd turned in Varin's destabilizer at the meeting room's check-in point; the rooms were too close to the palace to allow the presence of weapons.

The woman touched her jacket again, where a gun could have been holstered. Only she would've been searched for weapons as we had been.

That's it! She wasn't touching her jacket to warn us she was armed, but rather out of habit. She was as unarmed as we were.

I quickly reassessed the situation. Varin was tall and muscular. I was swift, nimble and unpredictable. The woman was heavier than I was; a little softer, a little slower. And Mackiel had the strength of a coat hanger.

I gave Varin a slight shake of my head. *We aren't leaving.*

Leaning against the metal table, I said, "I don't think so, Mackiel. We paid for an hour in this room, and I want my money's worth."

A small crease formed between Varin's brows, but he kept silent. Good Eonist.

Mackiel winked at me. "I'm afraid I'm not here for that, darlin'. But if we leave now, there may be time later."

I narrowed my eyes at him and his insinuation. "I'm not going anywhere with you. Our days in each other's company are over. *We're* over." He was going to have to drag me from this room, and I knew he didn't have the strength to do so.

A muscle flicked in his neck, the only sign of uncertainty. "Now, let's not be difficult, darlin'. You know I hate it when you're difficult."

I placed my hand on my hip. "Oh, but what is it you said? You made me, so you only have yourself to blame."

Mackiel bared his teeth like a wild animal. "We. Leave. Now."

"Or? You don't have anything I want. And I always need something in return, isn't that right?"

Varin shifted to my side, but I moved back toward the incinerator. I didn't want to be protected. I wanted to hurt. I wanted Mackiel to hurt. For what he'd said about my father, and for betraying me.

"Come on, Mackiel," I goaded. "Scared to take me on without your henchmen by your side? Sweet, innocent me? Your porcelain doll."

"I will hurt you." Mackiel spoke through gritted teeth. "If I must."

The woman moved toward me, but Mackiel flicked her away. He was angry. And when he was angry, he didn't think clearly. *Perfect.*

I pursed my lips. "I don't think you care that I ingested the chips." Mackiel continued inching toward me. "You only care that I disobeyed you."

"I was waiting for the day you would, darlin', but today is not that day."

"Today, tomorrow, the next—what does it matter? For you *never* made me," I sneered at him. "I wanted to be one of your dippers. I became one. I needed a place to stay. You gave me a room. Everything I wanted, you gave it to me. Like that—" I snapped my fingers. "I was *never* yours. And that day on the dock?" I leaned over the table toward him. "I wanted you to drown."

He leapt around the table and lunged for me.

In his rage he hadn't seen me flick the switch on the incinerator. When he reached me, I shoved his side, propelling him toward the wall and the incinerator drawer.

I'd lied. Of course Mackiel had made me. He made me

study my targets. Learn what made them tick. Learn movement. Gravity. Subtle shifts in weight to get what I wanted. And what I wanted was for him to lunge at me.

Mackiel went to brace his hands against the wall to prevent himself from bumping into it, but instead found the hungry mouth of the incinerator.

He was right. I was his. And, for many years, I'd thought he'd been mine.

But not anymore.

I slammed the drawer down and slid the lock across, trapping his hands within the surging heat.

He screamed as his flesh burned.

The woman rushed to release Mackiel from the incinerator.

"Go!" I pushed Varin's back. His mouth gaped open. "Go, you stupid Eonist!"

The two of us barreled out of the room.

"Get her!" Mackiel cried.

But we were already gone.

CHAPTER TWENTY-ONE

Marguerite
Queen of Toria

*Rule ten: The advisor from each quadrant must
be present in all meetings and involved in all
decisions to ensure the queens remain impartial.*

The inspector summoned the queens to his interrogation room first thing that morning. Marguerite hoped for good news. He'd been sniffing about the palace for two days; surely he had a lead by now?

Corra was already sitting opposite the inspector, her hands clasped together near her throat. Her gaze caught on Marguerite's black armband. Did sadness dull her brown eyes? She knew Corra would be hurting, regardless of what her quadrant had tried to stamp out of her. Even Eonists were allowed to grieve. In their own way.

She gave Corra a tight smile as she sat beside her. "How are you holding up?" she asked.

Corra was silent for a moment, as though she was vetting her response. Marguerite's heart hurt, wishing the Eonist queen would let her in, this one time. The queens needed to remain strong. Together.

"I only want the killer found," Corra eventually replied. It was an honest, and Eonist, answer, but Marguerite still knew she was holding back.

"As do I," Marguerite said. The bubbling anger within turned into a fire at the mention of the murderer. She wondered if anger could turn her organs to ash?

The inspector ushered the advisors out of the room, then closed the door behind them.

"The advisors must be present, Inspector," Marguerite said, standing. "Anything addressed to the queens must be heard by all. That is Queenly Law. There are no secrets within the palace."

The inspector gave her a pointed look before replying, "I'm sorry, Queen Marguerite, but I need to speak with the queens alone."

Marguerite's heart started to race, and she gripped the thick material of her skirt to steady herself. "But Queen Stessa is not here yet."

"I'll get to that," he said.

Marguerite glanced at Corra. What did that mean? She reluctantly took her seat, but her body was rigid, as though prepared for a physical blow.

"Have you found the assassin?" Corra asked, her hand still at the hollow of her throat, something Marguerite had noticed was a new habit of Corra's. "Please, tell us good news."

"I'm sorry, my queen." He took the seat opposite her and adjusted the recording device around his ear. "I'm afraid all I have is bad news."

"What is it?" Marguerite braced for the impact.

"A short time ago," he began, "Queen Stessa's body was found—"

He didn't need to finish. Marguerite was up out of her chair once more, her hand covering her mouth. "No. No. No. No. No."

"Please sit, Queen Marguerite," the inspector said, a downward turn at his lips.

"Dead?" Marguerite hated the word. It burned her lips on the way out. The inspector nodded.

"What happened?" Corra asked.

"She was drowned," the inspector replied, his eyes keenly watching their reactions. Scrutinizing.

"She drowned?" Corra asked. "How? Where?"

The inspector shook his head. "I said she *was* drowned, not that she drowned. She was found in the baths."

"*Queens above,*" Marguerite said, tilting her head back to the opening in the ceiling. "What is happening here?"

"That's what I'm trying to uncover," he said. "Did either of you know Queen Stessa couldn't swim?"

"No," Marguerite replied, taking her seat. Grief pressed her farther into her chair. *Not Stessa. Poor Stessa. She was so young. Close to the same age as my daughter. How could she be dead?* "I didn't know that, Inspector."

But Corra said, "Yes, I did." The inspector fixed his eyes on the Eonist queen, as did Marguerite. "She's Ludist. They don't swim. They don't know how."

"Oh," Marguerite replied with a nod. "Of course. I suppose I knew, then, too . . ."

The inspector fluttered an elongated hand at her. "I don't suspect either of you, which is why you're here. I wanted to inform you both of what happened to Queen Stessa, before the remainder of the palace is informed of her passing."

Marguerite raised her eyebrows. "You don't suspect us?" Last she'd heard, they were the only suspects.

"No," he said, and let out a small sigh. "With Queen Stessa's death, it has become clear what is going on."

Both the queens leaned forward, clinging to his every word as though they were life itself.

"This was not a vendetta against Queen Iris, but"—he cleared his throat—"I believe, a plan to rid Quadara of all its queens."

Marguerite flinched. That couldn't be right. "Why would anyone want us gone?" That would threaten Quadara's very foundation.

The inspector snapped two long fingers at her. "That is what I am here to find out."

Corra jumped up, startling Marguerite. "This is preposterous!" she said. "First Iris, now Stessa. You didn't stop the assassin. Who's to say he won't target us next? You'll have two more dead queens on your hands!"

Marguerite couldn't help but gape at her sister queen. She'd never heard Corra raise her voice, let alone show any kind of anguish or frustration.

The inspector didn't appear ruffled. "I understand you are worried—"

"*Worried?*" Corra huffed. "Iris was murdered! And now you're telling us Stessa was purposely drowned and now . . . and now . . ." But she didn't finish her sentence. "I'm sorry." She returned to her seat, her hand at her throat. "It's been a trying few days with little sleep. I don't know what came over me."

But Marguerite believed she'd seen the true Corra, the girl behind the rigid mask. And that girl hurt deeply. She took Corra's hand in hers. "You don't have to apologize, Corra," she said. "We're all allowed to grieve."

Corra gave her a swift nod, but kept Marguerite's hand.

"When did this happen, Inspector?" Marguerite asked. "What have you uncovered thus far?"

"Her body was found around thirty minutes ago." Marguerite felt Corra tremble under her touch. She gave her hand a reassuring squeeze. "She was supposed to be in her room, resting. Her young advisor was the one to find her. By the time he arrived at the baths, she was already gone."

"Lyker." Corra sighed.

"Could he have done it?" Marguerite asked the inspector.

"His clothes were wet when he brought her to me, but he'd pulled Queen Stessa from the pool. It's difficult to determine without further investigation."

"No," Corra butted in. "I don't believe he would have."

The inspector turned to her. "And why do you say that, my queen?"

"Because they loved each other," she replied. Her eyes almost glistened.

Who was this girl who spoke of love? It was not an Eonist concept, Marguerite thought.

"How do you know this, my queen?" the inspector asked.

Corra pinned him with her dark eyes. "Because I walked into her room yesterday and found the two of them together."

Marguerite gasped. Another Queenly Law broken. Was this why Stessa had pushed Marguerite away when Lyker had entered the palace, to protect her secret?

"Perhaps they had a fight?" he asked. "Most of the time, the murder victim knows their murderer."

"No. They were not fighting." She cleared her throat. "I can't be certain, but I don't believe he would've killed her."

"But he still lied to me, which means—" the inspector began.

"Ludists are not killers, Inspector," Marguerite said. "If Corra says they were in love, then I don't believe he could've harmed her."

"True, however, crimes of passion are not uncommon in Ludia," the inspector said. "Yet, with Queen Iris's murder, it is difficult to link the two killings to this young man, for what would he gain in that? Unless Iris knew about their relationship?"

Marguerite exchanged a glance with Corra, who shook her head. "I don't believe so."

He nodded. "Still, I will speak with him again, but I doubt his involvement."

"What do we do now?" Marguerite asked. She glanced at Corra. "Clearly the assassin is still roaming free. We are in danger if we stay." She had never once thought of leaving the palace since the day she set foot inside it, even when Elias had been revealed as a fraud and a cheat and her whole world had fallen down upon her. The palace was where Marguerite was meant to be, and being queen was what she was born to do.

"We're never to leave," Corra said, looking up at the glass dome. "If we do, we'll forfeit our throne, our reign tainted. We cannot have outside influence on our duties."

"Perhaps that's the assassin's plan?" The inspector pressed a flag on his recorder. "He does not have to kill you all, merely drive you out of the palace. Yes, that could be it," he said more to himself than the queens.

"Stessa also has no heir," Marguerite murmured. "She was too young."

"None of us do," Corra reminded her. Marguerite failed to meet her eyes, feeling the truth would be pulled from her. Corra's mother had been queen when Marguerite had fallen pregnant and supposedly lost her child. She knew nothing of Marguerite's daughter hidden in Toria.

Keep her safe. Keep her hidden. That is all that matters. The throne is your responsibility, not hers.

"We have increased the number of guards," the inspector said. "We will ensure the assassin does not have the time or opportunity to strike again."

"You said that before." Marguerite shook her head. "And now Stessa is dead."

"We thought we had the murderer contained in the processing room," he replied.

"Why don't you force everyone to leave?" Corra asked. "At this point, our protection is more important than finding the assassin, correct?"

Marguerite could not help but agree. "We must protect Quadara and Queenly Law, whatever the cost." And yet she would not reveal her daughter. No matter what happened to her. Her daughter had not been prepared for a life within the palace; she did not know how to be queen. She didn't even know her real parentage. Marguerite would not falter now. Her daughter would live a normal life. Most importantly, her daughter would *live*.

The inspector pinned the queens with his black eyes. "What if the assassin has been part of the palace all along? What if they were waiting for their moment to strike?"

Marguerite's tongue felt dry and heavy in her mouth when she replied, "Then we are doomed."

CHAPTER TWENTY-TWO

Keralie

W hat happened back there?" Varin asked as we ran down the stairs, away from the House of Concord. Away from Mackiel's screams.

I didn't look back.

Had I gone too far? Was Varin finally done with me? I was surprised he'd stayed around this long.

The Concord began to fill in preparation for the day's business. People stopped and stared as we fled. I knew we looked quite a sight.

Once we reached the center of the Concord, I halted and looked up. The Queenly Reports repeated the same news from yesterday. Nothing about the queens' murders.

What was going on? Why hadn't we heard anything? I understood the need to keep everyone calm, but surely something should've been leaked by now? Why was everyone acting like nothing had changed?

I took in some shuddering breaths. Everyone needed to know what had happened. I didn't want the two of us to be alone in this.

"Are you all right?" Varin asked, standing beside me but still keeping his distance.

I shook my head. I couldn't look at him. I could barely breathe. What had I done?

"What are we going to do now? We didn't learn anything," he said. He was right. We didn't know much more than what we'd already suspected. He let out a breath. "You could've warned me about what you were planning to do."

"How?" I said, finding my voice. "Mackiel was right there. I needed the element of surprise."

"You certainly had that."

"You can go now," I said. "It's over."

"What are you talking about?" He shook his head.

"I'm tired, Varin. I want . . ." I was going to say *I want to go home*, but I didn't know where that was anymore. Certainly not the auction house.

Varin stepped a little closer. "You're scared. Take a breath."

A laugh burst forth. "Scared? Didn't you see what I did back there?" If anything, Varin should have been scared of me. It was like I was back on my father's boat, steering toward the cliffs. I'd been enraged. I'd wanted destruction. So I lashed out.

There was a fury within me that I couldn't control. A darkness attached, like a long shadow. And whether Mackiel had created it, or whether it was always within me, I wasn't sure.

All of a sudden, the alley spun. Stars glimmered; the queens mocked me from above.

I fell toward the grimy stone.

An arm snagged my waist at the last minute. "Keralie?" Varin said, holding me inches from the ground. "Are you okay?"

The world spun again as he set me on my feet, keeping his hand on my arm. I looked down at his dermasuit-covered fingers, surprised by their steadiness and strength. Neither of us had flinched upon the contact.

"I'm fine," I replied.

"No, you're in shock. Take a moment."

Though I hadn't actually seen it, I imagined Mackiel's flesh falling from bone. How could I have done that to someone? Someone I once thought was my friend? And did I dare admit the truth to that day on the dock after all these years?

When we had jumped into the water, I'd expected Mackiel to struggle. I'd *known* he would. I'd wanted to show Mackiel that I belonged in his world, that I could be ruthless too. I'd overheard him talking about his new recruit to his father days earlier. He'd said I was soft but could be molded. It had maddened me.

So I dared him to jump, to see Mackiel flail and have a taste of weakness. But I'd saved him before his final breath.

I'd always thought I'd never meant to hurt him. That it was a game, and Mackiel liked games. But today wasn't a game. I wanted to hurt Mackiel, maybe more than I wanted to escape.

It was life or death, said a voice deep within. A voice that sounded suspiciously like Mackiel's. *Damn him!* I couldn't get him out of my head. Out of my life. Out of me.

I pushed Varin away. "I need to sit down." Sinking to the ground, I pressed my forehead against my knees.

Varin squatted beside me. "You did what you had to. You saved us."

"Yes, with no help from you."

He surprised me by letting out a low, chest-rumbling laugh.

"I'm not the quickest in a tight spot." His expression was soft. For the first time, he didn't appear to be judging me, and this was the one moment when I would've forgiven him for doing so. And he wasn't looking at me like I was broken. A porcelain doll. He looked at me as though I was strong.

"Truer words have never been spoken," I said with a small smile.

"Do you really want to quit now?" His dark brows were low over his eyes.

"We lost our evidence," I said, referring to the rerecorded comm chips. "And we still don't know how Mackiel is involved."

"We have enough information. I can go to the palace alone, if you want?" He was testing me. Did I want to help the queens or not? Did I want to do the right thing? Was I more than a thief?

Who do you want to be?

"I'm in this deeper than ever. But Mackiel will still want his cut." I ran a finger along my throat. "Unless you want out?"

Varin could disappear into Eonia; Mackiel and his henchmen wouldn't find him there. "I told you, I'm going to see this through." He raked his hand through his dark hair. "You're not the only one who needs something."

"HIDRA," I said. It wasn't a question.

He nodded, something behind his expression—hope?

Too bad we wanted the same thing. I could leave him here and venture to the palace for HIDRA on my own, but he could easily turn me in to the palace authorities. After all, who would the palace guards trust? A thief or an Eonist messenger?

I needed Varin on my side. Until I got what I wanted. I'd worry about betraying him later.

"We're in this together," he said. "But no more lying. No more tricks."

I held my hand out for him to shake.

"Together," I said as our palms made contact. "Promise."

He should've known better than to trust a thief.

There was only one place left to go. And it was as though we'd been drawn there from the start, for this was where it had all begun. My steps turned more determined as we walked back up the stairs to the House of Concord and through to the palace.

"We need a plan," he said.

"*We* are the plan." I grinned. "No one will suspect a silly little Torian girl and a young, naïve Eonist." I nodded at him. "We've got this. You and me. We go to the palace authorities and tell them we have information to trade on the queens' murders. We tell them all about Mackiel and the comm chips."

"How do you plan on breaking into the palace?" he asked, staring up at the golden dome. "There are Eonist guards defending the entrance and many more inside."

I shot him an annoyed look. "We're not breaking in."

His brow furrowed. "We're not?"

"You think that little of me?" I looped my arm through his, feeling his muscles tense on contact, but he didn't pull away. "Silly Varin. We're invited. Everyone is."

His eyebrows raised. "We're going to attend court?"

"We're going to attend court," I confirmed. "And we better look our finest."

He shook his head with a disappointed sigh. "So no to breaking into the palace, but yes to stealing more clothes?"

I snapped my fingers at him. "Now you're starting to get it."

225

CHAPTER TWENTY-THREE

Corra
Queen of Eonia

Rule eleven: The power of the queen can only
be passed on to her daughter in the event of
the queen's death or her abdication.

C orra returned to her rooms after meeting with the inspector. She couldn't believe Stessa was now also gone. She needed to reset. She'd allowed her emotions to take control and realized it a moment too late. There had only been one other occasion when Corra's emotions had bested her—the day of her mother's passing.

Corra hadn't expected to be queen until she was fifty-five, as her mother's death date was set to ninety years old, giving Corra plenty of time to perfect her hold on her emotions. By then she thought she might not even feel them. A true Eonist, ready to take the throne.

But her mother had begun rejecting her monthly medical treatments for her weak heart. In one of their few meetings, her mother had told Corra that she'd wanted to pass on to the next world so Corra could step into the light.

Corra had tried reasoning with her mother, but her mother wouldn't hear of it. A year later, her mother was sent to the palace infirmary to take her final breaths.

With her mother's death imminent, Corra had stole out of the palace for the first time in her life. It was important the Eonist advisor found her within Eonia—to ensure her upbringing inside the palace was kept a secret. During the few days Corra had spent in Eonia, she knew her mother had done the right thing. She had felt an affinity for the quadrant she'd only ever heard about, and she could not imagine feeling closer to Eonia had she grown up there.

When the Eonist advisor had arrived at the apartment her mother had given as Corra's address, she'd been ready to return to the only home she'd ever known.

After arriving at the palace, she had visited her mother in the infirmary. Corra held her mother's limp hand and whispered her words back to her. "I promise to be patient. To be calm. To be selfless. And rule with a steady hand. A steady heart." Tears fell down Corra's cheeks then. "I love you, Mother." She buried her face against her mother's side to hide her tears.

When she left the palace infirmary, she promised to leave her sadness behind.

But it wasn't as easy with Iris. And now Stessa.

Corra wanted to disappear. More than that, she wanted to be able to grieve, hurt—*feel* like everyone else. She hated how she dishonored Iris with every glib response.

How much longer could she keep the mask in place? And what was the point? Her life was at stake, as was Marguerite's.

Corra acknowledged the two guards posted outside her room before retiring. Sitting upon her bed, Corra let out an exhausted sigh.

A strange wailing, like an injured animal, echoed down the hallway. Corra thought of Lyker, shattered in his grief. He'd never be able to scrub the image of a limp and lifeless Stessa from his mind. Corra was glad she hadn't seen Iris that way; she'd turned her head when the body had passed during the death processional. It allowed her to hold on to the last image of her love, vibrantly alive, doing what she did best: ruling.

Corra would never wish the agony of losing a loved one upon anyone, not even an enemy. Not that Corra had enemies, but who else could be killing the queens other than some vile and unseen adversary?

Perhaps the assassin had been sent from across the seas? Hired by a rival nation who wished to see Quadara fall. But what nation? There'd never been any international rivalry, only the Quadrant Wars.

"What would you do?" Corra whispered to the silence, hoping Iris was watching from above. "What would you do if you were still here? Would you flee the palace to save your life?" She grinned in the dark. "No, of course you wouldn't. You'd stay. You'd fight."

A sob gurgled in her throat. "Why didn't you fight? Why did you let them snuff you out as though you were nothing? A flame in the darkness. Nothing more than anyone else." She shook her head. "But you were *everything*. I don't understand."

Her fractured heart pricked. She flopped onto her back, allowing her tears to freely roll across her cheeks.

"If I leave, I lose my throne. If I stay, I might lose my life." She rubbed her hand over her face. "What would you want me to do?" They were two very different things, what Iris would do and what Iris would want *her* to do.

"You told me we were in this together." She turned her face into her pillow and cried, the habit of hiding her emotions deeply ingrained. "Will I see you again?" she whispered. "Does the quadrant without borders exist for passed queens? Is that where we will be together? Together in the way we were never allowed to be in life?"

Corra's questions would remain unanswered, though she hoped they were not unheard by the queens above.

A bang against the door had Corra shooting up from her bed. "Who's there?" she cried.

"Don't worry, Queen Corra," one of her guards called through the door. "We have the situation under control."

"Let me in!" an angry voice wailed. "It was her—I know it was!"

Lyker.

"Stay back," her guard warned.

There was a loud thump, then a groan.

"Stop!" Corra cried. She flung open her bedroom door. "Don't hurt him!"

Lyker was on the ground, his nose streaming blood onto the polished marble floor. One of her guards had Lyker's hands tied behind his back. The other guard was rubbing his purpling knuckles.

"Please," she said to them. "He's grieving over Queen Stessa."

The guards, and Lyker, looked up at her in surprise. Lyker's eyes were red; she was sure hers were too.

She stepped to the side. "Let him in."

"Are you sure, Queen Corra?" one guard asked. He made no attempt to release Lyker. She nodded.

"You can leave," she said to the guards after they hauled Lyker to his feet and shuffled him into her room. They looked at her as if she'd grown a second head. "Now," she commanded.

"Yes, Queen Corra." They bowed and left the room, but not without a lingering glance at Lyker.

"I'm sorry," she said to him once they were alone. "You must be in a lot of pain."

But Lyker didn't look at her. He was staring at her bed and the tissues scattered across the blanket. Corra had forgotten to dispose of them in her incinerator.

"Lyker?" she asked after a long moment.

He finally glanced up, his face distorted in grief. "You did this." His voice was low but strong, and different from the boy she'd seen earlier with Stessa. The light had been extinguished from his eyes, replaced by something sinister and wild.

He locked the door. Before she could ask what he was doing, he launched across the room. He propelled her into the wall, his hands around her throat. Her head smacked into the wood, sending fresh tears down her cheeks.

"Stop!"

But he was too strong, his anger too fierce. "You killed her! You killed her! You killed her!"

"Queen Corra!" the guards thumped at her door. "Are you all right?"

No, she tried to say, but there wasn't enough air in her lungs. Her chest heaved. Black began to blot her vision.

"Why?" he cried, slamming one fist into the wall beside her face. He was much larger than she was, the biceps in his upper arm keeping her in place. "Why?"

"Let us in!" The guards continued pounding on the door.

Corra kicked, but the lack of oxygen made her legs feel weightless, as though she were submerged in water. Was this how Stessa felt when she died? Her chest burning, her throat raw, her body powerless, her head light?

She hoped so, for it wasn't too painful.

Lyker brought his face close to hers. Angry red flushed across his cheeks and neck, matching his hair. "You won't see her there," he said. Corra blinked. She didn't know what he was talking about. His swollen eyes filled with tears. "You don't deserve to be with her." His chest shuddered. "I won't let you."

He pulled away, and Corra collapsed to the floor.

She sucked in a painful breath, her throat numb and searing at the same time.

Lyker towered over her, his hands in his hair. He let out an agonized wail.

"Queen Corra!" a guard called through the door. "What's happening?"

"I'm fine," she croaked. "We're fine. I knocked over a lamp. That's all."

She crawled to her bed and pulled herself up by the blankets. Once she was sitting, she turned back to Lyker. He stared into the distance.

"I didn't kill Stessa," she said, hand at her burning throat. "I would never kill a sister queen."

He flashed her a look. "We threatened you."

Corra nodded. "You were scared. You wanted to protect . . ." She let out a ragged cough. "You wanted to protect your love. I understand."

He barked a laugh. "An Eonist understands love. Right."

"I loved Iris." Corra gasped, then smiled through her tears. It was the first time she'd ever said it out loud. "I loved her." She wanted to say it again and again, but it wouldn't bring Iris back. Still, to say it brought a little light into the darkness of these days.

"I would kill for Stessa." Lyker's fists clenched by his sides. "You thought we'd killed Iris. Would you not kill for your love?"

Corra studied him. Clearly, the boy was broken, as broken as her heart. Would she have killed for Iris? She wasn't sure. All she knew was that Iris had been her heart and now her heart was gone.

To kill for revenge was an act of the heart. No, she would not—and could not—kill for love.

"Come here," she said, patting the space beside her.

Lyker looked as though she might pull a destabilizer on him. She shook her head. "I won't hurt you."

He approached her cautiously. When he reached the bed, she held out her hands. They were shaking.

"I'm sorry for your loss," she said. "I'm sorry I thought you or Stessa were capable of such malice. Truly, I am." She held her hand to her hidden watch. "But I would never hurt Stessa, or anyone she loved. This palace has always been my home, and anyone within it is family." She had never spoken truer words. She wished Iris could see her courage.

"You're not like other Eonists, are you?" He squinted at her.

Corra tried to laugh, but her throat wouldn't allow it. "I think you'd be surprised by how much Eonists really feel."

"I wish I couldn't feel," he said. "I wish I hadn't loved her."

"Loving someone means risking your heart being broken," Corra said. "But those moments you are together triumph over any hardship."

Lyker sat beside her. "I'm not sure I believe that. Not now."

Corra knew how he felt; the pain was almost too much to bear. But then she thought of her mother. "In time, you will."

He hung his head, his coiffed hair flopping forward. "I don't know what to do without her. She's the reason I'm here. She's the reason for everything."

"What did you want to do before this?" Corra gestured to the gold-adorned room around them. "What did you want for your life?" She was treading on shaky ground, as Eonists were not meant to question their future or want more. But she didn't care. She needed to talk to someone about her grief.

"I don't remember wanting anything more than I wanted Stessa," he replied. Tears continued to stream down his face.

"But you had other passions?" Ludists were known for their wants and desires; surely there was something else.

Lyker studied his inked hands. "I wanted to be a world-renowned poet."

"Ah," Corra said. "And you gave it up for Stessa."

"And I would again," he said sternly, "if given another chance."

"I would choose Iris again and again."

They smiled at each other.

"You could leave," she said. "You could return to your Ludist life."

Lyker shook his head. "I can't, not now. Stessa wanted to be queen, but she was willing to give up the throne for me, for my happiness. Now that she's gone . . ." He swallowed roughly. "Now that she's gone, I have to do right by her. I have to be here, ensure everything she wanted as a queen and for her quadrant is not forgotten."

Corra held back tears, thinking how she had misjudged the youngest queen. She had hopes and dreams for her reign, and they were cut short, as were Iris's.

"Stessa would be proud of you," she said.

"Thank you, Queen Corra."

"Will you do me a favor?" she asked.

233

"Anything."

"I'd like some water for my throat."

"I'm sorry I—"

"You've apologized already." She cut him off with a wave of her hand. "I need water now, not apologies."

He met her eyes. "You sound like Queen Iris."

Corra smiled widely. "I do, don't I?"

———

AN HOUR AFTER Lyker had left, Corra woke to an excruciatingly raw throat, as though someone had run a blade back and forth across it. Her eyes were sealed shut from stale tears and sorrow. She'd fallen asleep in her gold dermasuit. Her crown was glowing hot.

She bolted upright, but Lyker was gone.

Her room was a haze of smoke.

She gagged, rolled off the bed and hit the floor. Beside her lay the glass of water Lyker had given her before she'd climbed under the blankets. She'd asked him to stay until she had fallen asleep.

"Lyker!" she cried, then coughed. "Are you here?"

She was met with silence and a strange crackling sound.

Fire.

"Guards!" she cried out. But her voice wouldn't carry. The damage to her throat courtesy of Lyker's grip and the smoke clogging her windpipe was too much; her voice was a whisper. She couldn't see where the fire had started, but she could feel it. Her dermasuit began puckering and blistering from the intense heat. It was coming from her bathroom.

"Guards!" Again, no response.

She pulled a strip of cloth from her blanket and mopped up

the spilled water by her bed. Placing the wet cloth over her mouth, she skittered across the floor, finding her way by memory. Her senses were full of smoke: her eyes, her nose, her mouth. The tiled floor was hot. The crackling grew louder.

But she would fight. As Iris would have. *Should have.* She wouldn't be the next in the list of dead queens.

A small sliver of light caught her eye. The gap under the door! She swallowed a few times to wet her throat—it was like swallowing acid—then she pressed her mouth to the gap and screamed, "Help! Fire!"

Shadows moved on the other side of the door. Her guards. Thank the queens above! They'd heard her.

The door handle jiggled somewhere above her head. She scrambled away, allowing them to open the door inward. The fire roared behind her. Something exploded and showered her hair in splinters. Her headboard. Her room was collapsing around her.

"Queen Corra! We can't open the door," a guard yelled above the roar. "Is something blocking it?"

Corra took a deep breath and stood, feeling around for the blockage.

She fell back to the floor. "There's nothing there."

The guards began throwing their bodies against it.

"It's locked!" someone shouted.

But she couldn't remember locking it. And although she wished she hadn't, she thought of Lyker. Had he changed his mind and locked the door again? Then how had he left?

"Can you unlock it from your side, Queen Corra?" a guard asked.

She launched herself upright once more and felt around for the lock. In the past, she'd only ever locked it when Iris visited.

Her gloved fingers scraped on something rough. There was no lock—the handle had been twisted clean off.

"I can't open it," she shouted. She moved to the window and banged on the glass. She could see silhouettes on the other side through the smoky haze. "Break the window!"

"Stay clear, Queen Corra," the guards yelled.

Corra fell back to the floor. "Hurry." The smoke took residence inside her chest, filling every hole, every cell, until her body felt like smoke and ash. "Hurry!" Her dermasuit tried to maintain her body temperature, but it couldn't fight fire.

A booming crack sounded from behind her, and though her vision was blurry, she could now make out the angry red flames.

She pressed herself into the far corner of her room, the rag over her mouth. It wasn't wet any longer, and her dermasuit began to melt off in pieces. She covered her face with her hands.

This is the end. She'd be reunited with Iris sooner than she thought. She would see her mother again. *I'm sorry, Mother.*

And now she understood what Lyker had meant when he'd said, *"You won't see her there."* He didn't want to kill Corra, as he didn't want her reunited with his lost love when he was still in the land of the living. Then who had set the fire?

An object collided into the bedroom window as the guards attempted to shatter it. The glass groaned, soon to break, but Corra couldn't lift her head. Heat encased her body and mind, and she was reminded of Iris's embrace.

I'm coming, she thought, her hand at the watch around her neck, above her broken dermasuit. But she wasn't scared.

Soon they would be together, no longer apart.

CHAPTER TWENTY-FOUR

Keralie

Why did they continue with this charade? When would the palace admit the queens were dead and there was no one to hold court? I didn't understand. Had they already located the royal ancestors? Who exactly was I in line to speak with?

"Stop fidgeting," I admonished, my hand on Varin's sleeve. "You look like you're up to something."

"We *are* up to something," he replied, his hands shuffling in and out of his coat pockets. His stolen outfit was too small, but I didn't mind his shirt stretching over his broad chest. My hands and eyes lingered unconsciously. He shifted away from me, his prominent cheeks darkening. He still wasn't used to being touched.

The process of gaining access to Queen Marguerite had taken the entire the morning. First, we signed in at the visitor processing room and were inspected for any weapons or dangerous items. Next, we were ushered into a theater with around one hundred other Quadarians who'd traveled to the palace. We were forced to watch all of this year's Queenly Reports to ensure we didn't approach the queens with previously rejected requests. Afterward, the guards separated the group into our quadrants.

We shuffled down an arched corridor with the other Torian visitors. Varin kept his head down, hoping no one would recognize he was too handsome to be anything but a perfectly engineered Eonist. He'd hidden his comm line in a safe place outside the palace, to maintain the illusion. He'd slicked his hair back in a traditional Torian style and the two-day-old stubble on his jaw roughened his look. Even I wouldn't have picked him out of the crowd as an imposter. Still, my fingers twitched, wishing to rake them through his hair—something I'd seen him do countless times—to free his longer locks.

Several crystal chandeliers dripped from the ceiling like icicles on trees in a winter storm. Everything else was dipped in gold. I struggled against the desire to touch the exorbitant wealth, keeping my hands tucked under my arms. I had to be good. Better. Like Varin. Maybe then they'd reward me with HIDRA.

Portraits of the past Torian queens followed us with their painted eyes.

"They're so lifelike," Varin murmured, his hands reaching out toward the paintings.

"Stop touching things," I said, repeating his words back to him from when we were in his apartment.

The left side of his mouth lifted but he didn't say anything.

The crowd pushed us forward, everyone desperate to see Queen Marguerite. They were in for a surprise. Varin darted glances at the Torians around us, as though he was appalled by our disorganization.

I had to admit, a part of me was thrilled to be inside the palace.

When I was ten years old, I would play the Torian queen—my throne made of ragged pillows—while Mackiel played the queen's advisor. A favorite game of ours. We usually ended up squabbling over who would rule what part of Toria. I'd always forced the Jetée and its various sordid businesses upon him, and took ownership of the wealthy houses and lawful businesses of the Skim for myself. Mackiel had said I was selfish. I had never argued otherwise.

We would play the game for days, until I tired of the storyline.

"Ruling Toria is boring," I would say, kicking down the pillow throne.

I don't remember Mackiel agreeing.

I twisted the comm case locket between my fingers. Had the childhood game meant more to him than a way to pass the time? Had he always wanted to tangle himself with palace politics, to prove he was more powerful than his father, *better* than his father, while I enjoyed the delights of being a dipper, having access to everything and anything I wanted?

I let the locket fall back against my wrist.

The crowd was funneled by the guards toward a vast opening, taking us along for the ride.

We stepped into a circular room where the high glass ceiling was the apex of the palace's golden dome. The sun gleamed down onto the elevated Quadarian dial, fracturing the light into streams and highlighting the words carved into the marble tiles around the room.

The throne room.

But we couldn't see the queens on their thrones—or whoever had taken their place. They were hidden by an ornate wooden partition, encircling the dial. There were four doors to enter through the partition, one for each queen, shielded by a guard.

The crowd gasped audibly behind us. Some Torians pushed forward, eager to see around the partition. The back of my neck prickled, desperate to know what the palace was telling everyone about the absent queens.

"The light of Quadara," Varin whispered, his eyes drawn to the light streaming down from the dome. "It's magnificent." His fingers fluttered as though he itched to paint it.

I nodded, words struck from my mind. Ancient Quadarians believed the nation was born from this very point, spiraling out in a clockwise direction. At first, the land had been fertile and lush due to abundant resources. This first region became Archia, once attached to the mainland. The land then developed to the south; resources were less available but provided an accessible coastline with bountiful seas. *Toria.* From there, the land changed. To compensate for having few natural resources, Ludists created man-made landscapes and canals and filled their idle time with entertainment. Finally, there was Eonia. As the region nearest to the north, with plummeting temperatures, crops and livestock were unable to survive. Eonia had no choice but to build their sprawling city and focus on technology to survive a mostly frozen land.

There was no denying the room had power.

"Wow," I breathed, forgetting our purpose. The weight of the room pressed upon me—its meaning and history. We neared the exact point where the quadrants once met. I could tell from the slack-jawed crowd that they shared the same sentiment.

We stepped toward the guard when it was our turn.

"One at a time," the guard said, holding up a hand.

I exchanged a glance with Varin.

"You can do this," Varin said. "You're doing the right thing. Just don't get yourself arrested."

"You worried about me?"

He pressed his lips together before replying, "Just be careful."

I nodded numbly. Something tumbled within my belly. I stepped forward, leaving Varin behind with the rest of the Torian crowd.

Was I about to meet with Queen Marguerite's advisor? Wouldn't it be obvious something had happened to her? Why hadn't they closed court while they waited for the new queens to take up their thrones?

Before I had time to practice what I was going to say one last time, the guard opened the door in the partition and ushered me through. I cleared my throat.

Here we go.

CHAPTER TWENTY-FIVE

Marguerite
Queen of Toria

*Rule twelve: As soon as a queen passes, her daughter,
or the next closest female relative, must be brought to
the palace immediately to ascend the throne.*

Marguerite's breathing grew ragged, color leaching from her cheeks, light dimming from her eyes.

"We're running out of time." People swarmed about her, hands fluttering at her arms, face and hair. "Tell us, Queen Marguerite. Please. Before it is too late!"

It is already too late, Marguerite thought. She leaned against the pillows, unable to keep her head upright. *No. I promised myself I wouldn't. I can't bring her into this. Not now.*

The palace doctor wore a silver dermasuit, a silver mask and a deep frown. The inspector stood beside him, watching every movement with detached interest. They whispered back and forth.

She's dying.

She did not require him to say it out loud. And yet they would not let her die in peace.

Poison.

The words were whispered among those gathered in the

infirmary. She'd been poring over her maps of the palace, trying to work out how the murderer had killed Iris, avoided being caught in the processing room when the palace went into lockdown and then murdered Stessa a day later, when her advisor, Jenri, had rushed into the room. He was covered in ash, a large gash across his arm.

Marguerite had bolted upright, her chair falling backward. "What has happened?"

"My queen," Jenri had breathed out. "There was a fire . . . Queen Corra didn't make—" But she did not hear him finish. She'd collapsed, her heavy skirts pillowing her fall.

At first Jenri had thought it was shock. He took her to the infirmary for observation. Then she started convulsing.

Poison—sprinkled over the parchment of her maps and absorbed through her fingers and into her bloodstream.

First Iris, then Stessa and Corra. The assassin . . .

Marguerite could not believe this was happening. It had been less than two days since Iris's death, and all the queens had been murdered. Now it was her turn to die. She hoped she would not be separated from her sister queens in the next life.

At least she'd had more years. Stessa, Corra and Iris—they were all so young. *Too* young. Like . . .

No! She would not utter a word. Her daughter must remain safe from the palace's influence. Especially now. It was far too dangerous to involve her in this mess.

"I need to sedate her," the doctor said, trying to maneuver his way to her bedside. There were too many people in the infirmary. "It might slow the poison."

"No," Jenri said. "We need her lucid. We need to know where her daughter is!"

The doctor glanced at the inspector and shook his head. "Then she is doomed."

Jenri's concerned face loomed overhead. "You are the last queen," he said. "Without your daughter, Quadara will be left with no one to rule—with nothing. Please, my queen."

"This is what they want," she managed to say, her voice startling her. It sounded like metal scraping against metal.

"Who?" Jenri asked, smoothing back her sweat-soaked hair from her clammy forehead.

She shifted her face away from him. "Whoever did this to us."

"Then don't let them win," her handmaiden, Lali, replied. She was tracing calming circles on the back of Marguerite's hand.

With her surviving family all men, Marguerite had feared this day would come. She knew she had to produce an heir; it was Queenly Law, after all. Luckily—or unluckily, depending on your point of view—all matchings since Elias had resulted in no further pregnancies. Marguerite couldn't bear the thought of choosing between her child and the throne again. And yet here she was, facing the same dilemma, seventeen years on.

Marguerite lurched forward. A bucket was placed under her chin before she retched up what little was left in her system. The doctor had given her a vapor to encourage the expulsions, hoping it would expel the toxin, but all it had done was make Marguerite weaker.

She lay down, her body weightless and her mind full of clouds.

Another spasm jerked deep inside. She curled into a ball and howled in agony. *Not much longer!* she begged to the queens watching silently from above. *Please. Make it stop!*

"I'm sorry, my queen," Lali said, her head bowed. "I had to tell the advisors about your daughter. For Quadara."

Marguerite wanted to rip her hand out of Lali's, but she didn't have the strength. She had trusted her. Trusted she would never utter those words again. *Your daughter.* But Lali had betrayed her, and now Jenri asked for the impossible. He had decided Toria was more important than her wishes, more important than her daughter's well-being.

But that was not his decision, nor her handmaiden's, to make.

"*Please,*" Jenri said. "You must tell me where she is. Tell me to save your quadrant, to save the nation."

"I cannot," she replied. "She is not prepared." But it was worse than that. Much worse, for how could her daughter be ready to take the Torian throne when she did not even know she was of royal blood? She would not thrust her daughter into this life without any warning. And the palace was no longer the safe place Marguerite had thought it to be.

But what would that mean for her beloved Toria and the rest of Quadara? Marguerite was a rare queen; when she'd first entered the palace, she found she could not focus solely on her quadrant. She wanted to be involved in all decisions. She wanted to make Quadara stronger, not only Toria. Now the nation was shattered, and the only solution was to give up her child's whereabouts.

"There's no one else," Jenri said. He looked truly remorseful for the situation they had found themselves in. "You know I would never ask something of you unless I had no other options."

"Anyone else," she rasped, her eyes wildly bouncing around the room. "Please, Jenri. If this happened to me, then it is sure to happen to her as well."

Too young. Far too young.

Lali knew how much this secret had cost Marguerite over

the years. She knew it was worth everything to her—to ensure her daughter was kept separate from this world.

How could she?

Someone gripped her chin as her eyes rolled into the back of her head. The pain in her chest was too much, and the fatigue too aggressive. Marguerite longed for stillness.

The machine attached to her started beeping wildly.

"We're losing her," the doctor said. "We have minutes left."

"Tell us, Queen Marguerite," someone begged. Marguerite's vision was tinted black. "Tell us to save Quadara!"

"There are no other female relatives," someone said. "We cannot find anyone to take the other thrones. Toria is our only hope. *You* are our only hope!"

Marguerite shuddered, breaths leaving her body in gasps. She couldn't give up her child to this wicked palace of darkness and death. She was a mother, and although she hadn't seen her child since her birth, she *had* to protect her daughter.

She was also a queen.

Sworn to protect Toria, sworn to keep the peace between the quadrants. With no queens, Quadara would fall to chaos. The nations across the seas would turn their eyes toward the wealthiest nation. Quadara needed to remain strong.

Could she continue to choose her daughter's future over the nation's?

"Queen Marguerite," the inspector began. "We need to—"

"No!" she cried. "Leave me be!"

But someone gripped her shoulders. Jenri. "We will protect her. *I* will protect her. I will not allow this tragedy to reoccur, but we need to protect Queenly Law. We need to save Quadara."

Marguerite wanted to laugh. Jenri had not stopped the poison from being sprinkled across her precious maps; the inspector had not stopped the assassin from slaying her sister queens. How could they stop a shadow without a name?

She closed her eyes and bit her lip as another spasm took hold. Was it her imagination, or did it feel less aggressive? Her body went numb, as though floating to the queens who awaited her arrival. Her beloved sister queens.

"Queen Marguerite," a voice called to her from this world, grounding her. "This is what you've spent your life working toward. Don't let it fall to ruin. Don't let the assassin win!" It was Lali. "Don't let them destroy Toria!"

You will make it up to them, Iris had said years ago when Marguerite had fretted over what she'd done to Toria by hiding her daughter. It was a decision that had haunted her every day since.

Was this the moment Iris had meant? A chance to redeem herself? But what about her daughter? Her safety? With an assassin loose in the palace, how could she knowingly bring her into this?

Marguerite rolled her head. "Do you swear it, Jenri?" she asked, her eyes trying to find him. "Swear she will be safe?"

"Yes, my queen," he replied from somewhere beside her. "She will be safe here, with me. I will go, alone, to retrieve her. I will not leave her side while she's here and until we find the assassin. I promise you. Toria and your daughter will be safe from harm."

If Jenri promised to care for her daughter, ensuring nothing happened to her, then they could still save Quadara.

Seventeen years ago, she'd placed her daughter's well-being above the nation's. She broke Queenly Law. Now was the chance to make things right. And she wouldn't only make it up to her people; she'd make it up to Quadara. She *had* to. With all queens dead, this was the only option. Jenri would bring her daughter to the palace and teach her the ways of the queens now passed.

She let out an exhausted sigh, barely able to focus her eyes on her advisor. "The map above my desk—" The map she ran her fingers along each evening before retiring to bed. Her body shuddered, her chest pressing upon her lungs. "Turn it over." With her last exertion, she pinned Jenri with her gaze—hoping to convey every emotion and thought tumbling in her heart. "It will show you where to find my daughter."

PART THREE

CHAPTER TWENTY-SIX

Keralie

I can do this. I can do the right thing. No one here knows who I am. Or what I've done.

Varin gave me a small encouraging smile before the guard closed the partition door behind me, blocking him from view. I took a steadying breath.

"How can I assist you, Ms. Corrington?" a woman asked.

That voice . . . A voice I'd heard on many Torian announcements. On New Year's Day. On Quadrant Day. The voice declaring the end of the Jetée. The voice I thought I'd never hear again.

I turned to face the throne. There sat a woman with pale skin, brown eyes and an ornate crown upon her graying auburn hair.

I stumbled in shock, my knee crashing into the marble floor.

"Queen Marguerite!" I gasped, righting myself. "It's you!
Alive! How?

"That is the general idea of court. You come to speak with your queen." Concern lit her brown eyes. "Are you all right?"

"Yes, of course." I pulled myself to my feet.

I shook my head slowly. How was she not dead?

Her brow knitted. "You look faint. Shall I call the doctor?"

Now that I was at the dais, I could see the other thrones. Next to Queen Marguerite sat a dark-skinned woman in a gold derma-suit, her braided black hair twisted high above her head.

Queen Corra.

On the other side sat a younger girl, closer to my age. She wore a lurid pink-and-orange-striped gown reminiscent of my stolen Ludist dress. Her black hair was short and spiky around her bejeweled crown.

Queen Stessa.

And beside her sat a small pale woman with the fairest hair I'd ever seen. A scowl on her face contrasted her pixie-like features. She glanced briefly at me, as though she detected my gaze. Her eyes were bright green.

Queen Iris.

My mouth popped open. I nearly fell to the floor again.

Alive. All of them.

Queen Marguerite looked alarmed. "Shall I get you a chair?"

Not possible. Not possible.

I had seen Queen Marguerite die. I'd seen them all die. I'd watched the life leach from their eyes as though I'd taken it with my own hands. And yet I was certain these women were not imposters. They were the rightful queens of the quadrants.

Which meant what? I'd been fooled? The comm chips were a lie? Another of Mackiel's games?

No. Varin had seen the memories as well. Which could only mean that . . . that what I'd seen wasn't a recording of their murders.

I'd seen the *plan* to murder the queens.

MY STEPS BACK to the palace processing room were buoyant, as though I wasn't quite touching the floor. Alive. The queens were alive.

"Is everything okay?" Varin asked, rushing toward me as soon as I entered the room. "You were gone for around half an hour. I thought something had happened. Did they believe you? They had to believe you, with all the queens dead and you knowing exactly how they died—but I couldn't see anything. I couldn't see how they reacted. What did they say? Will they grant us a reward? Who was upon the throne?"

It was the most I'd heard him say perhaps the whole time I'd been with him. His eyes were wide, his cheeks dark, his brows pinched together, and his slicked-back hair stuck up in odd directions as though he'd been running a hand through it. And while it had only felt like minutes since I spoke with Marguerite, the processing room's clock confirmed half an hour had passed. It must've been the shock, distorting my perception of time.

"They're alive," I whispered.

He leaned in, as though he'd misheard me. "The queens?"

I rolled my eyes. "Yes, the queens. Queen Marguerite was on the throne; she was the one I spoke to."

"How? You saw the chips twice, and *I* saw the rerecording." A muscle flicked in his neck. "I know what I saw." I didn't know why he was getting defensive.

"Comm chips record memories, right?"

"Yes, the recorder pulls images from your mind as you recall them."

"But what if the person had thought about the details of

the murders over and over, until it became a part of them, *like* a memory?"

He nodded slowly. "It's possible that could be recorded onto comm chips."

"Don't you see?" I fisted a handful of his Torian vest. "The chips weren't recordings of their deaths, but a *plan* for their deaths. None of it has happened!"

Something like relief washed over him; his shoulders straightened a little. "Did you tell Queen Marguerite about what we've seen?"

I shook my head. "Why would I? She's alive! They all are. I only told her about Mackiel and how he runs the black market."

"But—" Varin studied me as though he didn't understand my reaction, or perhaps he knew to expect the worst from me. "*Are* you going to tell her what we've seen? Tell anyone?"

"Tell them I've seen the queens murdered, including all the grisly details?" I shook my head again. "The palace would sooner lock me up for treason than believe me—I *stole* the evidence, remember?" I spread my hands wide. "Our proof was that the queens were dead, but they're not. And without the chips as evidence, I'm a criminal talking about slaying the queens."

"But that means the assassin has yet to carry out their plans." He pursed his lips.

A promise of a deal is not a deal done. While I wanted to be rid of Mackiel, his lessons had gotten me this far.

"We need more information before we can cut a deal with the palace," I said. "They'll hardly reward us for evidence of murders that haven't happened. And if we go back and tell them and then the assassin strikes, we'll be implicated. It's only our word that we're not involved. And what reason do they have to trust us?" I twisted my dipper bracelet around on my wrist. "I'm not saying anything until I'm certain I won't be arrested because of it."

"I'll tell them," he said. "I'm not a criminal."

Then I'd lose any bargaining power. "You can't."

"Why not? I'm not going to let the queens die." Now was not the time for Varin to grow a backbone.

I let out a frustrated breath and rubbed the back of my neck. "Please. Give me some time to find more information."

"You don't have to do this by yourself," he said quietly. "You're not alone in this anymore. We can trust the palace. We can trust the guards. If we tell them what we know, we can help find the assassin *with* them, and we can use our knowledge to prove we're on their side." He pressed his lips together. "You're not guilty until proven innocent, Keralie. We're here to help, remember?"

Except I was a criminal.

"I'll make sure nothing happens to you," he said. "I'll vouch for you."

My chest warmed. Even with Mackiel at my back, I'd never felt safe. I studied Varin's sincere expression, but it was clear this wasn't a game to him.

"It's the right thing to do," he added.

He seemed to believe there was some good left in me, that I wasn't beyond saving. But I'd always been willing to take what I wanted from others, regardless of the consequences, and with no guilt. And there was Varin, his expression unguarded, his voice hopeful. He was looking at me as though I was someone else. Someone I wished to be. Someone worthy of my parents' love.

"All right," I said. "We'll tell the authorities. And hope they don't throw me in jail."

He gave me a small smile. "They won't."

I'd have to work out what to do about HIDRA later.

"Come on," he said. We joined the queue leading toward the processing room exit.

I was mulling over what I was going to say to the guards about how I'd procured the comm chips in the first place when Varin said, "You're bleeding. What happened?" His eyes were narrowed on my skirt.

There was blood smeared across my stolen dress. "Shit." I rolled up the material. Fresh blood wept across my wounded knee. "I fell on it. It must've reopened the wound from yesterday." How had it been merely twenty-four hours since this all began? Since I met Varin?

"You need a dermasuit," he said, playing with the black material hidden under his shirtsleeve.

"Are you offering to strip for me?" I asked with a grin.

He groaned, although there was a hint of a laugh beneath his breath. "No. I was suggesting if you had a dermasuit, it would heal your wound."

"You're suggesting I impersonate an Eonist? Varin, you are full of surprises."

He didn't reply, his eyes focusing on something behind me.

"What's wrong?" I asked.

"We aren't moving."

I glanced at the crowd. It was crammed with people from different quadrants. Some were beaming, happy with their interactions with their queen. Others spoke heatedly with each other, hands waving. Eonists, as always, were the easiest to spot. Their monochromatic dermasuits and placid expressions contrasted with the lively conversations and colorful outfits. But he was right; we hadn't made any progress in the line.

"What's the holdup?" I asked the Torian man in front of me.

The man shrugged. "The guards are no longer letting people leave."

A weight pressed against my chest. I stumbled backward.

"Shit," I muttered.

A guard pressed a button by the exit. A metal wall lowered from the ceiling, blocking off the door with a clang.

"The palace apologizes for the delay." A guard had a comm line looped around his ear; he pressed a button, and his voice amplified throughout the room. It sounded like it came from everywhere and yet nowhere at once. "But we cannot allow anyone to leave the processing room at this time."

Everyone started speaking at once. Questions were shouted at the guards.

"Why?"

"What happened?"

"When can we leave?"

"I have plans this afternoon!"

"You can't do this!"

But the guards were Eonists; the questions didn't rattle them. They looked out to the crowd, defiant.

"I have to get out of here," I muttered.

"It's fine," Varin said. "They just need a bit more time."

"No, something is wrong." I searched the crowd. "Maybe Mackiel has found us."

"You said yourself that Mackiel is a wanted criminal. He wouldn't risk coming to the palace."

"But what if he's the assassin?"

The walls pressed in closer, and my head spun. The room was too small. Too packed. Not enough air.

There's a way in, but no way out.

Varin reached for me, his gloved hands lingering on my arm. "It's okay. He's not here."

"You don't know that."

He nodded. "Wait here. I'll find out what's going on."

He pushed his way through the crowd toward the guards. I tried to focus on my breathing and reminded myself of how this room was different from the cave. Much larger. Many more people. And I would not be left behind here, my father dying in my arms.

Varin's face had paled when he returned. "I overheard the guards talking. Queen Iris is dead."

"But I saw her in the throne room."

"That must've been why they've locked down the palace; they're hoping they've captured the assassin inside."

I glanced around the room, my breaths coming in quicker. "Mackiel." *He's here. I know it. I can feel him, his presence a pulse within the walls.*

"Take a deep breath. We're safe in here," Varin said.

Queen Iris wasn't safe in her own palace. "I'm not going to wait for him to find me caged in here."

"We don't have a choice. We can't act suspicious now. You were right. We need evidence."

I was too stressed to celebrate that I'd been right. "I'll go out there." I tilted my head to the entrance to the throne room. "I'll find the assassin before he strikes again. I'll stop him."

"If the guards find you roaming the palace halls, they'll think you're up to no good. You did work for Mackiel, after all."

"They won't find me," I said, moving through the crowd. Varin tried to follow, but he was too broad, too visible.

Now that I had a plan, my lungs began expanding. I was back in control. I could breathe again. I would search the palace hallways for Mackiel. Once I found him, I'd drag him to the guards and force the truth from his lips. Not only would I hand over the head of the black market, but a cold-blooded murderer. I would be rewarded with HIDRA. I would see my family again.

"Stay there," I mouthed back to Varin. "I'll be back soon."

I pressed myself against the wall and approached the nearest doorway. A guard was escorting an annoyed woman in from the adjoining corridor. I stuck my foot out as she stepped across the threshold. As the guards were distracted by helping her up from the ground, I slid out and back into the palace.

No one was better at locating and hitting a target than I was. And Mackiel was next on my list.

CHAPTER TWENTY-SEVEN

Keralie

The marble corridors were silent and still.

I crept along, my steps as quiet as the gold shadows cast from the dome above. No one would find me, not unless I wanted to be found. I'd been trained for this. I supposed I should thank Mackiel for that. I couldn't help feeling he wasn't far away, as if he was watching. He was always watching.

The hum from inside the processing room bled into the connecting corridors, and yet the rest of the building appeared abandoned. I moved deeper into the palace, the hairs standing on the back of my neck.

Voices pattered down the corridor like rain against glass. If I wanted to find out more about the assassin, I needed to move toward the sound of life.

The voices grew louder and more anguished. A wailing bounced off the marble walls, drawing me forward.

I broke into a run, keeping my tread light.

Rounding the corner, I stopped suddenly to hide from a gathering of people inside a walled garden.

The garden was green and lush, and bursting with flowers. Red dominated, ruby buds scattered throughout the emerald foliage. A piece of unbroken blue sky peeked in from above. The sight of freedom was magnetic.

The wailing women each wore large structured Archian dresses—the palace staff. Their faces were pressed into their hands, shoulders racked with sobs. Figures in dermasuits stood by, their hands on their destabilizers. Guards.

They leaned over to look at something . . .

And though a voice inside my head told me I already knew what they were looking at, I needed to see for myself. I took another step closer, holding my breath all the while.

As if the queens above had heard my thoughts, a guard shifted to the side, allowing me a clear view into the garden.

At first it looked as though she was merely sleeping, her body languidly splayed across a wooden settee, her face tilted toward the blue sky, white-blond hair spilling down the back of the chair in waves. But there was no ignoring the gash across her pale skin, dug so deep, white was visible.

Her spine.

I clenched my stomach and twisted back behind the wall. Before I could stop it, I doubled over and heaved. But there were no contents in my stomach. My last meal was yesterday.

What was worse than seeing her body slain like that was how the comm chips brought forth all the details I couldn't see with my eyes: the thin knife in the killer's hand, the feeling of the blade slicing through her skin like butter, the curtain of blood as it flowed down her neck and Queen Iris's hands as they reached for her bloodied throat, then for the murderer, splattering the greenery around her.

There weren't any red flowers. The red was blood.

I heaved again. And again.

My body convulsed a few more times until the shaking subsided.

With Queen Iris slain exactly as I'd seen it on the chips, it confirmed my suspicions. The comm chips were instructions on how to kill the queens, sent to the assassin from the person orchestrating the murders. Which meant that Mackiel had delivered the rerecorded chips to the assassin, or *he* was the assassin.

I had to tell Varin. The queens were being killed exactly as we saw it. The only question was who was next?

———

SINCE I'D LEFT the processing room, two guards had been posted on the outside door.

No one in, no one out.

Staying out of sight, I looked around for something—anything I could squeeze through and into the processing room. There had to be a way . . .

There. An air vent in the wall, low to the ground. There would have to be another leading to the processing room, allowing air into their makeshift prison hold.

I slid over the marble tiles, cursing as my split knee made contact with the floor. Varin was right, I needed it to heal, or I'd leave blood streaks wherever I went. I pulled my lock pick from my bracelet and began working the screws out one at a time. Once I'd removed the fourth screw, I lifted the grate and crawled through.

The ventilation shaft tunneled in two directions. I took the left.

The tumbling fear of small spaces was surprisingly comforting, momentarily blocking the image of blood splitting apart a pale neck and the red-stained hand that clutched the knife. If I kept moving, focused on something—even the pressure building in my chest—then I wouldn't break.

I hadn't seen that much blood since my father's accident. Guilt began clutching my sides with ravenous claws.

Focus, Keralie. Focus.

The voices in the processing room had hushed to a murmur as those held captive resigned themselves to the fact they'd be detained indefinitely. As much as I hoped the assassin had been caught in this room, I doubted it.

I shivered, feeling as though the assassin's shadow was attached to me, walking the palace halls and now shuffling through the ventilation shaft merely a whisper behind me.

The exit vent opened into the processing room at floor level. I couldn't see much from the ground, only pants, dress hems and shoes. Some people had sat down, indignant about their predicament. Others, mostly Eonists, refused to sit, standing still. Standing out.

Varin.

He wasn't far from the vent's exit, but too far for me to call out without attracting attention from the guards. I needed a way back into the room, and there was only one way to enter a room unnoticed.

Create a distraction.

This was going to require a more sophisticated trick than tripping someone. It needed to be something bigger. Louder.

The guards' amplifiers. *Yes.* That would work.

I quickly shuffled back along the ventilation shaft, ignoring the tightness in my chest, and unfurled out into the corridor. While it was still empty, life was returning to the palace; heels clicked and clacked against the floors, and voices carried from down the hallway.

Get in quick. Get out quicker.

Only two guards were posted at the entrance to the processing room. I grinned; they made this too easy.

I studied my bracelet before removing a ball-shaped charm. Mackiel had given it to me for my first job. "It will be like taking candy from a baby," he'd said. Which, of course, was exactly what he'd asked me to do. Something he'd already perfected at the age of six. "But you must take it without the baby realizing it's gone."

It had sounded easy enough at the time. A baby would have a short attention span. A baby wouldn't fight back. A baby couldn't have me arrested.

Only I hadn't realized that when a baby had something they wanted in their grasp—something they loved—it wasn't that easy to distract them. In the end, I had to buy another piece of candy to swap with the child. I hadn't known back then that Mackiel was always watching. I thought he hadn't discovered my trick. Years later, I realized he appreciated my resourcefulness.

He'd rewarded me that day with the small round charm. The first of many.

I threw the charm down the corridor to the right of me. It smashed into tiny fragments of glass.

"Bastard," I muttered under my breath. He'd told me the charm was a precious stone.

The guards immediately moved into action; one gestured to the other to follow the noise. As soon as he left, I was behind the other guard, my hand in his pocket, removing the amplifier.

The other guard called back, "It's just a piece of glass, must've fallen from a chandelier."

Before he had the chance to return to his posting, I was back inside the vent, the amplifier in hand.

CHAPTER TWENTY-EIGHT

Keralie

No one had moved inside the processing room, but someone had passed out cylinders of water, Eonist food bars and blankets. They weren't leaving this room anytime soon.

The guards continued to watch the crowd, their faces blank. I didn't know when the assassin would strike next. I had to act. *Now.*

I held the device to my mouth.

"Queen Iris is dead," I said in a low, authoritative tone. "All of you are to remain in the processing room until we capture the assassin." I paused to let that sink in. "We believe they may be in this room. We will not let them get away." I paused again, this time for dramatic effect. "Do not panic."

That was enough. Anyone who was sitting flew to their feet, faces flushing, mouths popping open in shock. Others bustled toward the guards, seeking answers. Everyone was shouting or screaming or fainting.

People pushed in on the guards, their voices and fists raised in anger and outrage.

"Is it true?" one person asked.

"Queen Iris dead. How?" another cried.

"An assassin? In this room? Let us out!"

"I don't want to die!"

"Stay calm." The guards used their own amplifiers and pushed back against the horde with their batons. Some raised destabilizers in warning. "Stay back!" But they wouldn't listen. The crowd was an ember within a box of matches and there was no undoing the flame.

The perfect distraction.

I scrambled out of the vent.

"Queen Iris was murdered the way we saw it." I slid in beside Varin, my voice low in his ear. "*Exactly* the same way."

His eyes shot to mine. "That was you?" His shoulders lowered, and he appeared relieved to see me.

I held up the amplifier. "People deserve to know the truth."

He pressed his full lips together as though he didn't quite believe my reasoning.

I scanned the embittered and enraged crowd. I almost felt bad for creating such chaos. "What have I missed?"

"They've been releasing people one by one." Varin nodded to the heavily guarded exit on the right side of the room.

I raised my eyebrows. "They're interrogating them, not releasing them. That's why we're here. The guards think they've captured the assassin."

"But you don't," he said without question.

"No. He's too smart for that."

"You really think the assassin is Mackiel, don't you? What about his hands?"

I swallowed roughly. "Then his henchmen are doing the dirty work, as usual. He's at the center of this, I know it." He'd do anything to save the Jetée and his father's business. Was killing the other queens just a diversion? So no one would suspect a Torian?

Varin sighed and ran a hand through his hair. "What are you planning now?"

"Who says I'm planning anything?" I broke a piece off his food bar and took a pull of water from his cylinder. My stomach gurgled in response, annoyed I hadn't eaten in over a day. I took a longer pull. Varin watched my lips cover the spout.

"I know that look on your face," he said.

I swallowed. "Okay, you're right. I'm going back out there to find our murdering friend."

"You're going to leave me behind again?"

I patted him on the shoulder. "You find out all you can from here. The palace guards are *your* people. Surely you can make something of that?"

"Are you giving me a choice?"

What needed to be done required a thief, not a messenger. "You use your skills. I'll use mine."

Without waiting for his reply, I pushed back into the crowd.

———

QUIET HAD CREPT upon the palace, as darkness crept upon the short winter's day. The openings to the dome overhead darkened to a rich amber; the queens would soon retire to their chambers. If the henchmen were behind these killings, then I needed a better disguise. And while I was good at skulking around undetected, it would be better if I weren't wearing a dress stained with blood from my split knee. In case someone found me.

Varin was right; I needed a dermasuit. And I knew of a place where I'd definitely find one. Queen Corra's rooms.

After an hour of slinking through the hallways, I noticed a pattern; the building was split in four, like Quadara itself. As I continued toward the east, the furniture became sparse—more practical and less frivolous and plush. Fewer chandeliers dangled from the gilded ceiling; they were replaced by cords of blue lights inset into the walls. It was like walking through a moonlit cavern. They were Eonist lights—drawing power from fibers embedded into the surface of the golden dome that absorbed the sun's rays.

As I rounded the corner, I saw two guards standing on either side of an entranceway. It was the first door I'd encountered with some kind of security. It had to be the entrance to Queen Corra's rooms. I slipped into the adjacent hallway and found what I was looking for. A vent. I unclasped my lock pick from my bracelet and made quick work of the screws.

Once the vent was open, I slipped into the room, silent as a shadow.

The narrow entrance opened onto what appeared to be the living quarters, although the furniture hardly looked comfortable. Like Varin's apartment, everything was streamlined: polished floors, sleek metal tables and basic white chairs. Even the Eonist queen didn't live in luxury—I supposed it would be contradictory to a quadrant determined to achieve and retain equality.

Unless you had a condition like Varin's.

My chest ached at the thought of him being killed at thirty as though he were some wounded animal. It wasn't right. Varin was a good person, and he had hardly begun to live his life. Surely there was a way we could both use HIDRA?

I slipped my fingers underneath a cupboard door when I heard a thump. I spun, crouching to the ground, prepared to be face-to-face with the ruthless assassin, a silver knife glinting in their bloody hands. But nothing moved. No flickering of shadows in the darkness. I took in a small, quiet breath and waited.

Nothing.

I searched the adjoining room for the source of the noise, my fists clenched. But the room was empty. The noise must've come from the guards outside.

There was a small panel I recognized beside the bed. I swiped my hand across it. A clothes rack slid out, four dermasuits of various shades of gold hanging from the metal bar. Touching the fabric between my fingers, a shudder ran down my back. Could I wear it, knowing the material contained conscious microorganisms?

Suck it up, Keralie. This is for HIDRA. And the queens. Do the right thing.

Quickly, I shed my Torian clothes, wincing as my starched skirt swept across my split knee. The wound had stopped bleeding, but it was still raw and angry that I hadn't given it the required rest to repair. The dermasuit would not only provide a good disguise but also prevent the wound from reopening. I shoved my Torian dress into the incinerator by Queen Corra's desk, then pulled a muted gold dermasuit over my head.

A strange feeling settled over my skin as it shrunk to fit me. A cool, soothing effect like the flutter of snowflakes on bare skin. Beads of perspiration, which made my old dress cling to my back, were absorbed instantly, and the ache of my knee immediately began to subside. I stretched my arms and legs, feeling my muscles flare with energy. I clipped on the gloves to complete the look. It was like slipping on a different skin.

Now I could walk around the palace without leaving a trail of my blood behind, for who knew who might follow it.

CHAPTER TWENTY-NINE

Keralie

I continued to scour the palace for the assassin. Or assassins. The more I thought about it, the more it made sense that Mackiel's henchmen were behind this. And I wouldn't have been surprised if Mackiel allowed them to take the fall for the murders, washing his hands clean of them.

After an hour or so, I'd still uncovered no sign of the henchmen. Perhaps they were in hiding with the guards now on alert. I decided to return to Varin to see if he'd discovered anything.

The storm I'd created in the processing room had escalated, allowing me to easily exit the vent. People were throwing the food and water they'd been given at the guards. The noise was deafening, and the room stank of sweat and piss. Were they not letting people out even to relieve themselves? It wouldn't be long before this room broke into a full-on riot.

Would they open the doors then? To keep the peace?

Varin was standing at the front of the room with the palace

guards. He'd removed his Torian disguise to reveal his dermasuit. He couldn't help but help.

I pushed my way to the front. "Hey," I whispered to him, standing close.

Varin startled, his eyes flashing over my body. "Keralie?" He was looking at me in a way he'd never looked at me before.

"What?" I asked, before remembering I was dressed in Queen Corra's dermasuit. Was he looking at me like that because I now looked like an Eonist—like him? His eyes roamed over my body. His response should've sent a flush of heat to my face, and yet I stayed cool, thanks to my new microorganism friends.

He cleared his throat and said, "You're back."

I ensured my voice sounded even when I replied, "What's happening here? What have I missed?"

"The guards refuse to give any further information." His face was cautious. "It seems your announcement was enough to start a war."

"Oops," I replied with a sheepish grin. "I was only aiming for a distraction. Trust me to overachieve."

"If the guards don't tell them something soon, I don't know what might happen. It's been hours since the guards were informed of any updates."

I glanced to the processing room clock; it was nearing nighttime.

"And when did they hire you as a palace guard?" I nodded to the guards who braced their destabilizers in the air, prepared to take down the next person who raised a fist.

"They didn't. They needed help in controlling the crowd. And I'm—"

"Eonist," I filled in.

"I was going to say strong."

I bit my lip, halting my retort. He didn't have to make it this easy.

"Did you uncover anything about the assassin?"

"Not yet. However, I did manage to acquire this lovely ensemble from Queen Corra." I tilted my hip out and waved my hands. "It's made it easier to move around the palace."

"You stole from the queen?" he hissed.

"You suggested it."

"I did not!"

"You said I needed a dermasuit."

"Keralie." My name was a sigh on his lips.

I grinned. "Don't worry, I won't tell anyone about Varin, the criminal mastermind."

Varin ignored me and jerked his chin over to the palace guards who were wrestling back the front line of protesters. "They allowed me to look at the list of everyone who entered the palace before Queen Iris was murdered."

"Mackiel?" I guessed.

"No." Why was a part of me disappointed?

"Who else could it be?"

He narrowed his eyes. "I don't know. But we won't find any answers in here."

"We?" I asked. "Nuh-uh. You stay here."

He stepped closer. "I'm not letting you back out there with an assassin on the loose."

"*Let* me?" I crossed my arms. "No one *lets* me do anything. I do what I want, when I want."

"Keralie. I'm worried about you." I couldn't deny the zing

that shivered up my spine when he said my name paired with that intense expression on his face. "And I want to help. This is as much my quest as it is yours."

"*Varin,*" I said, putting the same resolution into my voice. "You are too big and too broad to fit in that ventilation shaft. You will get us noticed, *and* arrested."

"I'm a messenger," he said. "It's my job to move quickly and quietly. And I can get us out of here without having to squeeze into that shaft."

"Sure." I snorted. "What's your genius plan, then?"

"Ask to be released."

"You're serious?" I studied his face. "Who am I kidding? You're always serious."

He held up a gloved hand. "Keep quiet, all right?"

"Why?"

"Because while you might look Eonist, *that*"—he pointed to my mouth—"is far from it."

I opened my mouth to argue but shrugged. He was right.

"Come with me," he said. I gestured I'd keep my mouth shut. This one time.

Varin approached a palace guard, who was speaking into a comm line in low tones. I wished I could hear the voice at the other end. Were they any closer to capturing the assassin? And if they did, what would that mean for me? For us?

"Christon," Varin said to the guard. "This is my colleague, Keralie." Christon looked over to me; I expected his expression to shift, but he gave me a stiff nod. "She has experience in dealing with criminals."

I covered my laugh with a cough. Varin shot me a warning

glance before continuing, "We think we can help in the investigation. But we'll need further access to the palace."

Christon studied me with his brown eyes—not pale like Varin's—and I held my breath. *Be Eonist, Keralie. Emotionless. Numb.*

"How can a messenger help?" Although Christon's tone was neutral, it was a cruel thing to say.

"Christon and I grew up together," Varin said, as though that would explain Christon's rudeness.

"Actually, Varin is no longer a messenger," I said. So much for staying quiet. I wouldn't allow Varin to be belittled. "He's leading the investigation in taking down Toria's notorious criminal district. The Jetée, you've heard of it?"

Christon shot a confused look to Varin. "But he was trained as a messenger."

"True. But his skills extend beyond delivering comm cases or merely standing guard like a statue." *Careful, Keralie; don't get personal.* "This was recognized by his boss, and he was given a rare chance for promotion. He works for Queen Marguerite now."

Varin shifted beside me, but I wouldn't let him ruin this with the truth.

"Varin leads the team," I said. "I follow." I tried not to laugh.

Christon asked Varin, "Is this true?"

Varin could let my story fall apart; he could continue to be Eonist and tell the truth. Or he could want more. For himself.

"It is," Varin said, squaring his shoulders.

I wanted to clap Varin on the back and throw my arms around him. Instead, I gave Varin a simple nod.

"All right," Christon said, clearly surprised. "I suppose the inspector could use the help."

"The inspector?" Varin asked.

"Inspector Garvin," Christon clarified.

"Of course," Varin said, although something flittered behind his stoic expression. "We'll report anything we uncover."

Christon escorted us to the exit of the processing room and nodded to the guard at the door to release us. Once we were alone in the palace corridors, I whirled on Varin.

"You did it!"

"*We* did it," he said. He seemed excited by the deception, although I doubted he'd admit that.

"What was that about the inspector?"

"I checked the list of everyone who entered the palace before Queen Iris died." He scratched his jaw, which was sporting a nice smattering of dark stubble. "Inspector Garvin was not on that list."

"Oh."

"Which means he was already in the palace before Queen Iris was murdered."

"Why would an inspector be in the palace *before* any murders?"

He looked down the corridor. "I don't know."

"Could he be involved?"

His eyes snapped back to mine. "I've heard of Inspector Garvin. He's . . ." He rubbed the back of his neck. "Different."

I could fill in the gaps. "*Tweaked.*"

"Yes, but that doesn't mean he's evil. It doesn't mean he's a killer." Steel lined his words.

I held up my palms. "You said evil, not me. But who would be controlling the inspector? If he is the killer?"

"Someone who has something to gain from having all queens dead."

We weren't any closer to knowing who that was.

"Come," he said after a moment. "Let's find the inspector. He's the only lead we have."

"What if we run into more guards?"

"We'll tell them what you told Christon."

"You agree to telling more lies?" I asked.

He stared at me for a long moment. "Perhaps you're rubbing off on me."

I pressed my body against him. Sadly, our dermasuits prevented any exchange of warmth. "If that's what you want, you need only ask."

"Stop it, Keralie." But he smiled, or at least, I thought it was a smile. It was hard to tell, as I'd never seen him do it before. Then a dimple appeared on each side of his lips and his white teeth flashed. For a moment, I forgot where I was and what I was doing. There was only Varin, and that smile.

CHAPTER THIRTY

Keralie

Varin and I stole through the corridors, avoiding the staff as the palace adjusted to their new blood-soaked reality. We explored every shadowed hallway and every dark corner. I shimmied through multiple vents, and Varin eavesdropped on conversations between guards. We searched and listened and waited for the inspector to make himself known. We checked every room, opened every door that was unlocked and every door that wasn't. And yet the inspector eluded us.

I was relocking one of the doors I'd picked earlier when two guards rounded the corridor. Their hands swiftly moved to unhook their destabilizers.

"What are you doing?" one guard asked, his gaze on the lock pick in my hand.

"I was—" I began before Varin interrupted.

"We're checking the doors," he said with such steadiness, even I would've believed him. "We're trying to work out how an assassin could've moved between many locked doors to get to Queen Iris's garden without anyone noticing."

"Exactly," I said, pointing at them with my lock pick. "We're testing the doors."

Varin shot me a look I was sure meant *shut up*.

"And who are you?" the guard asked.

I kept my mouth closed this time.

"We're helping Christon," Varin said. "You can check if you need to."

The second guard nodded and did just that, his hand at his comm line. I tried not to grin when Christon confirmed our story.

"What have you uncovered, then?" the guard asked, latching his destabilizer back onto his belt, deciding we no longer posed a threat.

"Any common criminal could have unlocked these doors," Varin replied. *Common?* I forced myself not to glower at him. "But moving about the palace unseen is the trickier part." He gestured to the two guards in front of us. "The security is unprecedented." It was true, we'd come across numerous guards. Some had merely nodded at us, our dermasuits the perfect guise; others asked if we were palace guards and what we were doing. Varin dropped Christon's name anytime we needed to douse suspicion.

"What's next?" the other guard asked.

Varin glanced at me before replying, "We're looking for the inspector. We need more details on how Queen Iris was killed."

I nodded solemnly, although more details were the last thing we needed. We had all the details on the event but none on the executor. Could it be this tweaked inspector we kept hearing about but had yet to see?

"Inspector Garvin is set up in the palace infirmary." The guard nodded down the corridor. "It's on the other side of the palace. We'll escort you there."

I shook my head slightly, hoping Varin got the hint. Our paper-thin lies were unlikely to fool an inspector.

"That's all right," he replied. "I'm familiar with the location. We'll finish up here, then head to the infirmary."

I jiggled the doorknob as though I was finishing something.

"Very well," the guard said. "Good luck to you both."

Once they'd disappeared around the corridor, I said, "You're getting good at this."

He grimaced. "I don't like the feeling of lying."

I cocked my head to the side. *"Feeling?"*

"You know what I mean."

"It gets easier. Soon you won't be able to tell the truth from lies."

A small crease formed on his smooth forehead. "You say that like it's a good thing."

I grinned, although my chest burned as if I'd swallowed something bitter. I didn't want to twist Varin into anything resembling me.

We quickly headed toward the other side of the palace in search of the inspector. I froze when we rounded a corner to find a large group of people gathered in a wide corridor.

I wanted to run. Hide. There were too many people. Too many eyes. Someone was bound to realize we weren't meant to be here. Perhaps the assassin.

The staff were sorrowful, their hands clutched together, their faces etched with grief.

"What are they doing here?" I whispered to Varin.

"I'm not sure."

The crowd shifted to either side of the corridor and faced inward. Facing us. I tried to move into an unlocked room, but people blocked the doorways.

They knew. Christon had discovered our lies. What was the punishment for deceiving guards and sneaking around the palace?

"We have to get out of here," I said, desperately searching for a way out.

"Calm down." Varin's hand was at my elbow. "They're not looking at us."

He was right. Their gaze was upon something moving down the corridor. Something inside a glass box.

A coffin.

"Queen Iris," Varin murmured.

Queens above. I didn't want to see her ruined body again.

The coffin was covered in melting candles and carried by her staff. And they were headed right toward us.

"We have to get out of here," I said again.

"It's the death procession." He shook his head. "It would be suspicious to leave. And disrespectful."

The last time I'd been to a memorial was for Mackiel's parents. He'd held my hand tightly during the entire service. How had everything changed in three years?

I'd only attended one other memorial. My grandfather's when I was six. I didn't remember much, except how everyone spoke of my grandfather as though he were still alive. When we got home from the service, I asked my parents when we would see him again. My father broke down. I'd never seen him in that much pain. Until the day I shattered his boat, his business and his life.

"Come on," Varin said, pulling me to the side with the rest of the palace staff. "Stand still and be quiet."

"I can't promise anything." I attempted levity, but the words felt sticky in my mouth. I didn't want to see Queen Iris again. I didn't want to be reminded of how I'd failed her.

But it was too late.

Her face was peaceful in death, more peaceful than the scowl I'd seen hours earlier in court. While I couldn't see the gash across her neck, I remembered it vividly. From both the comm chips and seeing her in the garden.

I hated that the last, lingering memory I would have of her would be her grisly murder. Was that all we were reduced to in death? A broken body? What about everything that came before? Mere memories that would one day fade altogether.

And though I tried not to, I thought of my father. Would I fail him again? Without HIDRA, he would pass to the quadrant without borders before summer warmed Toria's coast. He'd be lost to me. I doubted my mother would want anything to do with me once he was dead.

In a few years, what would I remember of him? Would I forget the sound of his voice? Would I forget him calling me a landlubber, someone unfamiliar with the ways of the ocean, while playfully tousling my hair? Would those bloody memories inside that horrid cave be all that remained of him?

My hands started to shake.

"It's all right," Varin whispered. He must've thought I was thinking of poor Queen Iris, but as always, I was thinking of myself.

Something touched my fingers, and I started. But it was Varin. He squeezed my hand in his.

But the scene was too close to Mackiel's parents' memorial, with Varin now taking the role of the consoler. I pulled away. I wasn't ready to trust Varin.

After Mackiel's betrayal, I wasn't sure I could trust anyone.

WE KNEW WE were heading in the direction of the infirmary when the murmur of voices drew us forward. A gathering of guards and staff blocked the entrance to a room. We glimpsed someone moving through the doorway dressed in a gray dermasuit.

"The inspector," Varin whispered.

"How do you know?" I whispered back.

"Gray dermasuits are only worn by inspectors."

I pulled Varin to the side. "We can't go in there now."

"Why not?"

"There are too many people. We need to watch the inspector without him knowing we're watching. Only then will he drop any pretense."

"*You never steal from someone without knowing more about the situation and person.*" He recited my earlier words back at me.

I nodded. "We need to wait till he's alone."

"We can't stand here till then. It's too suspicious."

He was right. We'd been lucky up to this point, but any more skulking around the palace, and someone was bound to realize we weren't doing anything official.

I examined our surroundings. I could fit in the vent and continue to move around the palace unseen, but Varin was too broad.

"Come on," I said, pulling him down the corridor.

I began twisting the doorknobs of all the doors on either side of the hallway.

"What are you doing?" he asked.

"Only locked doors hide something important. I'm looking for—" A door swung in easily. "Aha!"

Varin stuck his head inside the dim doorway. "A utility room?"

Luckily, the room was quite large; my chest didn't compress at the sight of it.

"Get in." I pushed him through the opening. "We'll have to wait for the infirmary to clear out."

The utility room was filled with mops and various cleaning products. Bleach pricked at my nose and eyes. I squatted, pulling my knees to my chest. There was no pinch—my knee had been almost completely healed by the dermasuit. I rested my head on a shelf.

Varin closed the door and squatted beside me. "You're exhausted," he remarked. "You should rest."

I shook my head. Fatigue was beginning to feel like a heavy blanket across my shoulders, but I needed to stay awake. I needed to uncover the assassin, or assassins, and earn access to HIDRA. I needed to save the queens.

"What if we can't uncover anything about the assassin?" I asked, studying his genetically perfect face in the low light. "What if you can't get access to HIDRA?" What if this was all for nothing, and we both left the palace empty-handed? And that wasn't even the worst outcome.

We could be uncovered as liars, posing as Queen Marguerite's guards. Or Mackiel and his henchmen could catch us, adding two more deaths to the body count. Or perhaps the inspector would find us and pull us apart with his Eonist implements.

"We'll find evidence on the assassin, Keralie," Varin said, his voice unwavering. "I'm sure of it."

"Because you hope so?" I waved my hands about. "That means nothing. We have nothing!"

"I know." He studied his feet.

Queens above. Why did I always have to be so rude?

"Hey." I linked his arm with mine—he didn't flinch. "I didn't mean that."

"Yes, you did." He lifted his face to mine. "You mean everything you say."

I mulled that over for a moment, considering my past jibes. Did I really mean them? A part of me did—the part that wanted to push Varin away to ensure he couldn't hurt me. Or so I couldn't hurt him. I couldn't hurt Varin like I'd hurt my father, or Mackiel. I didn't want to lose him too.

I needed to control my feelings around him, be more Eonist. But the more I looked into his pale eyes, the more that control slipped away.

"I'm sorry I'm such a horrid person," I said with a half smile. I spun my dipper bracelet around, the silver lockets tinkling together.

His brow furrowed. "You're not horrid, Keralie. You're . . ." A million words flashed through my mind as he hesitated. None of them were good. "Protective."

That wasn't one of them.

"Protective?" I repeated.

"Of yourself." His guarded eyes darted away. I didn't release his arm, as I normally would have. He glanced back after a moment. "I understand. You've been in Mackiel's employ for seven years, but you've really been alone that entire time. He didn't care about you. And you think you're to blame for this terrible accident with your father, but—"

"I *am* to blame."

"You may not be horrid," he said, "but you sure like the sound of your own voice."

I fluttered a gloved hand at him. "Go on, then. The floor's yours."

"This isn't a joke." He twisted to face me. "You need to forgive yourself. We all make mistakes. We must move on."

"No," I said. "Not until I fix it." Fix everything.

"How can you fix it?"

I bit the inside of my cheek. Now was the time to tell him how I wanted HIDRA for my father.

"I don't know," I said instead. "But I need to make things better. I need to right my wrongs. Start a new life." One far from Mackiel and the girl I used to be.

He took my hand, and my breath, with one gentle grasp. This time I didn't pull away. I trembled beneath his touch, shocked by it—it was different from the way Mackiel touched me. *He* was different. Varin wasn't using me, he wasn't playing a game, twisting me into something else. And even though there was no warmth, due to our suits, it meant more than anything I'd experienced in the last seven years.

The back of my eyes prickled. I swallowed down tears.

"You will, Keralie," he said softly.

I took a shuddering breath. "And you?" I asked. "What will you do if we fail?"

He tilted his head back and looked upward. "I'll have to make the most of the time I have left."

No matter what happened, I would make sure Varin wouldn't spend that time alone.

CHAPTER THIRTY-ONE

Keralie

I awoke with my head resting on Varin's shoulder, his arm around my waist. I didn't want to move, unless it was to shift closer, seeking his touch. For the first time in a long time, I was content.

Until I remembered where I was.

Something had been knocked over while I'd slept fitfully. I'd been unable to escape the palace, even in my dreams. The liquid had spilled onto my clothes and into my hair. The room now smelled of perfume, or chemicals, or both.

"Varin," I said, shaking his shoulder. "Wake up."

His lids flickered before he opened them. His pupils dilated and contracted. My heart rattled in my chest as he focused on me.

"What happened?" he asked.

I pulled my arm from around him. "We fell asleep."

He glanced around the room; the glass ceiling revealed the palace dome above. It was still light out. "We needed to rest," he said.

I let out a sigh. I didn't disagree, but it felt careless and callous to fall asleep while a killer planned to knock off the queens one by one.

Varin stretched, his muscles shifting against mine. "What should we do now?"

"We should—" My reply was cut short by a sound—a melodic whistling—something that contrasted with the gloom that hung heavy in the palace.

I cracked the door ajar, peeking through the opening as footsteps neared. The whistling grew louder, almost piercing, as a figure in gray walked past.

"The inspector," Varin mouthed.

We slipped out of the room, maintaining a safe distance as we followed the inspector back to the infirmary. The corridor was deathly quiet. The inspector pressed his palm to the door, his fingers extended like spider legs. So *that* was his tweaking.

The inspector stepped inside, leaving the door open behind him.

I nodded to Varin and whispered, "Follow me and stay low."

We slunk around the corner and into the adjoining room, crouching behind a cabinet, our dermasuits giving nothing of our movements away. I should've stolen a dermasuit years ago.

The inspector continued whistling as he pulled out sharp implements, each one deadlier than the next, and placed them on the table. Next to the table was a gurney draped in a white sheet; Queen Iris lay upon it, her wound exposed to the chill and medical tang of the room.

It had been bad enough seeing Queen Iris's blood coat the garden, but seeing her lifeless body displayed like some discarded thing made my stomach clench. Her blood appeared to have been drained: her lips were white, her skin a light blue, and the bloody gash now a thick flap of skin—as if she wore a mask and would sit up at any moment to tear off her face.

I pressed my fist to my mouth and forced myself not to flee.

The inspector stopped whistling and attached a comm line around his ear and pointed the microphone toward his mouth.

"A sharp blade killed Queen Iris," he said. I startled, thinking he was speaking to us, but he continued without pause. I shuddered as he pulled the skin at Queen Iris's throat apart with his gloved hands. "A very sharp blade." Now I understood his tweaking. His fingers were perfectly designed for this job.

I pressed my hand to my mouth harder, wanting to return to the processing room. The smell of piss and body odor sounded pretty good right now compared to this alien place. Varin squeezed my shoulder, although his face was also pale. He nodded once. We needed to find out more about this mysterious inspector and why he'd been here before Queen Iris was murdered.

"I doubt it was any of the other queens," the inspector said. "I've looked into their background, and none have any history of violence or training in weaponry. The only curiosity is Queen Corra." But the comm chips showed that Queen Corra was on the assassin's list. She couldn't be involved.

"I can find no information about her adoptive parents, merely a name. This could mean she has something to hide—perhaps she was raised by a family who opposes Queenly Law?" He pulled out a silver cutting saw. "And she is unemotional, and some would argue that's what is required to be a successful killer."

It was strange to hear an Eonist speak of his queen with a matching unemotional tone. I glanced at Varin, but his eyes were locked on the odd man before us.

"But," he continued, "it has been my experience that one kills for passion, for attainment, and what would Queen Corra have to attain by killing her sister queen?" He gestured to the body on the table as though he had an audience. "And yet the meticulousness of this kill does not display the crimes of passion I've seen when investigating other murders. This was a professional kill."

What did that mean?

He pressed a panel on the wall and another gurney rolled out. He pulled back a sheet and a strange aroma filled the room. "The second body also reveals no prints, although it's clear force was involved. Her drowning was no accident."

Queen Stessa dead? No! And when? Varin's wide eyes mirrored mine. We'd spent nearly all day searching for the assassin, and yet he hadn't broken his stride, murdering the queens as planned.

The inspector used his fingers to pull something from Queen Stessa's dress. "A hair," he remarked. "The color doesn't appear to belong to the queen; it could belong to our killer. I'll run further tests." He placed the implements on the table.

With that, he left the room, passing right by our hiding place. We waited a few moments before standing.

I looked at Queen Stessa's blue-tinged body. "When did this happen?"

Varin stood, shaking his head. "She must've been killed while we were sleeping."

"We're failing, Varin."

He brushed my hand with his, before moving into the room to study the inspector's implements. "I don't believe the inspector's involved."

"He's no closer to the truth than we are."

"No. It appears only the assassin knows the truth. And they—" He paused, his attention on the machines and implements hanging on the wall.

"What is it?" Dare I hope he'd found HIDRA? What if it was only one dose? Was I willing to condemn Varin for my father's health? Would I snatch it from his hands and run from this room? How would I leave the palace?

How would I live with myself?

He picked up a small silver tube, a sharp tip rising from the middle. "Nothing important," he said, but his voice was almost a whisper.

I scurried over to him to see what had him so transfixed. "Varin?"

"It's a gene test. The test that determines your death date." He stared at it for a long moment, his eyes closing briefly. He covered it with his hands, as though he wished it would disappear. How could something that small and insignificant cause such pain? "It determines everything." When he opened his eyes, they were unfocused. "I wish I could be something other than a messenger. I wish it were as easy as being good at my job, like you said to Christon."

"I'm sorry, Varin." I stepped closer to him. "The test must be here for when the queens give birth."

"What if we can't stop the assassin?" he asked, staring at his clenched hand. "What if we find nothing to bargain with?"

"But before you said—"

"What if I'm wrong?" That despair had returned to his features. I wanted to erase it from his face, from his life. But I didn't know how.

My hand hovered near his shoulder. "Varin, what's your—"

"We should split up," he said, interrupting me.

"What?"

He spun around, still holding the gene test, his face hard. "I'll go after the inspector, see what else I can uncover. You should go warn Queen Corra and Queen Marguerite."

"Now you want to split up? What happened to being in this together? To having each other's back?"

"We're running out of time." Clearly he wasn't only referring to the remaining queens. He placed the gene test back where he'd found it. "We don't know which queen is next. We need to cover more ground. You were right the first time." His expression softened.

"Can I get that recorded on a comm chip?"

He grinned. "Go, Keralie. I'll find you later."

"We'll get through this." I wasn't only referring to finding the assassin. "We'll make things right. There will be a way."

His grin drooped a little. "Thank you."

I gave his arm a quick squeeze before bolting from the room.

I would stop this.

PART FOUR

CHAPTER THIRTY-TWO

There was to be no further communication until the deed was done. Until they were dead.

All of them.

Still, that didn't stop her from pacing the room, wishing and wanting and waiting to hear something—anything. She longed to be in the palace when it happened. As though she could *see* the transference of power—to her.

She tuned the old house radio to the latest Queenly Report, preparing for the announcement. *All queens dead.*

Then they would come for her. Or that was the plan. But only if her mother caved and gave away her location. She would, though, wouldn't she? If she were pushed to the edge. Everyone caved at that critical moment, the moment before the end.

She couldn't wait. She'd had enough of playing peasant. Enough hiding. Enough pretending. Enough scheming. Enough dreaming. Soon she would be called forth to stake her claim to the

Torian throne. She would not only replace her mother, Marguerite, but all the queens.

Queen of Quadara.

She rather liked the sound of that.

SEVENTEEN-YEAR-OLD AREBELLA CARLONA had discovered she was next in line for the Torian throne when she was ten. To most children, this would've brought excitement. Dreams of feasts, flowing dresses, gleaming jewels and handsome suitors. But Arebella had learned another, if not more important, detail. She would never inherit the throne.

The cruelest twist of fate, for such a gift to be dangled in front of her but snatched away before she could reach it. And all because of her birth mother, Queen Marguerite.

Arebella had always known she was adopted, but had been told her mother had passed to the quadrant without borders in childbirth. She'd been raised by a teacher who had longed for children but never found the right time or man. Arebella didn't have anything in common with her older adoptive mother, but she appreciated the freedom granted to her, and that her mother never asked too many questions. When her mother died from heart failure when Arebella was fourteen, she wore a black veil for a month—the standard amount of time in Toria to pay respect to the dead. She rarely thought about her now. She doubted her mother even knew the truth of her heritage.

Luckily, there was a boy who did. A cunning and opportunistic young man.

When Arebella had learned the truth from this boy, she lamented the power that should've been hers. While she pouted and cried, he began scheming. He was good at that. In time, he helped Arebella realize her fate was in her own hands. She could go after the throne, if she desired it.

And she did. She wanted Toria as her own.

Arebella was obsessed with control. While she couldn't often regulate her own thoughts, she could regulate Toria. She wanted to make the rules. Change the laws. And she wanted the throne that was her birthright. She wouldn't allow her birth mother, who'd sent her away, to dictate her life.

But her plan didn't begin with the idea of assassinating the queens. Even a ten-year-old Arebella wasn't as diabolical as that. Instead, she used her curiosity, like any good Torian, to gather information. She sent out the boy to ask questions of anyone who could provide the right answers. It was imperative no one knew she was the source of the questions. Then no one would see her coming.

All Arebella had to do was be in the center of change. The center of the storm.

She was a bright girl. *Too* bright, if you asked her tutor. She had an unquenchable thirst for knowledge, more than any Torian child. Once Arebella started asking questions, and received answers, she wouldn't stop. *Know everything, and you shall know all*—a popular saying in Toria. And Arebella wanted to know all.

How do the queens inherit the throne?

How much control do the queens have over their quadrant?

What can the queens change?

What can't they change?

What influence do the queens have over another queen's quadrant?

She didn't know how to stop asking. A question filled her head as soon as the last one exited.

For four years, she merely acquired information. When her adoptive mother died and she inherited what little money the old woman had saved, she began her ascension to the throne. She knew her presence alone would not inspire a revolution. Instead, she would need to make powerful allies. The boy helped connect her with others who wanted to bring down the Torian queen. The proprietors of the Jetée.

Arebella attended each monthly meeting, their angry words adding fuel to an ember flickering inside her. She was outraged by the squalor they lived in when the queens resided in such grandeur. When Queen Marguerite announced on the Queenly Reports that she planned to demolish the Jetée, Arebella knew she had to intervene. These were Torians, after all—*her* people. People *she* should be ruling.

Soon Arebella's voice was the loudest in the revolt.

Arebella learned that Queenly Law dictated what could and couldn't be shared between the quadrants, and those who lived and worked on the Jetée wanted to share everything. They wanted Eonist technology; they wanted the freshest Archian crops and the latest Ludist fashions and toys. But the queens would not allow that.

During these monthly meetings at the Jetée, Arebella's focus widened past Toria's borders and to the other quadrants. She realized it would not be enough to rule one quadrant.

But the information she'd gathered from the Jetée was limited, and biased. Arebella used what remained of her inheritance to hire a former palace handmaiden as a tutor. The woman didn't know of Arebella's true heritage. No one else did.

After a few lessons, Arebella asked the one question she desired the answer to the most: "Has there ever been only one queen of Quadara?" She had grown tired of hearing about the Quadrant Wars of long ago.

Her tutor stopped and looked at her. "No, Arebella. We've only had, and only will have, four rulers. One for each quadrant. In the early years of Quadara, there was one king, but the nation is most successful, and peaceful, when there are four queens. You know this."

Arebella had shifted agitatedly in her chair. "Yes," she replied, her dark brows lowering over her serious hazel eyes. "But has there ever been a time when there wasn't anyone to inherit the throne?"

Her tutor had laughed, annoying Arebella further. "No. Since the inception of Queenly Law, we've always had four rulers. Ensuring the royal bloodline is of utmost importance to the queens."

Arebella had pouted. "*Could* there be a time when there are less than four queens?"

Her tutor didn't pause to consider why Arebella would ask such a thing, for she was used to her pupil's relentless questions, so she answered truthfully. "I suppose, if something happened to a queen before she had a child *and* if all her female relatives had passed to the quadrant without borders, then that quadrant would be without a queen."

Arebella had leaned forward in her chair. *This is getting interesting,* she'd thought. "Then what?"

Her tutor had looked through her for a moment, as though she weren't sure of the answer, for there had never been such an awful occurrence. "The other queens would fill in for that quadrant, I believe, until a suitable queen is found."

"The queens will inherit the power of the dead queen? They'll take over her quadrant?"

"Yes." Her tutor's expression had faltered then. "But don't worry, that's very unlikely to happen."

Arebella had been quiet for the remainder of the lesson, not listening to another word her tutor had said. The only thought running through her usually busy mind was that if all the queens were to die, the remaining queen would inherit their power and would rule all the quadrants. That queen could change not only Toria, but the entire nation, for the better. The queen could tear down the walls that separated the quadrants and prevented Quadarians from traveling and sharing resources as they pleased. Torians would then have access to all Eonist technologies and medicines to advance their cities and ensure another plague outbreak would not occur. They could visit Ludia for vacation and revel in the unlimited entertainment on offer. They could travel to Archia and eat produce fresh from the trees—not weeks-old apples imported from the lush isle.

Quadara would truly be a united nation. If it had only one queen.

And that queen could be her.

CHAPTER THIRTY-THREE

Keralie

I smelled the smoke before I saw it.

Mackiel had always praised my timing. I knew when to approach my target, when to begin the con, when to retrieve the prize and when to get out. *A gift,* he'd said, *not something that could be taught.*

Sure, you could teach someone to be more observant. Quicker. Quieter. But you couldn't teach the art of timing. Ever since I'd stolen Varin's comm case, my timing couldn't have been more off.

The drifting smoke reminded me of the time after Mackiel's parents had died, when he wouldn't leave his bedroom for weeks, and the power was cut due to unpaid bills. To stay warm, we pulled up moldy floorboards and burned them in the center of the auction house. Mackiel eventually took charge of his father's business, but the smoke lingered in the walls like an unwelcome memory for nearly a year.

The heady scent of smoke inside the palace was all wrong. As far as I'd seen, no windows opened to the outside world aside from Queen Iris's garden. Certainly no chimneys.

The palace was encased in a glass dome, and someone had lit a match within it. There would be no escape. I should never have left Varin's side.

I expected some kind of siren to go off, a warning, but nothing happened. I followed the scent down the hallway, all the while knowing exactly where it would lead.

Queen Corra's rooms.

Flames licked up the curtains of the internal bedroom window. Queen Corra's terrified face was pressed against it, her gloved hand banging on the glass.

A silhouette, surrounded by red flames.

Palace guards and staff had surrounded the entrance to Queen Corra's rooms, attempting to aid the doomed queen.

"Stand back!" a palace guard yelled to the audience gathered around him. He threw a chair at the glass. It rebounded, leaving the surface unscathed.

I ducked down to the floor to the vent in the wall I'd entered earlier and quickly unscrewed the latch, not caring if anyone saw. But the metal was too hot to touch, and my dermasuit fell apart when I placed my palms on the surface. A column of smoke swirled through the shaft toward me, a storm barely contained.

I gagged, standing upright, my lungs fighting against me. I couldn't go in there.

Too late. Always too late.

Someone rushed by, not noticing—or caring—I wasn't one of them, their focus solely on saving their queen. They carried buckets of water, but hung back, unable to subdue the flames through the glass.

My father's bloodied face flashed behind my lids. I couldn't do nothing. No, not this time.

"Give it here!" I said, grabbing a metal bucket from a slack-jawed staff member. She squeaked in protest as I tossed the water down the hallway. I gave her a look. "The water's no use if we can't break the glass."

And although I didn't want to—I didn't want to see—I stepped up to the window. Queen Corra's red-rimmed eyes were streaming rivers of tears, whether from the smoke or terror, I couldn't tell.

I swung the bucket as hard as I could. It hit the glass, reverberating across the window, down through my arms and into my chest.

A scratch left behind, nothing more. The glass must've been reinforced.

I took another swing.

Other staff members followed suit, dumping the water and slamming their buckets into the window. Again and again.

Queen Corra's hand clutched something below the hollow of her throat. Her eyes locked with mine. A moment passed between us. She knew this was the end. Her time was up.

My next swing nearly snapped my wrist. My bucket cluttered to the floor. Queen Corra's hand pressed against the hot glass, seeking comfort. I forced myself not to turn away, but I couldn't help the visions on the comm chips from washing over me, providing the details I didn't want to remember.

A heated flicker. Light. Burning flames. Coughing. Screaming. Tears. Skin bubbling and blistering. Crying. Begging. Brown skin covered in ash like dirt covering a grave.

The assassin watching as Queen Corra burned down to cinders.

Only this wasn't the comm chips; this was happening right now.

I glanced around wildly. The assassin was here, making sure Queen Corra's life was snuffed out. But where?

There were too many people in all different kinds of clothes—from different quadrants. It didn't matter that Queen Corra was Eonist; their faces all held the same horror, a queen dying in front of their eyes.

No one stood out. No one watched in glee.

But the inspector watched on, his long fingers at his comm line. Whoever he was notifying would be too late.

I stumbled back from the glass, my dermasuit suddenly too tight.

I was an imposter.

I'd stolen from a doomed queen. I'd been in her room only yesterday. I could've left a note, warning her about her future death. I could've done the right thing.

Varin and I had been selfish. We should've told the guards the details of the comm chips as soon as we entered the palace, regardless of our lack of evidence. Like Varin had suggested.

No. It was me who was selfish. I only cared about HIDRA. For my father. For myself. For redemption.

"Let me out. Let me out!" Queen Corra cried, her fists pounding against the glass. But I wouldn't meet her gaze. I couldn't watch a moment more.

I couldn't watch her die. Not again.

CHAPTER THIRTY-FOUR

Arebella

*H*e was here.

The thought sent a flurry of excitement through Arebella's veins even though she knew it wasn't *the* moment she'd been waiting for—for he wouldn't be the one to deliver the news.

Arebella's staff had informed her that he awaited her arrival in the main reception room. As she flew down the stairs, her questioning mind began to imagine why he was here and what he had to say.

There were many options—many different paths her plan could take. And he was a part of that plan. An integral part. She understood most people focused on what was in front of them, but Arebella thought of the past, present and future—all at once. It was often exhausting.

She'd first met him when he visited the house with his mother. His mother used to visit every few years. Arebella thought the woman was simply a friend of her mother's. She enjoyed the woman's company as she told her tales of her kind and intelligent mother, who had supposedly died in childbirth. On one particular visit, she'd dragged her son along. He was initially sullen and rude, refusing to play with ten-year-old Arebella.

When Arebella had called him an ignorant Jetée rat, an insult she'd heard her adoptive mother once use, he'd snapped and said, "At least I know where I'm from."

Arebella had been struck silent, her mind whirling through the possibilities of what he'd meant. She changed tactics then, deciding to befriend the boy rather than antagonize him. It took a few months, but eventually he told her.

Arebella was the daughter of Queen Marguerite.

He'd learned the truth while he was practicing sneaking through people's belongings and had found a letter from the queen herself hidden in one of his mother's locked drawers. The letter spoke of Queen Marguerite's daughter, named Arebella, who needed a home outside the palace and a parent who would never know of Arebella's claim to the throne.

While Arebella had thrown a fit, furious her mother had hidden the truth from her, he suggested she do something about it.

"Dream bigger," he'd said. "Want more. Don't ask. *Take* it."

Back then, he was all arms and legs with a hawklike stare. He took in everything, especially Arebella. In the years since, he'd grown into a charming young man, sharply dressed and immaculately presented. Arebella found herself longing for his visits, not only to discuss their plans to destroy Queen Marguerite's rule, but to see his face and hear his melodic voice. But his reputation proceeded him. She promised herself she'd guard her heart, yet as they'd grown closer and their friendship shifted toward the physical, she forgot that promise she'd made to herself. Her heart was no longer hers.

Before every meeting, she pictured what she would wear, what he would wear, and what they'd say. She mostly guessed correctly how people would respond, for she ran through countless possibilities, and one was bound to be correct. But not him. He always left her guessing. And that made it interesting.

Often, she wondered if he felt the same way about her. She thought he must, for why would he stick by her side and risk his life to enact their plans if he didn't care deeply? If his affection was only a game?

As she neared the main reception room, she wondered if today was the day he'd profess his love for her. Was that why he couldn't wait till the queens were all dead before seeing her again?

When she entered the room, she placed her hands within the folds of her skirt to hide her shaking. Most people saw trembling as a sign of weakness, but Arebella shook out of anticipation.

She no longer cared why he was here. She wanted news. Any news.

He had his back to her, but he wasn't facing the fire. His body was angled away from the flames. This was different. He always waited, his face open and receptive. Already this was more interesting than she'd imagined.

"Tell me," she said, unable to keep her voice from sounding shrill. "Is it done?"

"Not yet." He didn't turn around. "But I believe you will be summoned to the palace any day now."

She rubbed a hand across her mouth. "Excellent, then everything is going to plan." Why was he here? They'd agreed not to see each other until she was in the palace.

"Not everything, darlin'," he said, finally turning to face her.

Arebella gasped. "What happened to your hands?" They were blistered and blackened. Burnt. Now she understood his distance from the flames, though he still needed warmth in the chilly room. Since Arebella's adoptive mother had died, and left little wealth behind, she needed to conserve money. Soon those worries would be behind her and she could enjoy the constant warmth of the palace, conducted from the sun's rays that hit the golden dome. She would wear her favorite dress even in the middle of winter, the one with the short sleeves and the deep-cut—

"The plan hasn't been derailed," Mackiel said, bringing her back to the room. "But I need your help."

She glided toward him, her arms outstretched. "Who did this to you?" she asked.

"Keralie. But don't worry, she'll get what she deserves. In the end."

"Are you in pain?" She ran her fingers across his smooth jaw. How would his injury change the narrative? Would he still want to lie with her? She'd worn her best undergarments in preparation, as always.

He shook his head. "I've taken some heavy Eonist pain block- ers. But I could use a"—he grinned wryly—"hand." He pulled a roll of bandages from his pocket, his fingers shuddering.

Arebella nodded and began wrapping his hands gingerly.

Up close, they looked worse, charred and broken. They wouldn't heal. *Couldn't.* What was left of the skin smelled like coal. She wanted to scrunch up her nose and turn away, but she forced herself not to.

When she'd finished dressing his hands, she said, "Don't worry. When I'm queen, I'll provide a dose of HIDRA." Arebella wouldn't have to discuss her decisions with anyone else. She could make the rules as she wanted. "I'll heal you."

If he kept his charred skin, there was a chance to revive it, but if they amputated his hands, there would be no repairing them. And Mackiel was so good with his hands; it would be a shame to cut them off.

"I know you will," he said. "My queen."

Arebella's face broke into a beaming smile.

"Has the news spread to the people?" she asked, her hands wandering under his shirt to the skin beneath.

She sighed as she skimmed her hand across the smooth planes of his chest. The contact calmed her mind, allowing her to focus on one thought at a time—a powerful effect and one of the reasons she loved him.

She would help his pain by distracting him, and he could help her.

Mackiel moaned in reply. "No word has left the palace. They must be keeping the murders quiet until they find female blood relatives."

She moved her hands lower and his head fell to her shoulder, hot breaths against her neck. "But they won't find any female relatives."

"No . . ." he breathed out. "None remain. No one but you . . ."

"And our assassin?"

"Perfect," he managed to reply. "Swift, silent and deadly."

Hearing her plans coming to fruition was a blissful release, like rain after a sweltering summer's day. Her mind was cool, calm. She would do anything to keep that feeling. The plan she'd set in motion at fourteen was finally coming together. Her plan to save the Jetée. Her plan to tear down the walls and share resources across the quadrants. And her plan to be the one, and only, queen of Quadara. She trembled at the thought of how good that would feel.

Perhaps it would permanently calm her mind.

"It will be over before—" His voice faltered as she pushed her body up against him, careful not to touch his hands. "Before the week is out. It's been difficult with so many people in the palace. It could be sooner if the assassin has the opportunity to make the kills."

"As we planned."

"Yes."

"Good." She pulled his mouth to hers.

The rest was lost between heated breaths and low moans.

CHAPTER THIRTY-FIVE

Keralie

My body took over as my mind raced. I fled from the fire, from the images burning behind my lids. I wasn't sure where I was running to, but I needed space from Queen Corra's terrified eyes, in case she pointed a finger at me.

Too late. Too late.

People filled the passages as the smoke filtered down the corridor. Still, no one stopped me as I ran by. They scattered in various directions, their eyes wide, panicked, as if they'd never seen the palace passageways before . . .

The processing room! They were fleeing the processing room! How did they get out?

Now free, they shoved and screamed at each other as they bolted. But they were going the wrong way. There was nothing inside the palace but death. No wonder they weren't interested in me—I was another lost soul roaming the hallways.

I dodged the frantic bodies as I pushed against the tide. There was no hope behind me.

Get in quick. Get out quicker.

I'd been here far too long.

An arm snagged my waist, pulled me into an adjoining room and closed the door behind us.

"Varin!" I cried at the sight of him. My breath shuddered out of my lungs.

His eyes darted across my face, his cheeks flushed. "I lost the inspector in the crowd. But I ran into Christon. He said the palace visitors overpowered the guards. They couldn't escape out the shielded exit; instead they broke into the palace, hoping to find another way out."

"There is no other way out," I said. I'd created this chaos. I never should've informed them of Queen Iris's murder. If anyone else got hurt, it was on me.

Too much blood on my hands.

"Did you find Queen Corra in time?" he asked.

I shook my head. I didn't need to say anything further.

"This isn't your fault," he said.

I turned away. "It's always my fault."

Before I knew what was happening, Varin enveloped me in his arms. Instantly, my body went rigid, but the embrace was familiar, like a long-ago memory.

And it was a long-ago memory. My mother used to give me the best hugs. She'd stand with her arms around me, her head on top of mine, for minutes on end, with neither of us saying anything. She had the gift of communicating without words. I'd never felt more loved than when in her embrace. My father had been different. Even when we would argue, he'd always end the conversation with *I love you more than my boat loves a twelve-knot wind and a warm sea.* Back then, I'd claim to have no idea what he meant, but I'd been lying. Regardless of my choices, my parents loved me. Until the accident.

I pressed my cheek against Varin's chest. He smelled of pine and soap—the scent of his dermasuit. My eyes stung, and I squeezed them tight.

I never thought I'd be touched like this again.

"We don't have time for this." I reluctantly pulled away. "Queen Marguerite is the only queen left, and we know the least about her death."

He nodded slowly. "Only that she'll be poisoned."

"Right. We don't know anything more about the assassin than we did before entering the palace. It's almost been two days." Varin had been right all along; we should've gone directly to the authorities with what we knew, regardless of the consequences. We didn't have proof, but we could still save Queen Marguerite. "We *have* to stop this."

"It's not your job to save the queens," he said. "It's not your job to save anyone."

I knew *who* he was referring to. I jerked away. "What would you know?" I narrowed my eyes at him. "You've never loved any-one. How would you know what it's like to hurt someone you love? Don't tell me what to feel!"

His eyes flashed. "I know what it's like to be hurt."

"Because of your death date?" I harrumphed. "You think your own demise is painful? Imagine the feeling of being responsible for someone else's." I shook my head. "It's worse, much, much worse. If I don't get a dose of HIDRA for my father, then he's—"

"*What?*" he interrupted. "You never said anything about HIDRA. I thought you wanted money!"

I threw up my hands. "I lied, okay! Are you really that surprised? All I do is lie and cheat and steal. I'm not that different from Mackiel. He made me, remember?"

"Keralie." My name was a groan on his lips. "You should've told me the truth."

"I didn't want you to know we were both after the same thing. You might have turned me in to get what you want." It sounded ridiculous out loud. Varin was loyal, he'd proven that time and time again, even when I'd stolen from him, insulted him and dragged him into this mess.

"I wouldn't have turned you in," he said. "I would've allowed you to take the dose of HIDRA to your father. He needs it."

Well, that made me feel worse.

I smiled sadly. "I don't want you to sacrifice your future for mine—or my father's."

"Mackiel said your father was in a coma?" he asked, and I nodded. "Then his situation is more dire than mine. It's the right thing to do."

"What's your condition?" It was the question I should've asked when he'd first mentioned it. The question he avoided back in the infirmary. "Why is your death date set to thirty? Why do you need HIDRA?"

He surprised me by not flinching. "I'm going blind."

I gasped, my hand flying to my chest.

"I have a rare genetic condition," he said. "It's degenerative. I already struggle to see in bright sunlight and at nighttime, and my peripheral vision isn't great." He swallowed roughly. "I'll be completely blind by the time I'm thirty."

"But your eyes are beautiful." *Stupid Keralie. Such a stupid thing to say.*

He smiled. "A symptom of the condition."

"But HIDRA will cure it?" I asked.

"My condition has never been urgent enough to bump me up on the waiting list to be assessed. It's not like I'm dying. At least, not right now." One side of his mouth lifted.

Somehow it hurt even more that he was trying to make a joke about this.

"I'm sorry," I said. "I should've told you the truth from the beginning. But I'm not good at trusting others. Look at Mackiel." I let out a hollow laugh. "He was my closest friend, and he's tried to kill me. Twice."

He looked at me for a long moment. "You can trust me."

"Yes. Because you're Eonist. You're good, loyal, understanding, selfless, honest."

"No." He shook his head. "You can trust me because I'm your friend, Keralie. And *real* friends, friends who care about each other, don't lie."

I wanted to believe that, but I'd been burned before. Perhaps Mackiel *had* stolen my ability to care. Perhaps I'd become the girl he'd trained me to be. And there was no undoing it.

"Do you think people can change?" I asked. "Or do you think we're destined to follow a certain path?"

Varin sucked in a deep breath before letting it out slowly. I'd never seen him this ragged, tortured. I didn't want to hurt him with my words, but I had.

"I have to believe that we can change. I *have* to believe I can be more than a messenger, more than my quadrant requires of me, more than my death date. And you," he said, raising an eyebrow, "make me believe that my dreams of more are not in vain. That I can go after what I want. Even if only for a short amount of time."

His art. *Queens above.* Now it made sense that he'd never tried to pursue his dreams, for it would all be cruelly snatched away. Never to paint again. Once he lost his vision, the one thing that brought joy to his life would be impossible.

My heart constricted, and tears filled my eyes. "I want to believe there's more for you," I said. "For both of us."

"Thank you." There was a hint of dimples on either side of his cheeks.

"Come on," I said, wiping my tears away. "You can do better than that. Show me some teeth."

He grimaced, his teeth flashing white in the dark room.

I laughed. "Better, but it still needs work."

He stepped toward me, tentatively. "Mackiel didn't steal anything from you," he said quietly.

I didn't reply.

"Keralie?" he whispered. "If there's one thing I'm certain of, it's that you're your own person. No one can make you do anything you don't want to. Look at the way you've moved about the palace, with no one the wiser."

I studied the floor. "I'm not sure I know who I am without him. I'm not sure I can stand on my own."

"You already are." He placed his hands gently on my shoulders. "This is all your doing, not his. You want to help the queens. You want to help your father. That's all you."

I looked up into his eyes, and a breath lodged in my chest. His expression was heated, as if his gaze could cleave me in two and reveal the true Keralie trapped within.

Who do you want to be?

His eyes, like silver moons, moved across my face. My heart

slammed against my rib cage. In that moment, I didn't feel like Mackiel's best dipper. I didn't feel like the girl who had ruined her family. A girl you couldn't trust.

I didn't feel alone.

That was when I realized I didn't want to be anyone other than the girl standing in front of Varin. The girl he was looking at with such desire in his eyes.

I gripped his shirt and pulled him to me.

His lips were softer than I expected. Warmer too. All this time, I'd pictured him as though he were made from the same shiny metal Eonia seemed to love. Unfeeling and cold.

But he wasn't. Not at all.

His mouth moved against mine, taking both of my lips in his. His skin smelled salty and a little spicy. That was the real Varin, not what the dermasuit made him.

I ripped off my gloves and gripped the back of his neck, splaying my fingers underneath his locks. His hair was silky—everything about him was soft.

My heart sped faster, if that were possible, heat blooming wherever we touched skin to skin.

Then he let me go. In that brief moment of lost contact, we grinned at one another, surprised and electrified. I pulled at his neck, but he brought his hands up to stop me.

"I want to feel you too," he said, cheeks darkening at his words. My heart fluttered. He unclipped his suit at his wrists and pulled off his gloves. With his hands free, he brushed a strand of hair back from my face, his fingers shaking. Then he burned a line across my cheek to my lips. I was worried we'd lost our moment, but then his mouth returned to mine.

I gasped, already forgetting the gentleness of them—of him. No longer restricted by the dermasuit, his hands dug into the back of my hair, bringing me up to meet him. Now I could feel the *real* him. See the real him. And he was all warmth. And hands. And lips.

Hot and cold shimmered through me, fighting for dominance as the dermasuit tried to regulate my searing temperature. The tumbling in my belly was similar to fear, and yet I wanted to embrace the feeling, wrap myself within it and never let go.

He continued kissing me, and I wasn't sure when to stop. *Why* should we stop? We still had much to do—too much. Even so, I didn't want to pull away. He obviously felt the same, his hands roaming across my sides, his touch almost as intimate as the kiss. I shuddered at the thought of what it would be like to touch Varin without our dermasuits in the way.

His eyes held a flicker of longing, and I thought I might combust under his gaze. In that moment, I couldn't imagine kissing anyone else.

How did people kiss strangers with such abandon? Kiss without a care? How could they do something this intimate, this revealing, with someone they didn't want? Other dippers easily wielded the power of seduction as though it meant nothing at all.

Mackiel had tried to teach me the power of a kiss, to make men forget, and then steal from them. Now I understood, for it was a perfect plan—the perfect distraction. But I couldn't do it. I'd tried, and was close on a few occasions. But when it had come down to it, I couldn't. And now I knew why.

My first kiss was meant to be with Varin.

CHAPTER THIRTY-SIX

Arebella

T he eight most perfect words roused Arebella in the middle of the night.

"You've been summoned to the palace, Miss Arebella."

She bolted upright, not needing to be told by whom or why. *This* was the moment she'd been waiting for—the moment she'd been planning over and over again until her plans were a tangled mess in her mind. She looked out her window; it was still dark.

There wasn't time to waste.

"Dress me in my finest," Arebella said to her housemaid, leaping out of bed. She didn't need to rub sleep from her eyes, for she hadn't *really* been sleeping. Arebella was not familiar with the deep unconsciousness that others seemed to enjoy. A few shallow hours of quiet here and there were all she could achieve. Her brain was far too active. "And quickly," she added.

Her housemaid's hands shook as she laced up Arebella's corset and attached the large hooped skirt to her narrow waist.

Arebella huffed. "Now is not the time to be sloppy. Do it right or don't do it at all."

The mouse of a woman nodded, her hands steadying, although her lip was now trembling. Arebella cursed the woman's weakness. The housemaid had been her adoptive mother's and had never warmed to Arebella. She would happily have done without any help, but she couldn't reach the many buttons down her back.

She stilled the housemaid's hands in hers. The fragile woman flinched, expecting the worst. Arebella had never been cruel to her, but she'd also never been kind.

"Thank you for your help," Arebella said with a forced smile. Why not start practicing her cordialities now, before she arrived at the palace?

Once Arebella was dressed in the shimmering golden gown, she descended the stairs to the foyer, a lantern in her hand to guide the way. Candles had been lit to conserve power. It was not a grand house, for it was all a single income could afford, but it had three bedrooms and a reception room, where the palace staff would be waiting.

Her veins thrummed, and her heart trilled. This was the day—the first day of her new life—the life she was always supposed to have lived. She'd recited the words over and over in her head in preparation for this moment. She'd practiced her expressions in the mirror. Shock. Sadness. Awe. Disbelief. She had perfected them all.

When she entered the reception room and found only one man, she nearly turned on her heel. This wasn't how she'd imagined it. Where was the rest of her royal staff?

When a queen died, a convoy of palace staff and guards was supposed to journey through the main streets of Toria, ending at the palace. An announcement should've gone out on the latest Queenly Reports, informing the quadrant of where and when they could catch a glimpse of their soon-to-be Torian queen. It was tradition. And she had dressed for the part, knowing Mackiel would be waiting for her carriage to pass—to signal the next stage in their plan. She'd have to send him a message instead.

The man in front of her was younger than she'd expected. She had imagined what her advisor might be like. Perhaps she would be motherly and Arebella would befriend her instantly, taking her hand in a gentle, but firm, grasp. Or perhaps he'd be stoic, a father figure whom she'd win over with her ambition and intelligence.

Arebella blinked, but the scene didn't fade from her eyes. She couldn't control this. This was real.

"Lady Arebella," the tall, thin man said, then bowed when she made eye contact.

Lady? Although it wasn't *Queen* Arebella, not yet, she quite liked the sound of it.

"I apologize for calling on you at this hour," the man said. "My name is Jenri."

Would he still play the role of the stoic advisor? Arebella was thrown for a moment, her mind scrambling to reimagine her future.

"Good morning," she replied. "How may I help you?"

This would be the hardest part—pretending she didn't know who she really was. As far as she should be concerned, a visit from the palace was a grand and enjoyable occasion—at any hour. And so Arebella smiled widely.

Jenri swallowed audibly before stepping forward. "I'm the advisor for Toria."

"Oh?" Arebella placed a gloved hand to her chest; her heart

banged wildly beneath her fingers. "How fascinating! What brings you to my home?"

Jenri's discomfort made Arebella buoyant; she was succeeding in fooling him. She hadn't been sure she could deceive someone from the palace—someone trained to detect deceptions—until this very moment. She wished Mackiel were here to see her succeed.

"I'm afraid I have some difficult news," Jenri said, his face twisting. "You may want to sit, Lady Arebella."

She clenched her teeth in response. No one told her what to do. And soon she would be ordering *him* around. "I'm fine standing." She couldn't deny Mackiel's brashness had rubbed off on her. "Thank you," she added at the last minute.

Jenri nodded. "I've been told you are aware you are adopted?"

"Yes." *This is it,* she thought. *But don't smile. Look slightly concerned. Confused.* "But my adoptive mother died a few years ago. I inherited this home once she passed."

"I'm sorry to hear that."

Arebella nodded glumly. "But what does that have to do with the palace?"

"Quite a bit." Jenri cleared his throat. "I wish there was an easier way to say this. However—"

"You can tell me." Arebella stepped forward, her palms faceup. "I'm not as fragile as I look."

Would the words fall easily from his mouth, or would he struggle to spit them out? And how would he word it, exactly? Arebella bit the inside of her mouth. *Focus. Be in the moment. Remember everything. Every word.*

He smiled at her. "No, I don't suppose you are. It's in your blood to be strong."

"My blood?" Arebella was sure he could hear her pulse.

"Yes." He glanced to the floor for a moment before continuing. "You see, your birth mother, well, she was the reigning queen of Toria."

Arebella let out a well-timed gasp. "Queen Marguerite?" A smile spread across her face. "Truly?"

He nodded shortly. "I'm afraid the woman who took you from the palace did not inform you of your heritage due to her personal beliefs against the thrones."

Arebella swallowed a huff. He was going to blame Mrs. Delore for not informing her and pretend Marguerite had wanted her to inherit the throne? She wasn't sure if the deception made her like Jenri more or less. Would it be in her best interests to distrust him? Or rely on him? She'd have to mull it over tonight while everyone else slept. Her first night in the palace, how thrilling!

Focus, she admonished herself.

"That's surprising news," Arebella said after a moment of planned reflection. "I had no idea I came from a royal line. How exciting! Oh!" She scrunched her dark brows into a frown. "But with you here . . . Doesn't that mean . . . that she—" Her voice shook with excitement, although it could have easily been misread as fear. "You said 'was.' "

"Yes. I'm afraid Queen Marguerite has passed," he said, lowering his head. "I came as soon as I could."

She'd imagined those words countless times. She thought she might still be imagining them, but he hadn't worded it exactly right. Not how she wanted him to. She'd thought there would be more drama, more flair. More crying. And more people. But it was only this one advisor. How disappointing.

He awaited her response.

She dug her painted fingernails into her palms to prevent herself from drowning in thoughts. A technique Mackiel had taught her. *Pain is reality,* he liked to say.

"That's dreadful," she said finally. She went with *dreadful* over *horrible,* as *horrible* sounded too distant and *dreadful* was close to *dead*—the poetry pleased her.

"I'm sorry to inform you of this," he said, his face drawn with emotion and fatigue. "Usually the queens are raised with the knowledge of their ancestry and are prepared for how difficult this day will be."

A war went on inside her. Should she cry? Was that too much? She'd never met the woman, and supposedly had only now found out she was related to her. What was the appropriate reaction to someone passing if you were related but had never met? Someone you would only ever meet face-to-face when they were already dead?

Still, the woman had brought her into this world, which deserved some acknowledgment. She sniffled, then asked, "What happened?"

Yes, that was a good one. Much better than *Oh, queens above! Not my poor mother!* which had been her preference over the last few months. Sometimes simplicity was best.

"She was poisoned," Jenri replied, his lip quivering. "The doctors did their best to save her, but they were too late. I'm very sorry, my lady." *How interesting.* She hadn't known how the queens would be murdered, only that they would be taken care of and that her mother's death would be slow enough to allow for her admission. It was safer not to know. That way Arebella's responses would be more genuine.

Jenri stepped forward and placed a hand on her arm, wrinkles gathering around his eyes as he took her in. He was emotional. Warm. Soft.

Easy.

"I'm sure you did all you could," she whispered, deciding to mimic his softness in the hope that it would connect them. *Find something they want,* Mackiel would say, *then give it to them, and they'll be yours for the taking.*

"I'm afraid that's not all," he said.

"No?" She could hardly contain her excitement. He was about to name her queen of all of Quadara.

"The other queens are also dead." He cleared his throat. "Murdered."

Arebella shifted her shoulders up and down to appear as though she was breathing raggedly. "How is that possible?"

"We don't know all the facts yet, but you can be assured that you will be safe with me."

Arebella nearly laughed. Of course she would be safe. This was all her doing.

Her mother couldn't control her life from behind the scenes now. Arebella would finally get everything she ever wanted, and was owed. And Quadara would gain its best queen.

"Can I still see my mother?" she asked. "Just once?" It seemed like the right thing to ask, to allow Arebella to say good-bye. Such a strange Quadarian tradition—the day you were to meet your birth mother was the day you would say your farewells. Perhaps it was a Queenly Law she could change? She didn't want her own child to meet her on her deathbed.

Will I have children? Arebella wondered. *Do I want children?* She supposed she could change that law too, if she wished. Once she was queen.

"Yes, my lady," Jenri said, breaking her from her tangled thoughts. "She is presentable."

Arebella pursed her lips at the description of her mother's corpse as presentable. From what she knew of death, it was ugly, and ladies like herself should turn their faces away. Not that she planned to, but it was always good to know what ladies like herself *should* do.

"I will require you to come to the palace at once," he continued. "We can send for your belongings once you've arrived."

"I'm going to live in the palace?" Her voice was buoyant.

"You will be Toria's next queen." He gave her a small smile. "I'm sure you'll be a wonderful queen, and I'll be by your side every step of the way, as I promised your mother." His voice lowered. "As I was *for* your mother."

Hopefully not every step, she thought.

"Thank you." She looked up at him, her eyes glistening with unshed happy tears. *Let him think they're from grief.* "Take me there now. I'm ready."

And she was.

CHAPTER THIRTY-SEVEN

Keralie

A few hours later, I woke to the last of the stars twinkling through the glass dome. Another day starting and the beginning of my third day in the palace, four since I'd stolen Varin's comm case, and I was no closer to finding the assassin. *We* were no closer.

I turned and found myself curled on a dusty rug. I held back a sneeze to not wake Varin and sat upright. I finally took in our hiding place: the walls were covered in rolls of fabric, and on two long tables in the middle of the room sat several sewing machines and half-made dresses.

The palace's sewing room.

It looked like the seamstresses had left in a hurry, their machines' needles still pressed into lengths of material. No doubt they'd been running from the hordes of angry and confused palace visitors flooding the corridors, or because they'd smelled the smoke. No one cared about dresses while queens were being slain in the corridors.

I had to find Queen Marguerite before the assassin did. At

this point, I didn't care if I was arrested. As long as she would hear me out—long enough not to eat or drink anything without it being tested first. The assassin wouldn't win. I would do what I should've from the beginning. I'd tell the palace everything I knew.

I turned back to my resting place to wake Varin, but he wasn't there, and the space beside me was cold. Where had he gone? He wouldn't have abandoned me, but the sight of an empty rug made my stomach clench.

Had he been captured? Perhaps the inspector had found us in here and pulled him from the room. Had the assassin? Why hadn't he taken me as well? Was Mackiel still playing with me?

I shouldn't have fallen asleep. But I hadn't had a full night's rest in days.

I dusted myself down and pushed the door open a crack to see if anyone was passing by. Once convinced it was clear, I shifted into the hallway.

Why was it so quiet? Where was everyone? I squeezed my hands into fists.

Varin will be fine. Everything will be fine. Find Queen Marguerite. Stop this mess. Find Varin later.

I headed toward Queen Marguerite's rooms. On the way, I passed by the infirmary. The door was slightly ajar. I pushed the door open, then halted in the doorway. Four bodies lay on metal gurneys, sheets pulled high to cover their faces.

Four—four queens. All of them dead.

"No," I whispered.

My legs went weak, and I collapsed. Strong arms caught me from behind, propping me up.

"Varin," I breathed. "We're too late."

330

"It's not Varin," a gentle voice said.

I looked down. Strange long fingers splayed around my waist from where he'd caught me.

The inspector.

I shoved him off and scurried into the infirmary, weaving in and around the gurneys and toward the back wall. But there was nowhere to go; the inspector was blocking the only way out.

"Back so soon?" he asked, seemingly unsurprised to find me there.

"I'm helping Queen Marguerite," I said, repeating the lie we'd told Christon. "I'm trying to help uncover the assassin."

"Is that so?" He tilted his head, studying me.

I couldn't help but flick my eyes over to the fourth gurney. I'd failed her.

The inspector looped his comm line around his ear to capture our conversation.

Where was Varin? He could get me out of this mess.

"Yes," I said.

"And yesterday when you were listening in on my autopsy report, that was to help Queen Marguerite?"

He knew we were there?

"Oh, yes," he said, reading my confusion. "I've known you were in the palace for a while." He gave a little whistle, then smiled. "The only question remaining is *why* you're here."

"Why are *you* here?" I countered. "You were in the palace before Queen Iris died. Why would you be here before there were any murders to investigate?"

"That is untrue," he said. "I arrived after Queen Iris was slain."

"Your name wasn't on the visitors list!"

"Authorities are not required to sign in."

No. No. It couldn't be that simple.

"But you were here," he said with a frown. He opened a silver comm case from his waist and fluttered his fingers across the hundreds of comm chips. He must've asked Queen Marguerite to recall all the court interactions that day and recorded her memories. He selected one, closed his eyes and placed the chip on his tongue to ingest the memory.

When he opened his eyes, they were steely. "Yes, you were here from the beginning. You gave information on a wanted criminal called Mackiel. This was before Queen Iris was slain."

"Don't turn this around on me!" I pointed at him. "I was trying to help!"

The inspector looked at the covered bodies. "And did you?"

"This is not my fault!" *Where's Varin?* If anything had happened to him, I would never forgive myself.

"That has yet to be determined," he replied.

Footsteps sounded in the hall. While the inspector glanced out the doorway, I grabbed the nearest and sharpest scalpel.

"Hello," the inspector called out to whoever was walking by. "You're just in time. I believe I've found your Keralie."

I nearly dropped the scalpel in shock when Varin walked in, followed by several palace guards.

No! "Let him go!" I cried.

Varin's face was blank as he nodded to me. "Yes. That's her."

Before I had time to react, the guards surrounded me. One jerked my hands behind my back and clamped shackles around my wrists. I hid the scalpel up the sleeve of my dermasuit.

"What are you doing?" I asked. "What's going on, Varin?"

He shook his head, unwilling to speak, his expression heavy with emotion. Emotion he shouldn't feel.

"Keralie Corrington of Toria," one of the guards said. "We are arresting you for the assassination of Queen Iris, Queen Stessa, Queen Corra and Queen Marguerite. Your sentence will be determined at a later date."

"What?" I shrieked, whirling around, pulling against my shackles. "I haven't hurt anyone!"

"Well, that's not entirely true, is it?" a familiar voice asked.

Mackiel walked into the room and stood beside the inspector. Although I'd known he was involved, my heart skittered in my chest like a frightened rodent. I wanted to flee. I wanted to scream. And I wanted to laugh at the absurdity of it all. Mackiel and I both within the palace, like in our childhood games. But there was nothing childlike in his expression.

His brow was heavy over his kohl-lined eyes, his gaze piercing. The smoky smell was evident even through his bandages.

I swallowed. "Okay, I admit I hurt him"—*and he deserved it*—"but I didn't kill the queens." I jerked my chin at Mackiel. "He's your assassin!"

The inspector shook his head. "Mackiel only arrived early this morning. The queens were already dead."

That couldn't be true. Mackiel *had* to be behind this. Where were his henchmen? Gone now that the deadly deeds were done?

"But you said yourself he's a wanted criminal!" I said. Mackiel always said the palace knew his face and name. That was why he made me steal for him whenever we were near the Concord.

"*You* said that," the inspector replied. "After you made claims against him to Queen Marguerite, I requested he come to the palace. He has been very helpful, and he has cleared his name."

Of course! Another lie. Another game. The palace knew nothing about Mackiel. But why did he pretend they did? Was it merely to make me do his bidding?

Mackiel quirked an eyebrow, a twist at the edges of his full lips. "I wish I could say it's good to see you, darlin', but under these circumstances"—he lifted a narrow shoulder—"it's rather a shock to hear what you've done in my absence."

"What *I've* done?"

"Why don't you tell Keralie what you told me," the inspector said to Varin, who hadn't moved from the doorway.

My legs trembled. *No. It's not possible. Not Varin.*

"I have proof," Varin said, avoiding my eyes.

"Proof?" I asked. "What are you talking about? The re-recorded comm chips?" Someone tugged at my wrist.

"I've got it," the guard said from behind me.

I twisted around to see he'd pulled my dipper bracelet from my wrist. He handed it over to the inspector, who broke one of the lockets free. It was the charm Mackiel had given me when I'd successfully broken into the home of the Torian governor, who claimed to be above the Jetée and the pleasures it had to offer but was known to spend all his spare time drinking and gambling. It was the job I'd done two weeks before Mackiel had asked me to steal the comm case from Varin.

The locket was a small silver bottle.

"I don't understand—" I began, but the inspector twisted the top of the locket with his narrow fingers. The tiny bottle stopper popped off in his hand. "I didn't know it did that." I wasn't sure who I was talking to anymore.

The inspector held the locket upside down. "The guards don't check for jewelry." A few specks of powder fell from the tiny bottle lip. "The perfect place for hiding poison."

"No," I said, jerking my head at Mackiel, whose blue eyes were wide with mock surprise. "He gave that to me. I didn't know it opened!"

"And what about this?" the inspector asked. He pulled off a tiny book charm. He flipped it open and a flame sparked inside.

"No," I said again.

The inspector continued pulling off the other lockets, his black eyes narrowed, including my lock pick and the locket in the shape of a comm case. He placed them on the bench and began shifting them around.

I didn't understand what he was doing until the lockets began snapping together like a puzzle. It formed a blade—a very narrow blade, with the comm-case-shaped locket as the base of the handle and the lock pick as the sharp tip.

"I didn't know it did that either," I said softly.

The inspector took one long slash to the air with the newly formed weapon. "Quite a deadly blade you've got here."

I pulled roughly against my binds. "He did this!" I shrieked at Mackiel. "I work for him! He gave me each locket! He was the one who killed the queens!"

Mackiel simply looked at Varin. "Varin? Some clarity here, please."

My eyes snapped to Varin. *Don't tell me you betrayed me. Not to Mackiel.* He wouldn't. He *couldn't.* I trusted him!

Varin slowly lifted his head but wouldn't meet my gaze. "A few hours ago, in the sewing room, I fell asleep." I didn't understand. We'd *both* fallen asleep. "When I woke, you were gone. I found you in the corridor twisting the bottle back onto your bracelet."

That had never happened. Why was he lying? Why would he turn on me?

"Queen Marguerite was found poisoned a short while later," the inspector said with a nod.

"And the day before." Varin cleared his throat. "When we were in the utility room, you also disappeared. I thought you'd gone to the bathroom. When you returned, your hair was damp, and you smelled of perfume."

"When Stessa died," the inspector said. "The perfumed baths."

"You're paying him!" I spat at Mackiel. "Aren't you? You're giving him what he wants. He belongs to you now, doesn't he?"

How stupid! I'd thought I meant something to Varin, but I was wrong. Everyone could be bought, and Mackiel would find the price.

"No, darlin'," Mackiel replied with a shake of his head.

"You set me up," I whispered, my chest painfully tight. My vision blurring from tears. "All of you."

"You're wrong." Varin stared straight at me for the first time. "*You* set *me* up. You made me think you wanted to help. You made me believe in you, but you were lying this whole time. Lying about your father, lying that you cared. All you wanted to do was kill the queens. It was *your* plan I saw on those chips. All this time, you said you were the best. I should've listened to you." He laughed cruelly. "How well you played us all."

My head spun. I pitched forward. The guards pulled, yanking me back.

"And what's this?" Mackiel said, taking a step toward me. I flinched as his ashen fingers ran over the Eonist crest sewn on the shoulder of my dermasuit. He raised a brow, knowing perfectly well the suit wasn't—*couldn't be*—mine.

"That's Queen Corra's," the inspector said. "Her hand-maiden reported one of the dermasuits missing from her rooms."

Mackiel tsked. "The same Queen Corra who was burned to death by someone setting her room alight. From the inside."

It looked bad. I knew it looked bad. But it wasn't true! Why wouldn't anyone listen?

"Tell us," one of the guards said, his hot breath crossing my face. "Why'd you do it?"

I shook my head, hair flying across my face. "There's nothing to tell! I have no reason to kill the queens. Why would I? I have no motive!"

"No motive?" Mackiel spread his charred hands wide. "But what is it you always wanted as a child?" His face was grim, but his taut lips twitched. He wanted to smile. "All the wealth in the quadrant and to rule Toria."

I shook my head. That was a game. A game we'd played as children. It had meant nothing.

"No!" I jerked forward again, desperate to be free from the binds and these lies.

"I've seen Mackiel's memories," the inspector interrupted. "What he says is true."

Everyone was looking at me as though I was a wild and wicked girl. But I wasn't who they thought I was. I wasn't Mackiel's. Although I had to admit I looked guilty: I'd been skulking around the palace for three days; I'd been in the queen's rooms, with every opportunity to kill them; Varin had told them about the murder weapon—providing them concrete evidence—and Mackiel had given my motive a voice.

"What about this?" one of the guards asked as he shook my binds. A scalpel fell to the floor with a clink, sealing my fate.

"I told you," Mackiel said with a sad shake of his head. "She's ruthless."

There was nothing I could do or say to unscramble his lies.

The inspector held the dagger in one hand and picked up the scalpel in the other. He looked at me, his dark eyes piercing.

"Take her to the palace prison."

CHAPTER THIRTY-EIGHT

Arebella

Arebella didn't need to pretend once she arrived in the palace. Her surprise was real. Her excitement was real. Her admiration was real. She'd never seen such extravagance. Even at night, the palace was a golden-domed jewel. She imagined herself wandering the maze-like corridors, her arms spread wide to brush the gilded walls.

Beautiful. All of it.

She smiled down at her gold dress, knowing how well she belonged without even trying. This was her birthplace—her real home, and finally they were reunited.

Once she had settled into her rooms and been introduced to the rest of her staff, Jenri brought her to the palace infirmary. It smelled of chemicals, which burned the nose and stung the eyes. Arebella blinked, feeling tears form behind her eyes and at the back of her throat.

She expected to see four bodies laid bare, but there was only one covered in a white sheet. Her mother.

The inspector beckoned her forward with his long fingers.

It was strange, standing over the body of her mother, knowing she was responsible for her death. Arebella knew she should feel some kind of sadness, for this was the woman who had brought her into the world, but she felt only the acrid swirl of bitterness. No guilt. Her mother had thought Arebella would be weak, unable to shoulder the burden of the crown. She couldn't have been more wrong.

She nodded to the inspector. "I'm ready."

He lifted the sheet.

A cry escaped her. Mackiel had advised Arebella never to venture to the Concord to see the Queenly Reports, for fear someone would recognize her. Now she knew why. Her mother had the same long auburn hair, sharp jaw and dimpled chin. But her mother's brows were lighter, her nose longer.

"She looks like me!" she exclaimed. She covered her face with her hands. Something stirred within. And it wasn't bitterness.

A hand touched her shoulder. "I'm sorry, my lady," Jenri said.

That was all she'd heard today. *I'm sorry for your loss, my lady. My condolences, my lady. How are you feeling, my lady? How can I help, my lady?*

She was tired of it. When would they dry their tears and name her queen?

Arebella dropped her hands and looked upon her mother once more, letting a breath slowly escape her lips. "I'm fine. It's merely a shock to see someone passed." She had never seen her adopted mother in death.

She tried to convince herself that was true. A shock to see she looked similar to her mother. A shock that in death, she looked alive. She convinced herself it wasn't guilt—why would she feel guilt for someone she'd never met? Blood was simply blood. While it linked them, it meant nothing. Her mother had taught her that. She'd cast Arebella away, depriving her of her birthright. Clearly, their blood ties had meant nothing to her. After all, everyone bled, everyone died. Arebella had just made sure it happened at the right time. Her mother's death had been meaningful, allowing Arebella to ascend the throne, and that should count for something. Death was often meaningless.

"We'll give you a moment," Jenri said, nodding to the inspector.

Once they were gone, Arebella took the time to really look at her mother. She wondered what it would've been like to live under her love. It was not a scenario she'd played in her mind before. Marguerite had been a great queen—so she had heard from Jenri for the entire carriage journey to the palace.

The strongest, kindest and wisest queen.

Words that were meant to have brought peace to Arebella— so while her mother was gone, she'd made the most of her time upon the Torian throne. Yet the words brought an ache. An ache Arebella had never felt before.

"I'm sorry, Mother," Arebella whispered. She felt silly, but there was something about Queen Marguerite's expression in death that made her want to cut open her heart and spill her darkest desires. And this would be her one chance before the death processional. With the assassin arrested, the queens would soon be laid to rest in the underbelly of the palace, never to be seen again.

"I hope you didn't suffer too much," she said. She thought poison seemed like a simple way to die, but from the sound of it, it had been the most drawn out and painful. And for that, Arebella *was* sorry.

"I want you to know this wasn't personal," she continued, waving her hands to her mother's still body. "Your death was not in vain. One day, in the quadrant without borders, we'll meet and I'll explain why I did this. I'll explain why you had to die for me to truly live."

Words swirled through her mind, words that might've sounded better, more meaningful, but there wasn't time for a second chance. As there were none offered in life.

She shook her head to clear her mind.

"Good-bye, Mother."

The woman who lay on the table with chalked lips and lavender lids was nothing to her now.

CHAPTER THIRTY-NINE

Keralie

My cell was twice the size of the cave I'd been stuck in six months ago. I knew this because I'd spent four days examining every rock and crevasse. I knew how far I could stretch out my arms before I hit the walls. I compared the cell to the cave over and over, until I couldn't tell the difference between memory and reality. I was plagued by darkness and blood and darkness and blood, with only myself for company. I never would've imagined I'd want to be back in the cave, my father unconscious by my side, but it was better than this alternative. The tightness in my chest was the only reminder that I was still here. Still alive.

It felt as though weeks had passed since I descended into the darkness. Weeks since I'd seen Varin. Since he'd betrayed me. I still couldn't fathom the reason. Unless they'd offered him HIDRA to turn me in and cover for Mackiel and the henchmen. And yet, Varin had said he would offer my father the dose of HIDRA over using it himself. Was that a lie? Had I taught him too well?

I should've known better than to trust him. And I hated him for it. I'd let my guard down and had been betrayed, again.

Where was Mackiel now? What about the henchmen? Had Mackiel convinced the inspector of their innocence as well? Were they now sitting upon the queens' thrones, their gray, decaying hands gripping the mahogany wood?

While it had felt like weeks, it had only been two days. I knew this because of the six meals they'd offered me since my arrival. Tasteless gruel for what I could only assume was the morning, stale bread at midday and bland stew in the evening.

The cell reeked of sick—my sick. Only minutes after being thrown into the small room, the little amount of food and water in my stomach had propelled its way out of my body to coat the floor. They'd ripped Queen Corra's dermasuit from me, dressing me in rags from unfinished palace dresses. I had nothing to prevent the burning fear from surging through me, and the rags were constantly damp from sweat.

Perhaps the darkness was kind; I could pretend I was somewhere else—somewhere bigger. Somewhere where breathing wasn't painful, where I was not racked by nausea and heart palpitations.

Deep, ragged breaths in. Deep, ragged breaths out. I'm stuck in here. I'll never get out.

My fear of confined spaces had complete control over my body and mind. I curled into a ball, hoping to make myself smaller and not be crushed within the room. My light-headedness was a constant companion in the dark.

The day after I'd been thrown down here, the inspector paid me a visit. He asked the same question over and over.

Why did I do it?

No matter how many times I told him I hadn't, he wouldn't believe me. Mackiel had bewitched them all with his lies, as he'd bewitched me at ten years old. Funny that it took his betrayal for me to finally see the truth. He'd tended to the greed in my heart, which had blossomed into a twisted vine, touching every part of me.

My throat was raw from screaming my innocence. While there were several cells in the underbelly of the palace's prison, they were all empty—no inmates to keep me company. Had the guards removed them in fear of my superior assassination skills? Did they believe I could kill someone merely by looking at them? Guards were posted outside the door leading down to the prison, but they only visited to deliver my food with a side order of spit.

There was nothing to distract me from imagining myself rotting away. Skin turning to bones. Bones to ash. But that was silly. They'd kill me before that happened.

This cell was merely a precursor to the main event: my hanging. For a crime as serious as murder would be punished by their quadrant's preferred method. And Toria favored the gentle caress of a rope around the neck.

Lucky me.

I wished I had that dagger now—my dipper bracelet—because I knew what to do with it. Find a nice home between two of Mackiel's ribs.

Perhaps I was an assassin after all.

———

I KNEW THEY were planning to kill me the day the food started improving. It wasn't normal prison food. It was *we're about to kill you, therefore you might as well enjoy it while you can* food.

It was the evening of my third day in prison, and my sixth day within the palace. For dinner, they served me a piece of roast chicken with two gooey garlic bread rolls. My favorite.

I hurled the bread rolls across the room.

Mackiel. He must've told them my favorite meal. My final dinner.

He was playing me still.

I couldn't let him win the final game between us. I let my fury ignite within me. I'd get out of here. I'd show Mackiel how well he'd trained me.

This was another job. Mackiel's final lesson. The scenario: to be locked inside a cell with nothing but my wits. I didn't even have buttons or zips or laces; the cutoffs from the old dresses were intentionally unembellished. The stiff material chafed against my skin, which became more sensitive the longer I sat hidden from fresh air and sun.

I needed something to pick the lock. *Anything.* But the guards hadn't given me utensils; they knew all my tricks. I could use anything to escape. After all, I'd managed to break out of the processing room, sneak around the palace, and kill all four queens without anyone seeing me.

I laughed quietly to myself.

I ate the chicken and kept the small bones, hiding them under my bed. I would wait for them to harden until I could break them into shards.

Then break the cell lock.

I hoped there was enough time.

CHAPTER FORTY

Arebella

The days after the assassin's arrest were the best in Arebella's seventeen years. But she had to hide that fact. She needed to appear like a fish out of water, a grieving daughter, a fledgling queen, for a little while longer. Until it was acceptable to be the queen she was born to be. The queen she'd spent her lifetime becoming.

She'd waited this long; she could wait a few more weeks until her true capabilities showed. She'd run the scenarios through her mind late at night: days would be too short, but weeks wouldn't be suspicious. Months? Well, she couldn't wait that long.

Arebella knew her plot to rule Quadara wouldn't be without opposition. If any blood relatives were found, then they could rightfully take their places, but Mackiel had promised they'd been taken care of, and no descendants would step forward—*could* step forward.

Still, it made Arebella nervous. Even inside the palace, there was a chance everything could fall down around her. Her perfect plan ruined. And while everything had gone smoothly thus far, she felt unsteady. One unruly, and unexpected, card could topple the entire pile. She wondered who or what that card might be and how she could remove it without collapsing her entire plan. Yes, she was inside the palace, but she was still waiting. Forever waiting. She was soon to be named queen of Toria, but that had never been her ambition. To change Toria and improve their standing, she needed to be queen of all the quadrants. If not, everything she'd done had been for nothing.

At night, while her mind ran through the details of what had come to pass, and what was still to come, the image of her dead mother could not be forgotten. Sometimes she imagined her mother speaking to her from the world without borders. She would say that she understood, that she was sorry she'd denied Arebella what was rightfully hers. Other times, she imagined her mother's skin peeling back from a slice in her neck, black bile dripping from her lips, hair floating around her crown as though she were submerged in water, and red flames reflected in her eyes. She would point a bony finger at Arebella and open her mouth to scream, cursing her for everything she'd done to her and her sister queens.

But it wasn't due to guilt, Arebella told herself. No, it was merely shock. Her mother had been the first dead body she'd ever seen, and the image would likely never leave. After all, Arebella had always overthought things. Death would be no different.

She would replace that image with more important ones. Like being the first sole queen of Quadara, and her first ruling: to demolish the walls that separated the quadrants. Only then could Toria and Torians truly thrive.

CHAPTER FORTY-ONE

Keralie

I was considering the details of my hanging—would it be public, or would I disappear from this world, my mother and father never to know what happened to me?—when footsteps descended the stone stairs.

I looked up. The chicken bones had yet to harden. This could be my chance to obtain a weapon.

"Hello."

That voice. An electric lantern rose in the darkness, lighting Varin's expression. Good for him—he managed to look sorry. He must've spent time practicing in the mirror.

"Go away." I returned to my examination of the filthy cell floor. He wouldn't have anything on him that would help me.

"No." His voice was stronger, set. He placed the lantern on the ground between us.

"Fine. Stay for all I care, but I don't want to hear your traitorous apologies."

He let out a humorless laugh. "Me? A traitor? *You* played me, Keralie."

I wanted to block out the break in his voice. Even though I hated him, it still plucked at my heart, which I'd opened for the first time since I'd left my parents. *Stupid, stupid Keralie.*

"I'd rather not waste my last few hours alive arguing who played who better," I muttered. "But just for interest, what did Mackiel offer you to turn on me?" I stood, throwing my hands wide. "There's no one here to hear your lies. Tell me the truth. I deserve that, at least. What did you trade me in for? Did he offer you a dose of HIDRA? Did you see we were failing and found yourself a better deal?"

"He gave me nothing." He stepped forward, and I noticed his eyes were glimmering with unshed tears. "I didn't know he was even in the palace until after I spoke with the inspector. Mackiel verified what I'd seen you do."

"Enough!" I stepped as close to him as I could with the bars separating us. "Tell. Me. The. Truth!"

He grabbed the bars on either side of my face. "I've told you the truth! Why can't you do the same? Do you have so much pride that you can't admit what you've done? Tell me why you betrayed me!"

I stumbled backward—his fury tangible. "You think I'm capable of murder?" My voice crumbled to nothing.

"I didn't." His eyes pierced mine. "Until I saw you with that bottle of poison. Until everything pointed to you. I couldn't turn away from the truth."

I raked my hands down my face. "That *never* happened! And I didn't even know my bracelet could do that! Don't you see? It was Mackiel all this time. He framed me!"

He sighed and shook his head. "I came here to see if you would admit it and tell me why."

"Mackiel, your new best friend, told you why," I snapped. "Let's not cover well-worn ground."

"Not that." He shook his head again. "I thought . . ." His face softened. "I thought you and I . . ." He sighed, hands in his hair. "I guess I was wrong."

"And I thought you cared about me!" I filled in the gaps. "I guess we were both wrong."

We stared at one another. Words, conversations, days, moments that could have been spent together left abandoned. He'd shown me a path, a different life, one of honor and loyalty and, perhaps, love. But he had taken that away, from both of us.

"You really believe I did it," I said softly. "Why?"

"Because I saw you," he said, rubbing a hand over his eyes. How much sleep had he had since I'd been arrested? If he thought I was guilty, why did it still torture him? And why did I still care?

"Saw me do what?"

"Stop playing games!" he said. "You want me to doubt what I saw."

"I'm not playing any games. I'm trying to save my life!"

He swallowed roughly. "I can't argue with you anymore, Keralie. If you won't tell me the truth, then I can't make you. You're the best liar, after all."

His words were like a physical blow. I couldn't convince him I wasn't guilty. For some reason, he'd seen something to turn him against me. Something he believed in more than he believed in me.

How could he place faith in what he'd seen when he was going blind?

351

And yet I couldn't make him doubt himself. The words burned on the tip of my tongue, words that might free me but would break him. I couldn't tear Varin apart like that. I couldn't use his condition against him. I didn't really hate him, after all.

"You thought you were doing what was right," I said, understanding. "You thought I was the assassin. That's why you turned me in." I suppose that made it easier to understand, rather than Varin betraying me. I placed my hand on his on the cell bar, desperate for contact, but his dermasuit gloves were back in place. "But I didn't do it. Trust me now."

He glanced away. "I can't."

And although I understood why—he was Eonist, led to believe in truth and logic—my heart fractured at his words. I'd thought he was more than that. But he still hadn't learned to use his heart over his head.

"Here." He pushed something between the bars.

"What is it?" I asked, picking up a scrunched piece of paper from the ground. I didn't know what to expect, but I gasped when I flattened it to reveal an intricate pencil sketch. "It's me." My eyes reflected back at me, a sly smile upon my face. "When did you do this?" I asked.

"It doesn't matter." He studied his feet, his shoulders drooping forward. "It's a lie. Everything was a lie. You can add it to your collection."

Fat tears fell from my eyes, blotting the paper. I wiped them away, not wanting to ruin the drawing further. I looked happy. I looked beautiful. I looked like a good person. I looked like someone who had her whole life in front of her.

It *was* a lie.

"Why give this to me now?" I asked, wishing my voice sounded stronger.

"I don't need it." He didn't even want to remember me.

I swallowed down my tears. "Can you do me a favor?" I asked.

"I won't break you out of here."

"Not that." I took in a shuddering breath and let it out. "Find my parents—my mother." My father would be dead in weeks. "Tell her what happened. Tell her I was trying to make things right." Now I never would. "Tell her I'm sorry."

He nodded. "I will."

"Please don't tell her what you believe about me." I still couldn't put *assassin, the queens,* and *me* in a sentence together. It was too ludicrous. "They'll probably hear it from the Queenly Reports anyway."

He picked up the lantern, then headed for the stairs. Hesitating at the top, he glanced back one last time. "I wanted to believe it wasn't true, that I *hadn't* seen what I thought I had. But—"

"You don't trust me. You never did."

"That's not it. I do—I *did.* I trusted you. More than I've ever trusted anyone. More than I will let myself trust anyone ever again." His eyes glimmered with sadness.

What had he seen that had made him doubt me? How could he be so wrong?

"I'm sorry," I said. Even if it changed nothing, even if I was still to go to the gallows, I wanted him on my side. I wanted him to believe in us. I needed that perfect moment in the sewing room to carry me through to the end. I wanted to believe in the boy who'd drawn this beautiful picture of me. "I'm sorry I hurt you. But I didn't kill the queens. I swear it."

He let out a heated breath. "The more you deny it, the worse it is. It's like you don't even know what you did. You believe in your lies so much they've become your reality."

Was that true? Was I in denial? *No.* I didn't do this. Mackiel did. The henchmen did. I was set up to take their fall.

I dipped my head, unable to watch him leave. "Good-bye, Varin," I whispered.

CHAPTER FORTY-TWO

Arebella

F inally, the day of Arebella's coronation had arrived.
She had visualized this day more than any other moment in her life. To her, it marked the real change. Not
the moment her mother died, or when she entered the palace, but
the moment she was assigned the Torian throne and acquired the
power of all the Torian queens who'd come before her.

With the assassin in prison and her execution date set for
later that evening, it was time. Time the advisors moved on from
their grief and embraced their new queen, for Quadara needed her.
Now more than ever. The Quadarian public had yet to be notified
of the queens' murders, but would be, as soon as Arebella was on
the throne. That way, there would be no mass panic.

She couldn't wait to record her first Queenly Report for the
entire nation to see.

The palace seamstresses had made her an exquisite gown,
tailored to Arebella's every curve. She wondered if she would wear
it again. Perhaps she could wear it every day? Or would that be too

much? Or did she care? She was about to become queen, above all judgment.

She tried not to overthink it, and stepped into the dress as if stepping into another life—her real self emerging.

The dress was ice white, with lace from her neck down to her waist, where it met a large silk sash. When she turned and looked in the mirror, she saw the back of the dress gaped open, exposing her milky-white skin. The skirt fell to the floor with a long train behind her, which would run the distance from her rooms to the Torian throne—a coronation tradition representing where the queen had come from and where she was headed.

Arebella gave one final look at her reflection, tucking a strand of auburn hair under her golden crown, before setting out.

The palace staff greeted her as she walked the hallway, and the sun shone down from the dome above her, tinting her white gown gold. Jenri had invited the entire palace to participate.

"They need levity at this time," he'd said. "They need to celebrate."

They need to move on, Arebella had thought.

The staff sang the coronation tune: a combination of only four notes, sung in various patterns. Four notes to symbolize the four quadrants. And four queens.

Soon to be one, Arebella thought. While Jenri and the other advisors had yet to name her queen of all the quadrants, she knew it was the only remaining option.

Arebella couldn't contain her smile. She knew she looked radiant—more beautiful than she could've ever imagined. For a brief moment, she wondered what her mother would say. She swallowed down the thought and let the moment sink into her bones.

Be present. Be here. Be happy.

Mackiel stood in an adjoining corridor; he tipped his bowler hat with his bandaged hands as she passed, a cunning smile upon his face. Everything had gone to plan. More than that. Everything had gone perfectly. No one suspected a thing.

And her mind was calm. She didn't have visions of murdering queens, seducing black market traders or burying her ghoulish mother.

She would finally be a queen. And soon, the first queen of Quadara.

MACKIEL HAD WARNED her not to do this. He'd said Keralie would get inside her head; she was twisted like that. But Arebella needed to see her face, the girl who had fallen for Arebella to rise.

Arebella had often thought about the girl who sat in the palace prison. And although Keralie had served her purpose, Arebella struggled to leave her behind and focus on the future. Her presence troubled Arebella, like a pebble in her shoe.

If Arebella could see the girl, perhaps she could rid her from her mind.

Two guards escorted Arebella down to the palace prison. She asked them to leave her, but they refused, their destabilizers unhooked and armed. This was Jenri's doing, Arebella thought. He wouldn't leave her side during the day and posted guards at her door at night to ensure her safety. A promise to her mother, he'd said.

Arebella cursed her mother for controlling her life from beyond the grave.

"Hello," Arebella said to the prisoner.

Keralie looked up. An expression shifted across her face as she took in the young queen, dressed in her favorite golden dress, matching the golden crown on her head. "Who are you?" Keralie asked.

"Queen Arebella," she had the joy of saying for the first time.

Keralie studied her. "Queen Marguerite's daughter?" Arebella nodded. "I'm sorry about your mother."

Arebella tilted her head. "Sorry you killed her?"

Keralie harrumphed, but said nothing further. Clearly, she'd tired of arguing her innocence. "Have we met before?" Keralie said suddenly, tilting her head. "You look familiar."

"No." Arebella said firmly. She had to divert Keralie from this line of questioning, but she hadn't put much thought into this visit. She no longer had anything to plan for. She had everything she needed and wanted, and her questioning mind continued to remain blissfully silent. Mostly. Aside from the ghostly thoughts of her mother and this pebble in her shoe. At least she could be rid of one of them.

"I'm glad to see you have guards with you," Keralie muttered.

Arebella bristled. "Is that a threat?"

Keralie held up her hands. Her fingernails were stained green from something—food? "What could I possibly do to you, Queen Arebella?"

Arebella glanced at the guards behind her before replying, "You're a resourceful girl. I won't make the mistake of underestimating you. Not like everyone else has."

All those queens, slain by this little thing?

Arebella could see how preposterous it would seem. She was so . . . innocent-looking with her large blue eyes and small features. Even bedraggled, her blond hair curled into dirty little ringlets. She looked like a doll that had been left outside in the dirt and rain.

Mackiel had chosen well.

"I really wish I could take all of this as a compliment." Keralie waved her hands around the cell. "But the fact you all think I'm capable of succeeding in murdering the queens with no one seeing me is ridiculous."

Arebella stepped closer, her eyes widening. "*Compliment?* That's an interesting word to use."

Keralie let out a ragged sigh. "Tell me," she said. "Tell me what you came here for."

Arebella grinned. It was a ruthless smile. "Your execution is set for later this evening. And you will die by your quadrant's preferred method."

They lived by the quadrant's rules and died by them.

"*My* quadrant . . ." Keralie mused. "*Your* quadrant. How interesting. You know, you really do look familiar." She stared at Arebella with such intensity that Arebella had to glance away.

"Hanging," Arebella said, ignoring Keralie's pointed look. "You will die by hanging."

"Thought as much," Keralie replied with a shrug, although her expression showed she cared more than she let on. "Anything further, my queen?"

"Is that all you have to say to me?" Arebella asked, one eyebrow raised. She thought she'd feel some closure upon seeing the girl who had taken the fall, but she felt nothing. She hoped it would be enough to let her mind move on to something else. "Anything further you wish to say before your hanging?"

"Yes," Keralie replied, her eyes narrowing. "Keep those guards with you."

"Another threat?"

She shrugged again. "Only that the assassin is still in the palace. You better be careful, or you'll see your mother again sooner than you think."

Arebella pursed her lips to stop a smile. "Keralie, don't you think it's time you accept the truth?"

When Keralie didn't reply, Arebella turned on her heel and headed toward the stairs.

"Good-bye, Keralie." *And thank you.* "May the other queens meet you in the quadrant without borders." *Together, yet apart.* She grinned. "And let them have their revenge."

CHAPTER FORTY-THREE

Keralie

Later that day, I received another visitor. One who had me hissing and spitting like the stray cat I'd attempted to pick up outside the auction house when I was a child.

"Get away from me!" I cried as Mackiel closed the prison door behind him and walked down the stairs toward my cell. "Guards!" For once I wanted them down here. "Guards!"

"Calm, calm, darlin'," he said, voice as soothing as ever as he approached. "Haven't you missed me?"

"Why are you still here?" I asked. "You got what you wanted!" Queen Marguerite was dead; the Jetée would live on, his business was safe.

"Why would I leave?" He squared his shoulders. "I've been invited to remain in the palace by my dear friend Queen Arebella. I will be her royal confidant."

I shook my head. I'd never heard her name before I met her this morning.

"Oh yes," he said, reading the confusion on my face. "We've

been friends for many years." He gripped two of the bars, his hands unbandaged. And healed. I gasped.

"Oh, you noticed?" He wiggled his fingers at me. "I was granted permission by our lovely new queen to use a dose of HIDRA. This year's dose. Aren't I lucky?" He grinned.

I fought the urge to scream. My father was on the verge of death, Varin would be killed at thirty for going blind, and Mackiel was granted a precious dose of HIDRA? It wasn't right.

"Do you want to know a secret?" he asked. "You're stuck here, not long till your hanging, so why not?" He shrugged his narrow shoulders.

I pressed my lips together. I didn't want to know anything Mackiel offered willingly. It would only be a trick.

"Do you know why HIDRA is so rare?"

I didn't reply.

"HIDRA was once a woman. But she wasn't only a woman, she was a doctor. A *tweaked* doctor."

A *woman*? If a doctor could cure every injury and disease, why didn't she help more than one person a year?

When I said nothing, he fluttered a hand at me. "I know what you're thinking, like my henchmen, but no. She was something else." He grinned. "She was tweaked so she could work with the sick and diseased but never fall ill. One day, she helped remove a shard of glass from someone's abdomen, but it sliced her hand open in the process. Her blood dripped into the patient's wound. And *bam*"—he clapped his hands together—"the wound began to heal." His smile was as slow as my prison days were long.

I gritted my teeth. I wouldn't respond. I wouldn't let him see how his words hurt me.

"Sadly," he said without any sadness, "she died many years ago. But before she was buried, her blood was drained." He studied his hands. "They tried replicating it, but all tests failed. Instead, they diluted her blood to create more doses. But few treatments remain, and I doubt they'll help a criminal and an assassin."

My back hit the far wall of the cell as I scrambled away from him.

"Nice outfit, by the way," he commented on my rags. "Though I can't say the color does much for your complexion."

"Leave me alone," I said. "I have more important things to do today."

"I suppose you do." He sighed, then tugged at his collar. "My lovely Kera, how I wish everything had turned out differently."

"Differently?" I snarled. "You framed me! You were behind all of this, and your henchmen did the dirty work, as they always do. Today I'll die instead of you."

"Me?" He pointed a ringed finger at his chest. "Oh no, I didn't kill the queens. Neither did the henchmen. They're back in Toria minding the auction house while I'm here. I thought we'd worked this out? I'll be clearer. *You*"—he pointed at me—"murdered the queens."

"No one's here, Mackiel. Cut the bullshit."

"Darlin', you're wrong. On many levels. And I do wish everything had turned out differently; I never planned for you to be caught. That was your *boyfriend's* fault." His eyes turned steely at the word. Hatred slithered under his skin, close to being exposed, the true Mackiel hiding below the charming surface. "He'd told the inspector about you before I arrived. I had to change my plans."

"You admit it, then?" Finally, someone was speaking the truth. "You planned this? You bribed Varin?"

"Yes and no." He tilted his head; his bowler hat had been

replaced with a golden top hat—it didn't suit him. "I was involved, but I didn't bribe Varin. And I really didn't want you to be caught. I've invested far too much time and money in you to watch you die. Even after our little squabble." He twisted his hands in the low light as though he was checking for imperfections.

"I . . ." My legs threatened to fold. "What do you mean?"

"Kera." I wished he would stop saying my name. I didn't want him to be the last person to say it. Anyone but him.

"You were good, *too* good, at your job," he said. "Sadly, running away was never something you did well." He held out a hand. "I always tried to teach you . . ."

Get in quick. Get out quicker.

"No," I whispered. "I didn't do it." But the look on his face confirmed it. He wasn't lying.

He grinned. "I needed an assassin, but it's not easy to hire one. Not without having to share my plan with a stranger—someone who could easily betray me. About a year ago, I realized I already had the perfect assassin." A year ago . . . when Mackiel started acting strangely toward me. Distant. "I already had someone with the skills to get in and out without anyone noticing. My sweet little Kera. My best dipper. I'd trained you well."

"But I didn't kill them." I couldn't. Wouldn't. It wasn't possible.

"You did, darlin'. You just don't remember. Do these look familiar?" He held something out in his palm.

"Comm chips," I muttered.

Mackiel shook his head. "They're more than that."

"What are they?" I didn't want him to answer.

"Amazing little things." He picked up one of the chips and held it to his eye. "They're a new kind of comm chip, more

evolved. And illegal, as they have a few unwanted side effects."
He shrugged. "But you know my friends on the wall?" *Friends* was
hardly the word I'd have used for the wall guards Mackiel black-
mailed. "They were happy to inform me of the latest shipment of
this banned Eonist tech. The chips were to be delivered to a Ludist
official to see if they could be used for entertainment purposes. All
I had to do was intercept the delivery."

Then he had been telling the truth about the original recipient of the comm chips being dead.

"You did well stealing these from the messenger and ensuring
I didn't get my hands on them by ingesting them. Ingenious of
you, really. I was planning to force-feed them to you or hide them
in your food, but it was best you didn't know my involvement."

"I don't understand," I said.

"Poor Kera. Don't you see? It was the chips that contained the
plans to murder the queens. *My* plans. Before you stole them for
me, the chips were blank. Harmless. But things get interesting when
you record thoughts onto them." He flashed his canine teeth and my
stomach turned. "When I learned you were trying to redeliver the
chips at the House of Concord, I paid you a visit to ensure you were
going to head to the palace," he said. "You thought your decision to
come here was your own. You thought your mind was your own."

I'd stolen the chips for Mackiel. I'd ingested them to prevent
Mackiel from getting his hands on them.

Mackiel. Mackiel. Mackiel. It had always been him.

"What do they do?" My voice was barely audible, the truth
pressing down on me.

"They're a form of control." His deep-set kohl-lined eyes
watched me closely. "Once they've been ingested, you only need

to set off three little triggers." He tossed the chip into the air and caught it in his other hand. "Touch the murder weapon." He ran a finger around his bare wrist. "Enter the palace." He gestured to our surroundings. "See the queens." He grinned, wiggling four fingers at me. "Then nothing will stop you from enacting the plan—my plan." He knocked a finger down one at a time. "You, my perfect assassin."

Control.

I stared at my hands. They were shaking. "One of your games, Mackiel?"

His face softened for a moment. "I'm afraid not."

"Then I *did* kill them?"

"Yes. I know it's hard to understand, as you don't remember, but you did, and all the evidence proves you did. In fact, the inspector found traces of each and every queen's DNA on your dipper bracelet. They even found your hair on Queen Stessa's drowned body. That's what they were waiting for—concrete evidence—before you could be sentenced."

I remembered holding the knife in my hand as I sliced Queen Iris's throat, but that was the comm chips. I didn't feel the handle turn slick and warm as blood coated the blade. I didn't smell the rust of blood.

Not me. It couldn't have been me.

Only, Mackiel was saying the comm chips weren't merely instructions for the assassin, but controlled the assassin's body as well as their senses. And I couldn't deny what my bracelet could turn into. I'd been carrying a deadly weapon while I was in the palace. I'd had the weapon for months, made complete when Mackiel gave me the locket for successfully stealing the comm case. This was his plan all along, set in motion a year ago.

I began shaking my head wildly. "No, no, no, no, no."

I was the assassin. *Mackiel's* assassin. Varin had been right; he'd seen me with the bottle of poison because I *had* poisoned Queen Marguerite. My hair had been wet and perfumed because I'd drowned Queen Stessa. And my dress, splattered in blood—I'd thought it was from my split knee, but now I realized the truth. It was Queen Iris's blood. And I couldn't deny I'd been right there when Queen Corra had been consumed by smoke and ash.

I crumpled to the floor, wiping my hands frantically on my rags. "It can't be."

I couldn't have murdered the queens that violently, that thoughtlessly. I had my own mind. I was not a weapon. I never meant to bring any pain, shed any blood.

But I did. I broke things. I ruined them. Like I'd broken my father.

"That's one of the benefits of these little darlings." He twirled a chip around. "You dismiss the memories of the murders as the visions you saw. Because you carried them out in the exact same way. Who could tell the difference?" He winked at me. "Certainly not you."

I clutched my stomach. I was going to be sick.

What had I been thinking in those moments? When I'd killed each and every queen with my own hands? Had I any thoughts of my own? Or was I an empty vessel, ready for the taking? To be used by someone like Mackiel. The perfect assassin, he'd said.

A doll, that was all I was to him. Something to play with. Something to use. How long had he been grooming me for this, the worst possible act?

"Why?" I moaned.

"Now, now," Mackiel cooed as I trembled. "Don't fall apart. That's not the Kera I know."

No wonder Varin had turned me in. He'd seen what I'd done. He'd seen the truth.

Only it wasn't true—not the truth I held in my heart. Yes, I was selfish. Greedy. Vicious, even—at times. But I wasn't an assassin. Even Mackiel couldn't turn me into that.

For a moment, I was able to push back the disgust, the tumbling of my stomach at the sight of my hands, and remember that Mackiel had said he didn't want me to be caught.

"You're here to free me?" I asked, voice trembling. I could explain. I could tell the inspector I wasn't in control of my actions. That had to count for something, right?

He frowned. "I'm afraid not, darlin'."

"But you said—"

"I know." He held out his healed hands. "Believe me, I didn't want it to end this way. As I said, you were supposed to escape. The comm chips told you to leave after Queen Marguerite's murder, but your mind was torn. Instead, you returned to that blasted Eonist. He's what got you caught. And I had such grand plans for you—"

"More murders?" I sprung to my feet. "How dare you use me! How dare you make me kill the queens! Kill anyone! I thought you cared about me?"

"I do," he said, leaning forward, gripping the prison bars. "Don't you see, darlin'? I would never entrust such an important job to anyone other than you." His grin turned venomous. "But you were the one who turned from me first. You trusted that useless Eonist instead of your closest friend. You *cared* that he would suffer if he didn't deliver his comm case. *I* was meant to come to the palace with you. You weren't meant to care about anyone but me!" His eyes flashed, a storm breaking. "You forced my hand."

"*I* forced *your* hand? You forced me to kill!" Fury moved my body forward. I reveled in it. I wanted to forget what I'd done. "I wish we'd never met! You took everything from me!"

He tilted his head. "I suppose I did, seeing your final hours are almost up."

"Why did you come here if not to free me? Was it merely to gloat?"

He looked uncertain for a moment. "I wanted to say good-bye, I suppose."

"Good-bye?" I spat in his face. Everyone wanted their good-bye. They'd decided who I was, what I'd done and how I'd be punished.

Who do you want to be?

Well, I wasn't done. Not yet. "I reject your good-bye."

"Reject it?" He laughed. "You can't reject a good-bye. You can only receive it, darlin'."

"Really?" I asked. "Well, this is *my* good-bye." I grabbed his lapel and rammed his face into the bars. He let out a gasp. I struck a fist through the bars and into his stomach. He buckled forward, his coat opening.

My hands darted into the shadows of his coat pockets.

"Good, Kera," he said, wheezing. "Fight to the end." Then he grabbed my wrist. "But I'll be needing this." He pried his lock pick blade from my right hand. "Nice try, though."

"Damn you!" I wrestled against him.

"I'm sorry, darlin'. I truly wish I could let you escape. And I will miss you."

"Why?" I tore away from him, tears breaking through my resolve and streaking down my face. "Why won't you help me? After all we've been through." Was there nothing of the old

Mackiel left? Nothing that pulled at his heart when he looked at me? Nothing of our childhood on the Jetée?

He glanced upward, to the palace above. "In the end, one must make the best deals for oneself." He grinned at me. "You were my ticket to power, and I'm not about to undo it by releasing you."

"Queen Arebella," I said with understanding. "She orchestrated the murders!" *Accept the truth.* That was what she'd said when she visited, and it had struck me as an odd thing to say to someone you were convinced had killed your mother.

Not *admit* the truth, but *accept*. And now I remembered where I'd seen her before. The girl in the blue bonnet at the auction house that Mackiel had been helping to her seat. She'd been there all along.

Mackiel raised an eyebrow. "Did she?" he mused. "I guess you'll never know. But I'll have more power here as Arebella's confidant than I ever could've achieved back at the Jetée. And I'll ensure no one will threaten my business again. Not even a queen." His expression grew intense. "No one will *ever* forget my name."

Infamy. That was what this was about? Mackiel's father had always said he'd amount to nothing, and he was determined to prove him wrong.

My tears fell heavier now, blurring my vision. Blurring Mackiel. Blocking the hideous truth. "Get out!"

This time, he obliged. He tipped his gold top hat and left me sobbing on the prison floor.

Once his footsteps could no longer be heard, I wiped away the tears with my right hand. In my left was the second blade I'd stolen from Mackiel's pockets.

Yes, he'd taught me well.

CHAPTER FORTY-FOUR

Arebella
Queen of Toria

*Rule thirteen: Only a queen may sit upon
the throne. When she takes the throne, she
accepts the responsibility to rule the quadrant
until her dying day.*

Arebella took her throne, unable to avoid glancing at the empty thrones beside her. A tug lifted the corner of her mouth. Up on the dais, she could sense the power coursing through her. The power of ruling a quadrant—soon to be a nation. A nation no longer divided.

Mackiel had done his job; no living blood relatives could be found. Arebella would soon be named the only living Quadarian with royal blood. The next step was clear: she would become queen of Quadara.

Once she was seated, the entire palace staff and advisors took their seats opposite her. Some Torians still wore black, their faces covered by veils. It was clear from the advisors' tight expressions that they were unhappy with only one queen up on the dais. Their system was falling apart.

Arebella glanced at the Quadarian dial behind her. It was an overcast day; little light shone from the apex of the dome above, down to the golden jewel in the middle of the dial's face. The Queenly Laws were hardly decipherable in the low light, which was appropriate, Arebella thought, for the start of a new era. She would rewrite all the rules.

Mackiel grinned at her from the front row. They'd done it. They'd actually done it.

"You called this meeting," Arebella said to Jenri. "What's the agenda?" *Act surprised. Act outraged. Make them think this was never my intention. The final act.*

"Yes, Queen Arebella," Jenri replied. "I'm afraid to say we have failed." He cleared his throat. "We have failed to find any royal ancestors for Archia, Ludia and Eonia."

She raised her chin. "How is that possible? I thought it was part of Queenly Law to ensure the royal line?"

He exchanged a glance with the other advisors. "We do not know what's happened, but it appears that all traces of royal relatives have disappeared."

"What does that mean for me?" she asked, before realizing her mistake. "What does that mean for the *other* quadrants? Who will take the thrones?"

He let out a deep and exhausted sigh. Dark circles rested below his eyes. She doubted he'd slept since he found out about her mother's passing. But that was not her concern; in fact, it might work in her favor.

"Well?" she asked. "We can't leave the quadrants unruled. My Queenly Report is due to be broadcast this evening after the execution. We must act quickly. An unruled nation is a weak nation."

That's it. Lead them to the water . . . but don't push them in . . . Mackiel's voice was in her head. He nodded infinitesimally at her.

"You are right, my queen," Jenri replied. "We cannot wait a moment longer. The people will not be pleased to hear we've concealed the truth. Rumors have begun to spread that something awful has happened. We must announce the deaths of the queens, and your rise to the Torian throne, to keep the peace."

"Yes, yes." Arebella nodded a little too enthusiastically. "It must be done."

Jenri motioned to one of his staff. "Record a special Queenly Report detailing the murders to follow Queen Arebella's coronation announcement."

Arebella sat straighter in her throne. Waiting . . . Waiting . . . When he did not say any more, Arebella rose.

"My queen?" he asked. "Is there something else you wish to speak of today?"

Were they all fools? What were they waiting for?

"A decision must be made," she replied, her voice filling the cavernous chamber.

"A decision?" he asked, the bags underneath his eyes seeming to swell. "About what, my queen?"

Fools it was, then.

"For the other quadrants." She eased the frustration from her voice. "Toria is protected, but what about the others?"

"I'm sorry, my queen. But as I said, we could not find any living relatives. We will continue to search for other female descendants, those not directly related to the queens, but we'll have to run genetic testing on the entire population of Quadara. It could take years to find someone with royal blood."

373

"Years?" Arebella pressed her lips together for a moment. "We can't leave the other quadrants without a queen for that long, can we?"

"No," he said uncertainly, glancing to the other advisors, who shook their heads in agreement. "I suppose not."

"Then another system needs to be put in place. We have no choice." Her patience was wearing thin. Surely, he could see they were out of options. When he didn't speak, she added, "Temporarily, of course."

Jenri turned to the other advisors, and they began speaking heatedly. After what seemed like hours, he turned back to Arebella.

"You are the only surviving Quadarian with royal blood," he said. Arebella lowered her head sagely. "We could place you in charge of the other quadrants, however—"

"If that's what must be done," she interrupted. "Then I will endure the extra burden."

"But, my queen." Jenri's eyes were wide. "If you were to take their thrones, there is no undoing it. It would not be temporary."

Arebella knew all of this, but she forced her face to scrunch in confusion. "Why?"

"It is part of Queenly Law, something we must uphold. For if anyone with royal blood is to take the throne, then they absorb the power of that quadrant until their dying day."

"But that law was written for the queen's quadrant only," one of the advisors said. She was a tall woman with white hair. *Alissa.* Arebella remembered her from one of the many introductions over the last few days. She was married to Queen Corra's former handmaiden. "When a queen takes her throne, she is bound to that throne till her death."

"It is not stipulated that she can only hold one throne," Jenri said.

Yes. Yes. Finally, they are getting it.

"Jenri," Arebella said, bowing her head slightly, "I will do whatever my quadrant or quadrants want of me. Whatever is best for Quadara." She pinned him with her gaze. "It's what my mother would have wanted."

That's it. Play upon his weakness. Mackiel's voice was clear in her head.

Jenri addressed the other advisors. "We were planning to wait till we found a distant descendant, but Arebella proposes a quicker solution. If the choice is between the quadrants being notified their queen is dead and no one has yet to take the throne, or the quadrants being notified their queen is dead and the last royal will rule all the quadrants, then we have no choice but to place Queen Arebella in charge of all of Quadara."

"For all time?" Ketor, the old, stoic Eonist advisor, asked. "That is too much to ask."

"Until her dying day," Jenri clarified. "As Queenly Law states. We cannot read around the laws at such an unstable time."

This is it. This is it. Arebella bunched her skirts in her hands to stop from shaking.

"No," said another advisor. He had red hair, and it was clear from his bloodshot eyes that he'd been crying. *Lyker.* It had to be. She'd heard the palace staff whispering about his scandalous relationship with Queen Stessa. "That's not what Stess—that's not what Queen Stessa would've wanted. She wanted to protect Ludia and keep it separate from the other quadrants. What would this—" He looked at Arebella. "I mean, what would the queen know of the other quadrants' wishes? She just arrived here. She didn't even know she was a royal until six days ago. And she's so young!"

How dare he! He was barely older than her.

"I agree," Ketor said. "Queen Corra would also have been against this."

But she's dead. They're all dead. Arebella bit her tongue to stop from replying. Mackiel subtly held a hand up, palm facing her. *Take deep breaths. Don't let them know what you want.* She knew what he was trying to say.

"Then you teach Queen Arebella everything you know," Jenri said. "Ensure she rules wisely."

"What other choice do we have?" he asked when the other advisors didn't reply. "Queen Arebella is correct. We cannot wait years to find someone suitable. It is too risky."

"But Queenly Law . . ." Alissa lamented. She glanced at the walls around her, but the etched words were still unclear due to the little sunlight filtering in from above.

"These are desperate times," Jenri said. "We must do what is right for Quadara. The queens would all have agreed to that."

Alissa lowered her head. "Yes, Queen Iris would do anything for her quadrant. I suppose even if it meant sitting a Torian upon her throne."

Ketor nodded solemnly, while Lyker stayed quiet. Clearly, he did not agree with the other advisors.

"Queen Arebella?" Jenri's sullen eyes were back upon hers. "The choice is yours."

Yes. Yes. Yes.

"Of course," she replied. "I will do what is right for Quadara, for my people. And I will respect the memory of the passed queens."

Don't look at Mackiel. Don't look at Mackiel, she warned herself, for she knew she would be unable to hide her grin.

"Good," Jenri said. "You are already a queen; all that must be done now is to sit upon each throne and declare your loyalty to that quadrant."

Arebella rose. "I'm ready."

CHAPTER FORTY-FIVE

Keralie

I waited thirty minutes before enacting my plan. I had to ensure Mackiel had left, and I needed the extra time to collect my thoughts, and myself, from the floor.

I'd killed the queens. I couldn't hide from the truth any longer. Not if I wanted to get out of here. And everything finally made sense. Why I was always close to each queen's death, but too late to save her. How could I have saved the queens from myself?

I'd thought my timing had been off since I entered the palace, unable to save the queens, but I'd been right on schedule. Exactly as Mackiel had planned it. Me, his windup doll. The ticking-time-clock assassin.

But this wouldn't break me. All my other faults were on me. My parents' boat, my father's injury, my years of thieving and running away. But not this. Yes, I'd delivered death to each queen, but I wasn't culpable. I'd come to the palace to save the queens, not hurt them. My hand might've struck them down, but Mackiel controlled the blade. *He* was the guilty one.

I couldn't let him get away with this.

I was halfway up the prison stairs, ready to fight the guards outside, when soft footsteps padded from the adjoining corridor. I darted to the top and pressed against the door, waiting for the guard to round the corner and meet my raised fist. I wasn't willing to use Mackiel's blade on anyone but a locked door.

The guard opened the door; my first punch met his stomach, sending him to the ground. I launched on top of him, my second punch aimed for his temple.

"Stop," the guard said. "It's me!"

"Varin?" I paused, my fist hovering above his face. "What are you doing here?"

He rolled over and held up his hands. At first, I thought in surrender, but he was holding up a butter knife and fork.

"I thought you could use these," he said. "To escape."

"You came back to help? But you said—"

"I believe you," he interrupted. "I believe you didn't kill the queens. I don't know what I saw, but I know it wasn't you. It couldn't have been you." His pale eyes cut into me, sending my heart and head into a spin. "I was wrong. And I'll make it up to you. First, we need to get out of here."

"Well . . . I . . . ." How could I explain everything that *had* happened? He had no reason to question what he saw—he'd been right about me—about all of it.

"Can I get up?" he asked.

I was still straddling him, my fist clenched. "Sure." I blushed and scrambled off him. "Sorry."

We stared at one another. Before I could say anything more, he grabbed me, his arms encircling my waist.

"I'm so, so sorry." His words were whispered into my greasy hair. "Can you forgive me?"

I pushed him back, although I wanted to lose myself in the feeling of him. I'd thought I was never going to see him again, and now he wanted my forgiveness? Here he was, pushing logic and everything Eonist away and trusting his heart instead. Trusting in me. Against everything.

I couldn't find the words, my throat thick with emotion. I nodded instead.

"Let's get out of here, then." He grabbed my hand. "They're coming for you in less than an hour." But I couldn't let him do this without knowing the truth. If he was caught helping me flee the palace, then his life would be forfeit.

Could he forgive *me*?

"What?" he said. "What is it?"

I shook my head, tears threatening to fall. I didn't want him to stop looking at me the way he was looking at me. Like I was every-thing to him. His heart and his future. The girl in that drawing. I didn't want to destroy that. Destroy us.

"Keralie," he whispered, his gloved fingers on either side of my face. "We'll get out of here. Together. Don't worry."

"It's not that. You need to know the truth before you leave with me." I took a deep breath and let it out slowly. "I—I did kill the queens . . ." Saying it still felt wrong, even knowing the truth.

His posture changed immediately, his shoulders drooping, arms falling to his sides. His face blanked, as if he'd slammed a door on his emotions.

"Stop," I said quickly, reaching for him. "Let me explain."

I told him about the new Eonist technology and how Mackiel had used the chips to control me. Varin was quiet the entire time, only a flicker of emotion passing behind his eyes when I mentioned how I'd been controlled.

"Will you forgive me?" I asked, pain pinching my insides. I wasn't sure I could leave this place if he couldn't. It was one thing to help me believing I'd been framed. Now he knew the truth. I had murdered the queens. Perhaps that was too much to ask. He was Eonist. He believed in goodness and justice. He only knew how to see and judge what was in front of him. And yet he was still here. Still looking into my eyes.

"Yes," he said, though his voice was rough and cautious.

"I'll understand if you don't want to escape with me anymore." Would he push me down the stairs and back inside the cell? Would he want to see me hanged?

He pulled my face toward his and pressed a gentle kiss to my lips. I tangled my hands in his hair, feeling anchored to the world once more, and feeling more myself than I had in days. In years.

He pulled away. "Of course I want to be with you. You weren't in control of your actions. It's not your fault. It could've been anyone under Mackiel's control . . ." But his stoic mask was back in place.

I traced my hand across his rough jaw. "What are you thinking?" I wanted to pull the mask off and burn it.

"I was thinking we've wasted too much time." He grabbed my hand once more. "And that I'm going to kill Mackiel if I ever see him again."

"WHERE ARE ALL the guards?" I asked as we left the prison. It was odd, considering I was to meet my executioner in under an hour.

"I may have told them they were needed by the inspector," he said with a shrug, "to prepare for the hanging."

I shot him a surprised look. "And they believed you?"

He turned away, his voice barely audible when he replied, "I'm Eonist. Plus, I turned you in. They trust me not to help you."

I gave his hand a squeeze. "I forgive you, remember that."

He glanced at me briefly, hope lighting his eyes, and opened his mouth to say more.

I chuckled. "We can talk about it later."

We hurried down the corridor toward the Archian section of the palace. Before I could push them away, images of Queen Iris flashed through my mind.

"Why are we going this way?" I asked, digging in my heels. Even if I was willing to accept I hadn't been in control when I'd slit Queen Iris's throat, that didn't mean I wanted to return to where the deed had been done.

"The Archian garden is the only access to the outside world, aside from the processing room, and there's no way we can get through the barred door. Not even you can." He grinned. "We'll have to scale down the cliff and find passage in a boat and go where no one will find us."

He'd put a lot of thought into this. A life and future planned for both of us. A life on the run. I'd never see my family again—or what was left of my family.

He tugged on my hand. "Come on."

"No."

"No?"

"I'm not going."

His brow furrowed. "But this is the only way out."

"I'm not leaving the palace." His eyes narrowed. "I want to be free, but not until the inspector and the rest of the palace know the truth. I can't let Mackiel and Arebella get away with this. She killed her own mother! She can't remain the Torian queen."

"You're willing to risk your life for this?"

I was used to putting myself above everyone else. Stealing what I wanted, doing what came naturally. Looking for quick and easy wealth. Thinking that my wants and desires were more important than everyone else's. But now I had the opportunity to be someone different. Someone worth my parents' love. The girl they'd raised me to be.

Arebella couldn't be left to rule Toria. If she was willing to kill her own mother, what else was she capable of? And with Mackiel by her side, the darkness would spread from the Jetée to the Skim and even to the palace itself. While I couldn't bring the queens back, I could do this. It didn't matter what might happen to me. The queens deserved retribution.

"Let's find the inspector," I said, pulling Varin along. "We have one final date in court."

CHAPTER FORTY-SIX

Arebella
Queen of Toria

*Rule fourteen: It is the queens' duty to ensure
peace among the quadrants.*

Arebella sat upon the Archian throne first. It was only fitting, as Queen Iris had been the first to die. Mackiel beamed from the crowd, his gold top hat askew. There would be much to celebrate tonight.

Focus, Arebella admonished herself. This was the moment she'd dreamed of for two years. There would be time to enjoy Mackiel's company later.

Alissa stood in the crowd beside her Archian wife. She gave her a resigned look before stepping up to the dais. "Queen Arebella." She sounded uncertain, her voice barely filling the vast room. "Please raise your right hand."

Arebella did as instructed. She could not hide the tremble of anticipation. Jenri gave her a reassuring smile, misreading her shaking. *Too soft,* Arebella thought. She might need to replace him, in time.

"Repeat after me," Alissa said. "I, Queen Arebella."

"I, Queen Arebella."

"Promise to uphold all that my quadrant"—she shook her head for a moment before continuing—"*Archia* believes in."

Arebella repeated the words while smiling at her new Archian advisor. Time stretched out before her with an open hand. She'd win her over, eventually.

"And with this Queenly Pledge," Alissa finished, "my life is Archia's, and Archia is my life. Until my dying day."

Arebella swallowed. *This is really happening.* Archia was hers.

"And with this Queenly Pledge," she said clearly, her voice filling the grand golden room. A ray of light warmed her back as the sun attempted to break through the clouds. A new dawn. "My life is Archia's, and Archia is my life. Until my—"

The Archian door to court flew open. The inspector entered flanked by two people. Before she could see who they were, they were swarmed by guards.

"That's not necessary," the inspector said calmly. "They are here on my authority."

"Who is it?" Arebella rose from her throne.

The guards pulled the two intruders forward.

"Keralie," Arebella said, taken aback. Next to her stood her Eonist accomplice, his face set, shoulders squared.

Keralie lifted her lips into a snarl. "Queen Arebella."

Arebella ordered the guards to take Keralie away, but her words were drowned out by the inspector's when he said, "Keralie has some important information for the court."

No. No. No. Not now. Not when she was about to get everything she ever wanted.

"Finish the coronation!" Arebella cried. But Alissa wasn't looking at her.

"Queen Arebella," Keralie said loud and clear, "is your true assassin!"

CHAPTER FORTY-SEVEN

Keralie

M e? The assassin?" Queen Arebella asked with a laugh. She addressed Alissa. "Why are you letting her waste my time?" She waved her hand and sat back upon the Archian throne.

I tried to step forward but a guard clung to my arm, unsure who to believe. "But isn't everyone allowed to attend court, my queen?" I sneered.

"Take her away." She turned her face as though the mere sight of me stung her eyes. "She killed my mother and escaped prison. She's a criminal!" Her voice grew shrill. "Take her away!"

The guard tightened his hold and started pulling me backward. But I wasn't about to be silenced. "Yes, I *am* a criminal!" I shouted. "But I'm not an assassin, much as Mackiel wanted me to be. For *you*."

"She's lying!" Queen Arebella shouted back, leaping off the throne once more. "Why are you all gaping like fools? She admits to being a criminal, and yet you listen to her? *I'm* your queen. I order you to hang her! Now!"

Jenri glanced, bewildered, between Queen Arebella and the inspector. "What's going on here?"

The inspector stepped around the guards to approach the dais. "Apologies for the confusion." His voice was calm. "Keralie and this boy"—he nodded to Varin beside me—"found me in the infirmary. They shared some very interesting information. Information about the assassin that the court should hear."

"But you have undeniable evidence, Inspector," Queen Arebella interrupted, pointing at me. "She killed the queens."

"That is true." The inspector narrowed his black eyes at me. "Including evidence given by this young man." He pointed a long finger at Mackiel, who was sitting among the advisors, as though he belonged there. But he didn't belong anywhere but a prison cell.

Anger reverberated off Varin in waves. His stoic Eonist mask was well and truly gone.

"Then why are you wasting my time?" Queen Arebella asked.

"You admit it?" Jenri asked me. "You murdered the queens?"

"By my hand, they died. But not by my heart or mind." I shook my head. "I would never choose to kill another." It would take a long time to completely accept what had happened, but for now, I would push back the grisly memories and ensure my name was cleared. "I was being controlled. By comm chips. By *her*."

There was an audible intake of breath from the crowd. Queen Arebella merely scoffed at the suggestion.

"What is she talking about?" Jenri asked the inspector.

The inspector let loose a slow smile. "Before Keralie approached me, I had a theory on the assassin, but the puzzle was not complete. All the evidence pointed to this young lady"—he gestured to me—"and yet something didn't feel right. I began to believe her denials. I wanted further proof."

"I'm glad someone was listening," I muttered.

"I was"—the inspector nodded—"as I listened to everyone within the palace. Those old and new." He glanced between Arebella and Mackiel. "Keralie being controlled was the final piece of the puzzle to fall into place."

"What are you talking about?" Queen Arebella demanded. "Comm chips don't make people do things." She let out a forced laugh. "They're for recording memories. We all know that."

"Ah." The inspector raised a hand. "A *normal* comm chip can't, but there are some that can. I know all Eonist technologies, including the ones that have been banned from our quadrant. One such black-listed technology was a form of emotion control. Rather than having to undergo years of schooling, Eonist children would ingest chips that suppressed thoughts and feelings. But the side effects were too severe, causing the children to act strangely, not of their own will. They also reported periods of blackouts. The trials were abandoned.

"Even though they were banned in Eonia, they found their way onto the black market in the other quadrants. Allowing them to be bought at the highest price by the lowest of folk."

"Arebella hired Mackiel, and he tricked me into stealing the chips and ingesting them," I said. "They controlled me. They made me . . ." I took a deep breath. "Forced me to do their bidding. Then when all the dirty work was done, Mackiel came to the palace to revel in his success."

The inspector turned his gaze to Mackiel. "What do you say to this accusation?"

Mackiel tipped his gold top hat. "I know nothing of these advanced chips you speak of."

"Nor do I," Queen Arebella chimed in. "This is an elaborate tale from a desperate girl who should be on her way to the gallows."

I gritted my teeth. "It's the truth!"

Varin pressed against me for support, unable to touch me while the guards held his hands behind his back.

"It's a complete and utter lie," she replied.

"It is true that a person would do anything in desperation," the inspector said, approaching the Torian queen. "Isn't that right, my queen?"

"Yes." Queen Arebella nodded fervently. "Yes. That's right."

He looked up at her on the dais. "In desperation, a girl might even try to kill her own mother. Wouldn't you agree?"

Queen Arebella jerked as though her body had been destabilized. "What did you say?" She held on to the Archian throne for support.

Without glancing at her, he addressed the court. "A girl might orchestrate the murder of all queens to allow herself to rule. But she could not carry out the act herself, as that would be too obvious. Instead, she would need to employ someone who had the means for such brutal killings. Someone like him." He pointed to Mackiel. "An old friend of Arebella's. Who we now know controlled her." He pointed to me. "A criminal of his employ."

"More lies," Queen Arebella said.

"Initially, I was skeptical, but Keralie has allowed me to see the truth. She recorded her dealings with Mackiel, recounting how she was asked to steal the comm chips and later ingested them, not knowing the consequences. She had no control over what happened to the queens."

"What are you saying?" Queen Arebella's hand was at her throat.

"Do you deny your involvement?" The inspector turned his head to the side. "Even though you are the only one to prosper from the deaths of the queens?"

"Of course I deny it!" she shrieked. "Someone arrest the inspector for such lurid accusations!"

The inspector pressed his lips together. "I'd be happy to call in another inspector to check my findings, but he'll come to the same conclusion." He tapped the comm case strapped to his side. "My discoveries are all recorded here."

Arebella looked to her advisor. "Jenri, help me! He's lying!"

I stepped forward. "No, he's not." The guards had loosened their grip as the inspector had gone on. "Everything he says is true. Mackiel used me for Queen Arebella's bidding. They both controlled me and made me kill the queens. I'm not guilty—*she* is! If you wish to execute me, then Queen Arebella should hang by my side."

"No!" Queen Arebella's face had turned red. "I would never kill my mother. I couldn't!" It was easy to see Arebella as the young, indignant child she really was, as her lies began to unravel.

"That," the inspector said, "is the first truth you've said today."

Arebella's shoulders relaxed slightly. "Yes, yes. I didn't kill her."

"No, you didn't," the inspector said. "For she lives."

Gasps echoed throughout the room. I stumbled. *What?* Varin's eyes were as wide as mine.

A woman stood from the crowd, a black veil concealing her face. At first, I thought she was about to faint; then she pulled back her veil.

"Queen Marguerite!" Jenri gasped at the sight of the former Torian queen. "You're alive!"

CHAPTER FORTY-EIGHT

Marguerite
Queen of Toria

Rule fifteen: Each year, the queens will decide, in conference with their advisors, who will be granted a dose of HIDRA.

Marguerite realized she wasn't dead when she saw the face of the inspector leaning over her instead of her royal ancestors—long passed to the quadrant without borders. And while she could not speak, she nodded when he inquired if she was feeling well.

Well was a relative word.

As soon as the poison had touched her skin and sunk down through her tissue to taint her bloodstream, she'd thought it was the end. Her throat still felt raw and her insides as though someone had raked their nails against them, but she was breathing. She was alive.

The inspector explained that while the poison had already done some damage to her other organs, he had been able to prevent it from stopping her heart by using a dose of HIDRA.

Each year, Marguerite had been involved in deciding which critical patient was the most deserving to receive the life-saving treatment; she'd never thought she would be a recipient.

The inspector had explained that the palace doctor had

administered a dose of HIDRA when she'd fallen into a coma. Her infected blood had gone into a dialysis machine, was treated by HIDRA, then pumped back into her body to fix her internal injuries.

Marguerite hadn't known the woman who was HIDRA when she was alive. Now all that was left of her was twenty vials of perfect elixir blood. She wished the woman were still alive to thank.

As days went by, the blood did its work within Marguerite's body, and she had felt better. Lighter. Each breath was not as though someone had doused a wound with alcohol—the pain lessened and lessened. By the fourth day, she found her voice.

"Why have there been no visitors?" she asked the inspector. She worried the fire had taken more lives than Queen Corra's. Her chest tightened at the thought. The inspector had remained mostly by her side, but would disappear for long lengths of time.

He looked at her, his face grave. "Everyone thinks you're dead, Queen Marguerite."

She sat up in shock, not realizing until that moment she was once again in control of her body. "Why?"

He settled her back into the pillows around her. "For your safety. I worried the assassin would make another attempt on your life if they knew you'd survived."

"You still do not know who it is?"

A smile touched the inspector's eyes. "I have a theory that is coming together quite nicely." Marguerite wanted to ask more, but a wave of fatigue turned her limbs to lead.

"Sleep, Queen Marguerite," he said. "There is time for your questions. And for all the answers."

When Marguerite was ready to leave the infirmary, the

inspector explained his theory. While it was painful to hear, a part of it made sense. A part that rang true, deep to her bones.

That part was her ruthless, selfish and conniving would-be husband.

It was then that Marguerite remembered someone whispering to her over her still, death-like form, words she thought she'd imagined in her feverish recovery.

Whispers from her daughter, admitting she had killed her.

———————

"MOTHER?" AREBELLA WHISPERED, her voice soft but piercing as the advisors looked upon the queen, risen from the dead.

"I'm alive," Marguerite replied, but to Jenri. "No thanks to my daughter."

Jenri gripped Arebella's shoulder as she threatened to fall from the dais.

"I saw you dead," Arebella said. "In the infirmary. You were . . ."

Her mother smiled. "A ruse."

"Yes," the inspector said. "While I was able to save Queen Marguerite before the poison rotted her insides, I decided to keep her survival a secret. That way I could flush out those responsible for the deaths of the queens. When you saw her, she was in an induced coma. Sleeping, but very much still alive."

Arebella slumped against the throne, her legs unable to keep her standing. "Alive," she whispered.

The inspector faced his stunned audience. "I knew from the beginning the person responsible had to be someone who would benefit from the queens' deaths. But I didn't know who. Keralie was the first to come forth as a suspect, and while all the evidence pointed to her, her motive was not clear. Yes, she had the means, but why? Why kill all the queens?

"I told no one of Queen Marguerite's survival, as I feared it would only be temporary. I waited to see who would come forth to claim a throne, and in doing so, they would become my number one suspect. But strangely"—he fiddled with his recording device—"no other royal relatives were found. Which put you, Arebella, as the *only* suspect."

"Ridiculous!" Arebella shouted.

"When Queen Marguerite was well enough to speak, she told me how she dreamed her daughter had come to visit and apologized for killing her. But I could not arrest Arebella until I had proof. The hazy drug-induced memories of a convalescing queen would not be enough to condemn Arebella, not when all physical evidence pointed to Keralie. I needed more time for further investigation. Then Keralie found me in the infirmary and told me everything that had happened to her and allowed me to see her memories." The inspector nodded at Jenri. "And just in time. For it appears you were about to name Lady Arebella queen of all the quadrants."

"*Lady* Arebella?" Arebella muttered, tugging on her hair in irritation. "You mean, *queen*."

"No." The inspector focused his black eyes upon her. "You were never queen, don't you see? How could you be when Queen Marguerite was never truly dead?"

"Why?" Marguerite spoke up, her eyes full of tears as she took in her daughter. She was beautiful, the best parts of her and her father. At least on the outside. "I wanted a different life for you. A better life. Why would you do this? To my sister queens . . ." Her voice broke. "They would've loved you as their own."

"*Better?*" Arebella spat, her hazel eyes wide, cheeks flushed. "You denied me the one thing I wanted. You thought I was too weak to handle the power of the throne." She spread her arms wide. "But look at what I've done."

"You've achieved nothing but manipulating those around you to do your bidding." Her mother gestured toward the young boy in the gold top hat.

Arebella raised an eyebrow; her derisive expression was strikingly similar to that her mother often wore. "Like any queen would."

"Queens don't kill." How could her daughter be this morally corrupt?

"It was the only way to take what was rightfully mine! The throne!"

Her mother narrowed her eyes at her. "You were never meant to have it."

"Which is why I did what I had to!"

Marguerite's mouth opened and shut. There was no reasoning with the girl. Her logic was flawed.

"My queen?" the inspector asked Marguerite. "What do you want me to do?"

Behind the angry girl, Marguerite couldn't help but see the baby she had loved too much to allow her to be entangled within palace politics. And yet look at what had happened. Still, this was the little girl she'd longed to see ever since she'd given her away. She looked exactly as Marguerite had imagined: the same eyes, hair and face. But there was no warmth behind her eyes. Even now, knowing she had been exposed, she showed no remorse. Not even fear.

Could Marguerite have avoided this if she'd allowed Arebella to know the truth from birth? Or would they still be standing here, three queens slain?

"Take her to the palace prison," Marguerite said heavily. "I will decide her fate." She sighed. "In time."

The inspector nodded, and the guards moved from Varin and Keralie to approach the ousted queen.

"You can't kill me," Arebella said as she was put in chains. "You still have no other heirs. I will inherit the throne one day. You can't live forever!"

"No, I can't," Marguerite replied. "But I have enough time to ensure you'll never rule. For the only person who can change Queenly Law is a queen. A true Quadarian queen. And you have never been queen and never will be."

She thought her daughter would fight her, would spit words of hate, but Arebella was silent as she was dragged from the room.

"And Mackiel?" Keralie said, pointing to the narrow boy, who tried to appear small in the crowd.

"Don't worry," the inspector replied. "He will also answer for his crimes." He nodded to the guards, and they made to grab for the boy, but he pushed through the crowd, knocking people out of the way before anyone could catch him.

"There's nowhere to run," the inspector said calmly. "The palace is still closed."

But that did not stop the boy, whom Marguerite now recognized— not only from her memories from when he was a baby, but because he was the spitting image of her childhood friend. The friend she had given Arebella to, the friend who was to find a family and raise

Arebella far from the palace. What had happened to that sweet childhood friend who had stood by her side while the other children had called her names? How had Mackiel become something dark and twisted?

How had her own daughter?

Mackiel barreled down the aisle, his arms and legs spiraling frantically as he tried to avoid the guards. Rings flew from his fingers as he scrambled toward one of the court exits, his top hat falling behind.

But he wasn't the only person moving.

A figure darted through the crowd without touching anyone, like a fish in a stream, moving between invisible currents, or a shadow between gas lamps, light never touching them.

Mackiel hit the floor, the figure atop his back.

"Don't you dare run!" Keralie cried, pushing him farther into the ground.

The boy reminded Marguerite of a spider, all long limbs, squished to the earth.

The palace guards surrounded the two young Torians, extracting Keralie with some force.

"Curse you, Keralie!" he spat at her. "Why couldn't you just do what I wanted?"

Keralie kicked high; her foot collided with Mackiel's nose. He fell back into the arms of the guards, blood gushing from his face.

"Get rid of him," she said, before turning away, her shoulders trembling. "Don't let his blood sully this place."

Marguerite rushed down the aisle toward the girl. "It's all right," she said once she was beside her. Keralie slumped against a chair, her face flushed and wild. "It will be all right."

Keralie gaped at her. "I thought I killed you . . . I killed the other—"

Marguerite placed a hand on the frightened girl's arm. "*You* did no such thing. You must accept your part in this and understand it as no fault of your own."

She was staring at Marguerite's hand as if she were seeing a ghost. The poor girl. What had she been through?

"I don't know that I can," she replied, her eyes wet.

"You must," Marguerite said. "For life is not to be wasted. You must be strong."

"Yes, my queen," she said, but did not meet her gaze.

"Are you alone here?" Marguerite asked.

"No," said another voice. "She's with me."

Marguerite turned to see an Eonist boy a little older than her daughter. He carried himself much in the same way as Corra had, his posture stiff and face blank. A pang struck deep within for her sister queen—a hole in her heart, never to be filled.

"And you are?" she asked the boy with the strange eyes.

"Varin," he said. He pulled Keralie to her feet and placed his shoulder underneath hers to prop her upright. "My queen," he added.

Marguerite smiled at his formalities. "I'm glad to hear it. You'll need each other in this trying time."

The Torian girl glanced at Varin briefly, before nodding to Marguerite. "But, Queen Marguerite, what I did to the other queens—"

"Enough." Marguerite cut her off with a wave of her hand. "You will not live the rest of your life thinking of what happened here. You will leave and forget this place." The girl looked as though she were about to quarrel. "That is my order, as your queen."

Keralie studied her for a moment, before a smile took over her face, seemingly brightening from within. She was beautiful and full of life.

"I think that's one order I wouldn't mind obeying," Keralie said.

CHAPTER FORTY-NINE

Keralie

I had to see him. One last time. Then I'd be free.

I'd been forced to spend the last two days resting in the infirmary, ensuring I did not go into shock after discovering I'd killed the queens, according to the palace doctor. The dark circles that lingered beneath my eyes had started to fade as I tried to put the ghosts of this place behind me.

"Hello, darlin'," said Mackiel as I descended the prison stairs. He was sitting on the floor of his cell, his skinny legs stretched out, ankles crossed. He didn't look like the boy I'd known all these years; he'd been stripped of his fine—stolen—clothes and jewelry and was dressed in loose-fitting pants and a too-large shirt. Dirt was smudged on his pale cheeks like rouge, his black hair was lank from days without washing, and the kohl around his eyes had been rubbed free—from crying?

He looked tiny, insignificant. Powerless.

While I'd been in the infirmary, both Mackiel and Arebella

had been sentenced to life in prison. Mackiel would get his wish to remain within the palace after all.

"Mackiel." I stepped up to his cell, though not too close—I wouldn't make the same mistake he'd made when he'd come to visit.

"Here to rescue me?" He winked.

"Not in this lifetime or the next," I said.

"Who's that?" Arebella asked, her face peering through the bars in the cell next to Mackiel's. Her golden dress was gone, replaced with rags similar to the ones I'd been wearing only three days earlier. When she saw it was me, she scowled. "Oh, it's *you*."

"I've come to say good-bye," I said to them both, tilting an imaginary hat.

"Kera, darlin'—" he started, but I cut him off.

"I don't need to listen to anything more you have to say. I came here for you to listen to me."

"Oh?" he asked. "And what does my Kera have to say?"

"Thank you."

"Thank you?" Arebella let out a wild laugh. "Out of all the things I imagined you'd say, it was never *thank you*. Last night, I imagined the inspector visited, then you and . . . my mother—" Her voice broke. "Why hasn't she come to visit yet?"

"Because you tried to have her killed!" Mackiel spat toward the wall separating their cells.

I wasn't surprised Queen Marguerite hadn't visited her devious daughter. I doubted she could look her in the eye. Perhaps she never would.

"I thought she would let me explain," Arebella said with a sigh. "I could make her understand." She drew circles in the dirt on the stone floor. "Explain why I had to do what I did. For the throne.

For the nation. It was the only way. But she won't even hear me out! I've already imagined exactly what I'll say and how she'll—"

"Shut up!" Mackiel screeched at her, pounding his fist on the wall. "No one cares about your stupid *imaginings*. Just shut up!"

Arebella flinched, tears pooling in her eyes.

"Lovers' quarrel?" I asked.

He glared. Clearly, he had no affection toward her. And although I shouldn't, I felt sorry for the girl. Mackiel had used me too.

"Hurry up, Kera," he said. "Tell me why you're here."

A vein in my neck throbbed, but I took a deep breath to settle my nerves. "I wanted to say thank you," I repeated. "For you *did* make me who I am, and while many might see a wild and wicked girl, I am strong. I am resourceful. And because of that, I will survive what you did to me. And much more."

Mackiel opened his mouth, but I continued, "I am not your victim. I am not your friend. I am not your family. I am not *your* anything. And I thank you, because without your deadly scheme"—I locked eyes with Arebella—"I might have never left your employ. I might have never found myself—the person I want to be."

But he didn't deserve to know who that was. The only person I owed that truth to was me. And my family.

"Now I'm leaving you, and I'll never look back. But you'll always remember me"—I gave him my sweetest smile—"that I am sure of."

I bowed deeply. "And that is all."

Before he could reply, I darted up the prison stairs.

I turned at the top, smiled, then said, "Get in quick. Get out quicker. Right, Mackiel?"

With that, I left him behind.

BACK IN COURT, the true Torian queen sat upon her throne. She wore a deep red velvet dress with three black armbands to recognize her lost sisters. Her crown had rightfully been returned, the black veil pushed back over her long hair. The remaining thrones had been removed from the dais. I was happy to see guards posted on either side of her; the security had increased since the murders. Her advisor, Jenri, stood close behind her, his gray eyes never straying far from her face.

"Welcome, Keralie and Varin," she said with a smile as we entered the room hand in hand. "It's good to see you looking well."

No doubt she referred to my new outfit—the cutoff pants of a dermasuit with a deep blue corset and long overcoat from Toria, providing the best comfort from both quadrants.

"Queen Marguerite." I bowed, keeping Varin's hand within mine.

She smiled and asked, "Jenri said you wished to speak with me?"

I managed to unstick my tongue from the roof of my suddenly parched mouth. "Yes, my queen. If that's all right?"

She laughed, though not unkindly. "I know little of you, Keralie, but I would not have thought you shy. Go on."

I looked at Varin's serene face before turning back to the queen. "I know I have no right to ask you this"—I cleared my throat—"to ask you for anything—"

"Stop," Queen Marguerite commanded. "Have you already forgotten my order? You must move on from what happened here." She glanced at Jenri. "We all must."

"I haven't forgotten."

"Continue, then."

"My father was in an accident six months ago," I began. "An

accident I caused. And even though I don't deserve forgiveness, and to move on, *he* does." Before I knew it, tears were running down my face. "I turned my back on my family long ago, even before his accident. I turned toward something that was easy and gratifying and selfish. I didn't realize my choices would hurt my family; I only cared about what I wanted. What I *thought* I wanted. But I want more for my life now." I grinned at Varin through my tears. "I've seen so much while in the palace. Beyond the Jetée, beyond Toria." I spread my hands wide. Even without four queens, this room had a commanding presence. It spoke of our nation, of the divisions and the intersections. It spoke of our combined cultures. Our united desires.

The first four queens of Quadara had created peace with their walls, but had they misunderstood the power of this place? The potential of their nation?

There were no borders here.

"Are you all right?" Queen Marguerite asked, leaning forward.

Varin placed his free hand on my back, steadying me. If I hadn't stolen Varin's comm case, I never would've found out about Eonist death dates. I never would've understood how Eonists feel, and hurt. And Varin and I wouldn't have met; those walls would have kept us apart.

Arebella might have been destructive and dangerous, but she wasn't completely wrong about Quadara.

"I'm fine," I said firmly. "My eyes have been opened to a larger world. One I want to be a part of. But to do that"—I wiped my nose with the back of my hand—"I have to learn how to forgive myself. And I can't do that without my family. I can't."

At the mention of family, Queen Marguerite stilled. "What can I do?"

"My father is at the Eonist Medical Facility," I said. "He's been in a coma since the accident and has continued deteriorating. He has weeks—maybe less—to live. I was hoping . . . I would like to ask . . ." Why was this so hard? I was trying not to be selfish, but here I was, asking a selfish question. "I know out of all people, I shouldn't be asking anything from you, from the palace. I don't deserve it. But my father does. Please"—the tears flowed freely now—"please give him a second chance."

"You want to use a dose of HIDRA for your father?" she surmised.

I nodded. "I know there are few treatments left, but if you could spare it, I would be forever grateful."

Queen Marguerite looked to Jenri for a moment. A warm exchange passed between them, something extending beyond the queen and advisor relationship. What had happened here had highlighted what was important. I knew the feeling.

"Please, my queen. Please let me be a part of something good."

"With no other queens to deliberate over this decision," Queen Marguerite said, her eyes shifting to where the other thrones should be, "it is up to me, and me alone. We've been through many unspeakable horrors in the last two weeks. As have you. Without my daughter and the choice I made seventeen years ago"—she took a deep breath—"none of this would've happened."

"This is not your fault!" I interrupted. "My queen," I added quickly.

"Nor is it yours." Her words were stern but understanding. In that moment, I could see the wonderful mother she would've been. "I will grant you this, as you and your father deserve a new beginning. We all deserve that."

My knees buckled but Varin held me close. "Thank you, Queen Marguerite. Thank you. Thank you." The words didn't even begin to cover my gratitude.

"I will send a dose of HIDRA to the medical facility at once."

I pressed my face into Varin's chest and broke down.

"I've got you," Varin whispered against my shaking shoulder, "you're going to be all right." And for the first time in months, perhaps years, I believed my life could change for the better. *Had* changed.

After a moment, I pulled myself together and thanked Queen Marguerite again.

"You know," Queen Marguerite said, "I'm in need of additional advisors now that I'll be ruling Quadara alone." A darkness clouded her features whenever she mentioned the deceased queens. "I could benefit from someone who's been involved in interquadrant business."

I let out a surprised laugh. "Are you offering me a job, my queen?"

She raised an eyebrow. "Would you accept, if I was?"

"I don't know." I desperately wanted to start afresh and leave the palace behind, but everything that had happened in the past two weeks had changed me, irreversibly. "I'm not sure I could stay here."

"Not a problem!" She waved a hand. "I need a break from the palace myself. I'm currently organizing a tour of all the quadrants, spending a month in each, to ensure I understand the fundamental differences between them, but also the ideals we share. As the only queen of Quadara, I must respect what my sister queens believed in, while heralding change. Necessary change."

"I don't know what to say."

She leaned forward. "Say you'll help me. When I visit Toria, the final destination on my tour, help me learn all there is to know about your quadrant." I noticed she said *your* quadrant and not hers. She spoke for all of Quadara now. "Even the Jetée. The queens have been too long disconnected from our people. I realize that now, with all that's happened." She took a moment, her hand on her chest, before continuing. "I want to ensure everyone's voice is heard and placate any concerns. I cannot allow anger and hatred to cause such destruction, like what happened here with these murders."

"Yes," I said. "I would be more than happy to help." It was the least I could do for the palace and Queen Marguerite for helping my father. And it might help ease my guilt.

"Wonderful." She clapped her hands together. "Now on to Varin."

"Sorry?" He glanced at me. "My knowledge of the other quadrants is slim, my queen. I'm not sure I'll be of much help."

She smiled in response. "That's not quite what I had in mind for you. The inspector examined your background when he was investigating the murders."

If Varin was surprised, he didn't show it. "Yes, my queen?"

She pressed her lips together solemnly. "He learned about your death date." I squeezed Varin's hand. His chest rose and fell more rapidly as the queen went on. "I can't let Eonia continue to treat their people with such disrespect. While changing the laws there will take time, I can offer you something to ensure your vision doesn't continue to deteriorate."

"HIDRA?" I asked. Anticipation hummed under my skin. Were we both so blessed by the queens above?

Queen Marguerite shook her head. "I'm afraid not. You see,

Varin's condition is neither a disease nor injury. It's a genetic condition. And genes can only be manipulated before birth. I'm sorry, but we cannot fix his vision."

I couldn't believe what I was hearing. "I thought HIDRA could fix everything?"

Her brow lowered. "I checked with all our doctors. I'm very sorry. I wish I had better news."

Varin's expression stayed the same. I wanted him to scream, to yell, to break. I wanted him to feel, as I did in that moment. And I wanted to help endure his pain.

But he squared his shoulders and said, "I understand. Thank you for trying, my queen."

"Not all is lost," she said. "There is a treatment that will keep the degeneration at bay. And I've already put more funding into attempts to reverse genetic conditions *after* birth." When neither of us answered, she added, "There's hope, Varin. Please don't give up."

He nodded, but his hand felt limp in mine.

———

VARIN AND I sat on the House of Concord steps, my fingertips tracing patterns on the back of his hand. It had snowed overnight, coating everything with a dusting of white. The air had that crisp fresh smell of newly fallen snow, and the morning crowds were out preparing to do business.

The screens atop the buildings continued to play Queen Marguerite's latest Queenly Report on a loop. A few people stood, watching her solemn retelling of the past few weeks' events, four fingers pressed to their lips.

Quadara had been shaken, but it had not been broken.

Varin stared ahead at something I couldn't see. I worried he'd shut me out again without the possibility of HIDRA. But everything was different now. *He* was different.

"Are you okay?" I asked.

He turned and gave me a small smile. "Don't worry about me. As Queen Marguerite said, I have hope. That's more than I had before coming here. In fact." He lifted my hand and pressed a kiss to the back of it. "I have much more than hope. More than I could've ever dreamed of."

"What?" I said in mock solemnity. "A criminal record?"

He laughed, pressing my hand between his. The feeling of his skin on mine never failed to set my heart stuttering and stomach swooping. I hoped it never would. While he refused to put his gloves back on, he still wore the rest of his dermasuit. I didn't mind, for it was a good look on him. Anything, I'd decided, was a good look on him. Especially when he was smiling at me.

"Thank you," he said. "For staying by my side."

"Thank you for staying by mine. Now that you have me, you can't get rid of me."

"I hope that's a promise."

I grinned. "It is."

He glanced back at the palace behind us, the dome illuminating the Concord like a second sun. "Are you sure about helping Queen Marguerite when she travels to Toria? It will remind you of what happened here."

Something dark stirred within me, but I shoved it back down. I would keep the important part of my promise to Queen Marguerite—I would not dwell on the bloody crimes committed here. I would let those events belong to a girl who no longer existed. A girl who only cared about herself. The girl who belonged to Mackiel.

She was gone now.

I was a girl who cared for her family. Her friends. I was a girl who saw more than the Jetée, more than Toria. My eyes were open.

And I wasn't alone. I never had been. I'd turned my back on my family to chase wealth, to search for things they couldn't provide, things I thought I needed. But I was wrong. They'd provided everything I could have ever wanted. A life of warmth and love.

Looking at Varin, the word kept nudging in at the edges. *Love. Love. Love.* I loved this boy. And while he might not be there yet, I'd teach him how to love in return. He deserved it. As everyone does.

He let go of my hand. "Will you go home afterward?" he asked. He didn't need to say the words. After HIDRA. I couldn't believe the next time I saw my father, he'd be whole.

I knew it hurt Varin to talk about HIDRA, since it wasn't something that could help him. But as he said, he had faith in a cure, and in the meantime, he would visit the Eonist Medical Facility to slow the deterioration of his vision. He could continue his art and capture the beautiful, if complicated, nation of Quadara.

"I hope so." Uncertainty still flipped inside my belly when I thought about home.

He didn't reply. I studied his profile and the downturn of his lips. "What's wrong?" I asked.

"What about us?"

"You'll come with me, of course."

"A failed messenger and a retired criminal?" he mused. "It sounds like the start of some terrible joke."

"No." I shook my head seriously. "It sounds like a beginning. You can be whoever you want in Toria. Do whatever you want. For as long as you want."

His face grew serious. "I like the sound of that."

"It's a deal, then." I held out my hand for him to shake. The start of many promises I would keep.

He swept my hand back into his and held it to his chest. "I knew there was more to this world. More than the life I was living in Eonia. But I never thought I could be a part of it. You taught me I could. How could I ever leave you? You restarted my heart. You brought me to life, Keralie Corrington."

His words stole my breath away. I grinned through my unshed tears. "You made me realize I could change, that my past doesn't dictate my future. You saved me from myself."

He pressed his hot mouth to mine, sending a flare through my body. It was much better without a full body dermasuit between us—much more real.

When he released me, he was grinning widely. He'd never looked more beautiful.

"Here," I said, pulling something out from my coat pocket. "I thought you might want this back." It was the picture he'd drawn of me.

"You kept it?" he asked.

I nodded. "I wanted to have something of you with me. But I don't need it anymore. I have you."

He smoothed the piece of paper on his leg. "Thank you."

I leaned over his arm while he traced the intricate lines of his drawing.

"I want to be this girl you captured," I said. A girl of light and laughter. "I want to be worthy of your—" I wanted to say *love*, but it was too soon. "I want to be worthy of you."

"Worthy of me?" He scoffed. "Keralie, I thought I was alone in this world. I never thought anyone would care about me"—he smiled—"the way I care about you."

We kissed again.

When he pulled back, his gaze was focused on something behind me.

"They're here," he said.

A carriage pulled up at the House of Concord stairs, and a woman stepped into the snow. She glanced at the palace before her eyes settled on me. Her expression shattered into disbelief. As did my heart. She looked exactly as I remembered. And she was looking at me in the way I'd hoped, with love and forgiveness.

My mother.

She turned around and reached inside the carriage to help someone down.

The last time I'd seen him, he was covered in blood and bandages with a respirator wedged down his throat. I held my breath until he locked his eyes on mine.

When my father broke into a smile and opened his arms—ready to embrace me—my heart restitched inside my chest.

I was home.

ACKNOWLEDGMENTS

I like to think that I've been preparing to be an author all my life. As a child, I was always imagining fictional worlds, usually with my cats as my begrudging accomplices. While this isn't uncommon for kids, who thrive on untamed imagination, unruly magic and the unknown, we tend to grow out of these "childish fantasies." I did not. This book you hold in your hands is my lifelong dream come true. But I wouldn't be here without the following people.

To my amazing editor, Stacey Barney. Your wisdom, infectious laughter, and kind and supportive words made this already wonderful journey even more special. I've always wished for an editor who loved my book the way you do and I'm so lucky to have found you! Thank you!

I can never thank my fabulous agent, Hillary Jacobson, enough. You were my first "yes," setting my book and life on a course I'd only ever imagined. Knowing you have my back is such a wonderful and reassuring feeling. Thank you, thank you!

I'm so grateful for Jennifer Klonsky, Courtney Gilfillian, Kate Meltzer, Katie Quinn, and the entire Penguin Teen team, you are the best bookish crew an author could hope for! Thank you to Theresa Evangelista and Katt Phatt for creating the most gorgeous cover I've ever seen. And thanks to Virginia Allyn for making my childhood dreams come true by creating the magical map of Quadara. And a special thanks to the indomitable Felicity Vallence. You are the best in the biz!

The writing process can be a lonely one, therefore I'm so appreciative to have Sabina Khan, Tomi Adeyemi, Adalyn Grace and Mel Howard to share the ups and downs with. Thank you for always listening with a kind and open heart.

To Amie Kaufman, thank you for all your invaluable advice and being such a wonderful friend. Also, thanks to Nicole Hayes, Jay Kristoff, Shivaun Plozza, all of Hillary's Angels, Team Pusheen, EaF and The Wordsmiths for your ongoing support. Much love to the Literarians for their encouragement over the years. Raising my glass in your honor!

Hugs to the rest of my friends and family. I'm always taken aback by how excited you are about my book. It means the world! A special thanks to Jessica Ponte Thomas and Shannon Thomas for always being there for me.

To my Disney prince, Andrew Lejcak, thank you for putting up with all my book talk. I know it's not something you understand completely, and because of that, it means even more that you let me waffle on and on and on . . . I love that I get to share this journey with you. And *look*, I called you a prince! ☺

To Mum and Dad, you taught me that dreams don't always come true like in the movies; it requires more than wishing upon a star or a fairy godmother's *bibbity bobbity boo*. From a young age, I was determined to work hard to achieve my dreams. It's because of you that they're now all coming true. I'm so lucky to be your daughter.

Many hugs and kisses to my furry "workmates," Lilo and Mickey. Sitting at the computer all day and late into the night would've been lonely without you, although I could've done without you climbing all over the keyboard!

To Gary Rodney, my behavioral optometrist in Sydney. The years before I started your therapy were the hardest of my life, unable to read or write due to my poor vision. The words "thank you" are far too inconsequential for what you've done for me. You are my HIDRA.

I must also acknowledge and thank Walt Disney. Without you, I would not be the person I am today, and I would not believe in the power, magic and enchantment of storytelling.

Lastly, thank *you*! Even through the murder and mayhem, I hope *Four Dead Queens* has brought some wonder and joy into your life. Thank you for choosing my book!